W9-BVR-320

RECEIVED
SEP 06 2012
By _____

No Longer the Property of
Hayner Public Library District

HAYNER PUBLIC LIBRARY DISTRICT
ALTON, ILLINOIS

OVERDUES 10 PER DAY, MAXIMUM FINE
COST OF ITEM
ADDITIONAL $5.00 SERVICE CHARGE
APPLIED TO
LOST OR DAMAGED ITEMS

ALSO BY ANDREW PORTER

The Theory of Light and Matter

In Between Days

In Between Days

Andrew Porter

ALFRED A. KNOPF   NEW YORK   2012

THIS IS A BORZOI BOOK
PUBLISHED BY ALFRED A. KNOPF

Copyright © 2012 by Andrew Porter

All rights reserved. Published in the United States by Alfred A. Knopf,
a division of Random House, Inc., New York, and in Canada by
Random House of Canada Limited, Toronto.

www.aaknopf.com

Knopf, Borzoi Books, and the colophon are registered trademarks of
Random House, Inc.

Library of Congress Cataloging-in-Publication Data
Porter, Andrew, [date]
In between days / by Andrew Porter. — 1st ed.
p. cm.
ISBN 978-0-307-27351-2 (alk. paper)
1. Dysfunctional families—Fiction. 2. Divorced parents—Fiction.
3. Adult children of dysfunctional families—Fiction. I. Title.
PS3616.O75I52 2012
813'.6—dc23   2012019635

This is a work of fiction. Names, characters, places, and incidents
either are the product of the author's imagination or are used
fictitiously. Any resemblance to actual persons, living or dead, events,
or locales is entirely coincidental.

Jacket photograph by Lise Sarfati/Magnum Photos
Jacket design by Carol Devine Carson

Manufactured in the United States of America
First Edition

b2011123x

For Jenny and Charlotte

Part One

SINCE HIS DIVORCE, Elson has fallen into the habit of stopping by the Brunswick Hotel for a quick drink after work. He likes the Brunswick Hotel because it's one of the newest hotels in the city and because he knows that no one he knows will ever find him here. He likes the anonymity of it, of drinking here alone in the third-floor bar area, of sitting here at the window, staring out across the street at the futuristic office buildings, at their slick glass surfaces, knowing that behind these glass surfaces men and women in finely pressed suits are probably packing up their bags and briefcases, making plans for dinner or drinks. He likes to imagine these people leaving, likes to watch them as they walk out the door and get in their cars. There's something strangely soothing about it all, about this daily routine of watching the city empty out, of watching it grow quiet and dark.

Tonight, the barroom is empty, save for a few out-of-town businessmen, drinking alone, and outside the window, the city is quiet, a light rain coming down now, a cold winter rain, which is somewhat atypical for Houston this time of year. In an hour from now, he will be meeting Lorna Estrada, the woman he has been sleeping with for the past six months, the woman he met just after his wife left him, at a barbecue at his friend Dave Millhauser's house. Lorna is twenty-seven years old, and many years his junior, and yet surprisingly mature for her age. He sometimes speculates that this is because of her Filipino upbringing, because of the strictness of her parents, or other times because of the fact that she came to the States so young, that she got a firsthand glimpse of how cruel the world could be to a non-English-speaking adult, especially in a city like Houston. The first and only child in her family to ever receive a degree in anything, Lorna works as a curator at the Museum of Fine

Arts and shares with Elson a strange and fervent interest in minimalist architecture. That Elson is himself an architect was perhaps part of the initial allure, the fact that they could talk with ease about the work of Claudio Silvestrin or Vincent Van Duysen or Souto de Moura, but now, Elson wonders, what has that allure become? A few empty hours at the end of the day. A couple of drinks, maybe a movie. Mostly sex. And even that has become routine. In the early days of their relationship—if that is in fact what this is—they would go to the houses of Lorna's friends. They would sit around drunkenly discussing the state of the world, or art, just as he'd done back in college, and though most of these people were younger than him, some of them young enough to be his own children, he still enjoyed it. He liked to watch the flicker of the candles, the shadows playing along the walls. He liked to listen to the conversations from a guarded distance, with a vague sense of amusement or perhaps jealousy. How long had it been, after all, since he'd shared these types of convictions himself? Later, he had even started smoking again, joining a small group of them as they went out to the yard to have a cigarette after dinner. And as he stood there beneath the lamplight of the porch, or in the shadows of the garden, he would look over at Lorna and smile, and she would always smile back.

But what has happened since then? He often wonders whether he has maybe upset her or embarrassed her in some way. Or if it is simply the fact that he, Elson, is so indicative of everything that she and her friends despise. It has been a month since they've done anything but meet at Elson's apartment after work, and even when Elson has inquired about her friends, Lorna has been evasive. They are always too busy, she tells him, working on their projects or organizing some event or protesting some local politician. One night, earlier that week, he had stopped by her apartment after work to drop off a sweater she had left at his place. He had not told her he was coming, but he had expected she'd be happy to see him. He had knocked on her door several times, and when no one had answered, he had stood there for a long time and listened. Through the clear glass window, he could hear voices coming from the other side of the apartment, laughing. He stood there for a while longer, listening, and then knocked again. After a while, the voices grew quiet, and a light went off in the kitchen. He wondered what to do, whether to stand there and wait, humiliate them all when they eventually came out, or whether it would be better just to leave. Finally, he had decided to drop the sweater off in the doorway and leave. The following night, when Lorna came over to his place, she denied ever hearing him knock. She claimed that they were planning a rally about something or other and that they were probably too busy, too engrossed in their project, to hear him. Elson had shaken his head and smiled. *Whatever,* he'd said, borrowing an expression from Lorna herself, an expression that she often used when she wanted to dismiss him. And then he'd stood up and walked into the kitchen for a beer.

Now, sitting in the dim-lit glow of the Brunswick Hotel bar, Elson finds himself wondering whether he should have handled it differently or whether it would have even mattered. He looks over toward the bartender and motions at his glass. A moment later, the bartender walks over and fills it. He's a young man, this bartender, and fit. He reminds him of some of the boys that his son, Richard, used to bring over to the house.

"Looks like it's going to break," the bartender says, nodding toward the window.

"What?"

"The storm," he says. "Looks like it's going to be a bad one."

Elson stares out the window and realizes that the sky has darkened, the clouds from the east moving in over the city like a fog.

"Good," he says.

"Huh?"

"I'm glad."

"You looking for a storm?"

"You could say that."

The bartender stares at him quizzically, then smiles. "I've seen you here before, haven't I? Last Tuesday."

"Maybe," Elson says. "I come here a lot."

The bartender nods. "You know, I actually just started here last week." He smiles at him. "Just moved down here from Austin."

Elson nods again. He can tell that this bartender is looking for a conversation, maybe even wanting to ask him something personal, so he quickly turns away, staring at the wall on the far end of the bar until the bartender finally leaves.

When he comes back a few minutes later, Elson pulls out his wallet. "How much do I owe you?" he asks.

. . .

Later, as he stands outside the front lobby of the Brunswick Hotel, waiting for his car, Elson lights a cigarette and watches the sky grow dark, the palm trees in the distance swaying hypnotically in the wind. He wonders why he acted the way he had at the bar and whether or not he has ruined the Brunswick Hotel forever. He looks across the street and thinks of Lorna and realizes that the promise of the night has suddenly vanished. He wants to go home and sleep it off.

The valets are putting on rain parkas with the hotel logo printed on the back, and when his car comes up the ramp, they all swarm in around him, holding out their arms, swinging an umbrella above his head. He tips them generously and takes off, realizing it might be a long time before he returns here again.

Outside the edge of downtown Houston, he stops at a light and checks his messages. He is hoping for a call from Lorna, hoping for a last-minute cancellation or maybe a change of plans, but instead what he sees is a long list of messages from his ex-wife, Cadence, each one spaced out by a couple of minutes, most of them left in the past half hour. He pulls over on the side of the road and calls her up, feeling a sense of uneasiness, a sense of dread. The last time they spoke, almost a month before, he had vowed never to call her again directly, to handle all of their future correspondences through e-mail or perhaps a third party. The last time they spoke, she had called him a monster, a term that had stung him so deeply that it had taken him several days to shake it off.

He expects that Cadence will want to pick up where she left off the last time they spoke, but when she answers the phone, her voice is surprisingly calm.

"What's the emergency?" he says.

"What do you mean?"

"Well, you called me—let's see—seven times."

"Oh," she says and pauses. "No emergency."

"You just wanted to talk?"

"No," she says. "I wanted to tell you something."

Outside the window, the rain is coming down hard now, obscuring his view of everything. He turns off the windshield wipers and waits for her to finish.

"I wanted to tell you that Chloe is going to be coming home tonight and that she's going to be staying with me for a while."

"What do you mean?"

"I mean simply that."

"Doesn't she have classes?"

"Well, no. Not at the moment." She pauses. "She's been asked to take a leave."

"A leave from school?"

"Yes."

Elson feels his pulse quicken. "What are you talking about?"

"Just what I said. She's been asked to take a leave for the rest of the semester."

"She's been expelled?"

"Well, no, not exactly. It's more complicated than that."

Elson looks out the window and feels his body loosening, his mind swimming with possibilities.

"What I'm saying is it hasn't come to that yet. They're still in deliberations."

"Who?"

"The provost, the president, the dean of student life. Most of the Student Judiciary Council." She pauses. "As I said, we're hoping it doesn't come to that."

"Jesus," he says. "What the hell did she do?"

"Well," Cadence says, but doesn't finish. "Look, Elson, this is something she wants to talk to you about herself."

Elson sits there for a moment, silent.

"I told her I wouldn't tell you."

"You're keeping secrets from me now?"

"No," she says. "It's not like that."

"How long have you known?"

Cadence is quiet for a moment. "I don't know," she says. "A couple weeks, I guess."

"A couple *weeks*?"

"Look, Elson, I'm not going to talk to you like this, okay. I'm not looking for a fight. I just wanted to tell you that she's coming home tonight and that she's agreed to meet with you tomorrow if you're willing. She can explain the whole thing to you then."

Elson considers this. "Who's picking her up?"

"Richard."

"I'll get her."

"No, Elson, that's not part of the agreement. Look, I told her—I promised her—I wouldn't even tell you until tomorrow."

Elson grips the edge of the dashboard with his left hand, squeezing it until his knuckles turn white. "So, you're telling me that I can't even pick up my own daughter from the fucking airport? Is that what you're telling me?"

"That's what I'm telling you."

"Cadence."

"I'm hanging up now, Elson."

And before he can get out another word, the line goes dead.

He looks at the phone, then redials her number, but all he gets is Cadence's voice mail. He considers leaving her a message but decides instead to just hang up. He drops the phone on the floor and then feels his stomach drop. He wonders where his daughter is now, whether she's high above the earth in an airplane cabin, circling the tiny suburbs of East Texas, or whether she's still back at the airport in Boston, waiting for her plane. He tries to picture his daughter's face, tries to remember the last time they spoke, but the memory is vague. Instead what he sees is his daughter as a child, as a young girl, standing in the doorway of his study, asking him what he's working on, then coming over and sitting on his lap, watching him as he works on his latest blueprint, studying his hand as he makes tiny markings on the page, measuring things out with a ruler and pen. She smells like bubble bath, her hair still wet, her skin moist, and as he lights up a cigarette and turns to her, she makes a face, scrunches her nose, as she always does. *I thought you were going to quit,* she says. *You promised.* And he assures her that he will, that once his project is over, once he's finished, he will definitely quit, and then the memory is gone, and Elson is reaching into his pocket for a freshly opened pack.

A moment later, as he's driving past the gay bars in Montrose, he dials up Lorna's number, his fingers twitching so badly now that he can barely hold the phone.

When she answers, her voice is calm, guarded. She tells him that she's talking to someone on the other line.

"I'm coming to see you," he says.

"I'm not ready," she says. "I haven't even showered."

"I need to see you right now," he says. "Something's happened."

Lorna is silent. Then she says, "What's happened?"

But he doesn't answer. He realizes only now how upset he is, how he doesn't even have words to explain it.

"I'll tell you when I come," he says finally.

"Give me twenty minutes."

"Okay," he says, and then he drops the phone on the seat. Outside his window, the storm is finally breaking, the heavy clouds from the east rising up over the city, combining with other clouds to form a giant mass. He pulls over on the side of the street and parks. The rain is coming down quickly now, pounding the car, and in the distance he can see brilliant displays of lightning splintering along the horizon. He looks out the window to his left and notices a small row of brown stucco houses, all old and somewhat disheveled, and realizes then, with something like panic, with something like fear, that he doesn't actually know where he is, that he must have made a wrong turn somewhere, that somehow, in this city where he's grown up, this city where he's lived all his life, he is lost.

2

ON THE OTHER SIDE of Montrose, less than a mile from where his father sits helplessly in his car, Richard Harding is reading the final stanza of his latest poem to a small group of regulars at Dr. Michelson's house. The Michelsons' house is large, the room where they're sitting, dimly lit. An old baroque study filled with antique bookshelves and dusty books. At the far end of the table sits Dr. Michelson, a retired professor of English, a former professor emeritus at Rice University, who now spends his free time dabbling in poetry and leading a small, biweekly workshop for a group of recent Rice graduates. That Richard himself never knew Dr. Michelson at Rice doesn't seem to matter. He was brought in by his friend Brandon O'Leary on the second week of August last summer and has been a regular ever since.

It's no mystery to Brandon or any of the other students that Richard has quickly become Dr. Michelson's favorite, a fact that both delights and annoys Richard. He sometimes wishes Dr. Michelson wouldn't praise him so effusively in front of the others, that he wouldn't make it so obvious that he likes him. Sometimes, at the bar they go to afterward, the others will make a joke about it, pinching his side or mussing his hair. *So, the old queen's got the hots for you, huh?* Or *Hey, I think I spotted old Michelson sporting a woody.* Richard knows it's all in fun and probably just a result of their own insecurities, their own jealousy, but still, it makes him wonder how much of Dr. Michelson's praise is real. What are these comments, after all, but thinly masked truths?

Tonight, he reads slowly, quietly, the words of his poem overshadowed by the violence of the storm outside. The others seem distracted, more interested in the splitting thunder and the sudden streaks of lightning flashing across the lawn. But Dr. Michelson remains poised, his eyes focused on Richard, his head nodding each time that Richard looks up from his poem. When Richard finally finishes, Dr. Michelson looks at him and smiles.

"Thank you, Richard," he says. Then he turns to the group. "Any suggestions?"

The others are quiet, unsure of what to say. Normally a very vocal and spirited group, they are typically quiet whenever Richard reads. Maybe it's the fear of dissent, the fear of disagreeing with Dr. Michelson, or maybe it's just the fact that they've grown exhausted over time with the inevitable praise that always follows.

Finally, Eric Stevenson speaks up. "I thought it was kind of long at the end. You know, like it kept going on and on, repeating itself."

"You'd suggest condensing?" Dr. Michelson breaks in. Then he looks at the others. "What do the rest of you think?"

"I kind of agree with that," says another boy, very timidly, looking away as soon as he says it.

Michelson looks up at the boy. "Really?"

"Well, yeah," he says. "I guess."

A few other people chime in quietly, agreeing with Eric. Richard stares down at the poem he has written, a poem about his mother and father's recent divorce, a poem that he has to admit is probably a little long. After a while, the others begin to bring up other things. The clichéd imagery in the second stanza, the overly sentimental language at the end of the poem, the somewhat-oblique references to things that have happened in the parents' marriage.

Finally, Dr. Michelson breaks in, praising the group for their thorough critique, but also explaining that while their points are all fair, what they seem to have overlooked is the utter simplicity of the writing. The simple beauty of it, that is. The emotional honesty. He goes on for a while longer, but Richard zones him out. He has grown wary of this type of praise, these types of compliments. He no longer knows whether or not to believe them. The poem was something he had worked on for days, labored over, but in the end, what did it really mean? Even he couldn't say. He wonders sometimes whether any of this is even relevant, whether anyone but the person who has written the poem can actually say what it means. And if the person who has written the poem doesn't know what it means, then is the poem even valid? He looks down at his hands, unable to meet Michelson's eyes, even as he explains to the group that what they're looking at here is *real* poetry.

When Dr. Michelson finally finishes, the group adjourns to the kitchen, where Mrs. Michelson is waiting with a small tray of drinks. *Margaritas tonight,* she says to the boys and then winks. The boys circle in around her, thanking her profusely. Then a few of them head out to the yard. Normally, after one of these biweekly workshops, they all go out to the pool to swim. They swim there until eight or nine, drinking whatever Mrs. Michelson brings them, before heading off to the bar. But tonight they just stand there cautiously beneath the small overhang in the roof, watching the rain as it comes down in violent waves, the lightning as it crackles at the edge of the lawn.

After a while, one of the boys starts off toward the pool. It's Eric Stevenson, the one who didn't like Richard's poem, and as he does this, the others begin to cheer. He stands there for a moment at the edge of the pool, then pulls off his clothes and jumps in. A few of the others begin to follow, stripping down to their briefs, before Mrs. Michelson catches wind of what's going on and comes over to the door. *Better come in, boys!* she yells. *I don't think it's safe.* But before she can finish, the rest of the boys jump in, and the cause is lost. Dr. Michelson, who has just returned from his study, comes up to the door and laughs, perhaps a little too loudly, then takes a drink from his wife's hand and shepherds her away from the door.

"Let them play," he says. "They're young."

"It's dangerous," she says. "The lightning."

But Dr. Michelson just shakes his head and laughs. "Haven't you ever swum in the rain before?" he says, and then pats his wife's hand. "I know for a fact you have."

His wife looks at him but doesn't answer.

A moment later, Dr. Michelson turns on the pool lights, and the pool glows. A bright electric blue. The boys, all of them half naked, swim for Dr. Michelson's pleasure.

Richard moves across the room toward a small group of boys in the corner, trying to avert his gaze from Dr. Michelson. He knows that at some point Dr. Michelson will want to corner him, will want to tell him again how brilliant his poem is or remind him again about the application deadlines for summer fellowships. Lately, he has been talking to Richard about graduate programs in creative writing, something that Richard has little interest in.

As he approaches the boys, Richard can hear them talking about how crazy this all is, swimming around in the rain—not to mention in a lightning storm—how someone is probably going to die out there. At the far end of the pool he can see his friend Brandon O'Leary splashing about, waving to him. Richard waves back, then starts toward the door, trying purposely to avoid Dr. Michelson's gaze. He stands for a moment beneath the small overhang in the roof, waiting for Brandon, and when Brandon finally approaches, he smiles.

"Why don't you come in?" Brandon says, his body glistening and tan.

"Can't," Richard says. "Gotta pick up my sister from the airport."

"Chloe?"

"Uh-huh."

"What's up?" he says, smiling.

"Long story," Richard says. "I don't really understand it myself."

Brandon nods. "Well, you gotta come out later, okay? To Limelight."

Limelight. One of the newer gay clubs in the city, a poor excuse for a club, really. More of a bar than a club. A meat market. "There's someone I want you to meet," Brandon adds.

"A job?"

"No, not a job. A friend."

Recently, the only people Brandon has wanted to introduce him to have been jobs, what Brandon calls johns. Overworked businessmen looking for a hand job in the back of their BMWs. Men wanting to believe that they're only taking a little recreational vacation from their wives, a little break, relieving stress. That this has become Richard's life is a little perplexing, even to him. The son of a prominent Houston architect hanging out with a boy who gives out hand jobs for fifty bucks a pop in the backseat of some ophthalmologist's car. It sickened him the first time Brandon told him about it, amused him the second. But now it simply seems routine. Something Brandon does two or three times a month to supplement his income, his measly paycheck from Café Brasil.

"Who's this friend?" Richard asks.

"A guy I met. I think you'll like him."

"I'm not looking for anything serious."

"Dude, believe me, this guy isn't serious. In fact, he's the total opposite of serious."

Richard nods. "I'm not looking for anything, really."

"What do you mean?"

But Richard doesn't answer. "What did you think of my poem?"

"I liked it."

"That's all?"

"Well, no. I mean, it was sad. And I agree with Eric, it was maybe a little long. But it was good. I mean, all of your stuff is good. Michelson practically creamed himself."

Richard shrugs this off. "I don't know," he says. "Lately, I don't know what any of this stuff I've been writing means."

"You're getting better," Brandon says.

"You think?"

"Yeah," he says. "Definitely."

And then a moment later, there's a shout from the pool, and a group of the boys begins to beckon Brandon to come back in and join them.

"Better go back," he says. "Call me on my cell, okay?"

"Okay," Richard says, and then, as Brandon is turning around to go back to the pool, he yells, "Hey! What's his name?"

"Who?"

"Your friend."

Brandon smiles. "Beto," he says. Then he turns around and does a sort of sideways dive into the pool.

When Richard returns to the kitchen, Michelson is waiting, drink in hand. Richard explains that he has to leave, and Michelson says he'll walk him to the door.

"I was talking to some friends of mine," Michelson says as they move through the hallway. "One at Cornell, one at Michigan. I was telling them about you."

"Oh yeah?"

"They said that if you still wanted to apply, then you should go ahead and send your application directly to them. That way you'd be sure to get a fair read."

Richard nods again.

"Are you still thinking about applying, Richard?"

"Maybe."

"Maybe?"

"Well, yeah, I don't know." He pauses. "I mean most of those places are pretty hard to get into, you know, and also I'm a little strapped for cash these days. It's not really such a good time for me."

"It's never a good time," Michelson says. "But you're still young, you know. The older you get, the harder it becomes to do something like this."

Richard nods again. Then Michelson smiles and puts his hand on Richard's shoulder, massaging it lightly. For some time now, Richard has suspected that Michelson knows about him, about him and Brandon, and about some of the other boys in the group. At least half of them are gay, a fact that surely couldn't have escaped Michelson himself, though he never mentions it, never even brings it up, except in reference to their poems. Perhaps this is what years of being closeted has done to him, years of going out to cocktail parties with his wife at the dean's house. That poor, lovely woman, Richard thinks. How could she have endured it for so long? How could she have put up with this man for so many years?

At the edge of the hallway, Michelson slows down and stares at him. "I feel like I'm losing you, Richard."

"What do you mean?"

"I feel like something's changed."

"Nothing's changed," Richard says. "I'm just really busy right now, that's all."

Michelson nods.

"With work and stuff."

Michelson moves toward the doorway, and Richard suddenly feels bad, guilty for not explaining to this man what he can barely explain to himself. That ever since his parents' divorce, he can hardly bring himself to care about anything. Not work, not poetry, not graduate school. Not even the tiny apartment he shares with a few other boys from his year.

"Well, if you're interested," Michelson continues, opening the door now and letting the rain into the hall. "I have a friend coming into town next week. A minor poet who's actually pretty good. I think you'd like him."

Richard nods.

"Just let me know if you'd like to meet him and I can arrange for the three of us to have dinner together."

Richard nods, considers this, wonders about Michelson's deeper motives. "I'll check my schedule," he says. "When did you say it was again?"

"Wednesday," he says. "Wednesday night. There'll be a reading, of course, and then, if you'd like, we can all have dinner."

"Wednesday," Richard says, pretending to ponder this, pretending he's actually considering it. "Okay," he nods. Then he gives Michelson his hand, which Michelson holds a beat too long, says good-bye, and takes off through the rain, jumping over the puddles on his way to his mother's minivan.

3

EARLIER THAT DAY, before the sun came up, Raja had come to her dorm room and let himself in with the key she had given him. He had lain down beside her and put his arms around her and squeezed her tightly. He had been up half the night talking with the police, then his lawyer, then his parents. Technically, he was not allowed to be on the campus anymore, but he no longer cared. What else could they possibly do to him? he often reasoned. What else could they possibly do that hadn't already been done?

It was still unclear what would happen to him, or to her, what the charges would be, but that morning he had come into her dorm room and said that he didn't want to talk about it anymore. It was her last day, after all, and what he wanted to do now was make love to her, then take her out for breakfast, then drive her up to the airport in Boston. It would be a month, possibly two, before they saw each other again, and he didn't want to spend their last day together worrying about it. She had finally relented, agreeing not to talk about it, though it was hard for her to think of anything else. When he'd made love to her, she'd cried, and then afterward, she had sat there at her window and stared out at the empty quad, at the freshly fallen snow and the purple sky above it. In the corner, Raja had dressed quietly, then come over to her and sat beside her on the bed. He had squeezed her so tightly that she was sure he'd broken a rib, or maybe something else, something that would leave a permanent trace of him.

"I don't want you to talk about this with your parents," he'd said finally.

"I already have."

"I know," he said. "But I don't want you to say anything that you haven't already said."

"Why not?"

"I just don't," he'd said. "It'll be better that way."

"For who?"

"For both of us."

She'd nodded, though it bothered her how surreptitious he'd become, how guarded. Earlier that week, he had come over to her dorm room and demanded that she show him all of her e-mails, even the personal ones from friends. Then he'd made her delete each and every one, even though she'd made a promise to him long before that she would never talk about this stuff with anyone. Deleting the e-mails from him had been the hardest. It was like erasing a part of her life, a part of her past. Suddenly, aside from the few tiny letters she'd kept hidden at the back of her desk, there was no evidence, no sign at all, that she'd ever actually known him.

Later, on the way to the airport, they stopped at a diner for breakfast, and then afterward they'd driven the rest of the way to Boston in silence. When he dropped her off at the airport, he'd been quiet, evasive, just like he'd been on the way up. He'd helped her with her bags; then he'd stood there and hugged her tightly, though he hadn't cried. She had wanted him to cry. She had wanted him to show some sign of remorse, some sign of contrition for what he'd dragged her into, or, at the very least, some sign that he would miss her. But that was not his style. Instead what he'd done was patted her on the head and kissed her. Then he'd said, "It's gonna be okay."

"I wish I believed you."

"It will be," he said. "I promise."

"Do you have enough money to get back home?" she'd said. "I mean, for gas?" He almost never had enough money for anything.

He looked at her and shrugged. "I'll manage," he said.

"What if I never see you again?" she said. The thought of this had never even occurred to her before that moment.

"Then that would be a miracle," he'd said. "Or a tragedy." Then he'd started to laugh. "Or both."

Now, as she stands outside the empty baggage claim at Houston International, she wonders how long it will be before she sees him again. How long it will be before she hears his voice. Raja had been the first and only boy she'd ever loved. Before him, there had been Aiden Bell, and before Aiden, there had been Dustin O'Keefe, but neither of those boys had held a candle to Raja. It was only with Raja that she felt herself. It was only in his presence that she understood what women meant when they talked about love in magazines and books. There was a coolness about him, a detachment, that seemed to attract other people. He had more friends than she had ever had, and yet he never seemed to make the slightest effort to get to know them. They simply showed up at his room at all hours of the night, wanting to talk about books or politics or movies or wanting to tell him about the problems in their lives. That he'd chosen her as his girlfriend had been a miracle. He could have been with any woman he'd wanted to, practically. Any Indian woman, for sure. And yet, he'd chosen her, a suburban white girl from the South, his Indian parents' worst nightmare. On their first date together, he had taken her to Tommy's, the local hamburger joint off campus, and over chili fries and beer, he had told her about his life in Pakistan, then India. How they'd moved around a lot. How they'd never had enough money. How he'd shared a room with his brother and sister. He talked a lot about his father's jobs, most of which were part-time jobs in the pharmaceutical industry, and how he'd usually get laid off or canned just as Raja was making friends. They were always moving, Raja said, but certain things remained the same, remained constant. His mother's cooking, for example, the rich tandoori and vegetable curries she made, the flaky *parathta* and roti that she baked in a coal-fired oven. The way he talked about his mother's cooking made her feel guilty for wanting to eat the chili-cheese fries at Tommy's, for devouring them so quickly.

When he'd finally finished, she'd asked him if he thought he'd ever go back.

"To visit, sure," he'd said. "But not to live."

"Why not?"

He'd thought about this for a moment. Then he'd said, very earnestly, "That place is dead to me now."

She'd asked him what he meant by that, but he hadn't answered. Instead, he'd taken her hand and reached for the bill. "Would you like to see my room?" he'd asked.

.   .   .

Outside the baggage claim at Houston International, the rain is coming down thickly now, blurring her view. In the distance, she can see a long row of lights, headlights from the cars moving up along the thruway. She tries to imagine Raja's face, his lips, tries to picture him just as he looked that night at Tommy's, that first night they kissed, but as soon as she sees his features, as soon as she pictures his face, the image is gone, broken up by the sound of her cell phone ringing. She reaches into her purse and grabs the phone, and a moment later she hears her brother's voice on the other end.

"I'm here," he says.

"Where?"

"Look to your right."

Craning her neck, she sees her mother's minivan, and then inside it her brother Richard, sitting in the front seat, waving.

Later, when they're on the interstate, Richard looks her up and down evenly, almost like he's surveying her. Finally, he leans across the seat and pats her hand. "You look thinner," he says.

"You think?"

"Uh-huh."

She shrugs.

"You hungry?"

She shakes her head.

"Mom said I needed to feed you."

She looks at him and smirks. "Since when am I incapable of feeding myself?"

"I don't know," he says, hitting the gas. "I'm just telling you what she said. I think she's just kind of freaked out, you know."

She nods, looks out the window, straightens her dress. In the distance, she can see the skyline of Houston, looming along the horizon.

"So I guess you're going to be staying with us for a while now, huh?"

"Looks that way."

"Any chance you're going to tell me what happened up there?"

She doesn't answer.

"Mom said it was pretty serious. Something about a political disagreement."

"A political disagreement?" She laughs. "Really? That's what she said?"

"Yeah. Why? It wasn't?"

She looks at him but doesn't answer. She can feel his curiosity, his eyes on her. There is no one in the world who knows her better than Richard, no one else who understands her like him, and for a moment she feels transparent, exposed, like he can see everything she's thinking simply by looking at her. It has always been this way, though, their whole lives. There is Richard, and there is her, and then there is everyone else. For most of her childhood, he had been her best and only friend, her sole protector, her confidant, and even now she realizes that there is no one else in her life who she can trust with this information, no one else who she would even consider telling the story to. Still, thinking of Raja, she decides against it, decides instead to change the subject. "Where are you taking me anyway?" she says finally as they're moving toward the exit.

"Back home. Back to Mom's."

She looks at him. "Can't you take me somewhere else?"

"Like where?"

"Like anywhere. You know, anywhere but *there*."

He steadies the wheel. "Well, I'm going to a club later, but I don't think it's really your type of club, if you know what I mean." He looks at her and winks.

"I don't care," she says. "As long as they have booze, I really don't care. And besides, I like gay clubs. Gay men are about the only type of men who are nice to me these days."

He puts on his blinker, takes the exit.

"How are they doing anyway?" she says.

"Who?"

"Mom and Dad."

He looks at her and shakes his head. "Last week Mom got the locks changed on the house."

"Really? Why?"

"I don't know," he says. "I guess she didn't want him sneaking into the house anymore and stealing her stuff. He still has his key, you know, and so I guess he kept coming by during his lunch break and hanging out there. I caught him once. He was just sitting around the kitchen, drinking a glass of wine, reading the paper."

"God," she says. "That's depressing."

"I know."

She looks at him. "So, I guess they're not talking still."

"Nope. Not unless you count leaving hostile messages on each other's voice mail as talking."

She looks at her brother and sighs. In a way, she still feels guilty about it, guilty for leaving him here all alone to deal with their parents by himself, guilty for not being around when it all went down. It had been Richard who had had to deal with the brunt of it, Richard who had had to endure the fighting, the legal disagreements, the disassembling of the house. It had been Richard who had called her up that Sunday night in late October and told her the news, left that cryptic message on her voice mail: *World War Three here, Chlo. I'm serious. All's not well on the home front. Call me as soon as you can.* And when she'd called, he'd been sweet, almost apologetic about it, like it had all been his fault. He'd listened to her as she'd cried for half the night, comforting her, reassuring her. And then finally, when she'd finished, when she'd finally exhausted herself, he'd started to laugh. *Well, there's one good thing about all this, you know.*

What's that?

No more family meals.

It had been a joke between them. Family meals. The one thing they both hated. The one thing they both despised. Their father sitting at the far end of the table, carving the meat, their mother sitting beside him, pretending to love him. The two of them sitting around obediently at the far end of the room, pretending to be two well-adjusted children in a well-adjusted home. It had been the greatest hypocrisy of all. These family meals. The greatest charade.

At the edge of the exit, Richard takes a left onto a side street, and suddenly the city of Houston comes into view: the neon-lit supermarkets, the taqueries, the giant palm trees swaying in the wind. This old familiar setting, the tropical paradise of her youth, coming back into view. She leans back in her seat and takes it all in.

As Richard pulls onto another street, she looks at him.

"You know, I read those poems you sent me."

"Oh yeah? Which ones?"

"All of them," she says, smiling at him. "They're good."

"You think?"

"Well, yeah. I mean, I'm not an expert or anything, but they're definitely a lot better than that crap they publish in the literary magazine back at school."

He looks at her and smiles. "Thanks," he says. Then he idles the car at a stoplight. "You know, this professor of mine—this guy I'm working with—he's been trying to get me to apply to grad school in creative writing. For poetry, you know."

"You should."

"Right," he says. "Can you imagine what Dad would say?"

"Have you talked to him about it?"

"Well, no—I mean yeah, kind of. I mentioned it to him once and he was all, *What? They actually have schools for that?*"

Richard mimics his father's voice, his consternation, until she finally laughs.

"It's bad enough I'm gay. But a gay poet. I mean, I think that's just a little too much for him."

She laughs again and realizes then how long it's been since she's laughed like this. How long it's been since she's had a reason. She imagines Raja sitting in his motel room all alone, then his parents sitting in the room next door, spending their very last penny to get him legal counsel. She pushes this image from her mind, readjusts her seat, rolls down the window.

"I think I'm going to smoke," she says.

"Be my guest."

She reaches into her purse for the pack, just as a thin stream of rain comes into the car, dampening her lap. She pulls out a cigarette and lights it, then closes her eyes, letting the rain hit her face.

"You know," Richard says after a moment, "I don't know what happened up there at Stratham and, I mean, I don't really need to know. You can tell me whenever you want. I just want you to know that if you ever feel like talking about it, you know, I'm here." He looks at her. "I mean, you don't have to worry about me saying shit to Mom and Dad."

"I know that," she says and smiles. Then she pats his hand. "Thanks."

She leans back in her seat again and closes her eyes.

A moment later, Richard's cell phone rings, and after a few brief exchanges, he pulls over on the side of the road and takes out a pen from the glove compartment and writes down something on his hand. An address? A number? When he finally hangs up, he looks at her and smiles.

"Change of plans," he says.

"Oh yeah? What's up?"

"Well, it looks like that club thing's not going to be happening any-more. Something about the weather or something. Anyway, we're going to a party instead."

"Whose party?"

He turns up the radio and hits the gas, and for a moment she thinks she sees him smile. "Beto's," he says, winking. "This guy named Beto."

4

LORNA'S BEST FRIEND, Elise Henriquez, is standing at the counter, making tea, a cigarette dangling from her mouth. Elise had arrived only minutes before Elson, just as he was about to walk through the door and tell Lorna what had happened. There had been a blackout in Elise's apartment apparently, and so she'd brought over half her refrigerator in a cooler, all of the perishables, all of the meats. And now, as a sign of gratitude to Lorna, she is making them tea.

Elson leans back in his chair and watches her. Just moments before, he had given Lorna a look, a nasty look, which Lorna had ignored. Now he wonders if he should have played it differently, maybe been a little more gracious. He tries to catch her eye again, but she has turned away.

The apartment itself is dimly lit, the walls covered with original artwork given to Lorna by friends. There's a warmth to this place, a warmth to this apartment, that belies her own personal aesthetic for clean lines and barren walls. A minimalist in theory, but not in practice, Elson thinks. On the wall to his left, there's an enormous bookcase filled with books, more books than Elson has ever read, mostly political biographies and socialist rants, abstract discourses on the state of the world. On the wall to his right, there's an enormous painting of Lorna herself, a nude, painted by an old boyfriend. When they'd first started dating, he'd asked her to take it down, demanded that she remove it, and she'd refused. He'd told her that it made him feel uncomfortable, especially when her friends were over, and she'd laughed. To have her body laid out like that for everyone to see, he'd said, what would they think? She had told him that they were all artists and that they wouldn't think anything, and that had been the end of that. But now, as he looks at the painting, he wonders why he'd ever cared so much. The figure itself barely resembles her. It's a crude rendering at best. He leans back in his chair and considers this.

"How do you like your tea?" Elise says to Elson, turning around and taking the kettle off the stove. "With cream? Sugar?"

"I think I'll just stick with what I'm having," Elson says, nodding toward the gin and tonic on the table that he's just made for himself.

Lorna looks at the drink, perhaps noticing it for the first time, then at Elson.

They have a rule lately, or rather, she has a rule: no more than two drinks a night. A rule implemented after Elson drove his car into one of her neighbors' trash cans and spilled half of its contents onto the street. But Lorna doesn't know about the Brunswick Hotel or the two drinks Elson has had earlier, so for all intents and purposes, this is really his first. His first real drink anyway. The other two were starter drinks, what his wife would have called *relaxers*. And besides, he thinks, his daughter just got expelled from college, right? Didn't that warrant a drink?

He leans back in his chair and stares at the two women.

"So, I meant to congratulate you," Elise says as she and Lorna sit down at the table with their tea. "For that building you just built. That music building over at Rice. It's lovely." She smiles at him. "I understand you had a hand in that."

"Oh no," Elson says. "Not really." He picks up his drink and sips it. "They had me on it at first, but then they took me off."

"Oh," Elise says, looking down.

"It's not that uncommon," Elson continues, trying to recover. "Happens all the time in a big firm like ours. They think they want you on one thing, and then they decide they want you on something else. There's a lot of moving around, you know, a lot of reshuffling."

Elise nods. "I'm sure," she says. "I can imagine."

The truth was, it did happen all the time in a big firm like theirs. People were always being moved around, reshuffled. But it was also true that this had been happening to Elson more and more often lately. He had been reassigned twice in the past month alone, and when he had made a formal complaint about it to one of the partners, Ted Sullivan, Ted had told him not to worry about it, that they'd soon put him on something else, something better, which of course they never did. What Ted didn't tell him, and what Elson knew to be the truth, was that they no longer cared for his aesthetic. They felt he'd gone too far, that his buildings were too severe, too cold. There had been some complaints among some of the clients as well. One of them, a very famous movie actor, who had actually requested that Elson design his house, had threatened to sue the firm after seeing the final product. He claimed that the house itself had caused emotional distress in his marriage, that his wife had cried when she'd seen it, and that it wasn't the type of place where a normal human being could raise children. Never mind that Elson had won a prestigious national award in the late seventies that had brought in more recognition, and more clients, to the firm than ever before. Never mind that one of the first buildings he'd ever built, a small Presbyterian church on the outskirts of Houston, was still being used in graduate classrooms as a model of formal simplicity. Never mind that half of the interns who worked there had listed him as their number one reason for choosing Sullivan & Gordon. None of that mattered anymore. What mattered now were profits. The bottom line. And none of his buildings were bringing in profits anymore, or at least not like they used to. The materials he chose were too expensive, they'd told him, his timelines too long. It was for these reasons and others that he'd never made partner. That he'd remained an associate architect for twenty-two years.

He picks up his drink and takes a sip and notices that both Elise and Lorna are looking at him expectantly.

"Isn't that crazy?" Lorna says.

"What?"

"Weren't you even listening?"

And he realizes then that he must have zoned out, something that's been happening to him more and more often lately. "I'm sorry," he says. "I must have drifted."

They both stare at him. "Well, Elise was just telling me that Woody Harrelson came into their gallery today and bought three paintings. All by Guzman. Stayed, what—five minutes?"

"Five minutes," Elise confirms.

"Woody Harrelson?" Elson says.

"Come on, Elson. You know who Woody Harrelson is. The actor?"

Elson stares at them blankly.

"Jesus, Elson. Don't you ever go to the movies?" Elise starts to laugh.

"I don't like movies," Elson says.

They both stare at him in disbelief, and Elson feels a sudden need to rescue himself. "I like Godard," he says finally, "but I'm not sure if he's still making movies anymore. Is he still alive?"

They both smile at him, but before they can answer, the phone rings, and Lorna jumps up and runs over to the counter to answer it. She starts to laugh at something the caller has just said and then she says, "This is so weird. We were just talking about you." Then she looks at Elise. *It's Guzman,* she mouths. "Well, aren't you the little star," she continues, laughing. "Uh-huh. I know. It's totally nuts, right?"

Elson reaches for his drink and finishes it off. He tries to remember who Guzman is. He's met so many of Lorna's friends in the past year that it's hard for him to distinguish one from another. All wannabe artists, he thinks. Poseurs. Frauds. He looks at Elise and asks her for a cigarette, which she happily gives him.

"What are these?" he says, eyeing the soft turquoise pack.

"American Spirits," she says. "They're organic. No chemicals."

Elson looks at the cigarette, then lights it. In the background, he can still hear Lorna talking. "No, totally, it's fine. Sure. Come over anytime. We're just sitting here having tea."

Elson looks at her, and she looks away. A moment later, she's off the phone and back at the table.

"Guzman's coming over," she says. "He's blacked out, too. The whole east side of Montrose apparently. Anyway, he's bringing Carrie."

"Well, if we're having a party . . . ," Elson says, reaching for the bottle of gin, not finishing his sentence.

Lorna purses her lips.

"I love Guzman," Elise says.

"Who's Guzman?" Elson says, reaching for the tonic. He looks at Lorna, who's no longer looking at him.

"Oh, I'm sure you've met him," Elise says after a moment, trying to break the tension. "Tall gay man. Always wears black. Even in the summer. I think you met him at Carrie's, or maybe it was Stu's. Anyways, he's a brilliant artist."

"Apparently," Elson says smugly, drawing on his cigarette.

"Don't mind Elson," Lorna says to Elise. "He's just had a bad day."

"Oh yeah?" Elise says. "What happened?"

Elson downs the rest of his drink quickly, then reaches for the bottle.

"My daughter just got expelled from college," he says, looking at the back of Lorna's head.

Lorna turns around finally, her eyes suddenly soft. He can see her surprise. "Are you serious?" she says. "Chloe?"

"Yep."

"What happened?"

"That I can't tell you, my dear. Wish I could, but Cadence won't tell me a thing. All I know is that she's back at home for the rest of the term."

"So, it's not permanent?" Elise says.

"I have no idea," he says. Then he takes the bottle and starts to pour, forgoing the tonic this time.

"Why don't you slow down," Lorna says, grabbing his wrist.

"My daughter just got expelled from school," he says to her evenly, as if that would be the answer to every question she asked him for the rest of the night.

After a moment, Lorna lets go, and he continues pouring.

"Maybe I should leave the two of you alone," Elise says. "I feel really bad for being here right now."

"Nonsense," Elson says, waving her off. "We're just having a drink, right? We're just a bunch of friends having a drink."

"You're the only one drinking," Lorna points out.

"Okay," he says, "so I'm the only one drinking. Big deal. I'm also the only one who's about to stand up and go take a piss." And with that, he stands up clumsily, feeling the shift of the room, and starts toward the hall. In the background, he can hear Lorna apologizing to Elise. *His divorce*, she is saying. *His daughter*. He moves toward the bathroom and closes the door. He stares at his face in the mirror, its distorted image, then runs some water. Suddenly the room is tilting, the Mexican tiles changing shape. He sits down on the edge of the tub and tries to catch his bearings. He feels a little nauseous, a little ill, and then suddenly he's on the floor and crawling toward the toilet. In the background, he can hear some music coming on. Marvin Gaye? The Four Tops? As the singer sings *Oh baby, baby*, Elson vomits twice, very violently, into the bowl. The music goes off, and then he hears his name being called. He vomits again, this time so forcefully that he feels it in his gut, his stomach muscles tightening, and then he looks in the bowl and notices that there are tiny red specks on the porcelain rim. Others float around in the bowl. He wipes his forehead, loosens his tie, stares at the specks, then moves over toward the wall and tries to relax. As he slumps down on the floor, he can feel the dampness on the back of his shirt and feels faint. A moment later, there's a knock on the door, and then another, and then he hears his name being called. When the door finally opens, he can see Lorna's worried face looking in.

"Elson?" she says.

But he can't bring himself to speak, can't bring himself to say a thing. He stares at her for a moment, then closes his eyes.

"Elson?" she says again. "What the fuck is happening?" And that is the last thing he hears for a very long time.

Part Two

"WHAT WERE WE talking about?" Dr. Peterson says.

"When?"

"The last time."

"I don't remember."

"Cadence."

"I don't know," she says. "Honestly."

"I think we were talking about your husband," he says, looking through a file on his lap. "At least, according to my notes."

"We might have been," she says. "I don't really know."

The room they're sitting in is a large, high-ceilinged office with glass walls overlooking the skyline of downtown Houston. The room is aggressively air-conditioned and very white. The furniture is spare, modern. No doubt picked out by some Scandinavian designer with impeccable taste. Two palm trees sit in iron pots in either corner of the room, but otherwise the space is empty, save for the two tiny couches they're both sitting on. Across from her, Peterson taps his pen.

"Well, isn't that part of the reason we're here?" Peterson continues abstractly. "To talk about him?"

"I thought we were here to talk about me."

"Well, that too, of course. But I guess what I mean is *him* in relation to *you*."

"Not today," she says bluntly, looking out the window.

"Why not?"

"Just not today."

Ever since she got the phone call last week that her ex-husband Elson had been taken to the hospital in an ambulance, she has cringed at the sound of his name. The call had woken her up from a dream, a dream she'd been having about her father's farm, and after she had woken up from this dream, after she'd learned what had happened, she had gotten into her car and then driven all the way across town at three in the morning to St. Ignatius Loyola, which is where she'd found Elson, lying in a bed, his girlfriend at his side. His girlfriend had been the one who called her. Lorna. A thin wisp of a girl. Not much to look at, really. Still, she had been exceedingly nice to her, so nice, in fact, that Cadence had found it hard to dislike her. What was a nice girl like this doing with Elson? she'd wondered. Elson had been asleep when she'd arrived. Hooked up to a heart monitor. A tube in his nose. He had looked like a tiny child, an infant, helpless and alone.

As they stood over Elson's body, Lorna had tried to explain to her what had happened. He'd been vomiting, she said, vomiting pretty hard, and then at one point he'd passed out cold on the linoleum floor of the bathroom. By the time he'd come to, the ambulance was there, and so they'd taken him out to the hospital, to the intermediate care unit, which was where they were standing now. At the time she'd called, Lorna said, she'd thought it might have been more serious, maybe life threatening, but now she wasn't sure. They hadn't let her see him, she said. They were running some tests, of course, some routine stuff, but she hadn't known what to do, hadn't known who to call, so she'd decided to call up Cadence. Every time she spoke, this poor girl, she looked down, as if embarrassed by what had happened, ashamed for what she'd done, for waking up Cadence at three in the morning and making her drive all the way across town to see him.

Cadence had assured her it was fine, that she would have done the same, then she'd patted the girl's hand. She pushed from her mind any thoughts of what Elson and this girl might have done together on her own living room couch or what Elson might be doing now to support her, how he was probably supplementing her income with money he rightfully owed her, how he was probably paying her utility bills, her cable, her rent. She ignored all of these things and embraced this girl, pulled her tightly to her chest, and told her it was fine.

"I'm just glad he's not dead," she'd said and smiled.

As it turned out, what had happened to Elson hadn't been that serious after all. A torn esophagus is what they said. That had been the final diagnosis. A torn esophagus from too much puking, or from puking too hard, she couldn't remember. In any event, Lorna had claimed that it was probably from something he ate, an allergic reaction or food poisoning. *Not from something he* drank? Cadence had asked. *No, no,* Lorna had said. *Probably not.* She wondered, even then, why this girl was protecting him. Had he trained her to do this, or was it something else? Guilt perhaps? Guilt for letting this happen? Didn't she realize that Cadence knew her husband, her ex-husband, better than anyone? That if anyone was to blame it was obviously Elson? She suddenly felt sorry for the girl, sorry that she had had to inherit her misfortune, her burden, and as they parted ways, she'd squeezed her hand gently.

"Good luck with him," she'd said. "He's more than a handful."

"Yeah." Lorna had laughed. "I've noticed."

Then she'd patted her hand again, thanked her, and walked down the hall.

So this is what had happened. But what she couldn't explain to Peterson, what she didn't *want* to explain to Peterson, was that earlier that night, as she'd been driving across town to the hospital, she'd been almost paralyzed with fear. The thought of losing Elson now, after everything that had just happened, it was almost too much to process. She began to regret certain things she had said to him, certain things she had done. She began to feel guilty for the way she had treated him, the way they had fought. Then at one point—and this is what she couldn't explain to Peterson—she began to second-guess herself, began to second-guess the divorce. She began to wonder whether any of this would have ever happened had she simply treated him better, or forgiven him, or had they both tried a little harder.

Second-guessed her divorce? Jesus Christ. What would Peterson do with a thing like that? He'd have a field day with it. He'd bring it up for the rest of eternity. She knew how his mind worked. How he processed these things. She knew exactly what he'd think. For the past several months, Peterson had been needling her, probing her, trying to catch her off balance, trying to get her to reveal things she didn't want to reveal. His style was to sit back patiently and wait, to sit there and watch her, but recently she had given him almost nothing to work with, and she knew it annoyed him. Had she not just left another psychiatrist the previous fall, she probably would have left Peterson by now. But what else could she do? The man wasn't a dolt, just exasperating. His incessant pen tapping, his placid smile, his overreaching claims.

And now, as she looks at him, she wonders whether or not he will try to persist, but after a moment Peterson simply looks at her and smiles, then closes his file.

"Well, what would you like to talk about then?" he says.

"I don't know," she says. "Why don't we play one of those games you like? What's that one? Association?"

He stares at her, refuses to take the bait, adjusts his tie. "How 'bout we just talk about you today?"

"Okay," she says.

"How are your classes going?" he says finally, grasping for something to ask.

"They're fine."

"Anything new to report?"

"No," she says. "Not really."

"What about that man you were talking to. That man in your class. What's his name? Has anything developed there?"

"Developed?"

"Yes."

"I don't know," she says, pausing, trying to think how to put this. "I guess you could say that a few things have developed there."

"In what sense?"

"Well," she says, deciding now to throw him a bone, "I guess in the sense that I've slept with him."

Peterson looks at her, trying to hide his surprise. "Really?"

"Yes."

"I'm surprised it took you so long to tell me."

"Well," she says, smiling, "I'm surprised it took me so long to sleep with him."

He stares at her, then looks down at her file. "So would you say you're dating this man now?"

"No," she says. "I'd say I'm sleeping with him."

Peterson nods. "And does this man have a name?"

"No." Cadence pauses. "Not for now. For now, we'll just call him *the man*."

Peterson smiles at this, shakes his head. What he doesn't know, and what Cadence will never tell him, is that this man she's referring to is not another student, as he presumes, but the instructor of her class, an adjunct lecturer who has been teaching at Rice for the past two years on a part-time basis. That she's become involved with him is a surprise even to her, but it's also not something she wants to get into with Peterson right now. Not today.

"Okay," Peterson says. "So, this man, do you find him attractive?"

"I just told you I slept with him."

"I know, but that's not an answer to my question." He pauses. "Okay, let me put it another way. Do you like him?"

"In what sense?"

"In any sense."

She pauses. "I think so."

The truth is, she isn't sure if she likes him. All she knows is that when she goes in to Rice twice a week to take her evening business class she enjoys hearing him speak. She enjoys watching him stand at the front of the room and talk to the other students about abstract principles and hypothetical scenarios, knowing all the while that she's slept with him, that she knows where his scars are, that she knows where he likes to be kissed. They met on the first day of class, when she'd stayed late to explain to him that she didn't like to be called on in class. That it wasn't anything personal, but that she just didn't like it. As someone who was twenty years older than the average student in the room, she'd said, she felt a little uncomfortable about it, that's all. He'd smiled and told her that he understood, that he would feel the same. Then he'd asked her her name, why she was back in school, and all the rest. She had tried to be cautious at first, but soon found herself telling him all about Elson, about their divorce, and about how she was trying to go back to school now, after all these years, simply for practical reasons. To make herself marketable, she'd said. To become a viable option on the job market. He'd laughed and shook his head. *Ah yes,* he'd said. *The job market.*

He told her his name was Gavin, that she should call him Gavin, and that had been the beginning. The next week they'd gone out for coffee (his suggestion), then drinks (her suggestion), then back to his apartment in Rice Village. He told her that night that he had been divorced himself, twice, and that he hadn't had the best luck with women. Then he'd told her that he had a son from his first marriage who was mildly retarded. He told her that everything he did was for his son, to get him help, to get him assistance. She wondered, even then, if this was just a line, something he used on all the girls, but decided in the end it wasn't. He was young—maybe thirty-eight or thirty-nine—and had a nice body. In fact, the first time she'd touched his body, it had been like going back in time, like going back to an earlier time in her life, a time when Elson himself had been in shape, a time when he used to play tennis and jog twice a week.

So yes, in a way she liked him. But still, she wasn't sure what she was getting into, and she didn't want to get into it with Peterson. Not today. She knew what Peterson would say, how he'd react, how he'd interpret it. She knew all the questions he'd ask. This was Peterson's bread and butter, after all. His mode of inquiry. This is what he got off on. And she didn't want to give him the pleasure. So, as he sits here now, staring at her, she simply looks at him, smiling, giving him one-word answers until he finally stops asking.

"Okay," he says after a moment, shifting gears. "And how about your children?"

"They're fine," she says.

"Your daughter's back in town, right?"

"That's right."

"Any new developments there?"

"What do you mean? With her case?"

"Yes."

"I'm not going to be talking about that anymore."

"Why not?"

"She doesn't want me to."

"Never?"

"No," she says. "Never."

"You realize that everything you say here is confidential."

"I realize that," she says. "I'm just trying to respect her wishes, you know?"

She looks at Peterson evenly. Ever since she brought it up, she's sensed that Peterson has had a strange fascination with her daughter's case, that he likes hearing about it, that he enjoys considering all the moral complexities. It's almost like he's just sitting there, waiting for her to mention it, even as she's talking about something else. And now he looks deflated, annoyed. He taps his pen.

She smiles slyly. "You look disappointed."

"Why would I be disappointed?"

"I don't know," she says, and drops it.

"Let me ask you something, Cadence," he says after a moment. "Do you feel like you're getting anything out of these little sessions we have?"

"Yes."

"Are you sure?"

"Yes. Why? Are you suggesting I don't?"

"No," he says. "I'm not suggesting anything."

She stares at him. Peterson. Insufferable Peterson. She wonders what it must be like to be his wife, to make love to him. *Do you like it when I touch you here?* she might ask him, to which Peterson would reply, *I don't know. Do you like touching me there?* Every question answered with a question. This was Peterson. This was his mode of detachment.

Peterson fumbles through a few more questions, looking at her file, covering every topic he can think of, before finally throwing up his arms. "You're going to have to help me out here, Cadence," he says after a moment, sighing. "This street runs two ways, you know."

"I know that," she says. "I'm sorry."

She can tell she's unnerved him.

"I guess I'm just not in much of a talking mood today," she says finally, leaning back on the couch. "In fact, I think this might be a good place to stop."

"Really?"

"Yes."

Peterson looks at her, nods, then reaches for her file and starts writing something down, scribbling away. This is the second time she's done that this month, ended their sessions abruptly. Usually Peterson protests, tries to push forward, but today he doesn't seem to care. And neither does she. She's long since stopped caring what Peterson thinks of her. She watches him as he scribbles, then stares at the long row of filing cabinets on the wall behind him. All these screwed-up people neatly arranged in yellow files, she thinks, all alphabetized. She wonders where she ranks among them, where she falls on the general scale of screwed-up-ness.

When he finally finishes scribbling, she looks at him. "By the way, I'm not going to be coming in next week."

"Why not?"

"I have a test that night. Not for my business class. A different class."

"Maybe we can schedule a different time then."

"No," she says. "I actually think I'd like a week off from this anyway."

"Okay," Peterson says. "Fair enough." He looks at his watch. "We still have fifteen minutes."

She smiles at him. "Maybe you can give me a discount today."

He grins. "I'm afraid that's not how it works, Cadence."

"Well, then, why don't we just say I'm giving you those minutes. Okay? You can call up your wife. Tell her you love her."

Peterson looks at her, then finally concedes. "Okay," he says, smiling now. "Sure. I might just do that."

Then he stands up and shakes her hand and lets her out the door.

Without stopping by the receptionist's desk to pay her bill or to schedule another appointment, Cadence starts down the hall toward the elevator. Another pointless session with Peterson, she thinks. But as soon as she gets to the elevator, as soon as she gets in, she realizes she's crying. She has no idea where this sudden outburst has come from, or what it means, only that before she knows it, she is rubbing her face, drying her eyes. She reaches into her purse for a Kleenex. There's a woman standing beside her in the elevator, watching her, and as they get off at the first-floor lobby, the woman turns to her and reaches out her hand, touches her.

"Are you okay?" asks the woman.

In the distance, through tall glass windows on the other side of the lobby, Cadence can see the city of Houston, shimmering and bright in the mid-afternoon sun.

"Yes," she says, smiling at the woman, touching her arm. "I'm fine."

2

CHLOE HAD THOUGHT about her for years, had dreamed about her, and now it suddenly seemed important that she see her. She had called her up earlier that day to suggest lunch, and when she'd answered her phone it was like nothing had ever happened, like no time had passed, like they were still back in high school planning a trip to the mall. Her voice had sounded different, though. Chloe had noticed this. More serene perhaps, more removed. She'd suggested that Chloe stop by her store and that they eat there. She could make them something in the back, she'd said. Some tofu, or perhaps a simple salad. Nothing fancy. She'd opened up her store in the year after Chloe had left for college. It was a New Age store, as far as Chloe could tell, a store that sold books about spirituality and holistic healing, a store that sold herbal lotions and beads. Chloe had never been inside, but she'd driven by it once or twice and had read about it on the Internet. They offered back massages and meditation sessions and Tarot card readings. They offered retreats to the Hill Country for what they called spiritual replenishing. She wondered, even then, what had happened to her friend. The girl she used to go to Nordstrom's with, the girl she used to talk to for hours about boys in their class.

In the spring of their sophomore year, Simone had dropped out. It had happened suddenly, unexpectedly. Her parents had pulled her out, and the next thing she knew Simone was in Colorado at some counseling facility, a place for troubled youth. It was true that Simone had had some trouble that year, some trouble with drugs, an eating disorder, a boyfriend who didn't treat her well. But still, the whole idea of pulling her out of school seemed a little extreme.

Chloe had always suspected there'd been something else, something she didn't know about. She'd also always suspected that Simone would eventually return, return to school, but she never did. In the beginning she'd written her letters, mostly updates on the latest gossip at school, and occasionally Simone had written back. But over time those letters became less frequent, and after a while she just stopped trying. She fell in with a new crowd, started dating Dustin O'Keefe, and pretty soon it was senior year and she was off to college. Simone was back by then, back in Houston, but she hadn't heard from her. She'd heard through the grapevine that Simone was getting her GED and working at the Whole Foods store in Montrose, but she'd never seen her there, and then one day during the fall of her first semester in college, she'd received an e-mail from a friend with a link to Simone's store. The title of the e-mail had read: "Fucking Bizarre."

Ever since she'd received that e-mail, though, she'd been curious to see her, her former best friend, curious to hear about her life and her husband, who was referenced on the Web site. So she'd called her up that morning, out of the blue, and now she was here, sitting in her store.

When she'd first arrived there'd been a young guy working behind the counter, a boy her age, and she'd assumed at first that this might be Simone's husband, but when she asked her later Simone had corrected her. *No, no,* she'd said. *That's just Dupree. He works here.* Dupree. A strange name for a boy, a hippie boy no less. When she'd first walked in, Dupree had regarded her absently, then smiled and gone back to his work. There was something about him that disarmed her. She was glad, in the end, that he wasn't Simone's husband. As it turned out, Simone's husband was a sculptor, an artist. He had a little studio in the back of the store, Simone said, but that day he was away in Austin, setting up a show. She'd shown her a picture of him, and he'd looked old, Chloe thought, a little weathered. Maybe forty, forty-five. He had a tiny goatee-style beard and wavy hair. He looked like he'd been through the sixties, or maybe a war.

They had talked about him for a while, Simone explaining how they'd met at a ranch in Marfa and how he'd courted her for years, sending her twenty-page letters from the ranch. He was living on the ranch at the time, with a bunch of other artists, a sort of commune situation, an artists' community. Then one day he just showed up at her door in Houston and said that he was moving there. He didn't have an apartment or a job, so she'd let him move in. Two months later, they were married. And two months after that, she opened up her store. "He really broke me down."

Simone laughed. "But I'm glad he did. He's a gentle man, you know, a very kind soul."

Chloe had looked at her and smiled, told her how happy she was for her, but a part of her still couldn't get past what had happened to her friend, how different she seemed. Every time Simone spoke, it was like she was speaking from behind a veil, couching her words with euphemisms, casting everything in a positive light. Everything she spoke of was very beautiful, every person she mentioned was very kind, very nice. She wondered after a while if they were living in the same universe. She wanted to remind her of certain things they had done: sneaking out behind the gym to get high during seventh period, stealing her father's car to take a joyride with some boys from Montrose, lifting mascara from the Lancôme counter at Macy's. She wondered if Simone even remembered these things, if she ever thought about them, or if they'd simply been repressed, like so many things, at the back of her mind.

When it came time for Chloe to share her own news, she'd spoken calmly at first. She talked about her college, the classes she was taking, the professors that she liked. She had tried her best to steer the conversation away from Raja and what had happened, but inevitably the question came up: why was she back here in Houston in the middle of the term?

She didn't have an answer at first. Not a real one. She told her that she was taking some time off, a little break, regrouping. But eventually the conversation turned toward Raja, and she found herself talking about it, mentioning things that she hadn't mentioned to anyone. There was something in the way that Simone looked at her, a calmness in her gaze, that made her want to confess. She told her there'd been an incident, a serious incident back at school, and that certain people seemed to think that she had been involved in this incident. She told her that she knew the people involved and that one of them was her boyfriend, Raja, but that was as much as she said. She said nothing of her own involvement, her own complicity. The upshot was that there was a boy who had been hurt very badly during this incident and this boy was now lying in intensive care, recovering. He was in critical shape. She looked at Simone very calmly as she said this. She was trying to remain composed. But Simone didn't seem the least bit surprised or concerned. She just sat there, drinking her tea, a placid, almost vacant look in her eyes. She wondered what Simone was thinking, whether she knew that she was lying or only telling half the truth.

She went on to tell her other things, things she'd spared her father the previous day at lunch. She told her about the article in the school paper, the one with the fuzzy snapshot of her and Raja walking across the quad, and, beneath that, the picture of Raja's friend Seung. The article itself had been mostly lies, of course, but still, it had hurt her, she said, as had the headline above it: *"Busted!"* She told her about the aftermath, about the conversations she'd had to have with the police and later with the dean of students, the Student Judiciary Council, the Faculty Senate, and the Faculty Committee on Student Conduct. She told her about the endless interrogations, the questioning, the going-over of the facts. She told her about the tricks they'd tried to use on her, the ways they'd tried to trip her up, the ways they'd tried to get her to turn against Raja. Then she told her about the way that Raja himself had been arrested, handcuffed right in the middle of class, right in the middle of a giant lecture hall, right in front of all his friends, his professor—a calculated humiliation no doubt—and the way that she hadn't spoken to him, not really, since she'd been home.

By the time she'd finished, by the time she'd told her all about her own hearing, the verdict, the sentencing, the humiliating phone call she'd had to make to her mother, by the time she'd finished with all that, she was nearly in tears. And Simone, in the seat across from her, was simply watching, nodding.

After a moment, Simone reached across the table and put her hand on Chloe's cheek, then cupped both hands around Chloe's face and smiled.

"It's okay," she said.

Chloe was crying now.

"I'm glad you came here. I'm glad you're telling me these things."

Then Simone stood up and said that she was going to make some more tea and that she'd be back in a minute.

Chloe dried her eyes. She watched her walk out of the room, a tiny room in the back of the store filled with ceramic bowls and cups, a giant kiln, and a tiny window overlooking a yard. She heard her turn on the water, then turn it off. She heard her moving around some plates. Then, for a long time, it was very quiet. She kept expecting to hear the kettle go off, or the water boiling, but she didn't. She called out to Simone at one point, but there was no reply, and so she figured she was in the bathroom or on the phone.

That was over twenty minutes ago, though, and now she's beginning to wonder what has happened. Suddenly, she feels stupid for unloading on her, for telling her all the things that Raja told her not to tell anyone. She thinks of Raja, sitting in his motel room, how disappointed he'd be if he knew what she'd said. She thinks about the way his voice had sounded the last time they spoke, how depressed he'd seemed. She remembers what he said to her, how now, more than ever, it was important that she didn't say anything to anyone. He'd called her from a pay phone on the outskirts of town, near his motel. He'd said that he didn't trust his cell phone anymore, that it was probably being bugged, that he didn't want to implicate her any more than he already had. There was no reason for them to know that they were still in contact, he'd said. That was the way he'd put it. *Still in contact.* Then he'd told her what he'd told them, the police, that they had broken up, that she had broken up with him. She'd started to cry when he said this, but he told her it was for her own protection, her own good, a necessary precaution. The less they knew about her connection to him the better off she'd be. He was already talking like a guilty man, a man who had already been convicted and sent away, and it bothered her. She wondered what had happened to his initial optimism, his undying belief that things would work out.

When they got off the phone, she had sat in her room for a long time, crying, and that's when she'd thought about Simone. It occurred to her then that if anyone would understand what she was going through it would be Simone. But now, as she sits here, waiting for her, she wonders what she was thinking, what type of strange, convoluted logic she must have used to bring herself here, to convince herself that this was a good idea. Simone, after all, was not Simone. Not anymore. She was someone else, a walking zombie, a brainwashed moonchild, a concubine for some strange, aging artist. She sits up after a while and looks around the room. She calls out to Simone.

"How's that tea coming?" she says. But there's no answer.

After a moment, she stands up and walks into the kitchen, only to find it empty, abandoned. She looks around the room and notices that there's a tiny teapot sitting on the counter and, next to it, a small stack of paper cups. She starts back to the back room, the office, and there she finds a pile of cluttered papers lying on a desk, an empty chair, and a few watercolors hanging on the wall. But no Simone. She peeks inside the bathroom door, but the bathroom is empty. Understanding now that

Simone is gone, she turns around and starts back toward the front of the store. She finds the boy, Dupree, standing at the counter, flipping through a magazine. He looks at her from behind his shaggy bangs and smiles. Above his head are tiny mosaics, wind chimes, crystal vases filled with beads.

"Have you seen Simone?" she asks.

"She's not back there?"

"No. We were talking, I mean, she was making me some tea, and then she just vanished."

Dupree shakes his head. "Yeah," he says. "She does that a lot. Probably just stepped out."

"Really?"

"Uh-huh."

"And you think she's coming back?"

"Who knows?"

"You say she does this a lot?"

"What?"

"Steps out."

"Yeah," he says. "All the time." He looks at her. "Something about a low stress threshold or something. I don't know. I don't really understand. Too much intensity or something and she tends to bolt."

Chloe nods.

"She's got a couple screws loose, you know, but she's a good woman. As long as you don't talk about anything too upsetting or negative, she's fine."

"Oh." Chloe nods, looking down.

"Why? You were talking about something upsetting?"

"Yeah," she says. "I might have been."

"There you go," Dupree says, smiling. "But you know what? The old man's worse. Her husband? That dude's crazy. You complain about one little thing and he walks out of the room, or else he just zones you out, you know, starts humming to himself or looking through a magazine or something. It's wack." He smiles at her.

"So if they're so crazy," she says, looking at Dupree, "I mean, if they're nuts, why do you work here then?"

"I don't know," he says. "Just kind of fell into it, I guess." He looks at her. "They're actually not that bad most of the time. And besides, the pay's good. Really good." He smiles at her. "I thought at first they might have been dealers, or maybe growers—a lot of these people are—and so I thought I might be able to do a little business on the side, but it turns out they don't even touch the stuff. Say they don't believe in it." He laughs to himself then and shakes his head.

"So what does that make you then, a dealer?"

"Me? No. I'm no dealer, but I can get you just about anything you want, you know, if you're interested. Weapons, fireworks, you name it. You want front-row seats to Radiohead, I'm your man. You like weed? I got a guy on the inside. A guy who drives the stuff straight up from Mexico. Has a special little deal down there with the authorities. Border patrol. Has it all worked out."

She looks at him.

"Seriously. Anything you want, just let me know."

"Okay," she says. "I'll keep that in mind."

"What's your name anyway?"

"Chloe."

"Chloe," he says, reaching out his hand. "Dupree."

She takes his hand briefly, then drops it.

"So how do you know her anyway?"

She shrugs. "We used to be best friends," she says. "A long time ago. Back in high school."

"Oh." Dupree nods.

"She was really different then, you know, really cool."

"Yeah," he says. "So what happened?"

"I don't know," Chloe says. "I have no idea. I guess she just lost her shit, you know. This is the first time I've actually talked to her in, what, like five years."

"Man," Dupree says. "That's really sad."

"Yeah," she says, nodding, realizing the truth of this.

A moment later, Dupree reaches into his wallet and pulls out a card, then slides it across the counter toward her. "In case you change your mind," he says.

Chloe stares at the card. There's no name on it, just a beeper number. She picks it up, smiles, then puts it into her purse.

"Well, I should probably get going," she says. "You know, in case she wants to come back."

"Oh, I wouldn't worry about that," Dupree says. "She usually calls first."

"She does?"

"Yeah. Whenever she disappears like that, she'll call me like an hour later and be like *Have they left yet?*"

"You're kidding."

"No." He laughs. "Pretty nuts, huh?"

Chloe nods, considers this, feels a sadness in her gut.

"Well, I should be leaving anyway," she says. "It was nice to meet you, Dupree."

"Likewise," he says. "And just remember, anything you need, I'm your man."

"I'll remember that." She smiles and then walks out the door.

Outside, the city of Houston is bright, humid. She walks to her car, her mother's minivan, which she's been sharing with her brother, Richard, since she's returned. Inside, she turns on the air-conditioning and then wonders where to go next. If she had any money, she'd go to the mall. If she knew how to reach Raja, she'd call him. But she doesn't have any money and she doesn't know how to reach Raja, so she just sits there, staring out at the street. In the distance, she can see the overpass of I-10 looming along the horizon. She thinks about how nice it would be to just get on the highway and drive, maybe down to Galveston, down to the beach. She remembers going there as a child with her family, how pleasant it had been. Richard and her father trolling for redfish out in the ocean, she and her mother lying on the beach, playing cards. She wonders if they'll ever do anything like that again, just the four of them, as a family.

After a moment, she starts up the car and pulls out on the street, and just as she's passing by the small row of coffee shops and boutiques on the corner of the road, she notices a young woman sitting in one of the coffee-shop windows, staring out. She slows down the car, looks at the woman, and it takes her a moment, almost a full minute, before she recognizes the blouse, and realizes it's Simone.

3

"I DON'T REALLY see it that way," Richard is saying. "I mean, I don't really see the point."

He is sitting at a small outdoor café with Dr. Michelson and Dr. Michelson's friend Elan. They have ordered, eaten, and now they are talking about Richard, about his future and his promise. Richard himself is still feeling a little hungover from the night before, the party at Beto's, his third of the week. All around them, people are laughing and drinking, clinking glasses. In the distance, he can see the sun setting just beyond the palm trees at the far end of the street.

"Maybe you could elaborate, Richard," Dr. Michelson says.

Richard pauses, looks at the men. "I guess what I'm saying is that I don't really see the point of going to grad school to learn how to write. I mean, William Carlos Williams never went to grad school, right? Plenty of poets didn't."

He is making an argument he doesn't really believe, and perhaps Dr. Michelson senses this because he stops him after a moment and smiles.

"It's okay to be nervous, Richard. Anytime you put your work up for evaluation, you run the risk of being rejected, and that's a difficult thing to stomach for any of us. Believe me, I know."

Richard doesn't say anything to this. He tries to imagine the last time Dr. Michelson got rejected from anything.

"I was rejected forty-seven times before I ever published a poem," Elan adds.

Elan says this smugly, as if his own remarkable success should be evidence enough to Richard that these things are possible. But still, Richard wonders, what type of success has Elan really had?

Earlier that night he had sat in a small parlor on the Rice campus and listened to Elan as he read his poetry to a small group of Rice students. Afterward, Elan had signed copies of his book and answered questions from the group. The room had been set up for a much larger occasion, complete with a fully catered hors d'oeuvres table, and the whole time Michelson had just stood there, shaking his head, wondering what had happened. *I sent out an e-mail,* he said. *Put up some flyers. Maybe people got lost trying to find this place. Or maybe they got the dates wrong.* Strangely, Elan himself hadn't seemed nearly as distressed as Michelson by the poor turnout. In fact, he said he'd half expected it. And besides, he said, it wasn't about the quantity of the audience members, but the quality, and he had been very impressed by the overall quality of the Rice students. Richard had wondered, even then, if this was just lip service, a lame excuse for what had happened. He'd driven all the way down from El Paso, after all, just for the reading, and how many books had he sold? Three?

Afterward, they had driven to the café, and all through dinner Michelson and Elan had gossiped about people they knew, various poets and editors, various luminaries and high officials of the literary world, going on and on about who had slept with who, who had won what, who was publishing where. After a while, Elan had started talking about his own book and how difficult it had been to publish, and how the literary establishment wasn't accustomed to truly innovative work these days. He spoke as if he truly believed that the depth of his genius wouldn't be discovered until after his death.

Richard had only half listened to his story, thinking instead about Beto's and how much he'd rather be there instead of here. For the past several days he had been practically living at Beto's. He and about eight or nine other guys who seemed to camp out there in the evenings after work. Discovering Beto's house had been like discovering a lost oasis in the middle of a drought, a place that he had often dreamed about but never believed existed. A place where young people, just like him, could stay indefinitely. A place where no one asked you who you were or what you wanted to do. A place where there was endless booze and food and drugs. A place where you could lose yourself for hours on end, for days, for weeks, maybe even for years.

This is where he wishes he were right now, but instead he is sitting here with Michelson and Elan, talking about himself, which is the last thing he wants to be talking about.

"What I'm saying, Richard, is that the public side of being a poet, putting your work out there for people to read and evaluate, is just as important as the private side."

Richard nods.

"Look at Elan," Michelson continues. "I'm sure he wasn't too thrilled by the turnout tonight, but he didn't let it bother him, did he? No, he stood up there and he read his poems and he sold a few books."

Elan looks at Michelson, pulls out a cigarette from his pack. "I didn't think it was *that* bad," he says.

"Well, come on, Elan. It wasn't great," Michelson says and laughs.

Elan looks away and lights his cigarette.

"I know what you're saying," Richard says finally. "It's just that I'm not sure that I even want to get anywhere. I mean, I don't walk around like you guys, thinking I'm a poet. I just like writing poems, you know. And I like going to those workshops you have. That's all I really want to be doing right now."

The truth is, Richard isn't really sure what he wants to be doing right now. A part of him wants very badly to believe that what Michelson is telling him is true, that he has the ability to be a great poet, that he has the ability to go off to some distant city and study poetry writing among other great poets, but another part of him realizes that on the flip side of that is another very real possibility, the very real possibility of failing miserably and having to come back to Houston with nothing, with a worthless degree and a few thousand dollars of debt. He imagines having to explain this to his father, his friends. He imagines having to start over again at twenty-six or twenty-seven, having to reevaluate his life, having to reassess his situation.

A moment later, the waiter appears at their table with the bill, and Richard sees his opportunity to leave. As Michelson fumbles with his wallet, he stands up slowly and pushes his chair under the table. "I think I should actually be heading out," he says finally.

"You're kidding," Michelson says.

"Unfortunately not."

"But it's still early," he protests. "We have the whole night ahead of us."

"I have to meet my father," Richard says, which isn't really true. His father had called him earlier that day to set up a contretemps, a little meeting to discuss his sister, but he'd declined. "It was great to meet you, sir," he says to Elan, who smiles vaguely, still sulking.

"I'm going to be calling you next week," Michelson says. "You're not going to be getting out of this that easily."

"Okay." Richard smiles. Then he thanks them again and starts across the patio.

On the way home that night, he thinks about how different his life had been only a year before, how different everything had been. Only a few months shy of his graduation, he had had his whole future ahead of him. A degree from a prestigious school, a boyfriend who loved him, a family that was still functioning, a sister who was happily in college. And now, twelve months later, what did he have? What had happened? Marcus had gone off to Korea to study cooking, claiming it was only temporary but then breaking up with him a few weeks later; Chloe had gotten herself expelled from college; his parents had divorced; and his degree, as it turned out, wasn't as valuable as he'd thought. Working for six dollars an hour at Café Brasil wasn't exactly his idea of a promising life.

So now, armed with a worthless degree in English and no marketable skills to speak of, he wonders what he will do, what possibilities lie before him. According to his father he should be applying to graduate school in something practical, like business or marketing; according to his mother, he should be using his degree to teach English, to embrace what she calls "the noblest profession"; and according to Michelson, he should be pursuing a degree in creative writing, going off to graduate school and beginning what he refers to as his "career as a poet." And it is this last prospect, the uncertainty of it, but also the strange temptation of it, that most unsettles him.

Back when he first started writing poetry, his junior year in college, he had thought of it only as an idle hobby, a casual pastime, a temporary distraction from his other courses. But somewhere along the way, something changed. He'd become drawn into it, seduced by the idea of writing poems that other people might want to read, entranced by the daily pleasure of putting words together with other words. It had become the part of his day he most looked forward to, the escape he most cherished. Still, what he couldn't explain to Michelson or to Brandon or even to his sister was that the thought of leaving Houston to actually pursue a career in it was utterly terrifying to him. Not because he feared rejection, not because he didn't think he could handle the graduate-level coursework of an MFA program, but because he knew that once he left, once he defined himself as a poet, once he made that commitment, he'd never again be able to pretend he didn't care. He'd have to acknowledge that on some level this was who he was. He'd have to acknowledge to the world, and to himself, that he had something to say, and that he had something to say that he wanted other people to hear. For so long now, not caring had been his mantra. It had been the thing that defined him, the thing that had allowed him to work at Café Brasil for minimum wage, to date boys he knew he'd never love, to waste away his evenings at places like Beto's house. In so many ways, it would be so much easier to just continue the life he'd been living, to lose himself each night in a haze of alcohol and drugs, to spend his evenings passed out on other people's lawns, to continue writing poetry only as a casual hobby, an idle distraction, to tell people he was Richard Harding, a recent Rice graduate with no job prospects and no cares. He couldn't live this way forever, of course, but he could live this way for a while, at least for the next few years, and in the meantime, he could enjoy the comfort of not caring, the anesthetizing freedom that came along with a life defined by excess.

With this in mind, he turns the corner away from his apartment, away from the apartment where right now his roommate Clayton is waiting for him to return his car, and heads north toward River Oaks, toward Beto's house, where he is sure, even now, the party is starting.

4

MURDER. His daughter had actually used that word. She had actually mentioned that as a possibility. If the boy they had hurt didn't come through, if he ended up dying, this boy she had gotten involved with could be tried for murder, and she for conspiracy, for conspiracy after the fact, simply for knowing him, simply for being his girlfriend and for not reporting what she knew. It was a remote possibility, of course, highly unlikely, but still, just the idea of his daughter even mentioning this word to him, of her using it in a sentence involving her future, it was almost too much to bear.

Since Tuesday, when they'd met, he had been going over it in his mind, trying to figure out the best possible scenario, the best possible plan. He had talked it over with his lawyer, Albert Dunn, and Albert had told him that the best thing to do right now was to lay low and wait it out, to wait and see what happened. In all probability, he said, they were simply trying to scare her, trying to put her on edge, threatening her with prosecution as a way of getting her to testify against her boyfriend. To do anything too aggressive at this point, Albert thought, would only arouse suspicion. After all, Chloe hadn't even been questioned yet. Not officially. She had been asked a few questions about her boyfriend, about his friend, and about their involvement, but not about her own. As far as they knew, she had been home in her dorm room studying, which is exactly where Chloe said she was. But still, Elson had known when he'd talked to his daughter earlier that week that she'd been lying, or at least not telling the whole truth, that she was covering something up. She had that look in her eye that she used to get back in high school whenever she'd come home from a party with the smell of alcohol on her breath, claiming to have been at the mall. Back then, he used to laugh it off, smile or shake his head, but this was a different type of situation altogether. There were dire consequences here, dire stakes.

When he'd talked to Cadence about it earlier that week, she'd told him to keep his nose out of it, that there was a reason Chloe had waited so long to tell him. "She's afraid you'll muck it up," she'd said, "start making phone calls and inquiries like you usually do."

"Well, aren't you even worried?" Elson had asked.

"Of course, I'm worried. Do you think there's a minute that goes by when I'm not thinking about this?"

"I don't know," Elson said. "It's hard to say."

"What's that supposed to mean?"

"Just what I said. It's hard to tell if you're worried or not."

"Are you kidding?"

"No."

"I'm getting off the phone," she'd said and hung up.

He'd regretted that conversation, just as he'd regretted almost every conversation he'd had with Cadence in the past year. He'd wanted to tell her, first and foremost, that he was happy she'd stopped by the hospital to see him, that Lorna had told him that she'd stopped by, and that it had meant a lot to him that she'd done this. But, as usual, there seemed to be an enormous gap between what he wanted to say to Cadence and what he actually said.

And now, as he sits at the Ginger Man Pub, waiting for his friend Dave Millhauser to return from the john, he considers the extent to which his own family has cut him off. Even his eldest child, Richard, had refused to meet with him earlier that day when he'd called him up to set up a meeting. What had he done, he wonders, what had he done to warrant this type of mistreatment, this type of contempt?

All around him students from the university are sitting at tables, drinking beer and laughing. The pub itself is warmly lit, welcoming, a place where he has been coming now for almost a year, a place where he and Dave used to come to eat after their weekly tennis matches, but where they now just come to drink. Ever since Dave was denied tenure at Rice, he has lost his privileges at the tennis courts, but he still likes to come here to the Ginger Man to drink, still likes to hang out around the campus, still likes to believe, in his weaker moments, that he's still a professor.

Earlier that night, Elson had helped Dave move the last of the boxes from his old house into his new apartment, the new apartment that he and his wife, Cheryl, had been living in since they'd moved out of their house. A small dingy duplex on the west side of Houston. Afterward, on the way out to the Ginger Man, Dave had confessed to him that things were a little tight right now, that ever since he'd been denied tenure at Rice, they'd been having a little trouble financially. As soon as he finished his book, of course, things would change, things would get better, but for now, he said, they'd just have to endure. Endure? Elson wondered who else he knew who was still *enduring* at forty-six. And what about that book of his? Dave had been working on that book for more years than Elson could count, and yet he seemed no closer to finishing it now than he'd ever been. According to Dave, this had been the main reason he'd been denied tenure at Rice, but Elson knew there were other factors: his poor teaching record for one, his run-ins with the chair, his propensity to miss meetings and cancel class. These were all things that Dave had alluded to at one time or another, and yet Elson couldn't help wondering whether there was also something else, something Dave hadn't told him.

As he leans back in his seat at the bar, he hears a group of students behind him shouting something, chanting. There's a loud grunt, and then a few of them stand up and raise their glasses above their heads in a toast. Elson has to smile, a wave of nostalgia filling him up. He turns back to the bartender to order another beer, and just then, just as he's reaching into his wallet, he feels a heavy hand on his shoulder and turns to see Dave sliding onto the bar stool beside him.

"I thought of a way I could help," Dave says, bellying up to the bar. "Can't make any promises, of course, but I just remembered that I know a guy up there at Stratham, a professor in the art history department. Very nice guy. Did my master's with him up at Cornell. Haven't talked to him in years, of course, but I could make a couple inquiries if you'd like. Name's Jeff O'Connor."

Elson considers this. Ever since they arrived at the Ginger Man, he has been talking to Dave about Chloe, about her case, breaking his one promise to her and Cadence.

"I don't know," Elson says finally. "I don't really see what he could do."

Dave shrugs. "Me neither. Maybe nothing. Just thought he might be able to poke around a little. You know, make some inquiries. See if he can get an inside perspective on things."

Elson lights a cigarette and nods. "That could be good," he says, smiling. "Yeah, actually, that could be very good."

"Look," Dave says. "When I was at Hastings—that school I taught at straight out of grad school—they had a similar thing happen. Kid got caught with firearms in his dorm room. A whole bunch of antique rifles and stuff. Said he was a collector, but the administration didn't buy it. They expelled him a few weeks later, and then a few weeks after that he was being brought up on criminal charges."

"Chloe didn't have firearms," Elson says.

"I'm not saying she did."

"She might not have even been involved. In fact, I don't think she was."

"I know. I'm just saying you can never be too cautious about these types of things. They can escalate. That's all I'm saying."

Elson nods again. "My lawyer says we should take it easy, lay low, hope it all blows over."

"Yeah," Dave says. "Well, that's another way to approach it, I guess. I'm just saying that if it was my daughter I'd want to know everything I could, you know?"

Elson sips his beer, and then draws on his cigarette. He imagines what Cadence would say if she were here, sitting beside him, listening to him take advice from a man she'd always despised. Finally, he turns back to Dave. "All right," he says, quietly. "Why don't you just go ahead and call up your friend then."

"You sure?"

"Yeah," he says. "Just don't go saying anything about this to anyone else, all right?"

"I won't," Dave says, and then he pats Elson on the shoulder.

Elson pulls out another cigarette from his pack and lights it. Then he looks at his watch, remembering his dinner date with Lorna. On the ride home from the hospital that morning he was released, he had promised her that he would stop drinking, had promised both her and the doctor that he would try his best to take better care of himself, but nothing had prepared him for *this*. Nothing had prepared him for the utter shock of the conversation he'd had with Chloe earlier that week, a conversation that had sent him boozing, more or less nonstop, for the past few days. He knew of course what he was doing, knew the risks that he was taking, knew that he couldn't live this way forever. *If you keep treating your body like this,* the doctor had told him, *if you keep drinking, if you keep smoking,* but before he could finish Lorna had jumped in and promised the doctor that she would look after him herself, that she'd make sure he stopped. It had been a strangely tender moment, the way she'd squeezed his hand then, the way she'd pulled him toward her and smiled at the doctor. And later, on the ride home, he could tell that she was genuinely scared. At a stoplight, she had turned to him very earnestly and said, *Please promise me you'll treat yourself better,* and he had looked at her then and promised. He thought of the way that she'd lost her own father to cancer when she was ten, the way she'd spent most of her teenage years in a state of uncertainty and fear. He knew that this was what was on her mind that day as they drove home from the hospital. But now, as he stares at the unfinished beer before him, his third of the night, he wonders why it was he'd made a promise he knew he couldn't keep.

Pushing the beer away, he turns back to Dave. "Let me ask you a question," he says.

"Okay."

"Have you ever heard of this guy Woody Harrison?"

"Who?"

"I think he's a movie actor or something."

"You mean, Woody Harrelson?"

"Yeah, that's him. You've heard of him?"

"Of course," he says. "Who hasn't?"

Elson reaches for his beer again and takes a sip. "Well, apparently he's an art collector too."

"Huh?"

"According to Lorna."

Dave nods. It was Dave who had first introduced them, Dave who had befriended Lorna first. Dave who had warned him about getting involved with her. "You know, I wanted to tell you something about that too," Dave says after a moment.

"Huh?"

"About Lorna," he says, shifting in his seat, growing uncomfortable. "I was actually debating whether or not to tell you this for a while, you know, because technically I'm friends with both of you . . ."

"Just tell me."

"Okay," he says and sighs. "Well, a few weeks ago—this was the night that Cheryl had that thing at the Menil Gallery, you know, that thing for her students—well, we were coming home, and we decided to stop at Café Luz for dessert, and so we're sitting there at Café Luz, having dessert, and all of a sudden I look over and notice Lorna sitting on the other side of the café with that guy Hector—you know, that guy she used to date?"

"So?"

"So, I'm just saying I saw them together."

"Yeah, of course you did. They're friends still."

"Yeah, I know." Dave shrugs, then looks away evasively.

"What?"

"I'm just saying they didn't look like they were hanging out as friends, you know?"

"What do you mean?"

"I don't know," he says. "I'm just telling you what I saw."

Elson looks at him, tries to shrug it off, but a part of him feels unnerved. Only a week before he had had a conversation with Lorna about Hector, a conversation in which she'd denied any involvement with him whatsoever, in which she'd denied even talking to him. So what did this mean? Was she lying to him now? He tries to push the thought from his head, but a part of it has a hold on him. He can feel a sourness rising in his gut. He thinks of the painting in Lorna's house, the nude that Hector had painted of her just before he left.

"Look, I'm sure it was nothing," Dave adds. "I'm sure you're right."

"Who knows?" Elson says. "With that girl, it's hard to know anything."

"I shouldn't have brought it up."

"No, it's fine," Elson says. "Really." Then he looks at his watch. "I should probably be heading out anyway," he says, looking at Dave. "Mind if I call you a cab or something. I'm kind of running late."

"I could call Cheryl."

"No, no," Elson says. "Best not to bother her." Then he lays down a twenty on the bar in front of Dave.

"I have money," Dave says.

"I know you do," Elson says, pulling out his phone to call the cab. "I know."

5

OUTSIDE THE WINDOW of Gavin's first-floor bungalow apartment, Cadence can see the palm trees in the courtyard silhouetted against the late evening sky. The air outside is moist, cool, a light breeze blowing in through the open windows of Gavin's bedroom. Despite everything that has happened in the past twenty-four hours, Cadence feels calm, almost surprisingly calm, though a part of her can't stop thinking about Chloe and the two men who had stopped by the house earlier that day to talk to her.

In the corner, Gavin pulls off his T-shirt, then his boxers, and walks down the dark hallway toward the bathroom. A moment later, she hears the shower go on and lies back on the bed and then closes her eyes. She takes in the scent of the room, of Gavin's bedsheets, of his covers, a very male smell, a little musky, a little ripe. In a way, not that different from the way her son, Richard's, dorm room used to smell in college. She wonders how it is that men allow themselves to cultivate these smells, these odors, how they remain so oblivious to them. She opens her eyes to the darkened room and rolls over on her side, thinking once again about Chloe and the men.

When they'd first arrived at the house, they had introduced themselves to her as friends of the Beckwith family, and yet she'd seen through them from the start. They were clearly some type of private detectives or government men, not police types, but the privately hired kind. They were northerners, surely, East Coast men who were way too overdressed for the Houston heat. Cadence had wondered if they'd just flown in that morning but had been too afraid to ask. She had just come back from Peterson's office and was still feeling a little out of sorts, a little unhinged from her sudden outburst in the elevator, the public display of it all. Meanwhile, Chloe had come right to the door and started talking with them. It was a side of her daughter she had never seen before, a grown-up side perhaps, a cautious side. She had spoken to them in a very formal voice, explaining that she knew nothing, had spoken to no one, and had nothing else to say to them, not without a lawyer. The two men had stared at her for a moment, somewhat dumbfounded and clearly discouraged, then turned around and started back toward their car.

Afterward, Cadence had praised her daughter for her confidence and poise, but Chloe had just shrugged and started back inside the house, saying over her shoulder, "Don't worry, Mom. They'll be back."

For the rest of the afternoon, Chloe had lain out by the pool, sunning herself in a purple bikini and listening to her iPod, and Cadence had sat in the kitchen, paging through her marketing textbook, which she realized then she no longer needed to read.

Later, when Chloe came in, they'd had a quiet dinner together, just the two of them, and Chloe had told her about her run-in with an old friend, Simone Walsh. The whole ordeal, the whole elaborate narrative of it, had sounded strange: Chloe showing up out of the blue at Simone's store, Simone disappearing, then Chloe tracking her down at a small café along the street. Cadence had wondered what it meant, what it all added up to. She could barely remember Simone now, only that when Simone had disappeared from Houston, she had considered it a blessing. As had Elson. They had both disliked her, both distrusted her, and yet now Chloe was trying to rekindle a friendship with her? It didn't make sense. None of it did. Not with everything else that was going on in Chloe's life. Cadence couldn't help wondering whether this was perhaps a sign of something else, maybe an old impulse to rebel reemerging in her daughter. All week long she had seemed like a ghost in the house, drifting in and out of rooms without talking, barely acknowledging her own name when it was called. Somnambulistic. That was the word she would have used to describe her had anyone asked. And yet, that night at dinner she'd seemed different. More animated perhaps, almost angry, as if Simone's unwillingness to rekindle a friendship with her had unmoored her. It seemed odd to Cadence, odd that Chloe didn't want to talk about the real issue at hand, about the impending trial, about the two men who had shown up at the door, but instead wanted to talk about Simone.

"I feel like she's been brainwashed," Chloe had said, as they'd cleared the dishes for dinner. "Like someone went inside her head and sucked out all the personality."

"You haven't talked to her in years, honey," Cadence said, trying to be understanding. "People change, you know."

"Not like this," she said. "She's like a zombie, Mom. Seriously."

"Well, someone might say the same about you since you've been home."

Chloe stared at her. "What's that supposed to mean?"

"Just that you haven't been the easiest person to talk to lately. That's all."

"Would you be?"

"No, I'm not saying I would. I'm just saying that you might have caught her on a bad day, you know?"

Chloe opened up a beer then, almost defiantly, and then started toward the staircase at the edge of the kitchen. "I'm trying to tell you something, Mom," she said, turning around suddenly. "And you're not listening to me." Then she'd turned around and started up the stairs.

Cadence had sat there for a long time, staring out at the pool. She hated it when they fought, which was one of the reasons she'd let her be since she'd been home, hadn't asked her where she went in the evenings, hadn't asked her why she didn't want to talk about what had happened back at school. It was a way of giving her daughter space, she supposed, the type of space her own parents had never given her, and yet how long was she supposed to stand here along the sidelines and watch, especially when there were men showing up at her door wanting to talk to her daughter about who knows what, wanting to implicate her in something that wasn't her fault, wanting to take her away from the life that she and Elson had worked so hard to give her?

She'd left for Gavin's shortly after their little tiff, and now as she lies here in Gavin's bed, waiting for him to come out of the bathroom, she has the strangest sensation that something has happened to Chloe, that maybe those men have come back to talk to her again or taken her away, and suddenly she feels the need to call her up and talk to her. Still naked, she leans across the bed and reaches for her bag, then inside it for her cell phone. She dials the house with no luck, then Chloe's cell. The phone rings twice, then a third time, then Chloe finally picks up.

"Mom, I told you not to call me, okay?" she says. "I don't want to talk about it."

"About what?"

"Mom."

"What?" Cadence says, confused. "I have no idea what you're talking about, honey."

"Didn't you get my note?"

"No."

"Just read the note."

"What note?"

"I left you a note on the counter."

"Chloe, you're scaring me. Where are you?"

Chloe doesn't answer.

"Is this about Simone?"

"No, Mom. Look, just read the note, okay? I'll call you as soon as I figure this stuff out. Some things have changed, all right. That's all I'm going to say."

"What do you mean some things have changed? Since when? Since dinner?"

"Yes."

"What's changed?"

"I'm going to hang up now, Mom."

"Chloe."

"Just trust me, okay. I'll call you." And with that the phone goes silent. Cadence immediately pushes redial, her mind racing, but the call goes directly to Chloe's voice mail. She tries again, but again no luck. When she looks up, she sees Gavin, standing at the edge of the hallway, his hair combed back in neat rows, a cotton towel around his waist.

"Is everything okay?" he asks.

"No," she says. "I don't think so."

He comes over to the bed and sits beside her, places his hand upon her knee. If he weren't so gracious, so understanding, she probably would have left him by now, probably would have left him long before any of this stuff got serious, but something about his gentleness had disarmed her, had pulled her in. It was something she needed right now, something she hadn't had in a very long time.

"Tell me what I can do," he says, rubbing her back.

She looks at him, but doesn't answer. "I need to go home," she says.

"Right now?"

"Yes, right now."

He looks at her. "Do you want me to come with you?"

"No," she says, shaking her head and then getting up to turn on the light. "I think I should do this alone."

There was a time when she was too self-conscious to show her body in front of Gavin, to expose herself in the bright yellow light of his room, but now she no longer cares. What she cares about right now is finding her daughter and what she feels right now is only guilt, guilt for not being there, guilt for not being home when she should have been, guilt for standing here in this small, dusty bungalow apartment, completely exposed, in front of a man she barely knows.

"I'm coming with you," Gavin says, walking over to the ottoman and grabbing his jeans.

"Please don't," she says, dressing quickly, throwing on her blouse and then shoving her bra into her purse. "I'll call you as soon as I know what's going on, okay?"

Gavin stands there, still shirtless, zipping up his jeans. "I could follow you," he says.

But Cadence shakes her head and starts down the hall toward the door. She thinks she says something to him, thinks she says good-bye, but isn't sure. The only thing she remembers at that moment, as she races down the stairs to the parking lot, is her daughter's voice, the words that she said to her earlier that day: *I'm trying to tell you something, Mom. And you're not listening to me.*

6

AS HE LEANS BACK on the bed and closes his eyes, Richard can feel himself drifting, first upward toward the ceiling, then out into the nighttime sky. He cannot remember how many hits he has taken tonight, only that he has reached a perfect level of peacefulness, a complete sense of detachment, and in truth he would stay this way forever were it not for the persistent tapping on his leg. He reaches down with his hand to brush it off, but feels nothing.

When he opens his eyes, he sees a young blond-haired girl, no older than twenty, staring at him, and by the way she's looking at him he can tell that she's just asked him something.

"I'm sorry," he says. "What did you say?"

"Pass it."

"Huh?"

"The pipe," she says. "Pass it."

He looks down at the pipe in his hand and then passes it to her slowly. She rolls her eyes and then takes a hit herself.

They are sitting on a large white bed in a large white room with three or four other people, all men, two of them completely naked. The music from the other room—some type of rhythmic techno beat—is bleeding into the bedroom, and Richard suddenly realizes that he has lost track of time, that he can no longer remember how long it's been since he arrived here or how late it is now. He looks back at the girl, who is staring at him again. Her eyes are dilated and enormous, a deep, empty blue.

"You aren't also, are you?" she says after a moment, smiling at him.

"Huh?"

"You know, gay. Like every guy at this party practically is gay."

Feeling self-conscious, Richard smiles. "I don't know," he says. "I'm not really anything right now."

"What does that mean?"

"I don't know," he says, then looking to change the subject, adds, "So, how are you friends with these guys anyway?"

"With who?"

"Well, like with Beto, for example."

"I'm not," she says. "I just come to his parties, you know. I don't think I've ever even spoken to him."

Richard nods and feels a tap on his shoulder, the boy to his right passing him the pipe. He takes another hit, then passes it to the girl.

"Where is he anyway?"

"Who?"

"Beto."

She looks at him, and as she exhales a smile spreads across her face. Then she starts to cough. "Rome," she says finally.

"Rome?"

"Yeah, like on a business trip or something. I think he left this morning."

"So who's looking after the house?"

"The house?"

"Yeah."

She passes the pipe to one of the boys, then starts to laugh again. "Are you serious?"

"Yeah."

"Honey," she says, grinning widely. "This house never closes."

She leans forward then and touches his arm and he lets her. He watches her move toward him, watches her eyes until they close, and then closes his own and lets her kiss him. Her lips are soft, full, and the kiss is not unpleasant, just like all the kisses he'd shared with girls back in high school hadn't been unpleasant. Just different, unusual. And suddenly he has the sensation that he is real and that everything around him is fake, and then that he is fake and everything around him is real. When he opens his eyes, she is staring at him, blank faced.

"You are gay, aren't you?" she says.

"Huh?"

"Nothing," she says and laughs. Then she extends her hand to him, almost formally. "I'm Angel," she says.

"Richard."

And just as he's about to say something else, the door opens, almost violently, and Brandon enters, the music booming behind him.

"Shit," he says, shaking his head at Richard. "Where the hell have you been?"

Clad in swim trunks and a cotton towel, Brandon stands there, his hair still wet, his skin still dripping with pool water. "I've been looking for you for like an hour, man." Then he looks at one of the boys on the bed, the one holding that pipe. "Better put that shit away, dude," he says to the boy, and it's then that Richard hears the sound of police sirens below, out in the yard, or maybe down the street, a sound that seems to blend so perfectly with the music itself that it almost doesn't seem real.

"This isn't a joke," he says to Richard.

"What's going on?"

"Some chick cracked her head open on the side of the pool. It's a fucking mess." Walking over to the window, Brandon opens the white curtain and beckons Richard to join him. Richard slides off the bed, along with Angel and the others, and starts over to the window.

In the yard below, a large crowd has gathered around the edge of the concrete pool deck, and kneeling on the ground are two paramedics with a stretcher. Floating in the pool are three large amoeba-shaped patches of darkness, and it takes Richard a moment to realize what they are, that these patches are in fact blood from the girl's head.

"Is she going to be okay?" Richard asks.

"Don't know," Brandon says. "But look, man, we gotta get you out of here. This place is swarming with cops. And also there's something else."

"What?"

"Just follow me."

Looking back at Angel and shrugging helplessly, Richard turns and follows Brandon through the door, then down a long, dark hallway to a staircase that leads them all the way down to the side entrance of Beto's house. From there, staying close to Brandon's side, he pushes open the sliding glass door and follows him at a near sprint across the narrow side yard and then through a tall row of hedges into the backyard of one of Beto's neighbors. After that, they make their way stealthily toward the street, staying close to the shadows and out of view of the neighbor's house.

All along the street there are cars, cars that no doubt belong to the many guests at Beto's house, lined up neatly like they would be at a wedding or a funeral. Thinking of the girl in the pool, Richard feels nauseous, almost dizzy, and as Brandon takes his hand and leads him toward his car, he sees the flashing lights of the police cars in the distance, then one lone cruiser, coming toward them. Brandon pushes him down to the ground, and they crouch there behind the SUV until the cop passes, the gravel from the street digging into their knees. When the cop is finally out of sight, Brandon grabs his arm tightly and then says, "Come on, man," and lifts him up.

"I forgot where I parked," Richard says, realizing suddenly that this is true, that he has no memory of even arriving.

But Brandon pushes his finger to his lips and leads him around to the passenger side. "Don't worry about it," he whispers. "I'll drive. We'll get your car tomorrow, okay?"

Then he unlocks the door, and Richard slides in.

When Brandon gets in the other side, he starts the car and pulls out slowly, then waits in the middle of the street. A moment later a second set of headlights turns on behind them, a few cars back, and then the car pulls up behind them and stops.

"Who's back there?" Richard asks, turning around and squinting against the bright glare of the high beams.

But Brandon doesn't answer. He just pulls forward and then turns at the nearest cross street, as the other car follows. He turns on another street a few blocks down, and then another, and when Richard looks back again, the other car is still there. He stares at the headlights for a moment, trying to figure out who's inside, but can't see a thing.

Finally, he turns to Brandon. "Brandon," he says. "Who the fuck *is* that?"

7

STANDING IN THE DIM LIGHT of Lorna's kitchen, Elson takes another sip from the sweating bottle of Corona in his hand, then continues his interrogation.

"Twice?" he says. "Are you sure it wasn't three times?"

Lorna looks at him, exhausted. They've been at it now for nearly an hour. "It might have been three times. Who knows? What difference does it make?"

"It makes a difference to me," Elson says, walking toward her now, standing over the table where she's sitting.

"Would you mind sitting down?" she asks.

"I'd prefer to stand," Elson says.

Lorna rolls her eyes and picks up her own beer. "I never would have pegged you for a bully," she says.

"Is that what you think of me?"

"I think a lot of things of you," she says. Then she looks at him. "Can't we go to dinner, please? I'm starving."

"I've lost my appetite."

"Oh God," Lorna says, and stands up now, walking toward the other side of the kitchen to retrieve her car keys. "I'm going to dinner, okay. If you want to stay here, that's fine, but I'm bored with this."

"I just want to ask you one more question, and then I'll go. You'll never have to see me again."

"Is that a threat?"

"No," he says. "I just want to get to the bottom of this."

"We've been through this, Elson. Jesus. I see Hector sometimes. We're friends. And I don't tell you because I know how paranoid you can be. Because I know you'll act like *this*. And I really don't see the problem with it, honestly. I mean, he has a girlfriend now, and I have you—or at least I thought I did. And so we don't even talk about it. We don't talk about *us*. We talk about politics and art and the freakin' Houston Rockets. I mean, if you could tape-record our conversations, you'd probably be bored to tears."

Elson looks at her, wanting to believe her, sensing a sincerity in what she's saying, but also somehow doubting that this is all there is to it.

"So why don't you just stop seeing him then? I mean, if it's so boring, then why don't you just stop?"

"Because I shouldn't have to," she says. "Because it's the principle of it. Because I should be able to see whoever I want whenever I want and you shouldn't have a problem with it. Because that's how normal people act when they're in a relationship."

Sensing that he's suddenly losing this fight, Elson takes another sip of his beer and reaches in his pocket for his cigarettes, but by the time he's lit one, Lorna is already walking through the living room and unlatching the front door. He wonders if his sense of how normal people are supposed to act in a relationship is in fact skewed, or out of date, as Lorna suggests.

"I'm going to dinner," she says as she opens the door. "If you want to join me, great. If you don't, then just make sure to lock the door on your way out, okay?"

"One question," Elson says.

But Lorna ignores him. She stands there for a moment, waiting for him. This is not how he planned for things to go, but at this moment he cannot bring himself to capitulate, cannot bring himself to give in. Finally, shaking her head, she turns around and disappears through the door, glancing at him briefly before letting it slam behind her.

On the way over, Elson had promised himself he wouldn't do this, that he wouldn't let it come to this, that he wouldn't even bring it up. He knew that he was driving her away, just as he had driven away Cadence and just as he had driven away almost every woman he'd ever dated. It was a fundamental flaw in his character, he reasoned, his inability to trust, a flaw that he had inherited from his own father, a flaw passed down to him through blood. If she was telling the truth, of course, she had every reason to despise him, and yet how would he ever know? It was the not knowing that killed him, the not knowing that brought out this ugliness.

Walking over to the other side of the kitchen, he drops his cigarette into the sink and runs some water over it. Any second now he expects to hear the sound of Lorna's car returning, the sound of her walking back into the house and apologizing, but when several minutes pass with no sound from her, no sound at all from the front of the house, he begins to realize that she may in fact be serious this time. Making his way across the apartment, he stops at her desk, her makeshift study in the middle of the room, and sits down.

Aligned along the top shelf of her desk are various photographs of her family and friends: her relatives back in the Philippines, her coworkers at the gallery, the various artists and political activists she's come to know through her involvement in the Houston art scene. It seems strange to consider now, but despite the difficulty of her youth, despite the fact she'd lost her father at such a young age, she had managed to build a fairly nice life for herself here in Houston, a life filled with love, a life filled with the type of unconditional support and kindness that Elson had only dreamed of. In many ways it was this—the richness of her life—that had first attracted him. He could still remember the way she'd caught his eye that night at Dave Millhauser's party, the way he'd caught her staring at him from across the yard, and the way, later, she'd come up to him out of the blue and introduced herself, claiming to be a fan of his work, claiming to have been a longtime admirer of his buildings. It had seemed like such an easy conquest at first, a casual seduction. He had talked to her about architecture and art, and she had listened to him with the kind of rapt attention that one might normally associate with a smitten schoolgirl, and before long he had found his way into her bed, and she had found her way into his heart. But that was before all of this, before he had allowed his own insecurities and fears to take over, before he had allowed his own strange suspicions to push her away.

Turning now to her computer, her tiny laptop at the edge of the desk, it suddenly occurs to him that this is the first time she has actually left him alone in her apartment, the first time she has actually trusted him this much. He stares at the dusty monitor for a moment, then braces himself. Aligned along the top of the screen are three neat rows of files, most of them with somewhat banal titles like "Loans" or "Work Stuff," but others with more intriguing ones like "Things I Want" or "Vacation Plans." Then, in the bottom left-hand corner of the screen, he spots an icon for her e-mail account and clicks on it. And just like that, before he's even had time to consider the consequences, he is inside her account, scrolling through her messages, looking for some sign, some indication, that she's still in love with Hector. What he finds instead, however, are mostly work-related correspondences, a few e-mails from friends, and a lot of forwarded messages from her mother. He runs a search for Hector's name, but finds nothing. Not even a reference. Then he runs another search, using words like "love" and "sweetheart," but again finds nothing. Finally, feeling both discouraged and deflated, he leans back in his chair and sips his beer, and it is then, as he's staring at her account, that he first notices Cadence's name at the bottom of the screen, attached to an e-mail. He stares at it for a moment, almost in disbelief, then clicks on it without thinking. *Thank you so much for your e-mails,* it reads. *I'm so glad to hear he's doing better, and yes, I'd love to talk again. Yours, Cadence.* E-mails? Talk? He looks at the message again, but what he's thinking about now is not the fact that she has been in contact with Cadence, but the fact that she has somehow been hiding this from him. That she's never mentioned their correspondence before, or even hinted at it, incenses him. It's a kind of betrayal, he thinks, no better or worse than the betrayal he's committing himself by looking through her e-mail. How long has this been going on? he wonders. When did this secretiveness begin? First Hector, now Cadence. What else has she been hiding from him? Perhaps a whole other life, or several lives, intertwined and connected like threads of a web.

Suddenly he can feel the neat walls of his world collapsing, and it is then, as he's reaching into his pocket for his phone, ready now to confront Lorna, that the phone itself begins to ring, a sound so loud and unexpected that he almost drops it on the floor. Fumbling to open it, he answers curtly, but what he hears on the other end is not the voice he expected, not Lorna's, but Cadence's, and he can tell right away that she's pissed.

"Where are you?" she says.

"What?"

"Where are you right now?"

"I'm home."

"That would be impossible, Elson, as I'm standing outside your apartment right now."

"Look, Cadence, I gotta deal with something right now," he says, looking again at the e-mail and wondering if he should mention it. "Unless this is an emergency—"

"Chloe's gone."

"What?"

"She's gone. She's disappeared."

He stands up then and switches the phone to his other ear, trying his best to process what she's saying. "What do you mean she's disappeared?"

"I mean she took the car and she left."

"How do you know?"

"Because she left me a note, Elson."

"Well, where the hell did she go?"

"I have no idea. If I had an idea, I wouldn't be calling you right now, would I?" She pauses. "Has she contacted you?"

"No." He can feel himself going numb, the overload of information settling in, the thought of his daughter vanishing in the midst of everything else, it's almost too much for his mind to process at the moment. He reaches for his cigarettes.

"I think we should call the police."

"Hold on," Elson says, lighting his smoke. "Slow down a second. What did the note say?"

"It said to give her forty-eight hours, and to not call the police."

"Forty-eight hours for what?"

"I have no idea."

"That's it?"

"No. It also said that *the situation* had changed. That she'd call us in a few days and explain it all."

Elson can feel the clarity of the world, the room he's standing in, shifting.

"Look," he says finally. "Don't call the police, okay? We need to think this through. Jesus, this is crazy."

"Elson."

"Seriously. Don't do anything, all right?"

He looks at the computer again, the cryptic e-mail, then thinks again of his daughter. "Give me ten minutes, okay? Give me ten minutes to come over there and promise me you won't do anything in those ten minutes but wait for me, all right?"

Cadence says nothing.

"Honey?"

"Don't call me that."

"Ten minutes."

"Okay."

"Promise me."

"I promise."

Looking back at the e-mail, he rereads the message one more time, but his mind is elsewhere now, on his daughter and on the absurdity of what has just happened. Walking across the apartment, he drops his beer in the trash, picks up the remaining slices of lime, then brushes off the countertop and sits down to catch his breath. He can feel a panic attack coming on, or something akin to one, the rhythm of his breath quickening, his heart tightening. He thinks suddenly about the doctor's admonitions and tries his best to compose himself. Then he reaches again for his cell phone and dials his daughter's number, hoping beyond all logic that she might answer, believing, even when he gets her voice mail, that she might actually want to hear from him.

8

"WHAT'S HER NAME?" Richard says.

"Who?"

"The girl in the pool."

They are sitting in the parking lot at Taco Cabana, the motor running, waiting for the SUV that has been following them for the past ten minutes to pull around the corner. Brandon still hasn't told him who's inside the vehicle or what they want, and because of the glare of the headlights, Richard has only been able to discern that the vehicle itself is a large one, an SUV of some sort, or maybe a minivan. His best bet is that this is one of Brandon's clients or maybe someone from the party who has offered to sell them drugs. Once before Brandon had taken him on a little excursion to the Galleria parking lot at three in the morning, only to reveal to him once they arrived that he was there to buy weed. A few minutes later a young girl in a CR-V had pulled up beside them, tossed a tiny bag of weed into their car, grabbed a wad of cash from Brandon's hand, and driven off. This was the extent of Brandon's paranoia, of course, his cautiousness, as he called it.

"No idea," Brandon says finally. "Never saw her before." He reaches into his pocket, pulls out his pack of cigarettes, and lights one.

In front of them, the Taco Cabana parking lot is empty. Richard stares at the bright pink stucco façade of the building, the outdoor seating area surrounded by palm trees. He is thinking of the girl, the image of the blood in the pool, the sight of the ambulance lights and the people standing around dumbfounded, confused, stoned. He wonders if he knows her, if he has ever met her before. And then he wonders if the sadness he feels now is real or just a by-product of the pot, if he'll wake up tomorrow morning and feel nothing.

"Look," Brandon says after a moment. "I don't want you to freak out about this."

"About what?"

Brandon pauses, looks out the window. "Well, remember how I told you I was trying to find you at the party?"

"Yeah."

"Well, I was trying to find you because your sister showed up."

"At the party?"

"Yeah."

Richard looks at him, confused.

"She's in some type of trouble, I think. I don't know. I didn't really understand what she was talking about, but she was looking for you, I guess, and then she asked me if she could stay with me for a couple of days. Her and her friend."

"What friend?"

Brandon shrugs, draws on his cigarette. "Look, man, she can explain it to you better than me. She just wanted me to make sure you don't go freaking out and calling your parents."

"So that was her?"

"What?"

"Behind us."

Brandon nods.

Richard stares at Brandon for a moment, unable to process what he's telling him, unable to understand a single word of it. In the distance, he can see a young couple getting out of their car at the edge of the parking lot, then walking slowly toward the restaurant, their bodies silhouetted by the light from the lampposts. He watches them enter the restaurant, and then a few seconds after that he spots his mother's minivan pulling around the corner and parking. Separated by about thirty yards, he can only make out two vague shapes in the front seat. He watches them for a moment, waiting for them to get out, but they don't.

"What's this about?" Richard says.

"No fucking idea, man. I think she just wants to leave your mom's car here with you and then she and her friend are going to be coming with me."

"To your place?"

"Yeah."

"Why your place?"

"I don't know." Brandon shrugs. "I guess she thinks it's safer."

"Safer from what?"

Brandon looks at him. "That, my friend, you would have to ask her."

Richard turns back to the minivan, and this time the driver's side door opens and Chloe gets out. She is wearing a gray hooded sweatshirt with the hood pulled tight over her face and holding a Big Gulp. A moment later, the other door opens, and a guy gets out, a tall, lanky boy with dark skin and a baseball cap pulled low over his eyes.

Chloe raises her hand tentatively, and Richard looks at her, suddenly processing what's happening, then waves back.

"You know that guy?" Brandon asks.

"Yeah," Richard says, nodding, looking at his sister. "I think I do."

Part Three

I

DURING HER FIRST SEMESTER at Stratham College, Chloe had lived
in a small dorm on the east side of campus, in an old, ivy-covered brick
structure that looked out upon the Stratham River on the north side and
the central quad on the south. The building itself reminded her of the
way that colleges were often portrayed in the movies, the resolute sane-
ness of New England, the classic elegance of the East, but within its barren hallways she had sensed a broken promise, a corruption of the past.
She had chosen Stratham College precisely because it represented to her
everything that she'd once believed a college should be. It was situated in
a quaint New England town; it advertised a liberal arts curriculum, with
an emphasis on diversity and progressive education. It promised passionate professors, and even more passionate students. And yet, when she
thought back on it now, when she thought back on those first six months
at Stratham College, she realized that she'd spent the better part of those
six months in a kind of self-imposed isolation. For one, unlike the rest of
the students in her dorm, she had found it very hard to make friends at
first. And it wasn't because she didn't want to have friends or because she
wasn't social. It was only that she didn't like the type of socializing that
went on at Stratham, the way they all shepherded each other around like
sheep, moving in large herds, succumbing to the wishes of the group. It
seemed diametrically opposed to everything she had been told about college. What had happened to individuality? she wondered. What had happened to discovering who you were and what you wanted to do? All that
stuff they had preached about during freshman orientation and written
in the campus brochure?

And so, instead of joining up with one of the large groups of freshmen that had formed in her dorm, she had decided to go her own way

and, as a result, had found herself frequently alone. She went to the dining hall alone, went to classes alone, even sometimes attended parties
alone. Occasionally, she would be asked by a group of the girls on her
hall if she would like to join them for a drink after class, but she always
sensed that these invitations were being offered more out of sympathy,
or pity, than anything else, and usually she would end up turning them
down, claiming that she had too much work to do or that she had made
other plans. And on the rare occasions when she actually did go along
with these girls, she would simply sit there smiling, trying not to think
about how much she'd rather be home in Houston or trying not to think
about what she would say to Richard later that night when she got back to
her room. At that point, she was calling up Richard three or four nights
a week. He was her lifeline to the world of the sane. *The people here are
so moronic,* she would complain. *Honestly, if I told you how lame they were,
you wouldn't believe me.* And Richard would laugh or sometimes offer his
condolences or sometimes offer advice, assuring her that it would all
eventually get better, though Chloe herself was doubtful.

At the time, her only salvation had been her classes, which she had
poured herself into with a kind of renewed resourcefulness and vigor.
Class was the only place she felt at home, the only place she could be herself, and because of this, she spoke often, asserting her dominance over
the other students, kids who would otherwise not look at her on campus,
kids who would frequently ignore her when she tried to look for a place
to sit in the dining hall or who would snub her whenever she showed up
at a party unannounced. In fact, when she did go to parties, which was
rare, she usually stood off by herself in a corner, nursing a beer, looking
around the room for someone she might know, someone who didn't have
a personal vendetta against her or who didn't consider her a freak, but
usually the people she saw were people she didn't know or people she had
once known but who no longer cared to acknowledge her. By this point,
she had declared a major in history, and so she'd occasionally see some
of the other history majors at these parties, but even these students rarely
said more than a few words to her before turning around and going back
to their friends. After a while, she'd put her beer down on a table, or on
the edge of a windowsill, and slip out the back door, realizing, as soon as
she left, that no one in the room had even noticed.

Alone in her dorm room, she spent long hours reading Marxist theory, populist theory, books on French intellectual history. She read books

by Francis Fukuyama and Friedrich Nietzsche and David Kolb. She tried to ingest these books in the same way that the girls on her hall ingested Jell-O shots, but she found little sustenance in their pages. More often than not, she would find herself falling asleep on the floor of her dorm room or, later, when her roommate Lizzy got a boyfriend, in the annexes of the library. In the evenings, after the gym had emptied out, she would go there and work out for two or three hours. She liked the eerie quietness of it, especially late at night, the industrial sound of the Nautilus machines, the clanking of metal against metal, the shadows playing along the walls. Afterward, as the gym was closing, she would go into the girls' changing room and take a shower, then stand there in front of the mirror and stare at herself. She could see her body fat shrinking, her muscles gaining definition, her breasts getting smaller. She had never been a beautiful girl, never been a "knockout," as her father would say, but she'd always been cute, attractive, and now she was looking more and more masculine. To complete the picture, she decided one day to get her hair cut short, a style that was actually in fashion at the time, but which made Chloe look like a boy. That night, alone in her dorm room, she had cried herself to sleep while her roommate Lizzy was out at a party. She had thought about what her mother had asked her right before she left. *So what do you think college is about, honey?* she had said, posing the question somewhat casually, and Chloe had stood there, staring at her blankly, not knowing what to say. She wasn't sure what college was about, but she was pretty sure it wasn't this.

Later, she would wonder whether her sudden change in appearance, her sudden androgyny, was what had initially attracted Fatima Mukherjee to her. Fatima Mukherjee, a girl from non-Western history class, a girl who had walked up to her one day after class and asked her to dinner. Chloe had always admired the way that Fatima sat at the back of the room and didn't speak. Unlike Chloe, who spoke too often without thinking, who tried to answer every single question the professor asked, who tried to dominate almost every class discussion, Fatima sat quietly and listened. She chose her words carefully, and when she did speak, everyone stopped to listen. She was clearly very bright, clearly very knowledgeable, and seemed all the more so because of her cautiousness and restraint. Thus, when she came up to Chloe that day and asked her to dinner, Chloe didn't know quite what to say. She was a little taken aback, a little surprised, not only because someone was actually talking to her but because this person was also someone she admired.

"I'm Fatima, by the way," Fatima had said warmly, extending her hand. They were standing in the hallway outside the seminar room, students passing by.

"Yeah, I know," Chloe said.

"You do?"

"Well, yeah, you know, from class."

"Oh right." Fatima smiled, looking around. "Anyway, so how 'bout dinner?"

"Dinner," Chloe said, nodding. "Sure. Dinner sounds good."

The place where they went was called the Ambassador, an upscale Indian restaurant on the outskirts of campus that catered mostly to the college's professors and administrators. It wasn't a place that Chloe had ever been to before, but upon entering, she immediately fell in love: the rich smells of vegetable curries, the dim-lit atmosphere, the steady pulse of Indian sitar music. Fatima claimed that this was the only decent place in town to get authentic Indian food and that she only came here on special occasions. Then she looked at Chloe very evenly and smiled.

"I've wanted to bring you here for a while," she said.

"Oh yeah?"

"Yeah."

"Why?"

Fatima blushed. "I like the things you say in class," she said. "You have an interesting mind."

"You think so?"

"Yeah." Fatima nodded. "I do."

On the walk over, Chloe had gotten the sense that Fatima's interest in her might not be wholly platonic, and now her suspicions seemed confirmed. And yet, throughout the rest of the meal, as they talked about the professors that they liked, the courses they were taking, the people in their dorms, Chloe made no attempt to disabuse Fatima of the notion that she herself might not be straight. Instead, she listened intently, smiled occasionally, and spoke in oblique terms about her past relationships. She used non-gender-specific language when referring to her exes and simply rolled her eyes whenever Fatima brought up the issue of dating at Stratham. *Oh God,* she'd say. *Don't remind me.*

The truth was, she liked Fatima and didn't want to ruin the meal. It had been way too long since she'd done anything even remotely social, since she'd enjoyed another person's company like this, and she didn't want this feeling to end. So she just sat there and listened. She sat there and listened and smiled.

On the walk back to Chloe's dorm, as they strolled along the narrow tree-lined streets of campus, Fatima had explained to her that there was a band playing the following night at one of the bars near campus. She said that two of her friends were in this band and that they were actually pretty good. Sort of a postindustrial punk rock sort of thing, she'd said.

Chloe nodded.

"You like music?"

"I do."

"You should come then," Fatima said.

Chloe smiled and said she'd love to.

Then Fatima put her hand on Chloe's shoulder and squeezed it. "Great," she said. "I'm so glad."

Later, as they stood outside of Chloe's dorm, Chloe felt a sudden sense of remorse, a guilt for misleading her. She thought about her brother, Richard, and what he would say. They were standing now on the stone steps beside her dorm, the flowering scent of springtime foliage filling the air, the sun starting to set in the distance.

"I feel like I should tell you something," Chloe said after a moment, looking down.

"Okay."

"I don't really know how to put this, but I just wanted to let you know that I'm not gay. I mean, I like boys."

Fatima started to smile, then laugh. "You're kidding me," she said. "I had no idea."

Chloe looked at her. "Are you joking with me?"

"Of course, I'm joking with you."

"So you knew?"

"Of course, I knew."

Chloe, feeling suddenly relieved, started to laugh then herself. "God, I feel so stupid now," she said.

"Don't." Fatima smiled, then she reached out and touched her shoulder again. "So, tomorrow?"

"Yes," Chloe said. "Tomorrow. Tomorrow would be great. I'll see you then."

Over the next several weeks, Chloe and Fatima began to spend more and more time together. In the evenings after class, they would often hang out at the small house that Fatima shared with three other girls from her year. All three of Fatima's roommates were also gay, though this seemed to be a nonissue for them, and it certainly wasn't an issue for Chloe. Over lamb curry and wine, they would talk about gender politics, about Britney Spears, about the decline of punk rock. They drank a lot of wine, smoked a lot of cigarettes, and occasionally partook of the small stash of marijuana that Fatima kept hidden beneath her sink. Through her conversations with Fatima, Chloe had learned about the importance of graphic novels, about the ancient art of Indian cooking, about the difference between butch lesbians and femmes. She had learned that Fatima herself had not officially come out until her freshman year of college when she'd met a girl named Vanessa Holt, who had broken her heart so badly that Fatima still couldn't utter her name without cringing. She learned that Fatima despised her parents, that she rarely spoke to them, and that she was putting herself through college on a student work scholarship. She learned that Fatima one day hoped to be a tenured professor of contemporary political history and that she was already making plans to pursue a Ph.D. in the coming years. Chloe liked Fatima, the way she seemed so together and yet so sweet, so unpretentious. She liked the fact that Fatima never made her feel stupid or wrong, and she liked the way that her voice sounded, especially late at night, after they'd had too much wine to drink and were lying around on one of the couches in Fatima's house. She liked the way it lilted and rose, the way it fell into a soft and steady cadence, the way it lulled her to sleep, just as her mother's voice, as a child, had lulled her to sleep.

Of course, one of the fringe benefits of getting to know Fatima was the fact that Chloe now had access to all of Fatima's friends, and Fatima, she soon learned, had a lot of friends. She seemed to know everybody, but especially those students involved in the student government and all things political on campus. She was a member of several student groups, including the Student Union, the Asian Student Alliance, and the College Democrats. She was also a member and cofounder of a group called the Open Forum for Political Thought, which was the first group that Chloe had joined. Once a week in the evenings, they would meet up in a small, dim-lit parlor on the third-floor annex of the Student Union Building and discuss the various political topics of the day. Though touted as an "open" forum, a forum that invited all political perspectives, it soon became clear to Chloe that the majority of the students who attended these meetings were radically bent. These were the campus revolutionaries and nonconformists. The environmentalists, the feminists, the Marxists, and pagans. She found their discussions to be exhilarating, their rowdiness intoxicating. They seemed to be tapping into a kind of deeply repressed anger that she herself had never believed she possessed. She liked the way they ranted and raved, the way they talked about sit-ins and protests, the way they referred to the administration as "money-hungry sheep." The way they saw it, Stratham College was nothing more than a giant corporation and, as such, filled with the same type of bureaucratic bullshit that all giant corporations possessed.

Afterward, they'd usually go to a small bar near campus called the Cove and continue their discussions over tall pitchers of Miller Lite. Usually, Fatima was exhausted by this point, burned out from having to moderate the discussion at the meeting, and more often than not, she'd want to talk about other things, like who was dating whom on *Six Feet Under* or what had happened to Mira Sorvino's career or what type of lip gloss Chloe was wearing. Chloe would sit there and stare at her. She marveled at the way Fatima was able to shut off her outrage, the way she was able to suddenly shift gears. Chloe, who rarely spoke at these meetings, would be brimming with anger, wanting to continue their discussion, but Fatima would simply look at her and smile. She'd tell her that everything she was saying was true, of course, but that there was a certain point when you simply needed to stop talking about it.

By this point, Chloe had allowed her hair to grow out again, and she'd also gained back most of the weight she'd burned off that past winter. She was starting to look healthy again, even feminine. She had also begun to notice that various boys at the Cove would now come up to her after the meetings and want to talk. They'd slam down their beers on her table, put their arms around her, sometimes make a joke. They'd invite her back to their houses or sometimes ask her for her number or sometimes suggest going around the back of the Cove to smoke a joint. Fatima would usually look over at one of her girlfriends at this point and shake her head, or roll her eyes, and then one of her girlfriends would very discreetly lean across the table and explain to these boys that the girls at this table didn't like men. "We're batting for a different team," she'd explain, and then the boys would turn around, deflated and confused, and go back to their booths.

"I hope you don't mind," Fatima would sometimes say to Chloe, touching her arm. "I mean, you didn't like those guys, did you?"

And Chloe would shake her head no, though sometimes she did mind. Sometimes she found herself craving male attention in the same way that Fatima and her friends craved revolution. Sometimes she found herself resenting the lesbian force field that seemed to surround her.

In fact, given the strength of this force field, it was surprising to Chloe, even now, that she'd ever met Raja; though, of course, the specifics of how they'd met had always been a mystery to her. She remembered only that she had been sitting at the Cove one night with Fatima and some of her friends and that they had all been drinking a lot and that then, at one point, Fatima's friends had stood up and left the table, and then a few minutes later a group of boys had come over and joined them. These were boys from the Asian Student Alliance, boys who Fatima knew and approved of, and after a while they had all started talking about some protest that was coming up at the end of the week, a protest regarding the unfair dismissal of one of the most popular professors at Stratham, a man who also happened to be Asian American. Sun-Li Kim, a Chinese American assistant professor of American lit, was being denied tenure, they said, and the following day they would be staging a protest outside the English department in which they'd be presenting to the chair of the English department a signed petition with over three hundred names.

The boy who was explaining this all to them was named Seung, a Korean American boy who was good friends with Fatima. The other two boys at the table were Indian.

"Did they give an explanation?" Chloe remembered asking at one point.

"An explanation?" Seung said.

"For why he was being denied tenure?"

Seung rolled his eyes. "Yeah," he said. "The typical. You know, he hadn't published enough. He hadn't met the department's *requirements*. That type of thing."

"Well, isn't that kind of valid?" Chloe heard herself saying.

At this point, the table had grown quiet, and Chloe could feel Fatima's eyes on her. She could also feel the beer settling in.

"I mean, just for the sake of argument," she continued timidly, "let's say he didn't meet the department's requirements, okay. Let's say he didn't do what he was supposed to do."

"It's irrelevant," Seung said. "He's a great teacher, and besides, there's a bunch of other shit I can't even tell you about. Weird shit. I mean, the whole thing is just completely fucked. Trust me."

Chloe nodded and looked down, and then a moment later she felt the world spinning, the bar falling out of focus, her stomach growing nauseous. A few seconds after that, she felt a hand on her shoulder, and when she looked up, she saw one of the two Indian boys staring at her, the quiet, handsome one.

"You okay?" he asked.

She shook her head.

"Why don't we get you some air," he said, and then he reached over and helped her stand up and led her out of the bar.

Outside on the curb, she vomited twice into a large metal trash can while the boy held her hair and massaged her shoulders. He told her that it was fine, that she'd probably just had too much to drink, that it happened to everyone. Then he'd helped her sit down on the curb and given her a glass of water, which he'd brought out from the bar.

"Drink this," he'd said and held the glass to her lips, and then he'd smiled at her in a way that made her feel calm.

She didn't remember much else from that night, only that she had sat there with the boy on the curb for a long time and that they had shared a couple of cigarettes and that she had felt at once both embarrassed and strangely calm. And she remembered also that, at one point, he had told her that he'd agreed with what she'd said at the bar, about Professor Kim, that she'd made a good point.

"Really?" she said.

"Yeah," he said. "I mean, it was something I was thinking about, too."

"So why didn't you say something?"

He laughed and rolled his eyes. "Seung," he said. "When that dude's on his soapbox, it's best just to duck and take cover."

She smiled and then drew on her cigarette and then looked at him. She wanted to say something else, but before she could say a word, the bar door flung open and Fatima came out, shaking her finger.

"You!" she said, waving her finger drunkenly at Chloe. "You owe me, like, some serious cash, honey!"

She was laughing as she said this though, and teetering slightly, and Chloe quickly ran over and hugged her, apologized. By then, the other two boys had come out and joined the third on the curb. They were lighting up their cigarettes and laughing, and then at one point they all turned around and started to leave.

"We're going to be taking off now, ladies," Seung yelled back as they started down the street. "It's been a pleasure."

And just like that the boy was gone, and Chloe was left there, staring at the back of his head, watching it as it bobbed unevenly down the street.

"Hey," Chloe said, after they'd left. "Who was that?"

"Who?" Fatima said, trying to use the side of a mailbox to keep her balance.

"That boy I was talking to."

Fatima smiled at her. "Why? You interested?"

"No," Chloe said. "Just curious."

Fatima stood up then and continued to smile. "Well," she said. "That boy's name is Raja Kittappa, but I'm telling you, Chlo, you should stay away from him."

"Why?" Chloe said.

"Because"—Fatima smiled—"he's got a girlfriend."

2

IT WOULD BE several months before Chloe would hear from Raja Kittappa again. By then, she would be several weeks into the fall semester of her junior year at Stratham, a newly reinvented version of herself, a girl who now had friends, a girl who now had a social life, a girl who now had things to do on Friday nights. That previous spring she had gone out almost every single weekend, had made a habit of scheduling her study time around parties, and though she didn't have as many close friends as Fatima, she had begun to take some pride in the fact that people knew her now, that people waved to her when she walked across the quad or smiled at her when she entered the dining hall. It was true that she had met most of these people through Fatima, but still, it felt good to be embraced by them, to be taken into their circle, and to be considered their friend.

She would be out with some of these friends, in fact, on the night that Raja called her, though, even now, it seemed amazing to her that he had. At the time, she'd been standing in a small, dim-lit bathroom at the back of Le Café Rouge, a dark off-campus coffeehouse where Fatima and some of the girls from her advanced poetry class were performing spoken-word poetry and what they referred to as "impromptu verse." She had taken a break from the performance when she got the phone call from Raja on her cell, though she hadn't recognized his voice until he introduced himself. Once she did, however, it all came back to her, the memory of that night, and for a moment she just stood there, paralyzed, staring at herself in the mirror, not knowing what to say. Raja had spoken calmly at first. He'd said that he hoped she remembered who he was, then apologized for the randomness of the phone call and asked her if she might be interested in joining him for dinner the following night at Tommy's. He said that he'd been meaning to call her for a while but hadn't had the courage.

She stood there, motionless, still trying to process what was happening.

"I'm confused," she'd said finally. "I thought you had a girlfriend."

"I did," he said.

"But not anymore?"

"Not anymore."

She looked at herself in the mirror. "I think I saw her once," she said. "Your girlfriend." She thought then of the beautiful Indian girl who Fatima had once pointed out to her at the campus deli. "She's pretty."

"Yeah." Raja had laughed. "Well, she's a lot of other things, too."

There was a sudden bitterness in his tone that made her regret bringing it up.

"Anyway," he said. "So, tomorrow? Tommy's?"

"Sure," she said. "Should I meet you there?"

"No, no," he said. "I'll swing by your dorm first, say, around seven?"

"Sounds good," she'd said, and then they'd hung up and she'd run into the main room of the coffeehouse where, just then, Fatima was coming offstage.

"What the hell?" Fatima had laughed as Chloe rushed up to her. "Why the hell are you smiling so big?"

The next night Raja had picked her up at seven, just as promised, and they'd walked over to Tommy's and then, afterward, back to his dorm room on the other side of campus. Chloe had expected Raja's dorm room to be just as mysterious as he was, but it wasn't. In fact, it was almost surprisingly plain. A tall row of bookcases lined the far wall, and above his bed, a small futon in the corner of the room, there were tattered posters of various rock bands: Belle & Sebastian, the Jesus and Mary Chain, Guided by Voices. Chloe had sat down at a desk in the corner of the room and studied the small silver-framed photographs of his family—his mother and father, his younger sister—all dressed up in traditional Indian garb.

"Where are these from?" she'd asked at one point, picking up one of the photos.

"A wedding, I think," he'd said. Then he'd walked over to her and put his hand on her shoulder. It was the first time he'd touched her that night.

"Whose wedding?"

He looked at her. "No idea," he said. "Can't remember." Then he smiled at her. "Say, why are you so interested in my family?"

"I don't know." She shrugged. "They seem interesting."

"They do?"

"Yeah."

"Well, they're actually not," he said and laughed. "They're actually surprisingly uninteresting."

"Really?"

"Yeah," he said. "Really."

"Well," she said. "I wish I could say the same."

Up until that point, she had successfully avoided the topic of her own family, but now she felt she had opened up a door. Still, to her surprise, Raja didn't pry. Instead, he just stood there for a moment. Then he cupped her face in his hands and leaned down and kissed her, a soft, innocent kiss that sent a rushing through her.

"That was nice," she'd said afterward, and then feeling suddenly self-conscious added, "I mean, you know—"

Raja smiled at her.

She looked down and blushed.

"No, no," he said softly, touching her arm. "You're right. It was nice."

For the next several weeks, she and Raja were inseparable. They went to meals together, met for coffee after class, studied together in the library after dinner. She often made herself an overnight bag, which she'd bring over to his place in the evenings after dinner. They hadn't slept together yet, but every time she packed her overnight bag, she'd have this fleeting sensation that tonight might be the night. Still, Raja never pushed, never pressured her. He seemed to want to take things slow. He seemed to be waiting for the right moment. And this was fine with her. For now, she was content to simply lie there beside him on his futon, to spend her evenings in his arms, to fall asleep to the sound of his voice or to the sound of the music on his stereo. They spent a lot of their evenings like this, just lying in bed, talking or listening to music. Raja liked to tell her stories, stories about his life growing up in Pakistan and India or, later, about his teenage years as a high school student in New Jersey. Through these conversations, she'd learned that his mother had grown up poor, even poorer than his father, and that she still spoke little English. She'd learned that his mother had cried for almost a week when they first moved to the States, that she hated New Jersey, that she hated the U.S. in general, and that she often threatened to leave, especially during that first year they were living there. He'd told her how distrustful his parents had been of the American school system, how they often set up meetings with his teachers, how his father had once written a letter to the principal asking for the dismissal of one of his teachers. During that first year in the States, he'd said, everything was different. It was like his parents were still pretending they were living in Mumbai. He and his sister were only permitted to socialize with other Indian children, friends of his parents, and they never once went out to eat, never once ate American food. It was like living in a controlled environment, he'd said, though over time his parents had relaxed, loosened up. Over time they had started speaking English at the dinner table; over time they had started letting them rent American movies from the video store; and over time they had even started letting them stay over at their American friends' houses on the weekends. Still, it had always been there, he said, this strange distrust of the States, this longing for Mumbai. It was a kind of homesickness, he guessed, a kind of homesickness that just never went away. And he knew that eventually they'd go back there, that eventually, when his father retired and his sister was out of the house, they'd move back there for good. But when she'd asked him how he felt about this, he'd said very little, only that his parents' lives—his parents' decisions—were theirs, not his.

"But don't you care?" she asked.

"It's not about caring," he said, and then he'd looked away, and that had been the last time they talked about his parents for quite a while.

Still, despite the difficulty of his teenage years, Raja seemed to have enjoyed his time at Stratham so far. He had a lot of friends here, more friends than Chloe had ever had, and these friends often came over to his dorm room in the evenings after class. They seemed to gravitate toward him in the same way that other students gravitated toward professors. They valued his opinion, respected his advice, and often turned to him for counsel on the various problems in their lives. Chloe liked to joke that these friends of his were not really friends so much as "patients" and that he should be billing them at a competitive rate. "Maybe we could get a couch in here," she'd said one night. "You know, set up a receptionist's desk in the hall. I could be your secretary."

"Right." Raja had laughed. Then he'd looked at her strangely and frowned. "To be honest, you know, I have no idea why they even come here. I mean, honestly, I don't know why they think *I* can help them. It really should be the other way around."

But the truth was there was a part of Chloe that secretly enjoyed the fact that so many other students at Stratham seemed to look up to Raja, that they seemed to see in him what she saw: a kind and gentle soul, a boy who would do anything for the people he loved. She had never dated a boy like this before, never believed she would, though, of course, it became evident to her after a while that she was not the only girl at Stratham who seemed to feel this way. In fact, for every boy that stopped by Raja's dorm room in the evenings, there seemed to be at least twice as many girls, and it was mostly the girls that Chloe had a problem with. Usually, they'd come in unannounced, sit down on the edge of his bed, then begin to play with their hair or complain about their classes; or, other times, they'd just sit there at his computer and check their e-mail. Most of these girls were Indian, some of them very beautiful, and all of them clearly enamored of Raja. They seemed to regard Chloe with a vague disinterest, if they regarded her at all, and more often than not, they'd simply sit there and talk to Raja as if she herself were not in the room.

For the most part, she didn't mind, didn't let it get to her in the way she could have. She didn't want to be that type of girlfriend, the type who allowed her own insecurities and fears to come into the picture. But still, there were moments when these girls could be so incredibly cold to her, so cold that she would find herself wanting to cry, and one night in particular when she did.

This was a night in early October, a few weeks after they'd started dating. She and Raja had been hanging out in his dorm room, eating Chinese takeout with a group of students from his floor. Chloe didn't know most of these students very well, but she knew that at least one of them was a girl who had once dated Raja. For most of the night this girl had ignored her, but then at one point, after they'd had a couple of beers, she'd begun to probe into Chloe's past, begun to ask her about her freshman year. Wasn't she that freak girl? she wondered. That freak girl who always showed up at parties by herself? What did they used to call her? she wondered. What was her name? No one else in the room, including Raja, seemed to know what this girl was referring to, but Chloe did, and after a moment she stood up and ran out of the room.

Later, when Raja caught up with her on the quad, on the small wooded pathway outside his dorm, she was crying uncontrollably. Without even hesitating, he ran up to her and embraced her.

"I don't get it," he said, stroking her hair. "What did she say? What was she talking about?"

But Chloe didn't answer. It had been so long since she'd even thought about freshman year, so long since anyone had even alluded to it, that she'd allowed herself to believe that that part of her life was over, that it was behind her, that no one now even remembered it. But of course they had.

Later that night, as they lay in his bed, she told him the story. She told him about her first few months at Stratham. She told him about the weeks and months that followed, about the year and a half she spent in solitude. She told him everything with the sobering understanding that this might be the very last conversation she ever had with him. But, in the end, Raja didn't waver. His eyes remained focused on hers, his expression one of concern rather than disappointment. And when she finally finished, he simply leaned over and put his hand on her head, pulled her toward him.

"I'm glad you told me," he said, and then he kissed her on the lips. "I'm so sorry you had to go through that."

"You don't think I'm lame now?"

"Of course not." He'd laughed. "In fact, I don't think that would be possible."

Then he slipped his arm around her body and pulled her over on top of him. He gripped her tightly, and she understood then what was happening, what he wanted.

She'd only had sex once before, with her high school boyfriend, Dustin O'Keefe, a few weeks before they'd left for college. That time she'd told herself that she was simply doing it to get it over with, so she wouldn't have to enter college a virgin, but this time it was different. It still hurt a little, but it didn't hurt in the way it had with Dustin. It hurt in a good way, and Raja himself was so unbelievably sweet to her, so unbelievably gentle and calm, so confident in the way he touched her, that she almost forgot for a moment that she'd done this before.

Afterward, as they lay there sweating, Raja had leaned across the bed and mussed her hair. He'd smiled at her.

"How are you feeling?" he'd asked.

"What do you mean?"

"I mean, right now, how do you feel?"

"I feel good."

"Are you sure?"

"Yes," she said. "Why? Is there a reason I shouldn't?"

"No, no," he said, laughing, kissing her arm. "I just wanted to be sure."

The next few weeks seemed to pass in a blur. Later, Chloe would realize that these weeks had been among the happiest in her life: waking up next to Raja in the mornings, walking with him to morning classes, meeting up with him in the late afternoons for secret rendezvous in his room, going out at night with him and his friends to various bars and restaurants and private parties off campus. The rest of her life seemed to fall away. She no longer worked so assiduously on her papers, no longer worried so much about tests. She stopped checking e-mails, stopped answering phone calls, even stopped talking to Fatima, who would call her at least once a day and leave a message on her voice mail, asking her where she was. Everything else seemed to recede. Everything else except Raja. And for now, it seemed, Raja was enough.

It was impossible to explain, but she felt drawn to Raja in a way that she had never felt drawn to another human being before. And it didn't seem to have anything to do with logic. She would be sitting there, trying to play it cool, trying to be restrained, and then all of a sudden she would see her hand reaching over and touching him, almost like it was out of her control. At times, it felt like being in a dream, the way you believe in a dream that you are in control of your actions, but then at one point you'll see yourself doing something and you'll realize you're not. That's how she felt around Raja. It was like there was a force outside of her that was stronger than her, and that force made it impossible for her not to be around him, or for her not to touch him when she was around him.

At the time, one of her favorite things to do with Raja was to meet up with him in the evenings after class at his place of work, a small, dimly lit theater on the other side of campus, on the second-floor annex of the Dramatic Arts Building. As part of his work-study scholarship, Raja had been assigned the responsibility of screening films two or three times a week for the various film students and film classes at Stratham. Usually these films were obscure European films that Chloe had never heard of, but she still loved to watch them, and she especially loved to sneak up the back staircase of the Dramatic Arts Building and surprise Raja as he was screening them. Sometimes she'd bring along a large bag of popcorn and a six-pack of beer, and they'd sit there and stare down at the audience, bathed in the silver glow of the screen, transfixed by the images before them.

Afterward, once the audience had filed out, Raja would take her into one of the back rooms behind the projectionist's booth, a large, dusty room filled with aisles and aisles of film stock, the entire library of the Stratham film department. Here he would point out masterpiece after masterpiece, explaining to her at great length why each one of these films was important or how each one had affected his life. Then he'd turn to her very casually and ask her to choose one.

"Won't we get in trouble?" she'd asked him the first time he did this.

But he just smiled and shook his head. "I have the key," he'd said and then patted his pocket. Then he'd looked around the room. "So," he said, smiling, "which one will it be?"

And so, from the hours of midnight until four in the morning, at least two or three nights a week, they had watched some of the greatest cinematic masterpieces of the past fifty years. They had watched Bergman and Fassbinder, Truffaut and Godard. They had watched Michelangelo Antonioni's *L'Avventura* and Satyajit Ray's *Pather Panchali*. They had watched old documentaries by the Maysles Brothers and short independent films by American directors like Terrence Malick and John Cassavetes. They had watched these films with a deep reverence, perched there at the edge of the projectionist's booth, looking down over the dark theater, the quiet whir of the projector lulling them into a sort of hypnotic trance. Sometimes Raja would stop the projector at an important scene and add his own commentary, explaining why the camera angle was brilliant or how the lighting was sublime. Other times, she'd just look over at him, and he'd seem transfixed, mesmerized, by what he was watching. Though he'd declared a major in chemistry, Chloe had known for some time that this had been his father's decision, not his, and that if Raja had it his way, he would have majored in film. But still, she never mentioned this, never even brought it up. The one time she'd even alluded to it, Raja had grown sullen and cold. To change his major at this point, he'd said, would be absurd.

"But don't you ever think about it, though?" she'd asked as they walked along the quad. It was four in the morning, and they were just now returning from the theater, the campus around them silent and dark, everyone asleep in their dorms, the first brisk winds of autumn biting their faces.

Raja had been quiet for a long time after she'd asked him this. Then he'd looked at her sternly, the first time he'd ever looked at her this way.

"No," he'd said finally. "To be honest, I never think about it."

Later, when they got back to his dorm room, she'd apologized for bringing it up, and he'd said it was fine.

"It's just that you seem to love it so much," she'd said.

"I do," he'd said. "But you don't understand my family. For me to major in film, it would be an insult, a disgrace."

"Even if you became a famous director?"

"Yeah," he'd said, looking down. "Even if I became a famous director."

Later, Chloe would regret this conversation, as it was one of the few awkward moments in what was otherwise a time of perfect bliss. It was also one of the last normal conversations she'd have with Raja before everything else turned south. The next night, when she returned to her dorm room after class, she'd received that fateful message from Richard on her voice mail: *World War Three here, Chlo. I'm serious. All's not well on the home front.*

According to her brother, it had been building up for a while now, their parents' troubles. He had seen it coming, he'd said. Ever since she'd left for college, their fights had been escalating, the unpleasantness growing. Their mother had been locking their father out of the house, he said, their father had been breaking things. One day he'd come home to find their father lying in his underwear on the living room floor, hungover. Another night he had found their mother sitting alone in her closet, packing up her shoes into boxes and weeping. It wasn't just one problem in particular, he'd said, but the culmination of a lot of little problems, all of those years of unhappiness finally catching up with them. Or at least that's how they'd explained it to him the previous night at dinner when they'd told him what was going to be happening. He spoke very calmly as he told her this, but she could tell, even then, that he was worried. Not for himself, but for her.

"They're going to be calling you tomorrow night," he'd said, finally, "but I just wanted to give you a heads-up, you know, so you had a chance to prepare yourself."

Chloe said nothing. She hadn't started crying yet, that would come later; she was still trying to process it, still trying to understand what her brother was saying.

"Why don't they just get a separation?" she'd asked finally. "I mean, really, why does it have to be so final?"

"I don't know, Chlo," he said.

There was another long silence, and then she said, "Well, who was it?"

"What do you mean?"

"I mean, who was it who asked for the divorce? Mom or Dad?"

"I don't know, Chlo. I think they just kind of decided on it together, you know."

"That's impossible," she said. "It's always one person who asks, one person who brings it up first."

Richard was quiet for a moment, then he said, "I don't know. I mean, if I had to guess, I'd say Mom, but who knows? And, really, that's not what you should be thinking about right now."

"Well, then what the fuck should I be thinking about, Richard? I mean, really, please enlighten me."

And just like that, she lost it. Just like that, it finally hit her, and before she knew it, she was crying, convulsing, trying to catch her breath, while her brother, on the other end of the line, was trying to comfort her, trying to apologize, telling her it would all be fine. Stoic Richard. Sensitive Richard. Her perfect, angelic older brother, reminding her that they had seen this coming for a while, that this had been a long time in the works. And she knew that he was right, of course. She had seen it herself that past summer: her father staying out late with his friend Dave Mill-hauser almost every night, her mother complaining about him at almost every turn, the two of them fighting for hours on end, in their bedroom, with the door closed. But still, as silly and as selfish as it sounded, she would have still rather had them living together unhappily than living apart. And when she said this to Richard, he agreed. Then he sat there on the other end of the line for almost an hour, listening to her, as she did little more than cry.

The next morning, with only an hour's worth of sleep, she had decided to skip her morning classes and go over to the other side of campus, to a small, shaded park bench that overlooked the river. Here, sitting on the edge of the bench, she had smoked cigarette after cigarette and continued to cry. She thought about calling up Raja, but decided against it. Instead, she just sat there, thinking about the ramifications of it all, what this would mean for her now. She wondered what family holidays would be like now, what it would be like to go home for Christmas. She wondered where her parents would live, who would get the house, would they sell it? She wondered what it would feel like to see her parents with other people, if they in fact remarried, or what it would be like to talk to them now, separately, as adults. In the distance, she could see a group of students on the quad, tossing around a football in the leaves, the sky above them overcast and dark. For the first time in a long time, for the first time in almost a year, she'd wished she were home in Houston.

Finally, around noon, she had called up her mother but had caught her on the way to an appointment. There was a long pause on the other end of the line, and then her mother had expressed her anger at Richard for telling her. *This isn't how I'd wanted you to find out,* she'd said, but before she could finish, Chloe hung up. Later that day, when her father called, she'd let his phone call go to voice mail, then listened to his message over and over, his roundabout, circumspect explanation for why this had happened: *Your mother and I have been together for a long time, darling . . . We love each other very much, of course, but sometimes love isn't enough. Sometimes life gets complicated . . .* She wondered if he was drunk, if he was reciting this speech from a bar. In the background, she could hear glasses clinking, people laughing. She wondered if he was even living at home.

All day long she had been thinking about Raja, wanting to talk to him, wanting to tell him what had happened, wanting to answer the numerous voice messages he had left on her phone. Almost every hour for the past six hours he had left her at least one message or sent her a text, wondering where she was. But there was still a part of her that didn't want to get into it with him, to expose herself so openly at such an early stage in their relationship. So instead of returning his calls, she had called up Fatima and asked to come over.

"You're still alive?" Fatima had said sarcastically when she'd called. "Really? I thought you might have died." But then she must have heard something in Chloe's voice, maybe Chloe sniffling, because she stopped. "Hey honey," she'd said, softly now. "What's the matter?"

Chloe didn't answer.

"Honey?"

"Can I please come over?"

"Of course," Fatima said, her voice suddenly concerned. "Come right now."

At Fatima's house, Chloe unloaded. She told her everything, everything she couldn't tell Raja, how she hated her parents now for doing this, how she hated them even more for the way they were handling it, for talking to her in platitudes, for telling her brother first, for not trying harder to make it work.

"So you're having some trouble with your marriage," she'd said. "Big deal. Go to therapy then. Work it out. You don't have to get a fucking divorce."

And Fatima, whose own parents were divorced, sympathized. "People are weak," she'd said finally. "The older I get, the more I realize this."

And so, on and on they went, late into the night, drinking glass after glass of wine, smoking cigarette after cigarette, ranting and raving about their parents, sharing war story after war story, commiserating about their pasts, philosophizing about the pointlessness of marriage. Meanwhile, Chloe's voice mail was filling up with messages, messages from her mother, her father, Richard, Raja. Chloe ignored them all and kept drinking. And then, at one point, Fatima had pulled out the small stash of marijuana from beneath her sink and rolled a joint. Sitting at her kitchen table, they had smoked the entire thing down to its nub. Then they'd gone into her living room and tried to watch TV, but the images on the screen were moving too fast, and after a while Chloe began to feel sick. A few minutes later, she was out in the yard behind Fatima's house, getting sick on the lawn. In the doorway behind her, she could see Fatima, silhouetted by the light from the kitchen and then, a moment later, another figure, standing beside her. She squinted her eyes, trying to make out who the figure was, but she couldn't tell. Then the figure moved out of the shadows, and her eyes adjusted, and she suddenly knew.

"It's going to be okay," Raja was saying now as he moved across the lawn, and then, kneeling down beside her on the cool grass, he held her in his arms. "Fatima told me," he whispered. "I'm so sorry."

She was crying now, and he was holding her head, and suddenly the world was slowing down. He continued to whisper to her, things she couldn't remember, and she continued to cry. She could smell the stale odor of cigarettes on his jacket, the stench of beer on his breath. She asked him where he'd been, but he didn't answer. He just kept rubbing her shoulders, comforting her, just as he had that first night they met. And when she looked up at him finally, she noticed for the first time a cut along his cheek, a swelling around his eye.

"Hey," she said. "What the hell happened to your face?"

But he just shook his head. "We'll talk about that later," he said. "Another time. The main thing right now is that we get you home."

And she realized then, when he said this, that he meant his dorm room, that he meant his dorm room was home.

3

LATER, SHE WOULD WONDER whether any of this would have ever happened had she simply returned his phone calls that day, had she not gone over to Fatima's house. If he had been with her, instead of with his friends, then he would have never ended up at the Cove that night and would have never run into those boys. He would have never known who Tyler Beckwith was, and Tyler Beckwith would have never ended up in the hospital. But this was all pointless to think about now.

The truth was, at the time, she had no idea what had happened that night, and Raja himself had said little about it. When she'd asked him about it the following day, he'd been evasive, vague, saying only that there'd been an altercation, a misunderstanding, and that he didn't want to go into it. It wasn't worth recounting, he'd said. It was really pretty stupid. But through his friends, Seung and Sahil, both of whom had been there that night, she had learned other things.

She had learned that a boy named Tyler Beckwith had come up to Seung that night at the bar and gotten in his face. She had learned that Seung had been standing on the other side of the bar, talking with Tyler Beckwith's girlfriend—a short, pale-faced girl from his modern architecture class—and that Tyler Beckwith hadn't liked this. In fact, before Seung knew it, Tyler was up in his face, pushing him around, calling him shit. Yellow face. Chink. All the worst things he could think of. It was like something from a dream, Seung said. Totally unprovoked. The guy was clearly drunk. Anyway, at one point, Raja had stepped in and tried to defend him, had tried to break things up, and that's when Tyler had pushed Raja, and then Raja had come back at him full force. After that, what had happened had been a blur. All they knew was that Raja had ended up pinning this guy Tyler down on the floor of the bar and humiliating him in front of everyone, including his girlfriend. Even made him apologize, Seung said. Wouldn't let him up till he did.

"Don't forget," Seung added. "Our boy used to play rugby."

"Raja?"

Seung nodded. "You didn't know?"

"No," Chloe said, shaking her head, because she didn't. This was the first she'd heard of it, and like so many other things about Raja, it just didn't add up. None of it did. The picture that Seung and Sahil had painted of him was simply impossible to reconcile with her own image of him. She knew that he was physically strong, of course, and that he was much taller than most other boys, and yet she would have never pegged him for the type to get in a fight, especially a bar fight.

Still, whenever she brought it up to Raja, he'd change the subject or else claim that everything that Seung and Sahil had told her was bullshit, exaggeration.

"Well, is it true that you used to play rugby?" she'd asked him one night, as they were sitting in his room.

He looked at her then and finally nodded. "For a semester," he said. "My freshman year. Why?"

"I don't know," she said. "It's just that rugby seems like such a violent game, you know, and you seem like such a pacifist."

"I am a pacifist," he said.

"Except when you're beating up guys in bars, right?"

She winked at him, but she could tell he didn't like the joke.

"That was a mistake," he said finally, and then he turned around, and that was the last time they ever talked about it.

In fact, from that point on, she never mentioned it again. Instead, they talked about other things. They talked about the people in Raja's dorm who were hooking up, the various dramas on his hall. They talked about the shortcomings of the new administration, about the hypocrisy of certain professors, about the latest articles they'd been reading in the *Huffington Post*. They talked about everything, it seemed, but Raja's run-in at the bar and her parents' divorce. Chloe had told him one night, after venting for nearly an hour, that she didn't want to talk about the divorce anymore, that it was too painful for her, that it was easier for her to just forget about it, to ignore it, to put it out of her mind, and Raja, in his own indirect way, had respected this. *Whatever's going to make you feel better,* he'd said, and then she'd told him that the only thing that was going to make her feel better was to be with him.

Meanwhile, at home, the drama was unfolding: the hiring of divorce lawyers, the reallocation of assets, the dividing up of property, the negotiations over ownership. Chloe found out about these things only in bits and pieces, through Richard, or occasionally through her father, who would call her up every few days to complain about her mother and how she was "raping" him.

It was strange, but during this entire time she rarely thought about her father. Their relationship had been so strained for so long now. It had been so long since she could even remember having a normal conversation with him, a conversation that didn't end in a fight or involve a disagreement of some sort. Gone were those days when she used to stay up late at night waiting for him to come home from work. Gone were the days when she used to sit around the kitchen table, talking with him about current events, arguing about this thing or that. The U.S. involvement in Iraq, the energy crisis, the latest indiscretion of the Bush administration. Arguing about political events had been their way of bonding for so long. It had been a thing that they'd done together all through high school, and yet somewhere along the way something had changed. Their friendly disagreements had turned into something else, a full-on war that had nothing at all to do with politics and had everything instead to do with her mother and the way her father was treating her. The way he had disappeared emotionally. The way he had stopped coming home for dinner. The way he had started spending his weekends out in the yard, working on the garden for hours on end, ignoring everyone else, and stopping only at the end of the day to read the newspaper, by himself, at the edge of the pool.

One night, after class, she was trying to explain all of this to Raja as they sat over drinks at the Cove. Raja had nodded at her as she told him the story, but she couldn't help noticing something different in his face, his eyes. He seemed preoccupied, distant, and when she finally asked him if anything was wrong, he'd been evasive.

"I'm just tired," he'd said. "Too much chemistry, you know." Then he'd patted her on the hand and winked.

Later that night, they were joined by Seung and his girlfriend, Bae. Chloe had only met Bae once before and had never really liked her, but that night she seemed different. More animated perhaps, lively. She and

Seung had been drinking since noon, Seung announced when they first arrived, and perhaps that was part of the reason. They had been making the rounds of almost every bar in town, he'd said, and then he'd proceeded to recount their journey in exhaustive detail. Bar by bar, drink by drink.

Later, he and Raja had gotten into an argument about the latest president of the Asian Student Alliance. Seung seemed to think that this latest president was too relaxed, too complacent, too easy to please. He didn't have enough fire in him, he said. But Raja pointed out that the previous president, Samantha Cho, had done little more than alienate the entire administration with her constant protests and complaints.

"But at least she wasn't afraid," Seung had said. "At least she wasn't afraid to speak her mind."

"Oh, no." Raja had laughed. "I'll give you that. She definitely spoke her mind."

Raja and Seung often had fights like this—Seung accusing Raja of being too restrained, Raja accusing Seung of being too extreme—but usually Raja backed off after a couple of minutes, realizing that he could never win an argument with Seung, especially when he was drunk.

But that night something was different. Maybe it was the alcohol, or the lateness of the evening, but Raja didn't back down, and after a while Seung grew frustrated and started to brood. At one point, a full minute passed in silence, and then Seung finally looked up at Raja and said, "Look, Raj, it's like that thing with that sign on your door, you know. You're not going to do anything about that, fine, but that's the type of thing we should be bringing to the administration, you know. People need to know about that. People should be getting expelled over that shit."

Chloe looked over at Raja, but he was looking down.

"What sign?" she asked.

"It's nothing," he said.

"He didn't tell you about it?" Seung said. Then he looked at Bae. "Unbelievable."

"Can we please talk about something else," Raja said, shooting Seung a glare that seemed to silence him.

"Whatever," Seung said, throwing up his arms.

Chloe looked around the table, confused, certain that she was being left out of something, but no one spoke.

Finally, Bae said, "You know, I have to agree. I mean, you don't want to talk about it, Raj. That's fine. Whatever. But someone higher up needs to know about it."

Raja looked at Chloe then and pulled out his wallet. "You ready to go?" he said, putting down a couple of twenties on the table.

Chloe looked at Seung, who was shaking his head.

"Okay," she said.

On the walk home, she tried to ask him more about it, but he was evasive and clearly annoyed. It was nothing, he said. It was stupid. A stupid prank. The same type of thing he'd been dealing with all his life. They were walking very quickly now along the narrow, tree-lined streets that surrounded the campus, and Chloe could tell he was pissed.

"When did this happen anyway?" she said at one point.

Raja looked at her. "I don't know," he said. "Maybe a few days ago."

"A few days ago?"

"Yeah."

"Well, do you know who put it up," she said, "this sign?"

He shook his head, but she could tell he was lying.

"Well, will you tell me what it said, at least?"

He stopped then in the middle of the street and looked at her. "Look," he said, quietly now, calmly. "When you tell me you don't want to talk about your parents, I don't ask you about them, right?"

She nodded.

"Well, this is the same type of thing. This is something I just don't want to talk about right now, okay?"

She nodded again, and this time he smiled.

"Thank you," he said. Then he put his arm around her. "If it was something for you to worry about, I'd tell you. I promise."

And so they didn't talk about it, and life went on as normal for the next couple of days. Chloe had a paper due at the end of the week in her French Enlightenment seminar and spent the better part of that Wednesday and Thursday holed up in her room. When Friday rolled around, she handed in her paper and then went immediately to the Cove, where Fatima and Raja were already drinking. In retrospect, this was one of her best nights at Stratham, a night of endless booze and flowing conversation, a night when people kept coming up to their table and talking to them, a night when the crowd kept growing, the music kept booming, and nobody wanted to leave. In the dark, smoky haze of the bar, she had slid her hand underneath Raja's T-shirt and kissed him drunkenly. She had told him she loved him.

Later, she would want to freeze-frame this moment in time, make it permanent. She would find herself wishing that they had gone back to her room, instead of his, that they had found a way to give a perfect ending to the perfect night. But of course this hadn't happened, though, even now, Chloe had trouble remembering what had.

What she did remember was stumbling home drunkenly from the Cove, then practically crawling up the back staircase of Raja's dorm, using the handrail for balance, laughing all the way. She remembered stopping at one point in the second-floor alcove and kissing Raja for a very long time, then following him as he started down the hallway toward his room. What she remembered after that, though, was still a blur. All she knew was that at one point Raja starting running, running very quickly toward his door, and when he got there, he ripped something off, a piece of paper, a sign, and started cursing. When she finally caught up to him, he was visibly shaken, the crumpled-up piece of paper hidden in his hand.

"Let me see it," she said.

But he shook his head.

"Let me fucking see it," she said, and this time she clawed at his hand, pried open his fingers, until he finally released it.

"Who the hell wrote this?" she said after she'd read the sign.

But he didn't answer. He just stood there. He did nothing at all. And he'd continue to do nothing at all, even when the signs kept appearing, day after day, for almost a month, even when his tires were slashed, even when he feared for his life, even when everyone he knew kept begging him to do something, to tell the police, to file a complaint, to inform the dean of students. Even then, he'd continue to do nothing at all.

At least not for a very long time.

Part Four

THE CAFÉ TONIGHT is dimly lit.

All around him people are sitting in pairs, or small groups, discussing the problems of the world, sipping their espressos, lighting each other's cigarettes. In the corner, a young Asian girl from Rice, who does a weekly set of acoustic Radiohead songs, is setting up her mike, and just out of view, on the other side of the room, he can hear Brandon talking to a customer from his post behind the counter.

Since his shift ended at six, Richard has been trying to work on his poem, but every time he looks at the paper, his mind returns to his parents and what he said to them. He remembers the way they looked when they showed up at his apartment the previous day, unannounced, his father wearing a polo shirt and khakis, his mother in a sundress. It was the first time he'd seen them together since his father moved out, and it suddenly struck him how normal it seemed, how much it seemed like normal life. They'd come under false pretenses, of course, to see if Chloe was now staying with him, if she was now living there, though they'd claimed that they'd simply come by to take him to lunch. Before they left, his father had asked him if he could use the bathroom, and as he walked down the hall, Richard had spotted him looking suspiciously into each of his roommates' rooms. *She's not in there, Dad,* he'd shouted at one point, to which his father said nothing.

Later, as they sat over steaming plates of chicken enchiladas at an upscale Mexican restaurant downtown, his father began his interrogation. Had he seen Chloe at all? Had he heard from her? Did he know where she might be staying? Was she staying in town? And what about her friends? Did he know who she still kept in touch with from high school? Could he give them their names?

To each of these questions, Richard had responded obliquely, eva-sively, trying his best not to give away what he knew. He said that he hadn't seen her, that he hadn't heard from her, and that he didn't think that she still kept in touch with anyone from high school. Then he said that if he had to guess, he'd assume that she'd probably left Houston by now. This last part had been unnecessary, a lie, and he wasn't sure, even now, why he said it. He could tell it had frightened them, especially his mother. *Why would you say something like that?* she'd asked at one point, and then, when he'd shrugged, she'd stood up suddenly and run to the bathroom. When she came back a few minutes later, her eyes red and puffy from crying, he'd tried to backtrack, tried to explain to her that this was only speculation, a guess, but it was no use. The damage was already done.

Later, as he sat by himself in his apartment, he'd felt the full extent of his guilt. He'd called Chloe shortly after he returned and told her what he'd said to them, and she had thanked him and then apologized for put-ting him in such a weird position. He told her that it wasn't a problem, though the truth was it had bothered him much more than he let on. He couldn't stop thinking about his mother and the way she'd run off to the bathroom, or his father and the way he'd kept asking him the same ques-tions over and over, ad nauseam, like an aging lawyer trying to win a case.

But still, he'd wondered then, what other choice did he have?

Ever since the divorce, he had found it difficult to be in his parents' presence. It was hard to describe, but it had something to do with the way they spoke to him now. Everything they said seemed to be couched in hidden meanings, secret codes. He resented the way they tried to extract certain information from him, the way they tried to play him against the other. For so long, he had sympathized with his mother, had taken her side, and yet even his mother had begun to act this way. He didn't know what to make of it. All he knew now was that the allegiances were set. His mother and father were a team, and he and Chloe were a team. If he were to betray someone, it would never be her. But, even so, he still felt a slight tinge of resentment for having to lie for his sister, for being put in this position. As much as he sympathized with his sister's situation, as much as he feared for her future, he still couldn't help thinking that a part of her had brought this situation upon herself by getting involved with this boy Raja. When he first spoke to them that night at the Taco Cabana, he'd wanted to tell his sister to cut her losses, to sever ties with this boy and move on. But he could tell, even then, that whatever he said to her would be falling on deaf ears, that she'd made up her mind, and that, for better or worse, she was sticking it out. *I'm so in love,* she'd written him in an e-mail that past fall, *you have no fucking idea.* And he could see that night as they stood outside the Taco Cabana that she was.

Still, it seemed strange to him now how much they'd both changed. Growing up, she had always been three years behind him, close enough in age that they had shared many of the same interests and friends, but far enough behind that he had always felt strangely protective of her. When she'd first entered high school he had immediately taken her under his wing, invited her to come sit with him and his friends during lunch, told her which teachers to avoid, taken her to parties where there were mostly upperclassmen. He had been the one who had first introduced her to beer, and later to pot, the one who had shown her the fine art of rolling a joint. He had explained to her in great detail the various tricks for getting out of class without her teachers noticing, had shown her how to forge a note from their parents, how to cover for herself when she came home drunk from a party. At the time he had told himself that he was simply initiating her into a world that she would have otherwise discovered herself, and at the same time looking over her, protecting her, making sure she didn't do anything too crazy. Now, however, he wasn't so sure. Sometimes he wondered if he hadn't exposed her to too much too soon, corrupted her in a way she wouldn't have been corrupted otherwise. He sometimes underestimated the power he had over her, the extent to which she trusted him, the extent to which she looked up to him. And it occurred to him, too, that maybe none of this stuff with Raja would have ever happened had he simply looked out for her more, had he not shown her the path of his own bad behavior.

Returning to his poem now, he starts to scribble down a few of these disconnected thoughts, but before he can arrive at anything meaningful, the music starts up in the corner, the girl singing, and then a moment later Brandon appears at his table with a fresh cup of coffee.

"Got a cigarette?" he asks.

Richard looks up, smiles, slides him the pack.

"How's the poem going?" Brandon asks, lighting his cigarette.

"It's not," he says.

Brandon sits down, picks up the poem, and starts to read before Richard snatches it back.

"Don't be an asshole," he says.

Brandon smiles at him. "What's with you tonight?"

"I don't know." Richard shrugs, looking over at the other side of the room. "Nothing. Everything." He puts down his pen. "It's just all this shit with Chloe, you know. It's just totally freaking me out."

"Tell me about it," Brandon says. "At least you're not living with her."

Richard looks at him and suddenly feels bad for complaining. What Brandon is doing for them, for both of them, is beyond accommodating. Since Chloe and Raja moved in, he's been letting them use his car, giving them food, letting them go on the Internet whenever they want. From what Brandon has told him, they've been very appreciative, very nice, but he's also heard them talking late at night in hushed whispers, he says, sometimes crying, sometimes even fighting. Earlier that day, he had told him how he'd come out of his bedroom the night before and found Chloe lying on the couch in a ball, crying. When he'd asked her what was wrong, though, she'd said nothing. She'd just looked at him, then shaken her head and walked out of the room.

"How's she doing, anyway?" Richard asks.

"I don't know," Brandon says. "I mean, I don't see them that much. They go out of the house a lot, you know, or else they're just kind of hiding away in their room, talking, I guess."

"All the time?"

"Yeah, I don't know. At least when I'm there." Brandon drags on his cigarette. "Yesterday she asked me if they could stay with me for a few more days, and I was like, sure, but after that, you know, you guys are gonna have to find another place to crash."

Richard nods, understanding.

"I mean, I don't wanna be an asshole or anything. I love your sister and all, but it just seems like they're in some serious shit right now, you know, and I can't have that type of shit sticking to me." He looks at Richard and shrugs.

"Yeah," Richard says, sighing. "To be honest, I don't really know what's going on myself." He picks up the pack of cigarettes and lights one. Yesterday his parents had told him that the police had been calling them, telling them that Raja was now being looked at as a fugitive, but when he asked Chloe about this, she denied it. She said that it wasn't actually that bad, that their parents were exaggerating. Even now, though, he isn't sure who to believe. "She's not telling me anything," he says finally. "I mean, I know some kid up there at Stratham got hurt and all and that they're saying Raja did it, but that's about it, you know?"

Brandon nods. "Yeah," he says. "Well, they're not saying shit to me. That's for sure."

They both look over at the girl in the corner, who has just started singing "No Surprises" in a very low, melancholy voice. A moment later Brandon looks at his watch and says that he has to get back, that his break is over.

"You going to Beto's tonight?" he asks.

Richard shakes his head. "Probably not. I gotta meet Michelson."

"Where?"

"Here."

"*Right* here?" Brandon says, looking around suspiciously.

"Yeah. You know, in like an hour or so."

"Little late for a meeting, don't you think?"

Richard shrugs. "It's not like I'm his student, you know."

"Man," Brandon says. "Must be nice. That dude never wants to have meetings with me."

"Maybe if you were a little nicer to him," Richard says.

"Yeah," he says. "Or maybe if I sucked his dick." Then he smiles slyly at Richard. "Speaking of, I'm meeting someone later tonight if you're interested. I'm sure he's got a friend."

Richard looks at him and rolls his eyes. "You're joking, right?"

"Yeah," Brandon says, turning around. "Of course, I'm fucking joking."

By the time Michelson arrives, it's almost eight o'clock, the café suddenly packed with the late-evening crowd. For the past half hour, Richard has been paging through an enormous volume of collected letters from Wallace Stevens to his wife, a book that Michelson had actually given to him the last time they met. Though very formal in nature, these letters are among the most beautiful Richard has ever read. He wonders what it would feel like to receive a letter like this, or to write one. Then he thinks about the random, disjointed e-mails he'd received from Marcos when he'd first arrived in Korea, filled with non sequiturs and typos. Did anyone in his generation even bother to write letters anymore? he wonders.

Did they care? Was letter writing a dying art? It is this that he's thinking about when Michelson appears at his table, suddenly out of breath, a cup of coffee in his hand.

"So sorry I'm late," Michelson says, sitting down at the table with his coffee. "You weren't waiting long, were you?"

Richard shakes his head. "Just since my shift ended."

"Ah, that's right," Michelson says, smiling. "I always forget you work here."

"Brandon, too."

"Huh?"

"From our class? *Brandon.*" Richard points over toward the counter where Brandon is busy steaming milk and flirting with a customer.

"Ah yes," Michelson says after a moment, staring at Brandon uncertainly. "Brandon. Of course." Then he returns his gaze to Richard and the book in his hand, his eyes suddenly brightening. "Oh," he says. "I see you're reading the Stevens letters."

"I am," Richard says. "They're wonderful."

"Aren't they?" Michelson smiles. "I know. I knew you'd love them." Then he winks at Richard in a way that makes him feel uncomfortable, exposed, as if there's some type of hidden meaning in this statement.

He still isn't sure why Michelson has invited him here in the first place, what he wants. Earlier that day he had received a lengthy voice mail from Michelson, in which Michelson had explained to him that he wanted to meet him here later, that he had something very important to discuss with him, but when Richard called him back, Michelson had been very evasive about the nature of the meeting, saying only that he was looking forward to seeing him. Now, however, he wonders what Michelson wants, whether this meeting is just a pretense for something else, whether it's part of his master plan. He looks over Michelson's shoulder at Brandon, who is making moony eyes at him, laughing.

"So, I guess you're wondering why I invited you here," Michelson says after a moment, smiling.

Richard nods.

"Well, as it turns out, I have some very good news for you, Richard," he says. "Actually some good news and some bad news, but I'll start with the good news first, okay?"

Richard looks at him, says nothing.

"Remember how I told you I had that friend up there at Michigan?"

Richard nods.

"Well, I took the liberty of sending him some of your poems, and I have to tell you, he was very impressed. *Very* impressed. Even called to tell me so."

"You sent him my poems?" Richard says, his voice almost cracking.

"Well, yes. But listen to this. He said that it wasn't unprecedented for them to accept a student late, especially if that student showed exceptional merit, which he felt you did. He said it didn't happen often, but it did happen. In other words, he believed you had a chance." He smiles at Richard. "The bad news is that he'll have to get the unanimous support of the other faculty, which might take some persuading. He also said that you'd need to send him your transcripts and some type of statement of purpose by the end of the week." At this, Michelson pauses. "Richard, you look upset?"

"You had no right to do that."

"Well, no, but I thought you'd be happy."

"Why the hell would I be happy? Those poems weren't even finished. They were drafts."

"Well, yes. A few of them were a little rough around the edges, as you say, but I think they certainly display your talent."

"Jesus," Richard says. "I never even said that I wanted to go there."

"Yes, you did."

"No," Richard says. "I didn't."

Michelson pauses. "Richard, I don't think I need to explain to you what a rare opportunity this is."

Richard looks at him. For months, Michelson has been talking about the University of Michigan's MFA Program in Creative Writing and what this would mean for him, how it would place him in very good company and so forth, but whenever Richard thinks about Michigan, he sees only wheat fields and farmers, a vast, desolate landscape filled with endless distances. He sees bitter winters and frost-covered windows and an empty apartment with a dark bedroom and a lone, solitary desk in the corner. And, of course, he sees the prospect of failure, the prospect of public humiliation and disgrace, all things he'd rather not be thinking about right now.

"I really can't believe you did that," Richard says again, this time more emphatically. "I sent you those poems in confidence."

"Richard, I think you're missing the big picture here."

"I don't think I am," Richard says. "I sent you some poems, and then you took those poems and you sent them off to a total stranger without asking my permission. I think that's pretty much the big picture, isn't it?"

"You're right," Michelson says finally, sighing. "I probably shouldn't have done that. You're right about that. I probably should have asked you first. But I did it, you have to understand, with your best interests in mind."

"My best interests?" Richard says, laughing. "How the hell do you know what my best interests are? You don't even know me."

"No," Michelson says, "but I know your poetry."

Richard stares at him. He can see that Michelson is hurt, deflated, surprised by his reaction. He probably expected Richard to jump up and throw his arms around him, hug him. But right now Richard is too annoyed, too infuriated, to even look at him. He turns away.

"Look, Richard," Michelson continues. "Why don't you just sleep on it, okay? Maybe you'll see things differently tomorrow."

"I don't need to sleep on it," Richard says. "Honestly, I don't."

Michelson bristles at this. "You need to understand, Richard, that if you pull out at this point, you'll not only be hurting yourself, but you'll also be creating a very embarrassing professional situation for me. Do you understand that?"

Richard stands up then and, no longer able to control his anger, begins to pack his bag. He feels violated in the worst possible way, betrayed by a man he once respected. He looks over at Brandon, who is staring at him in disbelief, his face full of confusion.

"Look," he says to Michelson. "Don't go calling me anymore, okay? And don't go doing me any more favors, all right? Not unless I ask." Then he starts toward the door, passing the customers, ignoring Brandon as he follows him out on the street.

"Hey, Rich!" Brandon yells after him. "Where the fuck are you going?"

But it's too late. Richard is already running, running through the darkness toward his mother's minivan, running past the banyan trees and the tropical foliage on people's lawns, running past the garbage cans and the sprinkler systems and the overturned bikes, running as fast as he can, wishing for once he had an answer to Brandon's question, wishing for once he knew where the fuck he was going.

AS HE SITS across from his wife at the kitchen table where they've eaten now for nearly thirty years, Elson finds himself wondering what had happened to all of that early optimism. Where had it gone? What had happened to all of that excitement they used to feel back in the early days of their relationship, back when oil was thirty-nine dollars a barrel and everyone in the country was flocking to Houston, trying to catch a piece of the action, trying to ride the crest of the wave? Where had it all gone? Had it all been eaten up by the crash? Was there nothing left of it now? Was their marriage, like everything from that time, something ephemeral and vague, something as tenuous as the market itself? He tries to remember the last time he felt the type of lust he used to feel for Cadence back then, the type of lust that had made him want to screw in elevators or the backseats of cars or the bathrooms of restaurants, the type of lust that had made him cancel appointments or drive home early from work or call in sick. How can it be, he wonders now, that this woman sitting across from him is the same woman he used to spend hours making love to, the same woman he used to have to call three or four times a day just to make it through the workweek, the same woman he once flew to Amsterdam on a crazy whim simply because he missed her. What had happened between then and now to bring them to this place where they could barely be in the same room together for more than a minute without fighting?

Across from him, Cadence is paging through their daughter's notebooks and journals, which she's brought down from her room, searching through her address book for some clue of where she might be. So far, at Elson's insistence, they've respected their daughter's wishes and not contacted the police, though there have been some inquiries on the other end. A couple of police officers from the Stratham Police Department who had called them up the night before, wanting to speak to Chloe. Two men in black suits, who Cadence claimed she'd met before, stopping by the house that morning. So far, they've told them nothing, only that Chloe is out of town visiting a friend and that she hasn't spoken to that boy they're looking for. What they've found out, however, has troubled them. That this boy they're looking for has fled the jurisdiction of the Stratham Police Department, that he's broken his bail, that he hasn't been seen in several days, and that even though he hasn't been formally indicted, he's still being looked at as a fugitive.

For his own part, Elson has tried to remain composed, tried to be the type of steady anchor that Cadence has always wanted him to be. Since the night they found out, since the night that Cadence called him, they haven't argued once, and Cadence has kept him more or less in the loop through e-mails and phone calls. It occurs to him now that this is probably the longest they've gone without fighting in several months and certainly the most time they've spent together since the day he moved out. If he weren't so overwhelmed with concern for his daughter, he might even see this sudden civility between them as a tiny silver lining on a very dark cloud.

As Cadence picks up another journal, Elson leans forward and pours himself another drink. They've both been drinking since the early afternoon, when he arrived, and now, as the sun is going down at the far end of the yard, just beyond the palm trees and the cabana house, he can feel the alcohol settling in.

"Did you know that she used to smoke pot in high school?" Cadence says after a moment, looking up from one of Chloe's journals.

"You shouldn't be reading that," Elson says, looking out at the pool, thinking suddenly of Lorna's computer, her e-mail account.

"Did you know that, though?" she asks.

"No," he says. "I didn't."

Cadence shakes her head. "There's stuff about us in here, you know," she says, paging through the journal. "Especially you."

"Really?" Elson says, his interest suddenly piqued. "Like what?" He leans over the table, but Cadence covers the journal with her hand.

"I thought you didn't think we should be reading it."

"We shouldn't be," he says. Then he looks at her. "Just tell me."

Cadence looks at him, smiles, then slides the journal across the table. "You can read it yourself," she says.

But when Elson looks at the journal he feels something like panic rising inside of him, a sudden fear of what he might discover. After a moment, he slides it back.

"It's not all bad," Cadence says. "Honestly. Some of it is actually very sweet."

"I'm sure it is," he says, "but not all of it."

"No," she says. "Not all of it."

He looks out at the pool again. "I'd rather not know," he says, "to be perfectly honest." Then he thinks again of Lorna and the fight they had the previous night on the phone, how she accused him of being a sneak, of violating her privacy, and how he hasn't heard from her since. In retrospect, he should have never mentioned anything about her e-mail account or her correspondence with Cadence, should have never even brought it up. What he'd done was only confirm her suspicions about him, proven himself untrustworthy. As she put it herself, *I feel like I don't even know you anymore.* And as he sits here now, staring at Cadence's face, he wonders if he knows himself.

"She should be calling us any minute now," Cadence says after a moment, looking down at her watch. "She said she'd call at eight, and it's almost half past."

"Half past eight?"

"Yes."

Earlier that day, Cadence had received a text message from Chloe on her phone, a text message that had informed her that she would be calling them both at eight, and when Elson had learned this, he had come right over, only to find Cadence holed up in Chloe's room, knee deep in her personal belongings. When he'd told her that they probably shouldn't be doing that, that they probably shouldn't be going through her personal stuff, Cadence had looked at him for a very long time, then grabbed the journals anyway and started downstairs.

"Well, if she doesn't call by midnight . . . ," Elson says, but doesn't finish.

"Then what?"

"Then, I don't know. We might have to call the police."

"You think?"

"I don't know," he says. "What other choice do we have?"

Cadence looks at him and nods, sips her wine. "Don't worry," she says finally. "She'll call."

But she doesn't. Not for almost an hour, at least. Not until Cadence has made it halfway through another bottle of wine and Elson is half asleep on one of the couches in the den. He can't even remember how he made it from the kitchen to the den or what he and Cadence had been talking about before he left the room. All he knows now is that he had fallen into some type of dream, a semiconscious reverie, the memory of those early days with Cadence coming back to him in fragmented waves: the night they first met at his friend Brian Lowry's house, those early days that they had spent at his apartment in River Oaks, the long drunken nights and the endless stream of parties, the scandal he had caused by dating a college girl, the scandal they had both caused when she had finally decided to drop out of college and marry him.

It is this that he's thinking about as he sits up on the couch and tries to orient himself. The room itself is dark, and in the distance, on the other side of the house, he can hear Cadence shouting, shouting something at their daughter on the phone. Taking a moment to catch his bearings, he stands up slowly, then starts down the hallway toward the kitchen, but by the time he gets there, Cadence is no longer shouting on the phone. She is sitting on the floor, her arms draped loosely around her knees, the phone lying on the floor beside her. The room itself is dark, save for the bright oscillating pool lights from outside casting strange oblong patterns along the walls, and it takes him a moment to make out her face and realize she's crying.

"Cadence," he says.

But she doesn't answer.

Without saying a word, he walks over and gives her his hand, helps her stand up, embraces her for what seems like the first time in many months. She looks at him but doesn't speak. She lets him hold her.

"Can you tell me what happened?" he says after a moment, very softly.

She shakes her head. "I screwed it up," she says.

"What did she say?"

"I shouldn't have gotten angry," she says. "I should have just listened."

Elson reaches then for his cigarettes and lights one, and though she hasn't smoked in twenty years, Cadence motions for him to give her a drag, which he does.

As she exhales, she shakes her head again. "How is this happening?" she says finally.

"What?"

"*This*," she says, motioning toward the phone on the floor, the room. "I mean, what did we do wrong? What did we do to deserve this?"

Elson puts his hand on her shoulder, but she shrugs it off.

"Just start at the beginning," he says, sitting down now on one of the stools at the counter. "Tell me what she said."

"It's what she *didn't* say," Cadence says. "It's what she's *not* telling us."

"Okay," Elson says. "But she must have said something."

"She did. She said she needed more time."

"For what?"

"I don't know. She didn't say."

"Well, how much more time does she need?"

"Two more days."

"*Two?*"

"Yes, two."

Elson shakes his head at this. "Jesus," he says, losing his calmness now. "And that's it. That's all she said?"

"No. She also said that if we called the police, or spoke to anyone, we would be ruining her life."

At this, Elson stands up and begins to pace. "Is she still in Houston?" he says.

"I have no idea."

"Well, what were the two of you talking about?"

"We weren't talking. I was yelling at her. I don't know. All this shit, you know. What she's putting us through. I just lost it."

Elson walks over and picks up the phone. "I'm calling the police."

"Elson."

"Seriously. This is ridiculous."

"Not tonight," she says.

"Why not tonight?"

"Because I don't think I can take any more tonight," she says, and then pauses. "And besides," she says, looking down, "I have somewhere to go."

"Where?"

"I have to meet a friend."

"Which friend?"

Cadence says nothing.

"Which friend, Cadence?"

"Elson, one of the privileges of being divorced is that I don't have to tell you every fucking little detail about my life."

Elson stares at her, catching on. "You're dating someone?"

"I'm not having this conversation right now."

"Who is it?"

"Elson."

"Who is it?"

"It's no one you know."

At this, Elson can feel the ground beneath him giving way, his body loosening. He feels as if he's just been hit by a very large weight. Moving over to the other side of the kitchen, he sits down at the kitchen table and stares at Chloe's journal. He's known for some time that this was going to happen, that sooner or later Cadence would meet someone, but now that it's a reality, now that she's actually telling him it's a reality, he doesn't feel prepared to accept it.

On the other side of the kitchen, Cadence is quiet and perfectly still, perhaps preparing herself for an explosion, bracing herself for a fight, but Elson doesn't move. He doesn't do a thing. He is somewhere else now, outside of himself. He is back in the front seat of his car on that late-summer evening in 1981 when he first saw Cadence coming out the front door of his friends' house, moving slowly across the lawn. He is remembering the way her body emerged from the darkness, the way her face was suddenly illuminated by the lampposts along the street, and the excitement he felt upon seeing her, this beautiful woman, the future mother of his children, the way he knew, even before she spoke, even before she said a word, that something remarkable was happening.

3

IF SHE HAD TO BE HONEST, she hadn't expected it. She hadn't expected that reaction. She'd expected something else—maybe a fight, or an argument—but not that. She hadn't expected he'd actually cry. In all the years she'd known him, in all the years they'd been married, she had only seen him cry once, when his father died, and even then, he'd done it privately, in their bedroom, with the door shut. She hadn't known how to interpret it, how to react. She'd been expecting him to explode at her, to lose his cool, but instead Elson had sat there quietly, saying nothing, staring out at the pool. When she finally walked over to him, he looked up at her with something like desperation, and that's when she'd realized he was crying.

"Elson," she'd said and touched his shoulder, but he didn't answer. Instead, he just turned around and looked back at the pool.

"I should go," he'd said finally.

"You don't have to," she'd said. "You can stay. We can talk."

But he shook his head. And later, as they stood at the door, he'd said, "I'm sorry, Cadence. I've done some terrible things to you. I really have, and I'm sorry for that." Then he'd turned around and, without saying anything else, had walked down the pathway to his car.

After he left, she stood by herself in the kitchen for a long time, staring out at the pool, trying to process what had happened. For years, she'd believed she was incapable of hurting him, or that he was incapable of being hurt. Even throughout their divorce, he'd been impervious to her insults, her attacks, her accusations. He seemed to have this ability to deflect almost anything she said. He seemed to have this barrier around him. So what had happened since then? Had he really changed? Or had he always been this way? As much as she hated to admit it, she'd been strangely touched by it all, the whole scene, the sight of him crying, his grave, unexpected apology. She wondered what he was doing now, where he had gone after he left. For the first time in a long time, she found herself wondering if he was okay.

On the other side of the Hyatt Regency bar, Gavin is talking to the bartender, a slim older woman, who is making them drinks. Cadence is sitting by herself at a small table in the corner, watching him, trying to think up a good excuse for why she can't stay here tonight, hoping she doesn't have to, though of course it had been her idea to come here in the first place. She had actually insisted on it—*to spice things up,* she'd told him earlier—though in reality it had been much more complicated than that. Ever since she'd last made love to Gavin, she'd been dreading the idea of going to his apartment. She found it depressing, she realized now, the darkness of it, the smell of sweaty gym socks, the constant clutter around the room. Initially, Gavin had suggested another place, a small motel down the street from his apartment, where they could meet. It would be closer, he'd said, and cheaper. But she had bristled at this. *"I'm not a prostitute,"* she'd responded. *"If you're worried about money, I'll pay."*

He hadn't said anything to this but had eventually agreed to go to the Hyatt. Later, when they arrived, they'd gone straight up to the room and tried to make love, but Gavin had had some trouble, something he blamed on the medication he was taking, and so they'd finally given up and come down to the bar.

Now, however, as she sits here, staring at him, she feels only sadness, sadness and guilt. She feels guilt for the way she left Elson earlier, the way she didn't comfort him as she should have, and sadness for the way she yelled at Chloe, the way she ruined any future chances for reconciliation. She realizes now that ever since the night that Chloe disappeared, she's been blaming herself for what happened, for her disappearance and, more specifically, that she's begun to associate Gavin with this guilt. If she'd been at home, after all, instead of with him, this might have never happened. She might have been able to stop her. This isn't fair to Gavin, of course. He's been nothing but supportive. But still, she can't help it. Every time she looks at him, every time she stares at his face, she sees the evidence of her own bad behavior, her own guilt, and has to turn away. In retrospect, she should have just canceled with him the moment she got that text message from Chloe earlier that day, or at least after she'd spoken to her that night, but for some reason she hadn't. For some reason she'd thought that seeing Gavin might provide her with a temporary respite from it all, a little distraction, though now, more than anything, she simply wants to leave.

When Gavin finally returns, he places a vodka tonic down in front of her and shakes his head.

"Guess how much these cost?" he says, smiling.

She looks at him.

"Just guess."

"I have no idea."

"Twelve bucks apiece," he says. "Can you believe that?"

"I'll get the next round."

"That's not what I meant," he says defensively. "I'm just saying that that's a lot of money, don't you think, for a shot of vodka and a little tonic?"

She shrugs. Lately, his obsession with money, with the amount things cost, has begun to annoy her. Every time he looks at a menu, he'll shake his head in disbelief, or roll his eyes, and later, as they're eating, he'll say things like, *So how does that ten-dollar sandwich taste?* or *Hey there, how's that three-dollar latte?* It seems ironic to her. For someone who majored in business, who actually teaches classes in business, he seems to be constantly surprised by the concept of a free-market economy and cost-push inflation. In a way, that's why she chose the Hyatt. She wanted to test him, to see how deep his stinginess ran. Now, however, as he sits there silently, she feels bad for her rudeness.

"So you were telling me," he says, after a moment, "about your daughter."

She looks at him. "I was?"

"Yes."

"What was I saying?"

"That she called you tonight."

"Oh, right," she says, trying to remember how much she'd told him. Somehow the day's intake of alcohol has muddied her memory, sullied her thoughts, and she feels suddenly regretful for saying anything. Long ago she had vowed never to mention any of this stuff to him, to leave him out of it.

"You were talking about the cops," he continues, "how you were thinking about calling them now."

"Yeah," she says, nodding. "Well, I've changed my mind about that."

"You have? Why's that?"

"I don't know," she says, looking over at the bartender. "I just don't think we should."

He looks at her, sips his drink. "Oh yeah?" he says finally.

"She asked us not to."

He seems to consider this, says nothing.

"You disagree?"

"No," he says. "It's none of my business."

"You look like you disagree."

"I don't," he says. "I don't know enough about the situation, actually, to have an opinion." Then he pauses for a long time, and she can see that he's turning it over in his mind, processing it. Finally, he says, "It's just that she seems a little young, you know."

"Meaning what?"

"Meaning that you're putting a lot of faith in a girl who's only twenty-one."

"She's my daughter."

"I know that."

"Well, she's not a dolt," she says. "I trust her."

He looks at her, says nothing, and she realizes then that she might have misspoken, that by suggesting that her own daughter was not a dolt, he might have thought she was implying that his son was. His son, the kid with special needs. His son, the boy he never talks about.

"I'm sorry," she says. "I didn't mean anything by that."

"I know," he says. "It's fine." He picks up his drink then and turns toward the jazz trio in the corner who are setting up their instruments.

The truth is, he talks so little about his son that she often forgets that he exists. He had brought him up once, that first night, had talked about him for a while, about how he was mentally challenged and so forth, but ever since that night, he hasn't mentioned him. There are no pictures of his son in his apartment, no drawings on the refrigerator, no toys hidden in the closet. No evidence at all that he exists. In her weaker moments, she often reverts to her initial suspicion that he might have made this child up for the sole purpose of luring women back to his apartment, of gaining their sympathy and trust. It's a ridiculous suspicion, of course, but for some reason she feels it returning to her now, feels the weight of it on her mind. She stares at him for a long time, then finally says, "Can I ask you a question?"

"Of course."

"Why don't you ever mention him?"

"Who?"

"Your son."

"What do you mean?"

"You never talk about him."

"Yes, I do."

"No," she says, "you don't."

He stares at her, shrugs his shoulders. "I guess I'm just protective of him, you know."

"But you don't even have a picture of him."

"What do you mean?"

"In your apartment. There isn't one picture of him. Don't you think that's a little strange? I mean, there's nothing. No toys. No video games."

"He doesn't play video games."

She stares at him.

"What are you implying?"

"I'm not implying anything."

"You think I made him up or something?"

"I don't know," she says. "I don't know what to think."

"Why the hell would I make him up, Cadence? Jesus. What purpose would that serve?"

"I don't know," she says, raising her eyebrows now in innuendo. "Why don't you tell me?"

At this, though, she can see she's hit a nerve, that she's upset him, that she's gone too far.

"You're sick," he says.

"Gavin."

"Seriously. You're fucking sick. I know you're upset about your daughter and all, but Jesus, Cadence, this is too much." Then he reaches into his pocket and pulls out his wallet. She can see that his fingers are shaking. After a moment, he pulls out a picture and lays it down before her. The picture is of him and a boy standing outside a theme park in Houston, their arms draped loosely around each other, their faces beaming. The boy is a carbon copy of Gavin.

She stares at the picture and feels her stomach drop, feels such a deep sense of shame that she can barely speak. What made her think she could mention this? What gave her the right to express her deepest, most irrational fears? Was it simply the alcohol, or was it something else? Was she finally losing her mind?

"I'm sorry," she finally manages. "I feel like shit."

He shakes his head, says nothing, then excuses himself to the bathroom. But when he returns, a few minutes later, he seems fine. He says he understands, that he knows she's under a lot of stress right now, that he can't even imagine what she's going through. He suggests that they just forget about it.

His kindness, of course, makes her feel even worse. She doesn't deserve him, she thinks. Any normal man would have discarded her by now. She reaches across the table and grabs his hand. "I'm sorry," she says again. "Truly."

But he says nothing. He doesn't say a word.

To appease him, and to mollify some of her own guilt, she agrees to spend the night with him. Upstairs in their room, she allows him to undress her, to sit there on the bed and stare at her naked body as she stands before him, something that she knows he likes to do. When it comes to the lovemaking, however, Gavin is unsuccessful again, something that he blames this time on the alcohol.

They lie there for a long time in silence, but there is no warmth between them. Whatever warmth there once was is gone now. She studies his chest, the smooth hairless surface of it, the paleness of his skin. She runs her hand up and down his legs, across his ribs, but he doesn't move.

Later, after he's fallen asleep, she lies there for a long time feeling empty and worn out. Her thoughts return to Chloe and the question that's been bothering her all night: Should they have called the police, or should they just wait it out and trust her? What would a responsible parent do? What would her own parents do? Nothing she's ever read about parenting has prepared her for this particular dilemma. There's no guidebook for what to do when something like this happens. After all, if they did call the police, they might end up implicating Chloe even more than they wanted. Then again, if they did nothing at all, they might end up putting her in even worse danger. She leans back on her pillow and closes her eyes, her mind returning to Chloe's journal and a troubling passage she'd read earlier that day, a passage she'd decided not to show Elson, a passage written only a day before Chloe left:

I guess if he wanted me to, I would. I mean, if I knew we could be together afterward, I would. I would do it.

She thinks about these words, what they mean, then looks back at Gavin and the clock, wondering how much longer she has to stay.

4

FOR MONTHS, she had imagined bringing him home to Houston with her. She had imagined driving him around town, introducing him to her parents, showing him her old high school. She had always felt an affinity toward Houston that no one up at Stratham seemed to understand. To them, Houston represented big hair and cowboy hats and conservative politics, but to Chloe, it had always meant something else. Houston was the world of her childhood, a magical place, a place that she had always felt truly herself, and it was this side of Houston that she wanted to show Raja, and had circumstances been different she honestly believed that he would have embraced the city in the same way she had. Instead, however, they'd spent most of their time holed up in Brandon's apartment, arguing and complaining about the heat, and she could tell now that he disliked it, that he wasn't happy here, that he maybe even wished he hadn't come.

Of course, given the circumstances, he probably wouldn't have been happy anywhere. Ever since he'd arrived, he'd been sullen and removed. It was a side of him she'd never seen before, and it bothered her. They'd fought more in the past few days than they had during the entire course of their relationship, and though she'd found ways of explaining this, attributing it to the heat or to their claustrophobic living situation, she couldn't help wondering whether it was something else, if he had maybe grown tired of her, or if she had maybe disappointed him in some way. She wondered what else she could have possibly done for him. After all, she was essentially jeopardizing her own future to save his. But when she'd brought this up to him the night before, when they were fighting, he'd reminded her that it had been her idea for him to come down here in the first place.

She'd bristled at this, though she'd known it was true. A few days earlier she had called him up out of the blue and suggested it—suggested that he come down to Houston for a few days and hide out—but she hadn't actually believed that he'd do it. Even when he'd called her up from the Houston airport the night he arrived and told her he was here, even then, she hadn't believed him. She'd thought he was joking.

"Describe what you're looking at right now," she'd said, and then he'd proceeded to describe the giant bronze statue of George Bush Sr., and she'd felt her stomach drop.

That night, as they drove home, he'd cried for the first time since she'd known him. She'd tried to get him to explain what had happened back at Stratham to make him do this, but he said only that things had changed, that Tyler Beckwith had fallen into some type of unconscious state, and that Seung had now agreed to testify against him, and that things were looking worse and worse. He said that he believed his own official indictment was imminent and that he hadn't known what else to do. He'd panicked, he'd admitted later, and had regretted his decision the moment he stepped onto the plane in Boston, but by then it was too late. By then, there was no going back.

She'd taken him to her mother's house first, cooked him an omelet, which he hadn't eaten, then packed up some clothes and her computer and taken him over to Beto's, where she was sure she'd find Richard.

Later, when they returned to Brandon's apartment, Brandon had made them up a bed in his study, a small room with a desk and a computer and a few bookshelves against the wall. The bed itself was nothing more than an old futon mattress, which Brandon had laid down in the middle of the room.

After Brandon had gone to sleep, they'd lain there for a long time on the mattress, holding each other. Raja was wide awake, his body filled with adrenaline, his muscles stiff and tense. She'd tried to calm him down, suggested that he drink some water or a beer, but he'd shaken his head. He kept getting up every few minutes to go to the window and smoke. He'd light a cigarette, take a few drags, then put it out. Then he'd come back to the bed and let her hold him. He didn't want to talk, he said, but he couldn't sleep either. Finally, he began to wonder whether it was really too late to go back, whether he could maybe call up the Stratham Police Department the next day and turn himself in, promise to come back that evening. Would that be the best thing to do? he'd wondered out loud. Then he'd answered his own question by saying, no—no, it wouldn't. Technically speaking, he had just broken his bail, and even if he went back now, he'd still have to contend with that, with the consequences, not to mention the fact that he'd be immediately jailed and lose any chance of ever getting bail again. It would be a nightmare, he said. A nightmare bottom line.

This went on for most of the night, Raja getting up constantly to smoke cigarettes, Chloe sitting there silently, listening. She said very little that night. She knew that bringing up her own concerns would only upset him more, so she'd kept them to herself. It was funny how things had changed, how she'd now become the pillar of strength in their relationship, the stable force. He'd been so stoic throughout it all, so confident and calm throughout everything that had happened back at Stratham, and yet now he was clearly losing it. It worried her, scared her, but also made her feel an even deeper connection to him. It was the first time in her life that she'd felt that someone else was actually depending on her.

The next day they'd dropped Brandon off at his job at Café Brasil, then taken his car across town to a small sushi place on the other side of Montrose that Chloe used to go to back in high school. Here, over steaming bowls of miso soup, they had sat for nearly an hour without talking.

Later, when they got back to the apartment, Raja had started to speak. He said that they needed to figure out a plan, that they needed to figure out a logical course of action. He asked her how long she thought they could stay at Brandon's, and she had said a couple of days, maybe four or five max. He nodded, looked around the room. By now, he said, the authorities up in Stratham would be aware of his absence. They would have taken some action themselves. Maybe called up some airports, sent around his picture, contacted the Canadian and Mexican borders. She looked up at him. It was strange to hear him talking in this way. It felt like something from a dream or a movie. Up until this point she hadn't really considered their next step, hadn't really considered where they might go now. In retrospect, she realized then, she had been living only in the moment, but now it seemed that living in the moment wasn't going to be enough. As Raja paced around the room, she felt the sudden reality of it all finally settling in. This was actually happening, she thought, and it was actually happening to them. She felt her stomach tighten. She looked up at Raja and wanted to say something, but he kept going. He said that he'd taken some precautions himself, that he'd bought two plane tickets, for example, one to Newark, and then another one in Newark to Houston, and that he'd paid for both tickets with cash. This might throw them off for a couple of days, he thought, make it harder for them to find him, but eventually they would. They'd figure it out. And when they did, they'd press her parents, and then they'd question Richard, and eventually they'd find them. It was only a matter of time, he said. Maybe three or four days at the most. That was the window they were looking at. After that, they'd need another plan, or at least he would.

"What's that supposed to mean?" she'd asked when he said this.

But he hadn't answered.

"I'm coming with you," she said. "Wherever you're going next, I'm coming, too."

Raja shook his head. "It's not safe," he said. And then he explained to her that he wasn't going to let her implicate herself any more than she already had. It was bad enough that she'd already implicated herself this much. Anything more and she'd be jeopardizing her own future, her own life, and he wasn't going to let that happen. He was very adamant about this, almost belligerent about it, and for most of the night they had fought about it, Raja insisting that this was his problem now, not hers, and Chloe insisting that she wasn't going to let him go anywhere without her. The air-conditioning unit in Brandon's apartment was on the fritz, and it seemed that the more they fought, the hotter the tiny room became. Finally, growing exhausted, Raja had lain down on the bed and closed his eyes.

"I don't want to fight anymore," he'd said, sighing, and then Chloe had lain down beside him on the bed and kissed his shoulder.

"Me neither," she said.

"It's only because I'm worried about you," he'd said finally. "Because I don't want to involve you."

"I know that," she said, and this time kissed him on the lips.

They made love twice that night in the muggy heat of Brandon's tiny study while Brandon sat silently down the hall, watching TV. Later, after he'd gone to bed, they took a cold shower together and then returned to the room to talk.

For the time being, the issue of whether or not Chloe would be coming with him was going to be left off the table. They would resolve that later. For now what they needed to do was figure out a next step. Raja said that he had a close friend from high school who was now living out in California, studying at Stanford. He trusted this friend completely, he said, and was sure that he could put him up for a couple of days, but that wasn't really a long-term solution, was it? What he really needed to do now was get out of the country. That would be the safest thing. Unfortunately, he'd left his passport back at his parents' house in New Jersey, which made air travel, train travel, and even buses out of the question.

"Out of the country?" she'd said. "Are you serious?"

He looked at her, shrugged.

"Come on, Raj. I don't think we're really at that point yet, do you?"

He shook his head, then stood up and walked over to the window and lit a cigarette.

She could tell he felt trapped. She had seen it in his face that morning, and she could see it again now. Still, she kept talking, wondering whether leaving the country wasn't a little extreme. I mean wasn't that essentially admitting to their own guilt? Wasn't that essentially throwing in the towel? After all, what if Tyler Beckwith recovered? What if the charges were lowered? But the truth was, the thought of him leaving the country, of both of them leaving the country, was simply too hard to process. The thought of them living a life in exile, a life on the run, it seemed insane.

"You haven't even been convicted yet," she reminded him.

"No," he said, "but I will be." And then he reminded her of what the charges would be if Tyler Beckwith didn't recover, if he died. It was the unspoken word that had never passed between them, the word they never uttered. "I'm just dealing with reality here," he said. "I mean, that's the fucking reality."

She looked at him and felt suddenly sick.

"I think you should go back," she'd said finally.

He looked at her. "I can't," he said.

"Of course you can."

"I'm not going back."

"Why not?"

But he told her it wasn't an option anymore. Not now. He'd played his cards, he said. He'd made a decision, and yes, it was an impulsive decision, and yes, he regretted it, but what else could he do? What other alternatives did he have? He looked at her for a long time after he said this, and she realized then that he was serious, that he'd made up his mind, and that there was no way that she was going to change it.

"I mean, do you know of anyone," he said after a moment, staring at her, "anyone at all who might be able to get me out of the country?"

She looked at him for a very long time and then finally shook her head. No, she said, she didn't.

Of course, had she had an answer to this question then, she would have given it to him, but she hadn't. It wasn't until the next day, when she was going through her wallet and came across that small white card from Dupree, a small white card with a beeper number on it, that a thought even occurred to her, though even now, as she sits across from Raja in a small corner booth of the Alabama Ice House waiting for Dupree to return from the bathroom, she wonders if this solution is really a solution at all.

She had called up Dupree the previous day using Brandon's cell phone, had entered Brandon's number into his beeper, then had waited there for almost an hour for Dupree to call back. When he did, he seemed happy to hear from her and not at all surprised that she'd called. She'd told him a little bit about their dilemma, though nothing specific, and then Dupree had suggested meeting up at the Alabama Ice House the following day to discuss their situation in more detail. It would be better that way, he'd said.

When she got off the phone, she told Raja about it, and though he'd been skeptical at first, he'd eventually come around to the idea. She explained how she'd run into Dupree a few days earlier at Simone's store, how he seemed like a trustworthy guy, how he seemed to have a lot of connections, and so forth, and though she didn't know how deep his connections ran, she figured it was at least worth a shot. Raja had smiled at her and nodded. Maybe it was divine intervention, he'd said. Fate. Or maybe, she thought, this is what desperate circumstances could do to a person: cloud their judgment to the point where even the seediest of characters could seem like a savior.

And, of course, since they've been here, Dupree has told them very little, only that he has spoken to a guy who he thinks can help them out. He had arrived almost an hour late, his hair still wet from the shower, and then he had sat down at the table and proceeded to talk for the next twenty minutes. He told them that he didn't want to know anything specific about their situation. He didn't want to know what they had done, or who they were running from, or even where they were eventually planning to go. It would be better that way for all of them, he'd said. What he could do for them, he said, was put them in contact with someone who could help them out. Then he'd looked down at his beeper and excused himself to the bathroom, which is where he's been for the past twenty minutes.

After he'd left, she looked at Raja, who shrugged as if to say, *Let's just wait and see,* and then kissed her. Now, however, he's looking more and more concerned, and it suddenly occurs to her that they're putting a lot of faith into a boy they barely know.

On the other side of the Alabama Ice House, the bartender is pulling sweating bottles of Corona out of an ice chest and placing them down in front of the only other patrons at the bar, three elderly men in Mexican cowboy hats who laugh uproariously at almost everything the bartender says. Chloe watches the bartender as he slices the lime wedges for their beers, sprinkles salt on their bottles. The bar itself is very dark and otherwise empty. Country-western music bleeds from an old Wurlitzer jukebox in the corner, a slow, wistful ballad that Raja seems to enjoy. She reaches across the table and grabs his hand, and a moment later, she sees Dupree, returning from the bathroom with the phone in his hand.

When he sits down, he reaches into his pocket and pulls out a piece of paper and slides it across the table to her. The paper contains only a street address, nothing else.

"You show up here Tuesday night at midnight, and he'll take you down to Laredo. Get you across the border. After that, you can catch a bus to anywhere you wanna go."

Chloe looks at the paper. "You sure?"

"I'm positive."

"I don't think I even know where this is," she says, staring at the address.

"Downtown," he says. "Warehouse district."

Chloe nods. "How will we know what he looks like?"

"I'll be there, too," Dupree says. "To make the introductions, you know. After that, though, I'm out of there. I can't be involved with this shit."

Chloe looks at him and nods. "Sure," she says. "Of course."

Dupree pulls out a cigarette and lights it. "To be honest, I've never done anything like this before. I'm strictly small time, you know. Recreational narcotics. But you two seem like good people, you know, and you're friends with Simone, so I figured what the hell, I'll do what I can."

"We appreciate it," Chloe says. "Really."

Dupree shrugs and picks up his beer.

"So how much is this going to cost us?" Raja asks after a moment, looking around the bar cautiously.

"Yeah," Dupree says. "I was just gonna get to that." He sips on his beer. "Just talked to my friend last night and apparently it's gonna be four grand total. For the both of you."

Raja stares at him, his face suddenly filled with concern. "And what about for just one of us?"

"For just one of you," he says, "I guess that would probably be half. So what would that be—two grand?"

"Two grand?" Raja says, shaking his head. "And that's not negotiable?"

"Negotiable?" Dupree laughs. "Dude, this guy doesn't negotiate. And besides, he's already giving you a discount, you know, because I know him, because we've done business before. Normally, it would probably be twice that. Shit, maybe three times."

Raja looks at her then, and she can see the disappointment in his face. She knows that he's spent almost everything he has already, just to get down here, that there's no way he can get his hands on that type of cash.

"We don't have two grand," he says finally. "I mean, we don't even have one grand."

Dupree looks at him and shrugs. "Dude, I don't know what to tell you then. I mean, this type of thing isn't cheap."

Chloe puts her hand on Raja's, then looks at Dupree. "We'll get it," she says.

"What are you talking about?" Raja says.

"We'll get it," she says to Raja. "Don't worry about it."

Raja stares at her, then looks away.

"You sure?" Dupree says.

"Positive."

" 'Cause I can't be flaking out on this dude."

"Don't worry about it," she says. "Honestly. We'll be there, and we'll have the money."

Dupree nods, then looks again at Raja, who is looking down at his lap.

"All right then," he says and stands up. "So, I'll see you guys Tuesday night then."

"Tuesday night," Chloe says.

Dupree looks at her then and smiles.

"You know," he says, "I don't know what type of shit you're in. And, like I said, I don't really wanna know. But I hope it all works out for you two. I really do."

"Thanks," Chloe says and smiles.

Then Dupree turns to Raja and shakes his hand. "Adios, *mi compadre*," he says, and then he turns around and disappears out the door just as suddenly as he arrived.

As soon as he's gone, Chloe turns to Raja and pats his hand. "It's going to be okay," she says.

"How are we going to raise that type of money?"

"I don't know," she says.

"Then why did you tell him we'd have it?"

"I'll figure something out," she says. "Trust me."

He stares at her.

"I have a thousand or so in my savings," she says, "and I can get the rest from my parents."

"You can't ask your parents."

"Okay," she says, "then I'll get it from Richard."

He sips his beer. "You think he has that type of money?"

"I don't know," she says. "But I know he'll give me whatever he has."

He looks at the bartender, then shakes his head.

"We have three days," she says. "We can get four grand in three days. I mean, it's not going to be easy, but we can do it."

"Two," he says.

"Huh?"

"Two grand."

"No," she says, touching his arm. "Four."

5

ELSON HAD BEEN WORKING on the e-mail all morning, trying to put his situation in the best possible light, trying to explain to his boss, Ted Sullivan, something that he could barely explain to himself. That his daughter had gone missing, that he didn't know where she was, that he now needed to take a leave of absence to find her. After he'd sent the e-mail off, he'd sat at his desk for a long time, staring out the window. The rest of the office was empty today, most of his colleagues off on-site, and for a moment he had felt strangely calm. Now, however, as he stares at the computer screen in front of him, he feels that sense of anxiety coming back. In the bottom left-hand corner of the screen is the layout for one of his two current projects, a Mediterranean-style residence on the outskirts of Houston. He had followed his clients' specifications to a T, but there was still something missing. A lack of cohesion in the layout, a lack of warmth in the overall concept. A house was supposed to have a central living area, after all, and this house was simply an elaborate labyrinth of narrow corridors and hallways, sectioned off by bedrooms and studies. There was no common living space, no place for the family to come together as a unit. There was, he realized now, no soul to what he'd designed. Leaning back in his chair, he considers this, then closes the window and shuts down his computer.

As a grad student, Elson had once attended a lecture in which a famous contemporary architect had spent almost an hour discussing the intricacies of his own home, showing slides of every room, explaining how he had taken great care to see the project through from early sketches to final details, how he had overseen every aspect of the house's construction and design. He then explained that this house had been his greatest accomplishment as an architect, not because it was his most ambitious but because it was his most personal. *When you build your own house,* the architect had explained, *you're putting your soul out there on display for the whole world to see. It's the most terrifying thing an architect can do,* he'd added, *but also the most gratifying.*

At the time, this lecture had had a very profound impact on Elson, and even today he still thought about it, regretting the fact that he had never built a house for Cadence and himself. On several occasions he had actually drawn up some rough sketches, even looked into some properties outside of Sugar Land, but somehow he had never had the time or the money or the energy to actually see these plans through, especially after the children were born. Instead, he had fallen into line at Sullivan & Gordon, taking on whatever projects they gave him, never complaining about the hours or the workload or the neediness of the clients, allowing his own visions of simplicity and order, of form before function, to be superseded by the homogenous designs of his peers.

Of course, in the beginning, it hadn't always been this way. In the beginning, when he'd first joined the firm, it had been the height of the oil boom, the late seventies and early eighties, and as a young architect, Elson and the rest of the firm had enjoyed a period of unprecedented growth and prosperity. While the world-class visionaries, like I. M. Pei and Philip Johnson, were putting up skyscrapers downtown, Sullivan & Gordon were building three-story mansions for oil executives in River Oaks. Almost every single week, it seemed, the partners were bringing in new commissions, and Elson, who was only a few years out of grad school, who still hadn't passed all of his architecture exams, who still wasn't officially licensed, Elson, the rising star of the company, was being asked to oversee and manage three or four projects at once. At the time, he couldn't have imagined a better place in the country for a young architect to cut his teeth. He couldn't have imagined another firm in the country that would have allowed someone his age to have the type of responsibility and creative freedom he was given at Sullivan & Gordon. Within a few years of his arrival, in fact, he was already promoted officially to project manager and, a few years after that, to associate architect. One evening, while he was down at Ted Sullivan's beach house in Galveston, Ted had pulled him aside, and as they stood on his deck overlooking the ocean, sipping on margaritas, Ted had told him that if he kept producing the types of buildings he was producing, he could see him making partner in a couple of years. It's possible Ted was drunk, of course, but Elson had held on to these words, had held on to them for almost two decades, repeating them in his head like a mantra, wanting to believe that they might come true, even when all evidence seemed to point to the contrary.

It was this that he'd been thinking about earlier that morning as he sat at his desk, putting the finishing touches on the e-mail he'd been planning to send to Ted, an e-mail that he'd condensed from three lengthy paragraphs to three short lines:

Due to unforeseen personal circumstances, I'd like to request an unpaid vacation of indefinite length. I can have all notes and materials for current projects on your desk by the end of the day.

Yours,
Elson

He knew that Ted wasn't going to be too happy about this, of course, knew that he'd probably flip his lid, but at the same time he didn't really see what else he could do, what other options he had. Still, it had felt a little strange writing something so formal to a man he'd known for almost thirty years, a man who had attended his wedding and his children's birthday parties, a man who he used to consider a friend.

He'd sent the e-mail off just before ten while Ted was off at a meeting and then had spent the rest of the morning busying himself with the final details for his two current projects: the modest private residence outside of Houston and a renovated town house downtown. Neither of these projects was very interesting to him, nor rewarding, but he hadn't mentioned this to Ted in his e-mail. He hadn't wanted to seem ungrateful or unhappy. He hadn't wanted to give him the wrong impression. This had nothing to do with his past complaints, he'd wanted to emphasize. It had nothing to do with that. Still, he knew that Ted wasn't going to like it. They were already majorly understaffed in several departments and were already having trouble meeting the deadlines for the projects they currently had. If Elson pulled out now, they'd be in even worse shit. They'd have to limit their new commissions, ask others to work overtime, maybe even lose some of the commissions they currently had. Potentially, this could cost the firm a lot of money, he knew that, just as he knows now, sitting at his desk, watching the door, waiting for Ted's return, that this is not going to go well.

As it turns out, however, Ted doesn't return until almost three o'clock, and when he does, he goes straight into his office and closes the door behind him. It was strange, but Ted had always handled his business dealings at the office behind closed doors. Even in those early years, when things were a lot more casual, Ted had always stayed holed up in his office, leaving the social interaction, the rallying of the troops, the boosting of morale, to Lewis Gordon. Lewis would hang out in the break room, chatting with the interns, arguing about the Rockets, making plans for dinner or drinks after work. Meanwhile, Ted would be going over the numbers in his office, calling up the clients, trying to figure out who was expendable and who wasn't. Still, Elson had always felt a closer connection to Ted for some reason—maybe because a part of him pitied him, or maybe because it was Ted who had first hired him, or maybe it was simply because he had always seen in Ted a small part of himself. It is this that he's considering when he receives the phone call from Ted's secretary informing him that Ted would like to see him now.

Bracing himself, he stands up from his desk and adjusts his tie. Then he starts down the hallway toward the partners' offices, knowing what will happen now, knowing what Ted will say to him even before he says it. And when he enters Ted's office, he finds Ted sitting behind his desk, as usual, brooding.

"What the hell?" Ted says, holding up the e-mail, which he'd apparently printed out.

"I need a vacation," Elson says.

"No shit," Ted says. "We all need a vacation. Find me one person in this office who doesn't need a vacation."

"I mean, I need some time off," Elson says. "For personal reasons."

Ted stares at him. "Is this because of Cadence?"

"No, no," he says. "Chloe."

"Chloe?" Ted says, squinting at him. "What's going on?"

Elson shrugs. "Can't really say."

"Elson."

Suddenly he can feel Ted's eyes on him. "Well, she dropped out of school for one thing," he says, finally, looking down.

"School?"

"Yes."

"That's it?"

"No, no," he says. "It's more complicated than that actually, but I can't really get into it right now."

Ted looks at him, perplexed. If at all possible, he'd like to avoid telling Ted anything specific about Chloe's situation, knowing the type of scandal this would cause in the office, knowing the way this would undoubtedly reflect on him.

"You're gonna have to do a little better than that, El."

Elson looks out the window behind Ted's desk at the towering skyscrapers of downtown Houston, shimmering in the light. He considers his alternatives, what he might say, then finally shrugs. "Look, Ted," he says. "She's gone missing."

"What do you mean she's gone missing?"

"I mean, we don't know where she is."

Ted looks at him suspiciously. "Elson, come on now. This all sounds a little strange."

"I know it does."

"Have you called the police?"

"No," he says. "I mean, we can't really. It's complicated."

Ted sighs, shakes his head. "Jesus, Elson."

"But this has gotta stay between us, okay?" he says, feeling suddenly as if he's said too much. "This can't leave the office."

Ted nods and pauses for a long time. "I don't have to tell you what this is going to do to us, El."

"I know," Elson says.

"And I can't make any promises."

"What do you mean?"

"I mean, you said 'indefinite.' Depending on what 'indefinite' means, I can't make any promises."

Elson stares at him, not quite comprehending. Is he actually saying what he thinks he's saying? Is he making a threat? For some time now, Elson had known that his job was in jeopardy, that everyone's job was in jeopardy, but this had been more of an abstract thought, not something he'd actually believed. Still, looking at Ted now, he feels suddenly unnerved. "What are you saying exactly?"

"I'm not saying anything, Elson."

"Really? Because it almost sounded like you were making a threat."

"Nobody's threatening anyone here, Elson. Jesus. All I'm saying is that you need to put yourself in my position for a second, okay? I'm not saying I'm not sympathetic, but you disappear for a few weeks, and it's going to cost me money. That's the bottom line."

"I'm talking about two weeks," Elson says.

"You didn't say that," Ted says. "You said 'indefinite.'"

"Okay," Elson says. "Well, I'm saying it now. Okay? Two weeks. Can I please have off two fucking weeks to find my daughter?" He realizes now that he's standing up, shouting, that Ted is suddenly frightened. He tries to apologize, but Ted waves him off, looks away, shakes his head.

"Go home, Elson," he says finally. "Okay? Why don't you just go home."

"Two weeks," Elson says. "Okay? That's it. That's all I'm asking."

"Fine," Ted says. "Whatever." Then he turns around and begins to go through the filing cabinet behind his desk, busying himself until Elson finally leaves.

At five, Elson meets Dave Millhauser at a tiny German beer garden outside of Montrose. They sit at an outdoor table and smoke cigarettes, drink beer, order food. Though Elson had called Dave up in a state of panic, Dave spends the first half hour talking about himself, complaining about his dire living conditions, his bleak job prospects, his inability to get past what has happened to him at Rice. He talks about the fights he's been having with Cheryl, how he's gained weight, how he doesn't feel like himself anymore. He tells him how Cheryl has been spending more and more time away from the house, how he feels like he's losing her, how he suspects she might be having an affair. There's a tinge of paranoia to almost everything Dave is saying, and yet Elson just sits there patiently and listens, nods earnestly, waiting for Dave to change the subject, which he eventually does, and when he does, Elson takes this opportunity to tell him about Chloe and then to ask him if he's had a chance to talk with his friend up at Stratham. Dave pauses for a long time, staring out at the palm trees on the far end of the courtyard, then finally says yes, he has, and reaches for his beer and takes a sip. "But I have to tell you, El. It doesn't look good."

"What do you mean?"

"I mean it doesn't look good."

"Well, what did he say?"

"Not much. Just that those kids are in a whole heap of trouble, you know. Apparently the administration's having a cow over this shit. They're having to do some major damage control, you know, trying to keep the whole thing under wraps. I mean, something like this, El, it could kill a school."

Elson nods. "Did he say anything about Chloe?"

Dave shakes his head. "Not once. Just talked about the other two. The two boys."

Elson nods.

"My advice," Dave says, "is to keep her as far away from this shit as possible."

"I would," Elson says, "if I knew where the hell she was."

"You think she may have gone back up there to be with that boy?"

Elson shrugs. "Who knows? That's what Cadence seems to think. I mean, Richard said something about her leaving Houston, and so Cadence thinks that if she went anywhere she would have gone back there, you know, to be with him, but really, who knows?"

Dave reaches across the table and pats Elson's arm. "I'm sorry, El. Really. I wish I had better news."

Elson nods and reaches for his cigarettes. Across from them, on the other side of the patio, a group of kids roughly Chloe's age are laughing and talking, raising their glasses of beer in a toast. He feels something tightening in his stomach, a pinching, and then looks away.

For the next half hour they talk about various things unrelated to the current crisis in Elson's life, or the current crisis in Dave's life, but after a while the conversation inevitably comes back to Chloe, and Dave asks him how Cadence is taking the whole thing, how she's handling it. Before he arrived, Elson had decided not to mention anything to Dave about Cadence or the fact that she is now seeing someone else, but now that Dave has brought it up, and now that he's had a few beers, he sees no reason not to. As he tells him about what happened the night before, about what Cadence told him, he can see Dave's face softening.

"Jesus," he says finally. "So she's actually seeing someone else?"

"Apparently."

Dave shakes his head. "Man," he says. "So how do you feel about that?"

"How do I feel about it?" Elson laughs. "How do you think I feel about it? I feel like I've been kicked in the stomach."

Dave looks at him and nods. "You know who it is?"

"No," Elson says. "I was hoping you might be able to help me out with that."

"Me?"

"Well, yeah. I mean, I was hoping Cadence might have said something to Cheryl about it."

"Cheryl?" Dave laughs. "El, I don't think those two have talked in like six months or so. Maybe longer."

"Really?"

"Yep."

"They're not friends anymore?"

"Friends?" Dave laughs. "Are you serious?"

Dave shakes his head, and for some reason this makes Elson sad. For so long now, Cadence and Cheryl had been like sisters, even tighter than sisters, and it suddenly seems strange to him that Cadence had never mentioned it.

"It's funny," he says finally. "I didn't think I'd care this much, you know? I mean, I thought I could handle it. But I guess you never really know how you're going to feel until it happens."

"You think it's serious?" Dave says after a moment, picking up his beer.

"No idea," he says. "Probably not. Maybe about as serious as me and Lorna, you know." He looks at Dave. "And speaking of, she's not talking to me either."

"Yeah, I heard about that."

"She told you?"

"Well, she told me you were looking on her computer or something and that you broke into her e-mail account."

"That's not the whole story," Elson says.

Dave raises up his arms. "Look, El, I don't want to get involved."

"I'm just saying that there are two sides to every story."

"I'm sure there are," Dave says. "And I'm just saying that I don't want to get involved."

Elson looks at Dave and decides to drop it. "You think there's any chance she'll take me back?"

"Who? Lorna?"

"Yeah."

"If I was a betting man," Dave says and starts to laugh. "If I was a betting man, El, I'd have to say no."

"Great," Elson says. "So I'm screwed on all sides. Every woman in my life hates me."

"Chloe doesn't hate you."

"No," Elson says, sipping on his beer, feeling a sudden sadness in his gut. "I think you'd be wrong about that."

On the ride home, Elson thinks about calling Cadence but doesn't. He's still feeling a little embarrassed about the way they'd left things the night before, the way he'd just sat there like a stone, unable to tell her all the things he'd wanted to tell her. He wonders what she must have thought about it all, how pathetic he must have seemed. He wonders if he should have just given her what she wanted: a fight. Then he considers what it's going to be like from here on out, whether he'll actually have to meet this man, whether he'll have to see him on the children's birthdays or on special occasions. The thought of Cadence with someone else, someone other than him, is so unsettling to him, so disturbing, that he can barely think about it for more than a minute without wincing. And of course he recognizes the double standard in this—the fact that he feels entitled to date himself while incensed that Cadence might do the same—but that doesn't make it any easier to stomach. It doesn't make it any easier to accept.

The night before, after he'd left her at the house, he had driven over to the Brunswick Hotel by himself and sat for a long time at the bar. He had found himself wondering what would happen to him now and what would happen to him if he never met someone else to spend his life with, if he ended up all alone in an empty house with no one around to take care of him. What if he woke up one morning, he'd wondered then, and suddenly lacked the desire to get out of bed? Would anyone notice? Would anyone care? Or what if there were something physically wrong with him? Who would take care of him then? He likes to think that his children would, but would they really? Would Cadence? Hadn't he burned a few too many bridges there? And what in the end would he be left with? A couple dozen buildings he was proud of, two children who despised him, an ex-wife who had since moved on and remarried. At the end of the day, how would they sum up his life? What would they say about him? For so long he had cared only about making beautiful build-ings, and then only about Cadence, and then only about his children, but what in the end was he left with? What in the end did he have to show for it?

As he drives, he feels suddenly overwhelmed by the thought of what might happen to him now, by what lies ahead in his future. He thinks about the doctor's admonitions about drinking, about the damage he might be doing to his body, about the number of years he has left. He's been living like this for so long now—living like a twenty-three-year-old for so many years—that it almost seems normal, it almost feels like regu-lar life. Still, he knows that at the rate he's going he'll be lucky if he ever reaches the age his own father had; he'll be lucky if he ever gets to see his own children grow old. At a stoplight, he considers calling Cadence again, even dials the first six digits of her number, but when the light turns green, he loses his courage and drops the phone on the seat.

He cruises past the neon-lit daiquiri bars and tattoo parlors in his neighborhood, then turns onto his own street, a quiet residential street that seems nearly abandoned tonight. He is bracing himself for another night alone, another night spent in solitude, but as he pulls up to the curb outside his apartment building, he sees a lone, silhouetted figure sitting on the stairs. He thinks for a moment it might be Cadence, but when the figure stands up, he realizes it's not. It's Lorna. She's wearing a sundress, her hair pulled back in a bun.

Without even stopping to lock up his car, he starts toward her, mov-ing quickly along the walk, certain that she has come to reconcile, to apologize, but when he reaches the doorway, she moves away from him, to the side, then crosses her arms.

"I'm not here to talk," she says.

"Hey," Elson says. "Hold on." He tries to touch her arm, but she moves away.

"I'm just here to get your key."

"My key?"

"Yeah. To my apartment," she says, and then she reaches into her pocket and pulls out a key herself. "This is mine," she says. "To yours."

He stares at the key but doesn't take it. "You've been waiting here all this time just to exchange keys?"

"I haven't been waiting that long."

"How did you know I'd be here?"

"I didn't."

He looks at her. "I could have just mailed it to you, you know."

"Yeah, well I didn't want to give you the chance to make a copy."

"Are you kidding me?" He laughs. "You really think I'd do something like that?"

"Elson, at this point I have no idea what you'd do."

"Come on," he says, moving closer. "Look, I screwed up, okay. I admitted it."

"Screwed up?" she says. "You went through my entire hard drive."

"I didn't go through your entire hard drive," he says. "Just your e-mail account."

"Just my e-mail account." She laughs. "Really? And you think that makes it better?"

"I'm not saying it does."

She looks at him.

"It was wrong," he says. "Look, I admitted it. What else do you want me to say?"

"Elson, I'm not talking about this right now, okay? Either you give me the key, or else I'm going to have to find some other way of getting it."

"What's that supposed to mean?"

But she doesn't answer.

"Look, let's go inside, okay? Let's just talk for a second."

She stares at him, then steps away, and he can see something in her face shifting, softening.

"What is it?" he says.

"Nothing," she says.

"You look like you want to say something."

She looks down at her feet but doesn't answer.

"What is it?" he says again.

But she's already turning away.

"Lorna."

"Look, Elson," she says finally, turning back to him. "Just give me the fucking key, okay?"

6

EVEN NOW, CADENCE regretted not calling him. She owed him a
phone call at least, a chance to talk things out. He'd probably been sitting
around all day yesterday, just waiting for her to call, but for some reason
she hadn't been able to pick up the phone. For some reason, she hadn't
been able to bring herself to talk to him. The night before, as she lay in
her bed alone, she'd found herself wondering why she was so afraid, why
she cared so much. Was it possible that Elson had snaked his way back
into her heart? Was it possible that she'd begun to have feelings for him
again? It seemed absurd. After everything that had happened between
them, after everything they'd been through, it seemed ridiculous to even
consider such a thing. And yet, last night, as she lay in her bed alone,
she'd felt very acutely the absence of his body. She'd felt very acutely that
something was missing. After a while, she'd walked down the hallway to
Chloe's room and crawled into her bed. She'd lain there for a long time,
trying not to think about Elson, trying to think about anything else, trying
to remember all of the reasons they had broken up, all of the bad things
that had passed between them, and after a time, as she lay there in her
daughter's bed, taking in the scent of her sheets, pulling them closely to
her face, she'd managed to fall asleep.

Now, however, as she sits in her car in the bright morning sunlight,
she is thinking only about the fact that they have lost an entire day over
this, an entire day that they could have spent looking for Chloe or talking
to the police or doing something else, anything that might bring them
closer to finding her. Across the street from her, she can see the sign of
the store, its name and its promise written in bright blue letters: NEW
HORIZONS. She had found the store that morning on the Internet, had
marveled at the elaborate website Simone had designed. It seemed amaz-

ing to her that this was the same troubled girl who she had feared when Chloe was growing up, the same troubled girl who she had tried to keep her away from. How strange life was. Now, from all appearances, Simone was a successful entrepreneur, a self-made woman, a business owner, and what was Chloe? What had happened to her daughter? What choices had Simone made that Chloe hadn't? Or vice versa. What choices had Chloe made that Simone hadn't?

As she stares across the street, she takes a sip of her coffee, braces herself, then gets out of the car, wondering if the answers to any of these questions will be revealed to her when she finally talks to Simone, or if Simone will even be there. And if she is there, will she be able to tell her anything, anything at all, about what has happened to her daughter? Suddenly the whole idea seems a little crazy, a little half baked, but what other choice does she have? Who else can she turn to? She stares up again at the sign, then the front door, which is covered with flyers, and then finally, slowly, makes her way across the street.

Inside, the store is large and airy, sunlight streaming through the windows, the sounds of a waterfall, or running water, spilling from the speakers. She feels immediately relaxed, at ease. All around her there are bookshelves filled with books on spirituality, tables displaying sweet-smelling lotions and creams, wind chimes and mobiles swaying hypnotically from the ceiling. At the front of the store, there's a boy behind the counter, a boy roughly Chloe's age, who smiles at her warmly when she approaches. She asks him if she can speak to Simone, explains that she's the mother of one of Simone's childhood friends, then waits while he goes into the back of the store to get her.

When Simone finally comes out, she looks tired, exhausted, but immediately comes over and hugs her, tells her how nice it is to see her again, then invites her into a room at the back of the store. Simone looks basically the same as she did the last time she saw her, maybe a little older, maybe a little thinner, but otherwise pretty much the same attractive girl that Cadence remembers. As she sits down at a small table in the back, Cadence apologizes for showing up out of the blue like this, then pulls out a pad and pencil and lays them down before her.

"I mean, you must think it's a little strange," she says, smiling, "after all these years, you know."

"No, not at all," Simone says. "Can I get you some tea?"

"No," Cadence says, "but thank you."

"I was actually expecting you," Simone continues, sitting down at the table herself. "I think you were supposed to come here."

"What do you mean?"

"I don't know." Simone smiles. "I guess I just mean that whenever someone shows up from your past like this, there's always a reason. Something is unresolved. I knew that you would come, just as I knew that Chloe would come."

"You did?" Cadence says, raising her eyebrows.

"Yes. Of course."

Cadence stares at her, reluctant to pursue the topic further, certain that this is somehow rooted in teleology, or cosmic connectiveness, or whatever Simone happens to believe. On the wall behind Simone's head, she can see a chart with "Seven Rules for a Better Life." She studies the chart for a moment, then looks away.

"Chloe must have told you she came here," Simone continues.

"She did."

"I felt bad about that," Simone says, "what happened. But I'm glad she found me later. We needed to talk. We needed some closure."

"Closure?"

"Yes."

"And do you think you found that?" Cadence asks. "Closure, I mean."

"Perhaps," Simone says, smiling. "It's not for me to say." Then she looks at Cadence warmly and folds her hands. "But that's not why you're here, is it?"

"No," Cadence says.

"You're here because you're looking for her."

"You know about that?"

"No," she says, "but I'm not surprised."

Cadence stares at her. "I'm sorry. I don't think I'm following."

But Simone doesn't answer. She just sits there, smiling at her, her eyes a vacant blue.

"You're saying that you suspected she might be taking off?"

"No," she says. "I'm just saying that I'm not surprised that she did."

"And why's that?"

"Well, when she was here," Simone says, "she seemed very troubled. Very scared. She was looking for something, or perhaps running from something. I couldn't tell."

"Troubled in what way?"

"Oh, no particular way."

"Just *troubled*."

"Yes," she says. "Just troubled."

"Look, Simone, if you know something."

"I just told you I didn't."

Cadence purses her lips, tries to restrain herself, remembering what Chloe said about Simone's low stress threshold, her tendency to bolt. Still, she feels certain that the girl knows something, that she's hiding something from her.

"If you know anything at all," she continues finally. "Anything at all. Even if you have some suspicions . . ."

Simone looks at her, stone faced, says nothing.

"I mean, do you even know if she's still in Houston?"

"I have no idea."

"You haven't spoken to her since that day?"

"No."

"How about up north? Did she say anything about going back there? Maybe to see her boyfriend?"

Simone looks at her for a long time, then finally she says, "Mrs. Harding, I think you're asking the wrong questions."

"What do you mean?"

"I don't think that these questions will lead you to where you want to go."

"Well, where do I want to go?"

"It's not for me to say."

"Look, Simone, I just want to find my daughter, okay? That's all I want."

"I know you do," Simone says, patting her hand. "I know."

It was strange.

When Chloe was young, maybe eight or ten, she had gone through a period of not talking to people, a period of time in which she'd simply stopped engaging with the outside world. It had been a period of time that Cadence still thought about now, especially lately, and that she'd been thinking about more and more ever since Chloe had disappeared. The psychologist she had taken her to see back then had told her not to worry, that this was a natural phase that all children went through and that it would probably soon blow over, that it was probably just a case of

Chloe trying to assert her independence. And yet, even though it had eventually blown over, even though Chloe had eventually returned to her former self, it had always bothered her, had always seemed to her a worrisome sign of things to come, a willful defiance that would eventually reemerge. And now it seemed that this secret side of her daughter, this side of her daughter that could disappear within herself, was also capable of true deception, of engaging in what was essentially a criminal act.

She had left Simone's store in a state of frustration, and now, weaving recklessly through midmorning traffic, she is cursing Simone and then herself for believing that Simone might actually want to help her. Chloe had been right about her. The girl had been brainwashed. She'd been indoctrinated with some type of weird cosmological thought that took common sense and reasoning out of the equation. But still, she feels certain that she knows something, that she is hiding something from her, that she isn't telling her the whole story.

As she passes the shops on Montrose Boulevard, she can feel the full extent of her frustration kicking in, a rage blooming inside of her. She wonders how it is that they have come to this place, how it is that she has allowed the situation to get this out of hand. Had she not done the exact same thing at Chloe's age, had she not abandoned her own parents, had she not dropped out of school to marry Elson, had she not given up her college studies for the sake of a boy, she might even wonder why Chloe was doing this in the first place. But a part of her understands. A part of her understands more than she'd like to admit. A part of her understands how alluring a boy can seem at twenty-one. A part of her understands how easy it might seem to give up everything else for love. And, in the end, how could she blame her? How could she blame her daughter for doing the exact same thing she had done?

Thinking about this now, she feels unsettled. She tries to remember the last time she and Chloe had a normal conversation, the last time they actually talked about something real. Chloe had told her almost nothing about Raja, only that she loved him very much and that he had treated her far better than almost any boy she'd ever met. But there was also something else, something else that her daughter wasn't telling her, a hesitation in her daughter's voice whenever she spoke about him, a hesitation that she used to recognize in her own voice whenever she spoke about Elson. Was it possible that her daughter was afraid of this boy? Or did she simply feel trapped, tethered to a life she couldn't control?

Feeling suddenly discouraged, she tries to push these thoughts from her mind, tries to concentrate instead on the road. At a stoplight, she finally calls Elson to tell him that it's time to get the police involved, that this is getting out of hand, that they need to do something, but her call goes directly to his voice mail, and when she hears his voice on the message, she feels suddenly tongue-tied and hangs up.

At the next stoplight, she checks her messages and sees that there are two from Gavin, which she ignores, and one from Richard, which she listens to. Richard says that he wants to meet her for lunch and then suggests a place by his apartment. When she calls him back a few minutes later, his voice sounds nervous.

"Is everything okay?" she asks.

"Yeah," he says. "Everything's fine."

"This sounds kind of urgent."

"It is," he says, "kind of."

"Is this about Chloe?"

"No, no," he says. "It's not about that."

"Have you heard from her?"

"No," he says, and then he pauses for a long time. "Look, Mom," he says, "can you come meet me or what?"

The place where they meet for lunch is a small outdoor café near Richard's apartment. In the back, where they sit, the patio area is surrounded by lush tropical foliage: bougainvillea, birds-of-paradise, rhododendrons, and hibiscus. Birds flutter between the trees, a small fountain burbles beside them, waiters dressed in white shirts move gracefully between the tables. Richard orders a salad and a glass of wine, and she orders the same, then asks if he shouldn't eat something more.

"You're looking very thin," she says, and he is, almost unhealthily thin. She reaches across the table and squeezes his arm, but he pulls away.

"I'm fine," he says and lights a cigarette. "I'm just not that hungry."

"And you should stop smoking, too," she says, frowning. "I thought you were going to quit."

He looks at her, shrugs. "Dad smokes."

"Yeah," she says. "Well, your father does a lot of things that aren't good for him."

He smiles at her. "And didn't you used to smoke?"

"Sure," she says, "when I was young."

"Well," he says, "I'm young. When I'm older, I'll quit."

"Right," she says. "That's what your father used to say." Then she looks at him. "And besides," she says, "you're not that young anymore."

Their salads arrive, and they talk for a while about Richard's poetry. He tells her that he has an opportunity to go to graduate school at the University of Michigan in the fall. It's a good program, he tells her, a good opportunity, but he isn't sure. This is the first time she's heard of it, and she feels momentarily confused, alarmed, taken aback, frightened by the idea of Richard leaving Houston. She's already lost one child, it seems, and now Richard is thinking about leaving, too? It seems absurd. Still, she can see from the expression on his face just how desperately he wants her approval. It is the same way he used to look back in high school whenever he'd come home from school with a bad grade on a test. It was strange, but Richard had always seemed to need her approval more than Chloe, had always seemed to seek it out, whereas Chloe had always been content to go her own way, to do her own thing. For years, Chloe had accused her of favoring Richard over her, of doting over him, of nurturing him, and she wonders now if this is true. He had been her firstborn child, after all, her eldest, and they had always shared a special bond because of this, but still, she wonders now, where has that closeness gone? What has happened to that bond? For months, he has seemed like a stranger to her, a boy who drifted in and out of the house without talking, dropping off laundry, picking up books, leaving cryptic messages full of vague insinuations taped along the kitchen counter. And now, as he sits here before her, talking about graduate school, she wonders if this is it, the last act, his final departure.

"So," she says after a moment, staring at him. "The University of Michigan, huh?"

"Not necessarily."

"Well, you'd be closer to your grandparents," she says, smiling, thinking about her own parents back in Illinois and how happy they'd be to have Richard nearby. "That's for sure."

"Yeah," he says and nods.

"And if it's something you want to do—"

"I'm not sure if it's something I want to do," he says, "that's the thing."

"Well, why aren't you sure?"

"I don't know," he says. "It just seems like a big step, you know."

He looks at her and she can see how distressed he is. He reaches for another cigarette and lights it.

"I mean, what do you think Dad would say?"

"Don't worry about your father," she says. "I'll take care of him." She reaches across the table and touches his hand. "If it's something you want to do, then I think you should do it."

"Really?"

"Yes."

He nods.

"Is that what you wanted to talk to me about?"

"No, no," he says. "Not exactly." Then he looks down.

"What is it?"

He draws slowly on his cigarette. "I actually wanted to ask you if I could borrow some money."

"Money? For what?"

He pauses. "I can't really tell you."

She looks at him evenly. "How much do you need?"

"Two thousand."

"Richard."

"I know it's a lot."

"Richard, I can't just give you two thousand dollars without knowing why you need it."

"Forget it," he says and looks away.

She stares at him. "Are you in some type of trouble?"

"No."

"Are you sure?"

"Yes."

"Well, I can't see why you'd suddenly need two thousand dollars. I mean—" Then a thought occurs to her, a thought that sends her mind racing. "Is this about your sister?"

"No."

"Did she contact you?"

"No."

"Honey, I love you, but if she contacted you, if you know anything about where she might be and you're not telling me—"

"She didn't contact me, Mom," he says, his voice angry now. "Jesus Christ, not everything's about Chloe."

She looks at him, his words stinging her, but he's looking away now. After a moment, he stands up.

"I knew this was a mistake," he says, sliding his cigarettes into his pocket.

"Richard, please sit down."

"I have to go to work."

"Richard."

But he's already turning away, walking toward the front of the restaurant.

"Richard!" she calls after him, but he doesn't hear her, or if he does, he pretends not to. He keeps walking and a moment later is gone.

On the drive home, she considers stopping by Richard's apartment to apologize, but decides against it. She knows her son, knows when he needs some time to cool off, knows when he needs some time to process what has happened. In so many ways, he is so much like his father. A sweet boy, a responsible boy, but still a hothead. Even as a child, he could fly into a rage without the slightest provocation. *A highly sensitive boy* is what his seventh-grade art teacher had told her. *Much more sensitive than most boys his age.* Back then, he used to waste away his evenings, lying around his room, reading comic books, afraid to interact with other kids. She used to worry back then that she had babied him too much, indulged his tantrums and his moods, turned him into the type of boy who would have difficulty making friends. Chloe, on the other hand, was much more like her: a sensitive girl, but in a guarded way. She'd sooner lock herself in her room for half the night than tell you what was wrong with her. And yet, the two of them had always seemed so bonded, so connected, almost like twins. They had always seemed so attuned to each other's body rhythms, so cognizant of what the other was thinking at all times. When they were young, it had seemed endearing to her, even sweet, but later it had bothered her. They seemed to exist in their own private world, a world that did not seem to involve her or Elson, a world that they were not permitted to enter. And so she knew that if Chloe had ever told him anything, if she had ever confided in him, he would have never told her. And yet, he had reacted so violently to her suggestion that she might have that she didn't know what to think. What was one to make of any of it? What did any of it mean?

As she passes into her neighborhood, she considers her next step, the options that lie before her. She thinks about meeting Elson for dinner, of making a definite plan. She thinks about what they might do the next day, or the day after, if Chloe still hasn't contacted them. In front of her, the street is lined with towering live oaks and cypress trees, casting long, irregular shadows across the neighboring lawns. She watches a boy on a bicycle, weaving aimlessly in the middle of the street. Everything else is quiet. Quiet and still. Everybody hiding inside from the heat. She watches the boy for a moment longer, then turns around the corner onto her own street, and it is then, as she's pulling up around the corner and nearing her house, that all of the options she'd been considering before seem to vanish.

Parked at the front of her driveway is a dark blue Corolla, and sitting on the front steps of her house are two men in blue suits. Not the same men who had stopped by before, when Chloe was there, but different men, older men. She feels her mind racing, thinks for a moment about turning around and taking off, but instead pulls up slowly into the driveway and parks.

By the time she turns off the engine, the men are at her window, motioning for her to roll it down. When she does, they speak calmly, explaining that they are detectives from the Stratham Police Department. They tell her their names, but she's so panicked she doesn't even process them.

"Mrs. Harding," one of the men finally says, "if you could just give us a few minutes of your time, we'd like to ask you a few questions about your daughter."

She looks at them, suddenly wishing Elson were there, suddenly wishing she had some counsel.

"What's this about?" she says finally.

"Why don't we just go inside, ma'am?" says the other man.

She looks at him, says nothing.

"Mrs. Harding?"

She looks down.

"Mrs. Harding," the man says again, touching her hand this time. "Why don't we just go inside, all right?"

7

TWO THOUSAND DOLLARS. That's all he needed. And now Brandon is telling him that it wouldn't be that hard to get it, or at least half of it, if he was willing. They are standing behind the counter at Café Brasil, both of them working the late-afternoon shift, the sunlight from the cloudless Houston sky forming patterns along the walls, the sounds of Belle & Sebastian filling the room. The café is empty, or nearly empty, just a few out-of-work slackers scribbling feverishly in their notebooks, smoking cigarettes.

He'd just have to meet the guy, Brandon tells him, at his hotel downtown, have a few drinks, maybe dinner, and then spend the night with him. He wouldn't have to do anything that made him feel uncomfortable, he says. He could set the parameters from the start. Make the rules. The next day he'd wake up, and he'd have half the money he needed in his pocket, all for a night's work.

"And what about the other half?" Richard says.

"This guy isn't the only guy I know in Houston." Brandon winks.

"But I need the money by tomorrow night."

Brandon nods. "I could lend you the rest. You know, you could pay me back over time, in installments."

"What are you my pimp now?"

"You don't have to make it sound so crude," Brandon says. "Really, it's just business. You'd actually be surprised by how businesslike it is."

Richard looks at him, nods. It seems crazy to him that he's even considering it. If Chloe hadn't seemed so desperate, so afraid, if she hadn't held him so tightly when she'd asked, if she hadn't cried, he wouldn't even be considering any of this. But what else could he do? What other options did he have? If his mother hadn't lent him the money, his father sure as hell wouldn't. And what did he have in his own bank account? Maybe a thousand at the most, which he'd already promised her and which she'd already told him wasn't nearly enough. He wishes she'd told him why she needed it. All she'd said was that this was more important to her than anything else she'd ever asked him for, and he could see in her face when she said this that she meant it. He'd told her not to worry, that he would take care of it, but he wonders now why he said this. What made him think that he could raise two thousand dollars in a day and a half?

"Let me ask you a question," Richard says after a moment as Brandon stands in the corner, refilling one of the stainless-steel containers with cream. "Why do you work here?"

"What are you talking about?"

"I mean, if you can earn that type of money in a single night, and you don't care about it, why do you work here for minimum wage?"

"Tax purposes." Brandon smiles.

"Right. Tax purposes." Richard laughs. *"Seriously."*

"Seriously?" Brandon says. "Seriously, it's not like I do it all the time, you know. I mean, maybe once a month, sometimes twice, if I really need a little extra. It's not like this is my long-term career goal or anything." He winks at him.

At Rice, Brandon had majored in women's studies, a major that had seemed even less practical than Richard's, though it occurs to Richard now that Brandon has never actually told him what his long-term career goal is. He thinks of asking him now but decides against it.

"So what do you say?" Brandon says finally. "Should I call him?"

"No," Richard says. "I don't think I can do it."

"Really?"

"Really," he says, shrugging. "It's just not me."

"Okay," Brandon says. "It's your choice." Then he opens up his cell phone and starts to write something down on a scrap of paper. "Here's his number, though," he says, handing Richard the paper, "in case you change your mind."

Richard takes the paper, thinks of crumpling it up, but instead slides it into his pocket. He doesn't even look at the name.

"So what are you going to do now?" Brandon asks.

Richard looks at him, thinks for a moment, then shrugs. "I don't know," he says. "There's really only one other person I could ask." He looks at his watch. "You think you can cover the rest of my shift?"

Brandon looks around the empty café, laughing. "I don't know, man. I mean, it's pretty much a mob scene in here."

Richard smiles. "Thanks, Bran," he says, patting his hand, taking off his apron. "I owe you."

A half hour later, however, as he sits outside the large Tudor house where he has come twice a month for poetry workshops this past year, he wonders if this possibility is really a possibility at all. For months he had believed that Michelson would give him just about anything he asked for, but would he now? Had he burned a bridge with Michelson? Had he wounded him too severely with his outburst? And which was worse in the end? Was it more humiliating to come back to Michelson with his tail between his legs or to whore himself out to a man he'd never met?

One thing is for sure. He'll have to give Michelson something. An apology, for one, but also something else. He'll have to tell him that he's reconsidered his application to Michigan. He'd acted rashly, he'll have to say. He hadn't thought it through. He hadn't considered the true enormity of the opportunity. In some ways, of course, it pains him to even consider this, to consider what he'll be giving up, what he'll be relinquishing by doing this, but on the other hand he understands now that he has a bargaining chip, something that Michelson wants, even if he isn't sure if he wants it himself. Sometimes he wonders if Michelson is simply living his life vicariously through him, if he represents in Michelson's mind some sort of incarnation of Michelson himself as a young man, the youthful promise and potential he'd never actually had. Or maybe it is, as he'd always assumed, a form of seduction, a way of getting close to him. There is, of course, the fact of Michelson's betrayal, something he'll probably never forgive, but there is also now the strange new possibility that Michelson might have actually been telling him the truth all along, that his work might actually show more promise than he'd originally thought, that he might actually belong at a place like Michigan after all. Aside from talking to his mother about this, he hasn't mentioned it to anyone, not to Brandon, and certainly not to Chloe, but a part of him has to acknowledge that on some level he'd been flattered by what Michelson had told him. Once he'd gotten past what Michelson had done, once he'd settled down and considered it, he'd realized that Michelson had been right, that this wasn't an opportunity to be taken lightly, that this might in fact be the only opportunity he'd ever have to go to a place like Michigan.

Ever since he'd returned from the café that night, he'd been turning it over in his head, vacillating between excitement and fear. One moment he'd be picturing himself sitting over drinks with a group of fellow poets, talking about Wordsworth and Keats; and the next, he'd have an image of himself sitting in a darkened classroom, biting the inside of his cheek as his professor made it clear to the room that he didn't belong there. And of course he'd thought a lot about what he'd be giving up by leaving: Brandon and his other friends, the comfortable little life he'd created for himself here in Houston, the prospect of making a more responsible career choice, of pleasing his parents, of doing what other people considered the right thing. There didn't seem to be an easy solution here, an easy answer, and compared with what his sister was going through, it seemed silly to even think about, but as he sits here now, staring at Michelson's house, he has to wonder what it is that's really stopping him. What, in the end, is the worst thing that could happen?

As it turns out, Mrs. Michelson isn't home. This is among the first things Michelson tells him as he walks through the door, this and the fact that he's happy to see him again, though he says this last part with a slight trace of guardedness, as if he's still afraid that Richard might suddenly start yelling at him again.

Michelson shepherds him into the kitchen, offers him a glass of wine, which Richard accepts, then lays out some crackers and cheese. This is the first time that he and Michelson have actually been alone together in his house, and he can tell that Michelson is nervous. Maybe it's the sudden reality of it all, the fantasy he'd rehearsed so many times in his mind finally coming true. The spider caught in his web. Or maybe his motives are much more sincere than Richard thinks. Maybe he's got him all wrong. Maybe Michelson is simply trying to help him out, a concerned teacher trying to help out his star student. A man with a little too much time on his hands.

As they sip their wine, he explains to Michelson that he's sorry, that he was out of line, that what he'd said to him at the café had been wrong. Michelson listens to him patiently, nods, and then finally accepts his apology. There's something oddly formal about it all, the whole thing, something that reeks of the principal's office. Michelson is sitting far away from him, almost three feet, his arms crossed, his lips pursed, and he can tell that he's still afraid, or maybe just nervous. Eventually, he decides to throw him a bone, tells him in a quiet voice that he's actually reconsidering his application to Michigan, and at this, Michelson's face suddenly brightens.

"You're kidding," he says.

"No."

"Well, this is wonderful news, Richard," he says, raising his glass and coaxing him into a toast. "I can't tell you how happy this makes me."

Richard smiles at him, nods. "Well, it's not like I've gotten in yet."

"No, but I have a good feeling about this. I really do." Then he stands up and puts down his glass. "Hold on a second, okay? I'll be right back."

A moment later he disappears down the hallway into the other part of the house, leaving Richard alone in the kitchen. As he sits there, he wonders what will happen now, what he'll say to him, how he'll bring up the issue of money. As soon as he mentioned his application, he'd regretted it, felt those old reservations coming back. What if he is making a mistake? he wonders. What if this is all wrong? One thing is for sure. He can't go back now. Not at this point. Not after Michelson's reaction. He sips his wine, looks around the kitchen, braces himself for what will happen next.

"I wanted to give you this," Michelson says, returning to the kitchen, nearly out of breath. "This is my friend's address and the address of the graduate office. You can send your statement to him and the rest of your materials—your transcripts and so forth—to the graduate office."

He lays the paper down on the table in front of Richard, then picks up his wine again and sips it.

"I should do that this week?"

"Tomorrow, if you can. The sooner, the better."

Richard looks at him and nods, though the thought of doing this tomorrow, of not having time to reconsider, is terrifying. He tries to hide his concern from Michelson, but Michelson notices.

"Are you sure you're certain about this, Richard," he says. "About your decision?"

"I'm positive."

"You're positive?"

"Yes."

Michelson nods. "Well, okay then," he says, and sips his wine. "Can I ask you what changed your mind?"

"I don't know."

"It must have been something."

Richard shakes his head. "I don't know. I guess maybe talking to my mother about it. I thought she was going to be against it, you know, but she was actually really supportive."

"Parents can surprise you sometimes," Michelson says.

Richard nods.

"And your father?"

"My father." Richard smiles. "My father's not going to be too happy about it, but I'll deal with that later."

"I take it the two of you don't get along."

"No, no." He shrugs. "It's not that. I mean, he's fine. I mean, our relationship is fine, more or less. It's just that something like this, you know, it's just beyond his comprehension."

Michelson nods and sips his wine.

The truth is, he hasn't had a normal conversation with his father in over a year, but he doesn't want to get into this with Michelson, sensing that Michelson's interest is not entirely sincere. Is this his mode of seduction? he wonders. To form a bond with him, then to reel him in? Suddenly he feels the conversation getting away from him, moving in a direction he doesn't want. Michelson pours himself another glass of wine, then reaches for Richard's glass, and as he does this, Richard braces himself, prepares himself.

"There's actually something else I wanted to ask you," he says finally, trying not to look as transparent as he feels, trying to hide his unease. "I feel a little awkward asking you this, actually, and I'll totally understand if you say no, but I was wondering if it might be possible for me to borrow a little money from you. Just a sort of short-term loan."

Michelson looks at him, surprised. "Is this for your application fees?"

"No, no," Richard says. "Something else."

"Something else?"

"Yes."

"But you don't want to tell me what it is."

"No. I can't, really."

Michelson pauses, and he can see that he's soured the mood. "How much do you need?"

"Two thousand."

"Two thousand dollars?"

"Yes."

Michelson shakes his head. "That's a lot of money, Richard."

"I know."

"Have you asked your parents?"

"Yes."

"And they've said no."

"They have."

Michelson rubs his head. "Are you in some type of trouble, Richard?"

"No, no," he says, and then pauses. "But my sister is."

He hadn't meant to say this, but now that he has, he realizes he needed to, that he needed to give Michelson something.

Michelson considers this. "Can I ask what type of trouble your sister's in?"

"To be honest," Richard says, "I don't really know myself. I don't even really know why she needs the money. I just know she needs it."

Michelson narrows his eyes again. "Richard, if you'll forgive me, this all sounds a little vague."

"I know it does," he says. "I'm sorry."

"I'd love to help you out, of course, but I'm your teacher, Richard. I'm not a bank."

Richard nods and realizes then that the matter is settled, at least in Michelson's mind. He's given his answer. He considers pursuing it further, taking another angle, but something in Michelson's expression tells him it wouldn't be worth it. It wouldn't matter. He feels suddenly deflated.

"I'm sorry, Richard," Michelson says, touching his hand.

"No, it's fine," Richard says. "It's totally cool. I figured it was a long shot anyway." He looks at his watch. "I should probably be getting back to work now actually."

"You sure you don't want to stick around? Maybe take a little swim?"

"No, no," Richard says, standing up. "Maybe another time. Thanks, though."

Michelson stands up then, too, and walks him to the door.

"Don't forget about tomorrow," he says, as they stand in the doorway. "You'll want to get those materials off as soon as you can." He pats Richard's shoulder.

"I won't," Richard says, trying to smile, trying to hide his disappointment. "Thanks again," he manages. "You know, for everything."

"Richard," Michelson says, grabbing his arm now, smiling. "I hope you understand, you never have to thank me for anything."

Technically, he should be getting back to work now, finishing his shift, but instead he finds himself driving to a small used bookstore near his apartment and browsing the aisles. This is a place that he used to come to a lot when he'd first graduated from college, when he'd first started writing poetry, and later, in those days after he and Marcos broke up. There was something oddly comforting about this place, something oddly soothing about it, about being here, standing among so many books.

He'd often fantasized about what it might feel like to see his own book on one of these shelves, sandwiched somewhere between Donald Hall and Oliver Wendell Holmes, to pick it up and read from it, to study the tiny markings that another reader might have made in the margins, to wonder who that reader was. It seemed like such a remote possibility that anyone might actually want to purchase a book he had written, and yet it had still been fun to think about. He imagined giving readings, signing copies for his friends, giving a copy to his mother. He would get carried away sometimes, ignoring the absurdity of it, wanting to believe it could work.

Today, however, he is thinking only about Chloe and how disappointed she's going to be when he finally talks to her, when he finally tells her the bad news, when he finally tells her that he's failed to deliver on his promise. He'd never seen her as panicked as she'd been that morning when she stopped by his apartment. *I've never asked you for very much, Richard, have I? But I'm asking you for this. If there's any way you can get me that money, you'd be saving my life. Truly. You'd be saving my life.* Saving her life? What had she meant by this? The words had haunted him. He trusted his sister, of course, trusted her more than anyone else, and knew that she wouldn't be saying any of these things if she weren't deadly serious, but still, what did they mean? He'd tried to get her to explain, but she wouldn't. *Just do this for me, Richard,* she'd said, drying her eyes. *Please. If you do this for me, I'll never ask you for anything else. Honestly.* And Richard, being the person that he was, being the brother that he was, had held her, had told her not to worry, had told her that he'd do whatever he had to do to get her that money.

But now what had he done? He'd failed on all counts. There was Brandon, of course, but Brandon could only get him so much. He'd thought about selling his iPod, or maybe even his computer, but it seemed unlikely that he'd be able to get the type of money he needed for either under such short notice. So where did that leave him? What other choices did he have?

Sitting down next to one of the bookshelves, he pulls out the tiny piece of paper in his pocket, studies the number, the name. Then he pulls out his phone, but stops himself before he actually dials the number. He wonders how he'd feel the next day if he actually went through with it, if he actually spent the evening with this man, whether he'd feel as dirty if he knew that he was doing it for a noble cause, for his sister. He wouldn't have to sleep with him, Brandon had told him earlier. He wouldn't have to do anything he didn't want to do. He could set the parameters from the start. He could back out anytime. And besides, maybe it wouldn't even come to that. Maybe this guy would simply want to talk to him. Maybe he'd simply want his company. Brandon had told him how this happened all the time, how guys would take him out to dinner, maybe a movie, then just send him home. And maybe that's all this was. Maybe it was as simple as that. And he could handle that, couldn't he? Dinner. A little conversation. It wasn't going to kill him. It wasn't going to be the end of the world.

It's depressing for him to even think about such things, but even more depressing to think about the alternative, to think about going back to Chloe with empty hands. It's only one night, he tells himself. What can possibly happen in one night?

He stares at the bookshelves in front of him, wondering what the poets he admires would do, what anyone in his position would do. A moment later, he dials the number and, in a moment of haste, pushes SEND. A voice comes on a few seconds later, a friendly voice, and within a matter of minutes arrangements are made. A time is set. But it all happens so quickly, so abruptly, that he barely has time to process it. Already, it seems, his mind has gone numb.

8

LYING NEXT TO RAJA in the dim light of Brandon's tiny study, Chloe feels momentarily at peace. She feels a sense of resignation, an acceptance of what will happen now. If Richard comes through for her, which she knows he will, then they'll be gone from here tomorrow night. Their lives will change in ways she can't possibly imagine, but they'll be together. That's the most important thing. No matter what happens to them, they'll be together.

For weeks, she's been living like this, living only in the moment, not knowing what might happen from one minute to the next, not knowing what might happen in the next couple of hours, or days, to change her life completely. As much as she's been concerned, as much as she's feared for her future, there is another part of her that has found it strangely liberating. If you could shut out everything else, she thinks, if you could concentrate only on your current dilemma, your immediate circumstance, if you could concentrate only on the present, you could simplify your life completely. Suddenly all of the questions about your future would disappear. Where you would live after college, what type of job you would have, whether you'd marry. These things would all go away. They'd disappear. They'd be replaced by other things, by questions relating only to the here and now. Questions relating only to your immediate circumstance. You couldn't live that way forever, of course, but you could live this way for a while, and if they actually made it down to Mexico, if they were able to make a life for themselves down there, then they'd have to live this way for the next couple of weeks, maybe months.

As for other issues, issues relating to family and friends, she has decided to put those out of her mind. There is no point in dwelling on things you can't control. And besides, it's painful. To think about a life without Richard, to think about a life in which she can no longer talk to him, or to her parents, it's almost too much to process. Instead, she has chosen to focus on the alternative, a life without Raja, which at the moment seems even harder to fathom. If she had to choose, she'd realized earlier that night, if she had to choose between her family and Raja, she'd choose Raja. It wasn't even a question. As hard as it would be, as hard as it would be to give up everything else—her family, her friends, her lifestyle in America—she would sacrifice it all in a heartbeat to be with him, to be able to stay with him. And she knew that he would do the same. That was what love was, wasn't it? That was what love in its most absolute form was. If it was anything less, then it wasn't love. It wasn't absolute. And if this was a test, some type of divine test of her love for him, then she was determined not to fail.

Raja, on the other hand, seemed much more troubled by the uncertainty of their future, by what would happen next. For the past half hour he has been lying next to her on the mattress, shaking his head, talking about his parents and how he has shamed them or, alternatively, about Mexico and how they will fend for themselves down there. How will they get food? he wonders. Where will they stay? And what will happen when their money runs out?

We'll figure that out when we get there, she tells him. It will all work out. It will all be fine. She can tell he doesn't believe her, of course, but he's stopped trying to resist her, too, just as he's stopped trying to resist the notion that she will be accompanying him down there. They'd argued about it for most of the day, had argued about it to the point of tears, but finally he'd given up. *It's your life,* he'd finally said. *If you want to do this, then I can't stop you. There's nothing I can do. But I want you to know that it's not what I want for you, and it's not what I expect.*

I know that, she'd said, and then she'd held him, not wanting to say anything else, not wanting to give him any reason to suddenly change his mind.

In general, it seems, a part of him has given up. He has given up on fighting, given up on arguing with her, given up on any hope for a decent future. In all of the time she'd known him at Stratham, she'd never seen him like this. It had always been she who was having these little crises, she who was worrying about her parents or about some paper she hadn't turned in or about who had said what to whom. He had always been the voice of reason, the eternal optimist. But now she can tell that something has changed. He has fallen out of himself. He has dissolved. A part of him, a very fundamental part of him, has disappeared.

In the other room, she can hear Brandon, just back from his job, putting on music, pulling plates and glasses out of the cabinets. A moment later, there's a knock at the door, and he sticks his head in.

"You guys hungry?" he asks.

Chloe props herself on an elbow, smiles at him. "We actually already ate," she says, motioning toward the empty Chinese food containers on the floor. "But thanks."

Brandon nods, then stands there for a moment. "I actually wanted to give you something," he says, pulling a thick white envelope out of his back pocket and tossing it to her.

Opening the envelope, she sees a wad of cash inside, easily a thousand.

"What's this?" she says.

"My contribution," he says. "Richard should be getting you the other half tomorrow."

At this, Raja sits up and stares at the money, but says nothing.

"You didn't have to do this," she says.

"It's not really from me," he says. "It's more like a loan I'm giving Richard. He's gonna pay me back and stuff, you know, later."

She looks at him uncertainly, then back at the money. "Thanks, Brandon," she says finally. "But like I said, you really didn't have to do this."

He shrugs. "It's not a problem," he says. "And besides, it's your brother you should be thanking."

She nods and sits up on the bed, places the envelope down beside her, thinking about Richard, wondering where he is, realizing that now they're only a thousand short.

"Where is he tonight anyway?" she asks.

"Who? Richard?" Brandon shrugs. "Can't say." But he looks away when he says this, and she can sense that he's hiding something.

"He's not at Beto's?"

"Uh, he might be," he says, then he turns around and looks back at the kitchen. "Shit, I got water boiling. You guys wanna join me, you're welcome to." Then he turns around again and returns to the kitchen, closing the door behind him.

After he's gone, Raja looks at her and sighs. "We can't take this money," he says.

"Why not?"

"We barely know him."

"He's a friend of Richard's. And besides, Richard's gonna pay him back."

Raja shakes his head. "It doesn't seem right," he says.

And she realizes then that he's disappointed, that a part of him had probably been holding out hope that Richard wouldn't be able to raise the money.

"You're mad because now I'm gonna be able to come down there with you."

"I didn't say that."

"No, but I can tell."

"That's ridiculous."

"Is it?"

He looks down at his hands, shrugs, then finally stands up. "I'm gonna go out for a bit," he says, "to get some cigarettes."

"I'll come with you," she says.

"No," he says. "Stay here."

"Why?"

"I just want to be by myself for a while."

She looks at him, and she can see that something in his face is cracking, giving way. She walks over and holds him.

"What's the matter?" she says, rubbing his back, but he doesn't answer. "Honey," she says again, pulling him closer. "What's the matter with you tonight?"

"It's nothing," he says finally, then hugs her back. "I'm fine."

9

"WHY AM I EVEN HERE?"

"I'm sorry?"

"Why am I here?"

"Today's your appointment."

"I know, but I shouldn't be here."

"Then where should you be?"

"I don't know," she says, "but not here." She stares at Peterson, the mid-afternoon sunlight filling the white empty space around him, bouncing across the walls. Earlier that day he'd called her up and given her an ultimatum, told her that if she missed another appointment (it would be her third in a row), he'd have to give up her spot. But still, why had she cared? Why had she come?

"We were talking about Elson," he continues. "You were telling me how you spent the night with him last night."

"I did," she says, sighing, "but not in the way you're thinking."

"No?"

"No," she says. "I didn't sleep with him. He just spent the night at my house. We slept together in the same bed. That's all."

"That's all?"

"Yes, that's all."

Peterson looks at her, says nothing, and already she regrets saying anything about it. If she weren't feeling so vulnerable right now, so confused, if she had had her head on straight earlier, she would have never even brought it up. But suddenly she feels like she's lost all sense of judgment. As soon as she sat down, she'd blurted it out, almost on cue, and now she realizes that she's going to have to deal with the fallout, with Peterson, with his inevitable questions and probing.

"I was feeling vulnerable," she continues. "I didn't want to be by myself last night. That's all. I had a horrible day, you know, and he came over to talk to me about it, and then suddenly it was late, and it just seemed natural that he should stay with me. That's all it was. It was nothing more than that. There's nothing to read into here."

"No?"

"No."

Peterson nods, scribbles something down on his pad. "And that's all you want to say about it?"

"That's all."

"So why did you have such a horrible day?"

"That's another story."

"Humor me."

She looks at him, considers what she's told him already, then sighs. "It's about my daughter," she says finally. "Chloe. Things have gotten worse with her situation."

"Worse?"

"More complicated."

He nods.

"Yesterday some men came by the house to talk to me about her. Some detectives."

Peterson leans forward, suddenly interested. "Detectives?"

"Yes."

"And that's why you were so upset?"

"Yes."

"And did these men talk to Elson, too?"

"No," she says. "Just me. They're going to be talking to him today."

Peterson puts down his pad. "And I don't suppose you're going to tell me what you talked to them about."

"We've been through this."

"You can't."

"No," she says. "I can't, and I won't."

"Because of your daughter."

"Because of me."

Peterson leans back now, picks up his pad, and then puts it down again. She expects him to be mad, but he's not. He's surprisingly calm. "Well, I'm glad you came by here at least, Cadence," he says finally. "I think that's something."

"You do?"

"Yes," he says, smiling, picking up his pen. "I actually do."

Driving home, Cadence has a sudden desire to call up her own mother and talk to her about it, to tell her what's happened. Throughout it all, she's told her nothing, has barely even spoken to her. She and Elson had both decided to keep their parents out of it. But suddenly she feels a need, a desire even, to talk about it, to get another perspective. A perspective other than Elson's or Gavin's or Peterson's. A female perspective, a mother's perspective. The perspective of someone who might actually understand what she was going through.

Ever since her divorce, she's found herself longing for female company. It was strange. Usually after a divorce, one person got all the friends, or the friends were split up evenly, but in their case, neither of them had ended up with any of their friends, which had made her wonder whether any of these friends had actually been friends to begin with. Most of their friends had been couples, and what they had done with them had been couples' things. Now, however, she realized that nobody wanted to invite a single woman over to dinner, nobody wanted to bring a third wheel out on a date. There'd been an initial outpouring of support, of course, from the women she knew, but after a couple of months, that support had dwindled, their interest had waned. Even Cheryl Millhauser, her former best friend, had stopped returning her phone calls, had stopped answering her e-mails, had stopped inviting her over for lunch. Was divorce really such an uncommon occurrence? she wonders. Such an unforgivable offense? Or was it something else? Was it simply that she was a symbol now, a reminder of the unhappiness in their own lives, their own marriages, of what could one day happen to them?

Had she had someone to talk to, what would she have even told them about yesterday, about what happened? Even now, it seemed like a dream, something surreal, an imaginary conversation she'd had with two imaginary men. Not a real-life conversation she'd had with two real-life detectives. She'd invited them inside, and she'd been surprised at first by how friendly they'd been, by how they seemed almost apologetic about having to be there. Everything they said involved a "please" or a "thank you," a "yes, ma'am" or a "no, ma'am." She'd even made them some tea, shown them some pictures of Richard and Chloe as children. But then at some point the conversation had changed. She couldn't really remember, but at some point their friendly dialogue had turned into a formal inquisition, and "a few minutes of her time" had turned into almost half an hour.

Initially, she had almost wanted to tell them everything, but after a while it became clear to her that they were not here to help her, nor to help Chloe. They had told her some horrible things about the incident itself, about how Raja and his friend had broken into the dorm room of Tyler Beckwith and terrorized him, how there'd been a fight, a terrible fight, and how Tyler Beckwith had come out on the losing end of that fight. They'd told her about how Tyler had been rushed to the hospital, about the concussion he'd sustained, about his facial lacerations, about his three broken ribs. They'd told her about the blood they'd had to excavate from his chest cavity, about the swelling in his brain, about the heart monitor that was right now tracing his heartbeat, the ventilator that was right now, at this moment, keeping him alive.

They'd told her some other things, too, details she'd chosen not to remember, but it had been enough to unsettle her, which was perhaps the point. Finally, they'd said that they now believed that her daughter was involved. Not in a direct way, but still involved. What she was doing, they believed, was harboring a fugitive, which in itself was a crime. A felony. A third-degree felony, to be frank, and this could involve jail time, not to mention the fact that she might be embroiled in conspiracy charges if the Beckwith boy didn't recover. They looked at her very solemnly as they said this. So, that's where they were, they said. The Kittappa boy was gone, that much they knew, and since she could give them no explanation for where Chloe might be, they could only assume that she was helping him. It was that simple, they said. Basic logic. They didn't have any proof, of course, but they had a strong suspicion, and usually when they had a strong suspicion, that suspicion was right.

Cadence had sat there, listening to them, nodding her head, very aware that anything she might say could later be used against Chloe. They told her that they now had evidence that the boy, the Kittappa boy, was down in Houston. They'd followed a trail of airline tickets he'd bought, and that trail had led them here. Had she talked to her daughter recently? they wanted to know. Had she had any contact with her at all? Cadence, now realizing that her daughter's safety was at risk, had decided to tell them the truth, or at least what she knew of the truth. She told them about the last time she'd seen Chloe, about how they'd fought, about how Chloe had seemed very upset. Then she'd told them about the text message she'd sent her, her phone call, and how she was now worried she might have left Houston. When they asked her why she thought she might have left Houston, however, she'd said very little, only that it was just a suspicion she had.

The two men had looked at each other and nodded, clearly not buying this last part, but not persisting either. Was there anyone else, they'd finally asked, anyone else who might know where Chloe might be? Cadence had paused at this, thinking first about Richard and how he would inevitably be dragged into this as well, how he would inevitably be questioned. Not wanting to implicate him, though, she told them instead about Simone and gave them her address, hoping they might have better luck with her than she'd had, hoping they might be able to crack her shell.

Seemingly appeased, they'd finally stood up and thanked her, explaining that they'd probably be in touch again in the next couple days and that they'd be talking to her husband as well.

"My ex-husband," she'd said as she walked them to the door.

"Right," the taller one said. "Your ex-husband."

"In the meantime," the shorter one said, "if you hear anything at all, you need to let us know, okay? You're required by law to let us know."

Cadence nodded.

"Believe it or not, we're not out to lynch your daughter here, Mrs. Harding. If there's any way for us to help her, we will. Trust me. But at the same time, she needs to cooperate with us, okay? All of you do."

Cadence nodded again and took the men's cards and then watched them as they walked to their car. As soon as they were gone, she'd closed the door behind her and then collapsed into a chair in the hall, and that's when she'd thought about Elson. It was strange, but his name had been the first that popped into her head.

As it turned out, Elson had not been able to come over right away. He had to work late at the office, he'd told her when she'd called. He had to make sure that everything was in order before he took his "leave." This was the first time she'd heard of his leave, and it surprised her. Throughout their marriage he had always been so busy, so preoccupied, with his work, that he'd rarely even taken a vacation, let alone a leave, and now he was taking off several weeks, he said, all for their daughter, and for her. To support them.

With nothing else to do, and with her mind racing, Cadence had decided to make them both dinner, and when he arrived, they'd eaten together out by the pool. She'd told him about the detectives, about what she'd said, and about how she was now worried she'd said too much. She'd expected him to be angry at her for saying what she had, for breaking their promise to Chloe, but he wasn't. Instead, Elson had just sat there, listening to her earnestly, patiently, perhaps sensing her uneasiness, her fear, and he hadn't persisted either, hadn't pushed, as he usually would. He had just sat there, listening to her, occasionally patting her shoulder or touching her hand. If he was still feeling wounded about what had happened the other night, he didn't show it. He didn't even allude to it. He just smiled at her and then told her that it would all be fine, that she'd done the right thing, and that what they needed to do right now was stay calm, take stock of their options, and figure out a plan.

Tomorrow, he said, he'd be talking to his lawyer, Albert Dunn, and after that, to the two detectives. Depending on what Albert said, he'd shape his answers accordingly. The point was to work with these detectives, but not *for* them. They needed to remember that these detectives were not their friends. They were not out to help them, as they'd promised, but to find Raja, and they would use whatever methods possible to find him, even if those methods hurt Chloe. Then he reminded her of what Albert had told them the previous day, that these detectives were simply trying to scare them, that they wouldn't actually be prosecuting Chloe because prosecuting her would mean losing her testimony, which they'd need later on to prove intent. It was all just a ruse, he'd said. A mind game. This was what they needed to remember.

It was strange. Hearing Elson talk in this way disarmed her. She wondered why he'd never acted this way during their marriage. Had it taken a crisis of this proportion for him to finally grow up? Or had he always been this way, deep down inside, and she'd simply never noticed? A part of her didn't trust it, not completely, but another part of her found it oddly endearing. As much as she hated to admit it, his presence in her life these past few days had been a calming one. He'd seemed to have genuinely changed. Perhaps his contrition the other night had been sincere. Perhaps he'd seen the error of his ways. All she knew then was that she didn't want to be alone that night, not with everything that had just happened, and she didn't want Elson to leave either, so finally, after dinner, she had opened up another bottle of wine and then asked him if he would stay with her.

It was late by then, they were both a little drowsy, and it had seemed, at the time, a natural thing to suggest.

He'd looked at her, a little perplexed, but said nothing.

"You shouldn't be driving home tonight," she'd added.

"I'm fine."

"No, you're not," she'd said. "And besides, I'd like you to stay."

"You would?"

"Yes," she said. "I would."

He'd looked at her again, and she could tell now that he was genuinely confused, and so she'd taken his hand and led him upstairs and then down the long hallway to her room, to *their* room, where she'd taken off her shoes and then lay down on the bed. After a moment, he'd lain down beside her, and they'd remained like that for quite a while, both of them fully clothed, saying nothing, until she'd finally turned off the light.

"Don't go getting too comfortable," she'd said after a while. "This is only for tonight, okay?"

But he'd said nothing to this, and she had wondered then what he was thinking, what was going on in his mind. There was only a foot and a half between them, but somehow, at that moment, he seemed farther away. She had an inclination to reach over then and touch him, to pull him toward her, to embrace him, but she didn't.

It wasn't until later that night, after he'd fallen asleep, that she'd finally nestled up close to him and put her arm around him. She'd pressed her body against his, hoping he wouldn't wake, and he hadn't. She'd told herself that this was only for tonight. She'd told herself that none of this had anything to do with anything.

10

SITTING ACROSS FROM the two detectives in the dim-lit bar area of the Brunswick Hotel, Elson is second-guessing his choice of meeting places. He'd initially chosen the Brunswick Hotel because he considered it a neutral location. A neutral location, but not too neutral. It was a place where he felt at home, a place where he felt in control, comfortable, but he realized now it was also a place that he felt strangely protective of, a place that he considered his own, a place that was now being sullied by the memory of a conversation he'd rather not be having.

At Albert Dunn's suggestion, he'd told them almost nothing so far. Nothing they didn't already know. Nothing that Cadence hadn't already told them. Anything you say, Albert had warned him, could be potentially damaging to your daughter. At the same time, he'd said, you don't want to lie. Lying could be even worse. The best thing to do was to play it cool, tell the truth, to give them something, but not too much. Albert had asked Elson if he'd like him to join him, if he'd like him to be there while he was questioned, but Elson had told him it wasn't necessary, that he thought he could handle it. Now, however, he isn't so sure. He can tell they're getting antsy, frustrated, discouraged. They've been sitting here now for almost an hour, going over the same details ad nauseam, going over the same facts again and again.

"And that's all you have to tell us, Mr. Harding?" the taller detective says finally. "That's it?"

"I've told you what I know."

The two detectives stare at each other, then share a knowing smile.

"Let me ask you something," the taller detective says after a moment, picking up his iced tea. "Would you describe your relationship with your daughter as a good relationship?"

"What's that supposed to mean?"

"Just answer the question, Mr. Harding."

"I just don't see what that has to do with anything."

"Please, sir," the shorter one says. "Just answer the question."

"How would you define *good*?"

The two detectives stare at him, but say nothing.

"Good?" Elson says. "Good? I can tell you I love her very much."

"That's not what we're asking you, sir."

"Well, I don't really see what you *are* asking me."

"Let me put it another way," the taller detective says. "Would you say your daughter trusts you?"

Elson stares at him, unsettled by the question. The honest answer is no. No, she hasn't trusted him in years. Not since she entered high school. Not since she was old enough to drive. But why are they even asking this? What does this have to do with anything? He sits there silently, refusing to answer.

"You and your wife got divorced this year. Is that right?"

"That's right."

"And how did your daughter take that?"

"What do you mean?"

"I mean, was she upset by it?"

"This is ridiculous."

"Mr. Harding."

"Of course she was upset by it. What do you think?"

"And how would you describe her emotional state at that time?"

"Her emotional state?"

"Yes."

"I don't like this line of questioning," he says finally. "I don't like what you're implying."

"We're not implying anything, Mr. Harding. We're just trying to get some information here."

"Yes, and the information you're trying to get is totally irrelevant."

"Why don't you let us decide what's relevant and what's not, sir."

Elson looks at them, then turns away.

"Look, Mr. Harding. Do you understand what obstruction of justice is?" the taller one continues. "Do you understand that that's a crime?"

"How am I obstructing justice?" Elson says, angered now. "Are you kidding me? You're asking me a personal question about my daughter, and I'm choosing not to answer it. I'd hardly call that obstruction of justice."

"You've answered virtually none of our questions, sir."

"Because I don't *know*," Elson says. "If I knew, I'd tell you. But I don't."

"You know, Mr. Harding, we have other ways of getting your testimony."

"What are you talking about?"

"Have you ever heard of a grand jury summons?"

Elson stares at him.

"We can compel your testimony, sir. You and your wife's."

"And what if we refused to speak?"

"Then I'm afraid you'd be held in contempt of court."

"Contempt of court?" Elson laughs. "Are you kidding me? Really?"

The detective stares at him, then turns to his notepad and writes something down.

"What are you writing down?" Elson says, peering over the table, but the detective turns over his pad before he can see.

"Look, Mr. Harding. I want to explain the situation to you, okay? I want you to understand the true severity of what we're dealing with here. We have a boy who's in very bad shape, and if that boy should die, God forbid, we're talking about a felony offense here for your daughter. Hindering apprehension or prosecution is a felony offense when a felony is committed. Do you understand what I'm saying, Mr. Harding?"

To this, Elson says nothing. He can feel his fingers tingling, his breath quickening, the onset of a panic attack coming on.

"My daughter's done nothing," he finally says. "She's not involved."

"Perhaps you believe that, Mr. Harding. And I can understand why you'd want to believe that. I do. But we happen to believe otherwise. And—"

"I'm done here," Elson breaks in, and he realizes now that his fingers are shaking, almost uncontrollably. "I've told you what I know, and I'm done."

He reaches into his pocket then, fumbles for his wallet, and lays down a twenty. Then he pulls out the card that Albert Dunn had given him earlier that day and lays it on top.

"Anything else you want to know, you're going to have to talk to my lawyer, okay?"

The two detectives look at him blankly.

"This is harassment," he says. "What you're doing to me is harassment."

Then he turns, without saying good-bye, and starts across the bar area toward the elevator and then, once he's downstairs, across the lobby and through the revolving door and out onto the street. It's early evening, the sun already starting to set in the distance, and everything around him is vague. He feels disoriented, confused, and before he knows it, he is running, the adrenaline inside of him pumping, his heart pounding. He makes it almost seven blocks before he has to stop and catch his breath, before he realizes, with something like shame, with something like embarrassment, that he has forgotten his car.

CHLOE HAD PACKED only the bare necessities: a toothbrush, a comb, her makeup bag, a few changes of clothes, clean underwear, tampons, and a wallet containing a little over five hundred dollars. She'd stuffed all of these things into a backpack along with her passport, which Richard had managed to find in her bedroom earlier that day.

Apparently, he'd stopped by while she and Raja were out getting lunch, but he had left her an envelope with Brandon, an envelope containing her passport, the money, and a short letter in which he'd told her to be careful with the money and to not do anything stupid. Given the fact that she'd just asked him to get her passport for her that morning, he must have surmised by now that they were planning to leave the country, but he hadn't said anything about this in his letter. He simply said to be careful and that he loved her very much, and as soon as she'd read those words, she'd felt a sinking in her chest, realizing then how long it would be before she saw him again and suddenly regretting that she hadn't said good-bye.

Now, however, as she sits in the backseat of Brandon's car next to Raja, staring out across the street at the blinking neon lights of Montrose Boulevard, she is thinking only about Raja and about what lies ahead of them tonight, about the long trip, the risky crossing, the uncertainty of a future in Mexico. She grips Raja's hand tightly, squeezes it until he finally squeezes back. Since they'd left Brandon's apartment, he has said virtually nothing to her, has given only one-word answers to her questions. She tries to meet his eyes, but he is staring out the window now, expressionless.

As they pass the high-rises in downtown Houston, Brandon takes a right onto a side street, then looks down at the directions that Chloe had printed out for him earlier that night. He shakes his head.

"Never heard of any of these streets before," he says finally. "In fact, I don't think I've ever been to this part of town."

"Yeah," Chloe says. "Me neither."

"You sure you don't want me to pick you up later?"

"No, no," Chloe says. "We'll be fine." Then she thinks about where they'll be later, how far away from Brandon and Richard and everyone else they'll be. Traveling along I-10, perhaps, or parked outside the border patrol station or possibly even in Mexico, surrounded by thousands of strangers.

"And you're sure you have a place to stay?" Brandon asks.

"I'm sure."

Brandon looks back at her in the mirror, meets her eyes, then smiles. "You know, I feel really shitty about kicking you guys out like this."

"You're not kicking us out," she says. "And besides, you've done enough. More than enough. Seriously."

Brandon looks back at the road, takes another right. "Well, the offer still stands, you know. If you change your mind, you can always come back. At least for a couple of days."

She reaches forward and pats his shoulder. "Thanks, Brandon," she says. "We appreciate it."

Then she leans back and puts her hand back on Raja's hand and looks out the window. Around her, the landscape of Houston is suddenly changing. Dark, poorly lit streets filled with enormous industrial-sized buildings, warehouses and textile mills, dry-good suppliers, and hardware manufacturers. There are no restaurants here, no bars or convenience stores. Just darkness and emptiness, the hollow structures of industry, she thinks. She puts her head back on Raja's shoulder and closes her eyes. She can hear his heart beating rapidly now, his breathing shallow and tight.

"You know, I think it's up here," Brandon says after a moment, turning. "The street."

And when she opens her eyes again she can suddenly see a large truck in the distance with its headlights on and, beside it, another small truck with its headlights off, parked diagonally across the street. She can also make out two figures standing beside the trucks, and as they approach, she begins to realize that one of these two figures is Dupree.

"You can pull over here," she says to Brandon when they're about a hundred yards away.

"You sure?" he says, looking back at her. "I could take you closer."

"No, no," she says, "this is fine." Then she grabs her backpack and opens the door, and Raja does the same.

"Thanks again," she says. "If there's ever a way for us to repay you for all of this, we will. I promise."

"Hey, it's my pleasure," Brandon says. "Really. No worries." Then he looks at her. "But look, just take care of yourselves, okay? Be safe. If anything happens to you guys, your brother's going to kill me, all right?"

"We will," she says, and then, though she doesn't know why, she leans into the car and kisses Brandon on the cheek. "You're a good guy, Brandon," she says. "Truly."

He laughs and shakes his head. "Well, I know a lot of people who would disagree with you, but thanks."

Then he puts the car into gear, and as she closes the door, he winks at her. Stepping back, she watches his car until the taillights are only tiny specks, tiny fireflies, flickering along the horizon.

Dupree is standing next to the truck, one hand in his pocket, the other holding a cigarette, swaying back and forth nervously. He is wearing a poncho with a picture of Jimi Hendrix printed on the front and has the hood pulled tight over his face. When they're close enough to hear him, he says, "Who was that?" And when Chloe doesn't answer, adds, "In the car?"

"Oh," she says, putting down her backpack. "That was just a friend, a friend of my brother's. He was just giving us a ride."

Dupree nods. "Does he know why you're here?"

"Nope."

"You sure?"

"I'm positive."

Beside Dupree is a short olive-skinned man with ruddy hair and a goatee-style beard, presumably their driver. He looks about forty, maybe forty-five, and is neatly dressed. He looks at Dupree and nods, and then Dupree turns back to Chloe. "This is Teo," he says, looking at the man. "He'll be driving you two tonight. Teo, this is Raja and Chloe."

Teo nods at them both, but says nothing, doesn't even extend his hand.

"So you got the money?" Dupree asks, turning back to Chloe.

She opens her backpack, then hands him the envelope. Dupree opens it, studies the bills for a moment, then hands them to Teo, who proceeds to count them.

"Here's what's gonna happen," Dupree says, speaking quietly now. "You two are gonna ride in the back, okay?" He motions toward the truck, a white cargo truck, which resembles a U-Haul in its setup. No windows or doors. Just a large, empty box used for transporting goods, it seems. "It's gonna be a bit of a tight fit, okay. He's got a bunch of other shit back there, you know, but it's only gonna be for a few hours, all right? Three to San Antonio, and then another two to Laredo. And we got some other stuff for you back there. Some food and water, blankets, stuff like that."

Chloe nods. Then she looks back at the truck, suddenly concerned. "How are we going to breathe back there?"

"Oh right," Dupree says. "No worries about that. He's got some holes in the floor, and another small one on the side." He looks at her. "You'll be fine." Then he reaches into his pocket and pulls something out. "And another thing. You'll want to hold on to this." He hands her a small temporary cell phone, a cheap plastic thing like the ones she used to buy in college when her own cell phone was on the fritz. "I'm assuming you two aren't carrying phones on you right now."

Chloe shakes her head.

"Good," Dupree says, "because people can track that shit, you know." Then he takes a drag on his cigarette and places the phone in her hand. "Anyway, anything goes wrong back there and you use this thing, okay? It's got one number programmed into it, and that number will get you Teo. Aside from that, though, you shouldn't be making any other calls, okay?"

Chloe looks over at Teo, but his head is still down, counting.

"And one last thing," Dupree adds. "Teo's gonna make two stops. One outside of Houston to pick up a friend, and then another one in San Antonio to pick up this girl, some chick who'll be riding with you for the last two hours, okay? If the girl's not there, then you might have to wait another couple hours in San Antonio, but Teo's gonna let you out if that happens, okay? Otherwise it's gonna be a straight shot right through. If everything goes as planned, you'll be eating breakfast in Mexico tomorrow morning."

Chloe nods, feeling suddenly overwhelmed, then looks at Raja, who seems concerned.

"And where's he going to drop us off?" Chloe asks.

"Bus station," Dupree says. "There's one right on the other side of the border. From there, you two can go anywhere you want."

Dupree tosses his cigarette on the ground and grinds it out with his sneaker. She can tell that he's nervous, anxious, that he wants to get this over with as soon as possible. He motions for them to follow him around the side of the van, and then he opens up the back door and steps onto the bumper. The space behind him is dark and filled with large cardboard boxes and crates, a veritable barricade of illegal cargo, it seems.

He motions for them to step up into the van, then leads them down a narrow center aisle between the boxes. In the back, there's a space no more than six feet wide with a couple of dirty blankets, laid down like a rug, a flashlight, a few bottles of bottled water, potato chips, and a bucket, a bucket that, Dupree explains, they're supposed to piss in if there's an emergency.

"I know it's not exactly the Ritz-Carlton," he adds, "but look, it could be worse, right?"

Then he points to a series of tennis ball–sized holes in the floor and one on the side of the wall, where he insists they'll get more than enough air. Chloe stares at the holes uncertainly, then she puts down her backpack and sits down on one of the dirty blankets, and a moment later Raja sits down beside her.

Dupree puts his hand on top of one of the boxes, then looks back at the open door nervously. "Look," he says, leaning down now, whispering. "There's one other thing I gotta tell you guys. And I didn't want to mention this shit to Teo, because, trust me, the dude would've dumped your asses a while ago. But look, this morning—" He pauses to double-check the back door. "Look, this morning some cops were hanging out around the store, talking to Simone."

She looks at him. "This morning?"

"Yeah."

"And did she tell them anything?"

"Who the fuck knows?" Dupree shrugs. "With that girl, who the fuck knows what goes on in her mind?"

Chloe sits up.

"And another thing," he adds. "Your mom was around the day before that. You know, just talking to her."

"My mom?"

"Yeah."

"She was talking to Simone?"

"Apparently." He looks around him. "Anyway, I just thought you two should know."

Chloe nods, though this information has terrified her.

Dupree stands up straight again and takes a step back. He puts his hands together. "Okay, amigos. I gotta split. Any other questions?"

"Just one," Raja says, speaking for the first time since they arrived.

Chloe looks at him, still trying to process what Dupree has told her about Simone.

"You feel like you can trust this guy?" Raja continues. "Teo?"

"Trust him with my life," Dupree says.

Raja nods, seemingly satisfied.

"And don't worry," Dupree adds. "The cross will be smooth. They'll probably open up the back door or something, but they're not gonna look around. Like I said, he knows these people. As long as you don't make any noise, you'll be fine."

Dupree looks at them then expectantly, waiting for something else, but Chloe has nothing else to say. Should she thank him? she wonders. Give him a hug? She feels like she should say something, but suddenly she can't bring herself to speak. She's thinking only about Simone and her mother and the cops, how they're all involved now.

Dupree takes another step back and pushes two of the boxes into the center aisle, then another two, making a barricade behind him, trapping them inside.

"This is just so they can't see you," he explains as he continues to move the boxes. "Hope you're not claustrophobic or anything."

Chloe says nothing. She grips Raja's hand, and he squeezes back.

When Dupree finally finishes, she can no longer see any part of his body, just the pointy top of his hood.

"Okay, amigos," he says, pulling down the door halfway. *"Vaya con Dios!"* Then he yanks down the door the rest of the way, letting it slam behind him, and suddenly everything is dark. A moment later, she can hear him putting on a padlock, then tapping the back of the van three

times with his fist. She lets go of Raja's hand, then fumbles for the flashlight, turns it on, and looks at Raja.

He's shaking his head. "There's something not right here," he says.

"What do you mean?"

But he doesn't answer. He just says it again. "There's just something
not right."

Part Five

IT HAD BEEN an accident. That's how Raja had explained it to her afterward, when he came home from Tyler Beckwith's dorm room, covered in mud. It had been an accident, he'd said as he sat there in the middle of his own room, naked, holding his knees to his chest.

There were no scratches on his body, no bruises, no signs of a struggle, but his eyes were strangely blank. His body was covered in sweat, his muscles tense. Behind him on the floor lay his clothes, the jeans and T-shirt he'd been wearing earlier, crumpled up in a ball.

What the hell had happened? Chloe wanted to know. Where was Seung? But Raja didn't answer, and suddenly she felt guilty, guilty for not being there, guilty for running away.

She was supposed to have waited. She was supposed to have waited outside the door with the two cans of shaving cream, ready at any moment to enter. But she hadn't. As soon as she'd heard the screaming, as soon as she'd heard the sound of Tyler Beckwith's voice, she'd run, bolted down the hallway, then down the staircase and out the door.

Had anyone seen her? Raja wanted to know.

She shook her head no, but then she remembered. Yes, she said, one girl. A girl she didn't know. But she wasn't worried about it. And she wasn't. At the time, she wasn't worried about it, though later this girl would come to testify against her in front of the Student Judiciary Council, would describe in detail the two cans of shaving cream she'd been holding in her hands as she fled from the dorm.

"Is everything okay?" she'd asked Raja.

But he shook his head. "I don't know," he said. "It was dark. I couldn't see. But no, I don't think so. I think it might be pretty bad."

"Really?"

He nodded.

And that's when he told her how he'd called up the campus police, and then the EMTs, from one of the emergency telephones on campus. It had all been anonymous, he said, but Seung had still freaked out, had tried to pull the phone out of his hand, and then later, after he'd hung up, had tried to wipe down the receiver with his shirtsleeve, removing their fingerprints. He'd called him crazy, he said. Seung had. Had chewed him out. Then he'd pushed him down on the ground, had tried to fight him, and that's where the mud had come from. From their fight. After that, he couldn't remember what happened. All he knew was that Seung had fled off into the shadows behind the Psychology Building, and that was the last he'd seen of him.

"Where do you think he went?" she'd asked.

But Raja just shook his head. Finally he said, "I don't know, Chlo. I don't know where the fuck he went. All I know is this is going to be bad. I think this is going to be really, really bad." And then he stood up and walked over to the window and looked down at the quad, as if expecting to see someone he knew standing down there, waiting.

But to go back.

Months earlier, long before any of this had happened, Chloe had stopped by Raja's dorm room one night while he was off at his job. This was the story she'd tell people later, when they asked, when she wanted to explain to them what had happened. He had been screening a series of short independent films that night for a group of senior English majors in the Drama Building, but she had begged off, claiming to be tired, and then had gone to his room to wait. She had her own key by then and had let herself in and then lay down on his bed and took a nap. This was something she did two or three times a week, a kind of ritual she had whenever he was working. She had lain there for a long time that night, sleeping, falling in and out of a dream, and then at one point there'd been a knock at the door, a loud knock that had woken her, and when she'd stood up to answer it, when she opened the door, she had seen a boy darting around the corner at the end of the hall. She couldn't make out his face, but she could tell that he was tall, white, and athletically built. His hair was blond, and he was wearing baggy jeans and a navy-blue peacoat.

She hadn't thought anything about it until she'd turned around and seen the noose, a small frayed noose thumbtacked to the door right above the dry-erase board that Raja used for messages. Written on the board below were three words: GO HOME JIHAD.

She'd felt her entire body freeze at that moment, had almost wanted to scream, but instead had run back into Raja's room and looked out the window. On the quad below, she could see the boy running back across the snow, his face buried in his jacket, his body silhouetted by the light from the lampposts along the path.

Her first thought had been to call up campus security, to let them know, but she had known how Raja would react if she did this, so instead she'd just gone back to the door, removed the noose, and erased the words the boy had written with the side of her hand.

It had been six weeks since that night in late November when they'd come home from the Cove and discovered the sign on Raja's door, six weeks during which they'd taken their final exams, gone home to their respective families for the winter break, and then returned to campus for the spring semester. During that entire time, there hadn't been another instance, hadn't been another sign on Raja's door, as far as she knew, and they had both come to believe that it had all blown over.

But now it was January, and it was starting up again. Or so it seemed. She felt sick with the thought of it. And as she lay there that night on his bed, waiting for him, she found herself debating whether or not to tell him. If it was only a onetime thing, she thought, maybe he didn't need to know. Maybe she could spare him the pain and grief. But there was another part of her that seemed to understand that this wasn't going to end. She wondered who this boy was, what he wanted, why he had chosen Raja. Anything even remotely racist was so frowned upon at Stratham that it seemed impossible to imagine that any one of her fellow classmates could have done something like this. But at the same time, she thought, how well did she actually know any of the people she passed on a daily basis? How well did she know what went on in their minds?

Lying on Raja's bed, she stared at the noose on the floor beside her, wondering what to do. She felt something sour rising inside her, an anger in her gut. If she had that boy right here, she thought, if she had him right here, right now, what would she do to him?

Later that night, when Raja got home, she had tried her best to control her anger. In an even tone, she had told him what had happened, then showed him the noose. He stared at it in disbelief, then shook his head. She could see something like fear in his eyes. After a moment, he walked over to the minifridge in the corner of his room and opened a beer.

"So what are you going to do now?" she asked.

He shrugged, then sipped on his beer.

"You're not going to do anything?"

"I didn't say that," he said. Then he looked at her. "You said you got a good look at him?"

"I guess," she said. "Not really." Then she proceeded to describe what she had seen: the blond hair, the navy-blue peacoat, the way he had darted around the corner.

"How tall?" he asked.

"I don't know," she said. "Like six feet or so."

He nodded.

"You think you know him?"

"I don't know," he said. "Maybe." Then he put down his beer on the edge of the windowsill. "Remember that guy from the bar? That guy I got in a fight with?"

"Tyler Beckwith?" she said, staring at him. "You think it's him?"

"I don't know," he said, "but I've had my suspicions, you know, for a while now."

"So why don't you report it?"

"What good would that do?"

"Well, it might make him stop for one thing."

"We don't have any proof," he said. "No evidence. It's my word against his."

"What about fingerprints?"

"Come on, Chlo, this isn't TV. We're talking about campus security here."

She looked at him. "Then call the police."

"I'm not calling the fucking police," he said. "And besides, they don't like to touch anything that happens here on campus anyway. You know that."

She stared at him, infuriated now, annoyed by his stubbornness. "Raja," she said. "He hung a fucking noose on your door."

"I realize that."

"And you don't see that as a threat?"

"I don't know," he said and looked out the window. "To be honest, it's probably nothing."

"Probably nothing?" she said. "How can you say it's probably nothing?"

He stared at her, something in his face changing. "You think this is the first time in my life I've been threatened?"

"I don't know," she said. "Is it?"

He walked over to the window, disgusted. "Forget it," he said. "You wouldn't understand."

"Why?"

"You just wouldn't."

She looked at him. "Why? You mean because I'm white?"

"Yes," he said. "Actually. If you want to know the truth, yes, because you're white."

She stared at him. "I don't think that's fair."

He laughed, and she could see now that he was angry. "Fair?" he said. "Do you really want to talk to me about what's fair? I mean, is that really the conversation you want to be having right now?"

He was staring at her now in a way that frightened her, that made her realize it was time to stop. Up until this point in their relationship, they had rarely talked about race, at least not directly, at least not as it pertained to them, and yet now she could see that something had changed, a wall had gone up, and she was not going to be permitted to scale this wall. Not tonight.

"So, that's it?" she said finally. "You're just going to let it go? You're not going to do *anything*?"

"I'm going to wait," he said.

"And then what?"

"And then we'll see."

That night, she went home alone and slept by herself in her own room. She could tell that Raja needed some time alone, some time away from her, some time to process what had happened. As much as he'd tried to play it off like he didn't care, she could tell that it had affected him, angered him, maybe even frightened him. She even thought he might actually try to do something about it this time.

But the next day, when she met up with him on the quad for lunch, it was like nothing had ever happened. He was calm again, even relaxed. He didn't even mention it, didn't even allude to it. He just sat there and talked about his classes, complained about a paper that was coming up, a professor who was trying to screw him over, and so forth. It wasn't until later that night, as they were sitting over drinks at the Cove, that he began to talk about it again, though even then he did so obliquely. It was strange, he said, strange that Tyler Beckwith would still hold such a grudge against him, strange that he would still be so angry. It was true that he had humiliated him in front of his girlfriend, and it was true that Tyler's girlfriend had broken up with him shortly after that night, or so he'd heard, but was Tyler really blaming him for this? Did he honestly believe that Raja was responsible? It seemed absurd. There had to be something else, he thought. Something else he hadn't considered.

The Cove was empty that night, or nearly empty, and they both had about five beers apiece. Chloe was nervous about speaking, nervous about reigniting their fight from the night before, so she mostly just sat there and listened, listened as Raja speculated about why this was happening, and by the time they'd ordered their final round, he was starting to get loose, talking about things he had never mentioned to her before, things that he claimed upset him: the stuff he'd had to deal with after 9/11, for example, the way people had refused to look at him in the hallways at school, the way they'd refused to sit next to him during lunch, even though he was Indian, not Arab, even though he had made it clear to them from the start that he had never had anything but utter fondness for the United States.

You have no idea what it was like to ride the subway or travel on an airplane after that happened, he said. The stares he got from white passengers, the terror in their eyes. And never mind the things he was called in school, behind his back, or sometimes to his face: rock chucker, rag head, camel jockey, jihad. For a long time they had nicknamed him Osama, a nickname that had stung him so deeply that he'd once filed a formal complaint to the principal, a complaint that had gone largely unnoticed. It was totally hysterical, he said. It was out of control. It was like living in an alternate universe.

At the time, he said, his only salvation had been the cinema. It was here that he could lose himself for hours on end, here that he could disappear from the world around him. In the dark, he said, it didn't matter who you were or what you looked like. For a few brief hours at least, you could be anyone, and for a few brief hours, you could go anywhere. You could be transported to French-occupied Europe or to London in the sixties or to the rolling plains of east Missouri. Every Friday night, he would go there by himself, to the Dollar Cinema in Newark, or sometimes, on the weekends, to the film festivals at NYU or to the special screenings they had at the Angelika Theater in New York. It was here that his education in film began, he said. It was here that he'd first discovered Godard.

It was strange to hear him talking in this way, strange to hear him talking so openly about things he had never mentioned to her before, and though a part of her wondered if he was finally losing it, another part of her found it strangely endearing, the fact that he was willing to open up like this. At one point she had asked him about his family, about his parents, and how they had handled it, and he had simply sat there, staring at her. The stuff he was dealing with in high school, he said finally, he never mentioned it. Not to them. It would have only upset them, he said. It would have only made his father feel guilty, guilty for bringing them here, for subjecting them to this. And besides, it wouldn't have mattered anyway. He knew what his father would say, how he'd react. He'd tell him to keep his head down and his mouth shut, to not retaliate, to just ignore it. He'd tell him that violence would only bring him trouble. His father was a pacifist, he said, a pacifist through and through, and believed strongly in the notion that an eye for an eye left everyone blind. His father saw violence as a sign of human weakness, he said, a sign of moral depravity. It was the lowest insult one could pay to another human being.

"So that's why you don't want to do anything about it," she'd said after a moment. "About the signs. You're trying to respect your father's wishes."

"I didn't say that."

"No," she said. "But aren't you?"

"I'm not my father," he said and suddenly seemed angry.

"But you believe in pacifism."

"I believe in pacifism to a point," he said, staring at her.

"Okay," she said, pausing. "So when, in your opinion, is violence justified?"

"It's never justified," he said. "It's just sometimes necessary."

"Like when?"

"Like sometimes."

"Like when you defended Seung?"

"No," he said and stared at her. "Like I said, that night was a mistake."

.   .   .

For the next several days they kept a cautious distance from each other. In the evenings after dinner, she'd still go over to his dorm room to study, but more often than not, once she'd finished, she'd go home alone to sleep.

By then, the signs were becoming a daily occurrence. Signs full of racial slurs, allusions to 9/11, warnings to other students that a terrorist was among them. Raja had stopped hosting nightly parties in his dorm room, had stopped providing counsel to his fellow students. He kept his door shut at all times, shut and locked, and after a while, nobody even bothered to knock. It was like the person living inside had suddenly died.

Meanwhile, Chloe had begun to spend more and more time with Fatima, rekindling a friendship with her, turning to her for advice. She often went there in the evenings after class, before she went to see Raja or sometimes after. Raja had made her swear to him several times that she would never mention any of this stuff to anyone, and especially not to Fatima, but one night, while they were smoking pot at her house, Chloe had blurted it out. Had told her everything. About the signs. About the noose. About how, just the other day, Raja's tires had been slashed.

"His tires were slashed?" Fatima said, suddenly alarmed, leaning forward now at the kitchen table. They were sitting in the dark, a small candle in the middle of the room casting shadows against the wall, the sounds of the Cure in the background.

Chloe nodded.

"That's a crime," Fatima said. "Everything you're talking about here is a crime."

"I know that."

"And he's not doing anything about it?"

Chloe shook her head. "He'd kill me if he knew I told you."

"People need to know about this," Fatima said.

"I know," Chloe said and stared at her plaintively.

Fatima was silent, and she could see now that she was thinking, turning it over in her head, and suddenly regretted telling her.

"And you don't know who it was who did this?"

"No," Chloe said, though just the day before she had seen Tyler Beckwith in his navy-blue peacoat, walking across the quad, his blond hair waving. It had been the same navy-blue peacoat she'd seen that night in Raja's dorm, the same blond hair she'd seen darting around the corner, and she felt certain now that it was him. Still, when she'd told Raja about it, he'd simply shrugged and looked away, saying under his breath that he wasn't at all surprised.

"This has to be known," Fatima was saying now, leaning forward at the kitchen table adamantly.

"Look, let's just drop it, okay?"

"How can you tell me to drop it?" Fatima said. "How can you tell me something like this, and then tell me to drop it? I mean, this is maybe the worst thing I've heard of since I've been here."

Chloe stared at her, feeling suddenly light-headed from the pot, but also fearful of what might happen now, what Fatima might do with this information.

"I think we should bring this up tomorrow," Fatima said.

"Bring it up?"

"Yeah, at the Open Forum meeting."

"At the Open Forum meeting? Come on, Fatima, are you kidding me?"

"I won't mention his name," Fatima said. "I'll keep him out of it. But I think people need to know about this. Seriously. People need to know that this is happening."

Chloe stared at her. "Please, Fatima," she said. "If you bring this up—I mean, if he found out that this was brought up at the meeting—you'd essentially be destroying my relationship with him. Seriously. I mean, this is something he just wouldn't forgive."

Fatima reached for the bowl and seemed to consider this. "You really think so?" she said finally.

"I know so."

Fatima shook her head, then lit the bowl.

Chloe could see that she was disappointed, but she also knew that when push came to shove, Fatima would always choose her close personal relationships over a cause. In Fatima's world, friends came first, social injustice second. In this way, she was fiercely loyal.

"You know, I wish you hadn't told me," Fatima said finally, putting the bowl back on the table, shaking her head.

"I know," Chloe said, touching her hand. "I wish I hadn't either."

But, in the end, Fatima kept her promise. The next day at the meeting she didn't mention it. Nor did she mention it the following night when she met up with Chloe and Raja for drinks. Still, it was probably asking too much that Fatima wouldn't tell *anyone*, and within the next couple days Chloe soon found out that she had not only told two of her roommates, both of whom had come up to Chloe on the quad and expressed their sympathy, but that she'd also told Seung. Chloe could understand why she would have told her roommates, she'd even half expected it, but she couldn't for the life of her figure out why she'd told Seung. Didn't she realize that Seung would immediately go to Raja and confront him? Didn't she understand that this was essentially like lighting a fuse beneath a powder keg? That everything that followed would be disaster? In fact, if there was one person in the world who she absolutely should not have told, it was Seung. But maybe that was her point. Maybe this was her own indirect way of bringing the issue to a head, of making it public, without actually having to do so herself.

Whatever her reasoning, by the time Chloe found out that she had done this, by the time she'd discovered that Seung knew, it was already too late. The night it all happened, she had come over to Raja's dorm room with the intention of giving him a gift, an obscure book on the films of Wim Wenders, which Raja had been looking for on the Internet for months, a book that Chloe had serendipitously found in a small used bookstore in Houston over the winter break and which she'd been secretly hiding away for a special occasion. She had wrapped the book up in newspaper that afternoon, had tied a bow around it, then had gone over to Raja's room with the intention of giving it to him. In her mind, she had imagined a night spent lying on his bed, listening to music, drinking wine, a night when they might actually make love again, a night when he might actually want to touch her, but when she arrived at his dorm room that night, they were already going at it, Seung and Raja, their voices so loud that she could hear them shouting from the end of the hall. When she got to his door, she stood there for a moment, then knocked tentatively. Nobody answered, so she knocked again, louder. This time the door cracked open, and all of her worst fears were confirmed. Seung stood there, staring at her, and behind him on the bed, she could see Raja, a cigarette dangling from his mouth, his eyes looking down.

"Come in," Seung said. "We were just talking."

But when she entered the room, Raja looked away. She walked over to the bed and put down the present and wine, but he ignored her. There was a tension in the room, something she could feel, something that unnerved her. Finally, Raja looked up.

"You know, I wanted to thank you, Chloe," he said finally. "Really."

"I didn't tell him," she said.

"No, really," he said. "Thank you."

"She didn't actually," Seung added. "Fatima did."

"And let me guess who told Fatima," Raja said, turning to her.

"I'm sorry," she said. "Look, I just—"

"Whatever," he said, throwing up his arms. "It doesn't matter now."

"Don't get mad at her," Seung said. "It's not her fault."

Raja looked at him, then back at Chloe. "Like I said, forget it. Who cares? It's all over now. Everyone knows."

Chloe wanted to point out that not everyone knew, that only a few people knew, and that these people were his friends, but she kept her mouth shut. Instead, after a long silence, she said, "Look, do you want me to leave or something?"

Raja shrugged, then looked away.

"No," Seung said finally. "You should stay. You should hear this."

"Hear what?" Chloe asked.

Seung looked at Raja. "You haven't told her?"

Raja shook his head.

A moment later, Seung walked over to Raja's desk and pulled out a piece of paper, then held it up to her. It was another sign, this time with a photocopied picture of Raja's family on it and, beneath it, in bold letters, the words AMERICA'S MOST WANTED. Chloe felt her stomach drop, realizing that this was the same picture she'd seen in a small silver frame on Raja's desk, the same picture she had studied on the first night they kissed.

"How the hell did he get this?" she said, and then she looked at the desk and noticed that all of Raja's photographs were gone.

"Broke in," Seung said, then, looking at Raja, added, "When was it? Last night?"

"I don't know," Raja said. "I guess."

"He broke into your room?" she said. "Jesus."

"Jimmied the lock," Seung said. "I mean, these old doors, it's not that hard."

She shook her head, then looked away.

"I mean, you hang up some signs on the door, that's one thing," Seung continued. "But you break into a dude's room and you steal his personal shit. You steal pictures of his family, and then you disgrace them. I mean, that's taking things to a whole nother level. That's getting fucking personal."

She looked back at Raja and she could see that something had changed in his face. The old passivity was gone, replaced by something else, a new anger perhaps, or maybe something else, something deeper than anger, a hatred perhaps. She knew that if there was one thing Raja couldn't condone, one thing he couldn't forgive, it was someone disgracing his family. His family was the one thing no one else was allowed to touch.

"Too far," Seung was saying now. "He's taken this thing way too fucking far."

Raja nodded.

"Have you called security?" Chloe asked.

"Security?" Seung laughed. "Really? What the hell is security going to do?"

She looked at him.

"We have a better idea," Seung said. Then he looked at Raja.

"No we don't," Raja said.

"Oh, come on, dude."

Raja shook his head.

"Look, what I'm talking about here, what I'm talking about is just a little payback. Retribution. You fucked with us, now we're going to fuck with you. That type of thing."

"He didn't fuck with *you*," Raja said. "He fucked with *me*."

"Whatever," Seung said. "You mess with one of us, you're messing with all of us."

And suddenly Chloe could see that for Seung this wasn't personal at all. It was political. It was the fight he'd been fighting ever since he got here.

"I'm not lowering myself to his level," Raja said. "Seriously. I'm just not going to do that."

"Lowering yourself?" Seung said. "You think when people fight in a war they're lowering themselves? You think when my grandfather fought against the fucking KPA, all those fuckers in the North, he was lowering himself?"

"This isn't a war," Raja said.

"No?" Seung said. "Well, you could have fooled me."

Raja nodded and sipped his beer, and Chloe suddenly noticed that there was a pile of empty beer cans on the floor behind him, that they'd probably been drinking here for quite a while.

"Look," Seung continued, "you know as well as me that if you're a person of color in this country, if you're not pasty fucking white, then every fucking day of your life is a war. And that's all I'm talking about. If you let people keep messing with you, they will. That's all I'm saying."

Raja looked at him, and Chloe could see that a part of what Seung was saying was starting to sink in, that he was starting to hear something he wanted to hear.

Later, she'd wonder if she should have stopped it, if she should have seen it for what it was—a knee-jerk reaction—if she should have prevented Seung from fueling the fire. But at that moment she was so filled with anger herself, so overcome by it, that she could barely think straight. And the room itself was almost electric with it, with all these crazy emotions flying around, these crazy thoughts, the three of them on tilt, it was hard to know what was right and what was wrong. It was hard not to see the utter simplicity in what Seung was saying.

"So, what are you talking about specifically?" she asked.

"I'm talking about messing with him," Seung said. "I'm talking about going over there to that dude Tyler's room and messing with him. Roughing him up a little. Scaring him. I'm talking about letting him know that we're not gonna lie down over this shit. If you want to play rough, that's fine with us. Then we're going to play rough back. But we're not gonna just sit here and take this shit, you know. That's not going to be happening anymore."

Chloe could see in Raja's eyes that he was starting to get salty, that he was starting to understand the simple logic of it all, but she could also tell that he was drunk, that they both were, and when Raja stood up, she noticed that he needed to use the edge of the windowsill just to keep his balance.

"So what do you say, Raj?" Seung said, raising his beer, smiling this time. "You want to fuck with this guy or what?"

DAYS LATER, WHEN RAJA was brought in for questioning, when they'd finally gathered enough evidence to bring him in, he'd say nothing of Seung's involvement. It was only later, when a witness stepped forward, a boy from Chloe's American Politics class, a boy who had been in the hallway that night and had seen them both leaving Tyler's room, it was only then, when this boy stepped forward and identified them both, that Seung would eventually be brought in, too. But, even then, it seemed that Seung was simply being looked at as a peripheral figure, a casual bystander, an unwilling accomplice. It was Raja, they believed, who had masterminded it all. It was Raja, they believed, who had a bone to pick with Tyler Beckwith.

The day that Seung was brought in, Chloe was approached herself, though not because they believed that she was involved at this point. They had brought her in for questioning simply because she was close with the suspect, they said, because Seung had told them that they were dating and that she had seen him on the night that everything happened. They had brought her into the station that evening, had given her a soda, and explained that she was not under suspicion herself. They were simply following protocol, they said, trying to cover all the bases. They were actually surprisingly friendly to her, so friendly, in fact, that she let down her guard, so friendly that she didn't even consider asking for a lawyer. This is what Raja had done, of course, had asked for a lawyer almost as soon as they brought him in, though not before they had gotten him to admit that he had been there that night, in Tyler's dorm, and that there was a history of bad feelings between the two. Still, she was not feeling overly worried at this point. It had been an accident, after all. An unfortunate accident, but still an accident, and she figured that

Seung would have told them the same, if he had told them anything at all.

The room where they had brought her was filled with photographs of historical buildings in Stratham, some of which belonged to the college itself, a large oak desk, and several potted plants. There was a soda machine in one corner, a microwave, and several filing cabinets covered with magnets and bumper stickers. There were flyers on the wall, advertising an annual potluck dinner, a weekly poker game, a St. Patrick's Day bash. If this was an interrogation room, she thought, it didn't feel like one, and it was maybe for this reason that she began to loosen her guard, that she began to believe that what was happening here wasn't as serious as she'd initially thought.

They had left her with her soda for almost twenty minutes, had left her to consider, perhaps, what she might want to say. Then one of the two officers who had picked her up earlier outside her dorm, a man who had introduced himself to her as Detective Sprague, had returned to the room with a notepad and a pen and a small handheld tape recorder, which he'd placed down on the desk before her. Sprague was an older man, maybe in his early sixties, a man with graying hair and a potbelly and a warm, avuncular smile. He made her feel immediately relaxed.

"So, how do you like this weather?" Sprague asked, winking. It had been snowing all day, and there was talk of a blizzard approaching the following morning. "Probably a lot different from what you're accustomed to, I'd guess."

"I'm sorry?"

"Back in Texas."

"Oh," Chloe nodded, suddenly understanding. "You knew I was from Texas?"

"Your friend Mr. Cho told me."

Chloe nodded again, though she suddenly wondered how much Seung had told him.

"Mr. Cho was actually very helpful to us," he continued, "and we're hoping you will be, too." He winked at her. "Just so you know, we're just trying to get the facts straight here. Just trying to get a handle on what actually happened. Your boyfriend's not in any type of trouble right now. You should know that. Neither is Mr. Cho. We're just trying to fill in a few of the hazy spots in the story, okay? And that's where you come in. We're hoping you can help us out with that."

Chloe nodded, feeling a little nervous still. "I'll do my best," she said.

"Well, that's all we can ask for, right?" Sprague smiled again. Then he reached for his pen and turned over the first sheet on the pad. "Mind if I write some of this stuff down?"

Chloe shook her head.

"Great," he said, then he proceeded to write something down at the top of the pad. "It's just that when you get to be my age, your memory doesn't work like it used to, you know." He laughed heartily to himself, still writing, then finally looked up at her. "Okay," he said. "So why don't we just start at the beginning, okay? Why don't we just start with what happened that day. The day of the accident."

That he was using the word "accident" relaxed her a little, but she still felt a tightness in her chest. "You mean like that whole day?"

"Sure. Why not? Why don't you just start with when you woke up?"

"Okay," she said, looking at her lap. "Well, you know, I woke up around noon, I guess."

"And this would be in your own room?"

"Yes."

"Not in Mr. Kittappa's room."

"No."

"And Mr. Kittappa wasn't with you?"

"No."

"Okay. Sorry. Keep going. Like I said, I'm just trying to keep the facts straight."

Chloe nodded. "Okay," she said. "So I guess I went to class around twelve-thirty, and then I was in class until about four or so. And then I went to dinner by myself at the dining hall. And then I went to the gym and then, you know, back to my room, I guess."

"And what time would that be? When you got back to your room?"

"Seven-thirty or so."

"Okay. And you didn't have any contact with Mr. Kittappa during this time?"

"No." She shook her head.

"Not even a phone call?"

"No," she said and shrugged.

"Okay," he said. "So then when exactly did you see Mr. Kittappa that evening? After you got back to your dorm?"

"Yeah, about a half hour later. I took a shower, and then I walked over there to his dorm to give him something. A present."

"A present?"

"Yes, a book."

"Any occasion?"

"No," she said. "It was just something he'd wanted for a while. The book."

Sprague nodded and continued to write. "Okay," he said. "So this would be around eight p.m. or so?"

"I guess so."

"And when you got to his dorm room, can you describe what you saw?"

Chloe tried to picture it, but her memory was hazy. Suddenly time felt very fluid. "He was there with his friend Seung," she said finally. "They were talking, you know. And they weren't really expecting me, so I guess you could say they were a little surprised."

"Surprised?"

"Yes."

"And do you know what they were talking about?"

"No," Chloe lied.

"And how did Mr. Kittappa seem when you arrived?"

"I'm sorry?"

"I mean, did he seem upset? Angry?"

"No," she said. "He seemed normal. You know, like, relaxed."

At this, Sprague reached for his tape recorder. "Mind if I turn this on?"

Chloe stared at him, then shook her head.

Sprague pressed down the button, then announced to the room the exact time and date, who he was speaking to, and his own name and rank. "Okay," he said, smiling at Chloe. "So approximately how long would you say you spent in Mr. Kittappa's dorm room that night?"

"About forty-five minutes, I guess."

"And what did you do while you were there?"

"Talked mostly."

"About?"

"I don't know." She shrugged. "Lots of things. Friends, you know, class, stuff like that."

"Stuff like that?"

"Yes."

"Tyler Beckwith?"

Chloe paused. "Yeah, I guess his name might have come up."

"In what context?"

"I don't really remember."

"You don't remember?"

"No, I mean, you know, he'd been harassing Raja and all. Leaving signs on his door and stuff, so I guess we were kind of talking about that."

"And you're sure it was Mr. Beckwith who had left these signs?"

"Yes," Chloe said. "Positive." Then she told him about the navy-blue peacoat she'd seen, and how she'd seen Tyler Beckwith wearing that exact same coat a few days later.

Sprague looked at her then and nodded. "And did Mr. Kittappa seem angry about it? About the signs?"

"No," Chloe lied. "I mean, he wasn't happy about it, of course, but I wouldn't describe him as angry."

"And did he seem inebriated?"

Chloe peered at him now, suddenly feeling uneasy. "Inebriated?"

"Yes, Mr. Cho mentioned that he and Mr. Kittappa had been drinking some beer. Is that true?"

"They might have been," she said, "I'm not really sure. I mean, they might have had a few before I got there."

"But they weren't drinking when you were in the room?"

"No," she said.

Sprague paused for a moment and stared at her evenly, his friendly expression suddenly gone. "So when exactly would you say Mr. Kittappa decided to go over to Mr. Beckwith's dorm room?"

At this, Chloe felt her stomach tightening, thinking immediately of Seung and wondering what the hell he had told them. She stared at Sprague but said nothing.

"Mr. Cho told me that at one point the three of you decided to go over to Mr. Beckwith's dorm room and play a prank on him. Is that true?"

Chloe stared at the tape recorder. "Can you turn that off?" she asked.

"I'd rather not," Sprague said. Then he smiled at her weakly. "So are you saying that you didn't accompany them over there?"

"No," she said. "I'm not saying that." Then she thought of Raja and wondered what he would want her to say.

"So, you did accompany them over there?"

Chloe sat there for a moment, staring at her hands, then finally nodded.

"For the record," Sprague said. "Is that a yes?"

Chloe stared at the tape recorder, then quietly said, "Yes."

"And what were you planning to do once you got there?"

"What do you mean?"

"Well, if you were planning to play a prank on Mr. Beckwith, what type of prank were you planning to play?"

"I don't know," Chloe said. "It wasn't really something they'd thought out."

"So you're saying that it was Mr. Kittappa and Mr. Cho who came up with this idea?"

"Yes." Chloe shrugged. "I guess so."

"And what was your role going to be?"

"My role?"

"Yes, why were you accompanying them?"

"I don't know," Chloe said. "I was just kind of there, I guess."

"So you weren't planning to participate in this prank?"

At this, Chloe paused for a long time, her breath very shallow now, her mind racing, everything in the room feeling suddenly smaller. She thought of the two cans of shaving cream she'd brought along, the way she'd stood outside the door and waited for them. Was she on the record now? Were these things that could be used against her?

"Ms. Harding," Sprague continued. "What I'm trying to figure out here is whether or not you were in the room when the accident occurred."

"No," Chloe said, shaking her head. "I wasn't in the room."

"You weren't?"

"No."

"So, if you weren't in the room, then where were you?"

Chloe paused again. She weighed the pros and cons of telling him the truth. She stared at the tape recorder. "I was out in the hall."

"Outside the door, you mean. Outside Mr. Beckwith's door?"

"Yes."

"And how close were you to the door?"

"I don't know," she said. "A few feet, I guess."

"And the door was closed?"

"Yes."

"Could you hear what was happening inside the room?"

"No," she said. "Not really."

"And how long, approximately, would you say you were standing outside the door?"

"I don't know," Chloe said. "Probably less than a minute."

"And what was your reason for being there, for standing outside the door, if you don't mind me asking?"

"I don't know," Chloe said, thinking again of the cans of shaving cream she'd been holding. "Just waiting, I guess."

"For Mr. Kittappa and Mr. Cho?"

"Yes."

"So why then—if you were waiting for them—why did you leave so soon?"

Chloe felt suddenly dizzy, the room around her shifting, her stomach growing nauseous. All at once the air felt very thick. "I think I need to use the bathroom," she said.

"Ms. Harding, we're almost done here. If you could just answer a few more questions."

Chloe clutched her stomach, tried to concentrate.

"What I'm wondering specifically, Ms. Harding, is whether you heard the sound of Mr. Beckwith being hit?"

"Hit?"

"Yes, with the cricket bat."

Chloe looked at him, confused.

"You're aware that Mr. Beckwith is in the hospital, right? That he's in critical condition."

"Yes, of course."

"But you didn't know about the cricket bat?"

"No," Chloe said, shaking her head. And she didn't. This was the first she was hearing of it.

"So, Mr. Kittappa didn't say anything to you about hitting Mr. Beckwith with the cricket bat?"

Chloe felt the sickness in her stomach returning, tried to picture what Sprague was describing. It seemed absurd. "He wouldn't have done that," she said.

Sprague smiled. "We're not saying that he did it on purpose."

"No," Chloe said. "What I'm saying is that he wouldn't have done that. Period."

"Ms. Harding—"

"I don't know what Seung told you, but he's a fucking liar. That's something you should know about him." She could hear herself shouting now, could feel her body standing up.

"Look, Ms. Harding, please sit down."

"Where's the bathroom?"

"Ms. Harding."

"I'm gonna be sick," she said. "Do you want me to get sick in here?"

At this, Sprague finally stood up and opened the door, pointed down the hall. Chloe was moving at a near sprint now, and when she finally got to the bathroom stall, vomited twice very quickly. She could feel the room spinning, could hear herself crying, and though she'd eventually catch her bearings, eventually collect herself, she understood at that moment, as she stood there above the bowl, that she was done talking to Detective Sprague, that she was done talking to anyone at all for that matter, not without a lawyer.

3

WHAT THEY NEVER talked about afterward, even in the days that followed, even as the world around them seemed to fall apart, what they
never talked about was the guilt they both felt. The guilt they felt for
what had happened. The remorse they felt for the boy who had once
tormented Raja, the boy who had humiliated his family, the boy who had
caused him endless pain, the boy who they had both hated. It was impossible now to feel anything even close to hatred for him. It was impossible
now to feel anything but a deep, profound numbness, a sobering regret.
Still, it wasn't exactly sadness. Sadness was harder to muster. Sadness
would come later. What she felt now, more than anything else, was simply remorse. The boy had a family, after all. He had friends. He was planning to major in French. He was planning to be a teacher. These were
things that all came out in the school newspaper afterward, in the same
article that implicated Chloe and Raja and Seung in the "crime." These
were also things that would be brought up later, when Chloe was called
before the Student Judiciary Council and forced to defend herself. Did she
know that Tyler Beckwith had volunteered at a homeless shelter in high
school? they wanted to know. Did she know that he had been a National
Merit Scholar and a star lacrosse player? The picture they painted of him
was so angelic, so sublime, that she almost wanted to correct them at
times, almost wanted to remind them of the signs that he had written, of
the noose that he had hung on Raja's door, of the way that he had slashed
his tires. But she never did. Her own guilt was so profound that all she
could do was sit there and nod. Apologize. Take her licks. In the end, they
decided that since her involvement was only tangential at best she would
not be formally expelled. Instead, she would be put on temporary proba-

tion, suspended for a semester, then reassessed the following fall. At the time, the sentence seemed surprisingly harsh.

As for Raja and Seung, they were immediately expelled and handed over to the Stratham Police Department. This was now a criminal matter and not something that Stratham College wanted to touch. In fact, they seemed to go out of their way to keep the story under wraps, to keep it out of the local papers and away from the national media. They downplayed its severity to outsiders, then played it up on campus. They were "very concerned" they had written in a campus-wide e-mail the following week. They were "very concerned" and "very troubled" by what had happened. They were doing everything they could to resolve this situation in a "satisfactory" way.

During this whole time Raja was living in a motel room near campus. He was forced to stick around until the investigation was over, but was no longer allowed on the campus "grounds." In the evenings, before his parents came up to join him, Chloe would visit him there, and they would order pizza or Chinese take-out and talk. Raja was always reassuring, always optimistic, never depressed, but still, she could tell he felt responsible for what had happened, that he was carrying a burden of guilt far greater than hers. He never came out and said it, but she could tell by the way he talked about Tyler, by the way he gave her nightly updates on his progress, that he was deeply troubled by it, that he blamed himself, and that the severity of the accident had devastated him.

They talked surprisingly little about the case, however. Nor did they talk about Seung, who was now staying in a much nicer hotel on the other side of campus and whose parents had hired a high-powered attorney to defend him. For all of his talk about repression and marginalization, Seung had come from considerable means, it turned out, had grown up in a wealthy suburb of Connecticut, and had gone to a fancy private school. All things he had kept hidden from Raja and Chloe.

Still, his unconscionable betrayal of Raja was not something that Raja could forgive, nor understand, and it was not something he ever wanted to talk about. The closest he even came to mentioning it was the night after Chloe was sentenced by the Student Judiciary Council, the same night that Richard, back in Houston, had informed her that her father had finally moved out. The combination of these two events mixed with everything else that was happening at the time had sent her into such an abrupt tailspin that by the time she made it over to Raja's motel room she was already in tears. He had taken her inside, poured her a glass of beer, then sat down next to her and listened to her as she told him about what had happened that day. Surprisingly, he didn't seem as upset as she had been by her suspension. Under the circumstances, he said, it was actually not that bad. In fact, she could have gotten a lot worse. If anything, he felt the Student Judiciary Council had been surprisingly lenient to her. She nodded and considered this. He always had a way of relaxing her, of putting things in perspective. And besides, with what he was going through right now, with what he was facing, it seemed pretty absurd to complain. Still, she couldn't get past the fact that none of this would have happened had Seung not implicated her, had he not told the police. Sure, there was a witness who had seen her leaving the dorm, but there was no other way of linking her to the actual incident without Seung's testimony. And now they were telling her that she might be facing conspiracy charges if Tyler Beckwith didn't recover, if he died, conspiracy charges simply for being there, conspiracy charges that could result in jail time, not to mention a criminal record. It made her sick just to think about it.

"Don't you ever get angry at him?" she asked, swirling her beer, "for what he did? For what he told them?"

Raja shrugged. "It would have come out anyway," he said.

"Maybe," she said. "But he didn't have to tell them everything. I mean, he didn't have to mention the cricket bat, for example."

Raja looked away then, and she could see that the topic was making him uncomfortable, but she could also see something else, a shifting in his eyes that made her realize that she might not know everything, that there might be more to this story than he was willing to admit. And that's when she asked him point-blank for the first time what she'd always wanted to ask him, what she'd always been too afraid to ask. She asked him then whether it had actually been him who hit Tyler.

He looked at her for a long time and then finally said yes, very quietly.

"I don't believe you."

"Then, no."

She looked at him. "Which is it?"

"Whichever you want it to be."

"What's that supposed to mean?"

"Whatever you want it to mean."

She sat up. "Why aren't you answering the question?"

"Because I don't think you're asking a question and because the answer to that question is totally irrelevant anyway."

"Why?"

"Because in the state of Massachusetts it doesn't matter. In the state of Massachusetts it doesn't matter who did what. Just the fact that I was there is guilt enough."

"Not if you're innocent," she said. "Not if you agreed to testify."

"I'm not testifying."

"Why not?"

But he didn't answer her.

"If you didn't do it, Raj, then you need to testify."

He looked at her earnestly then. "I never said I didn't do it."

So what had happened? A part of her felt like she'd never know. She'd never know for sure. And a part of her didn't want to know. If it had been Raja, would that change how she felt about him? Would she no longer feel as safe in his presence? Would she no longer trust him? Wasn't it easier just to believe it wasn't him? Wasn't it easier just to believe that it had all been an accident?

Sometimes, late at night, she'd try to reconstruct it in her mind from what she knew. She'd picture the three of them leaving his dorm room that night, moving swiftly across the quad, through the snow-covered grass, their faces hidden beneath baseball caps, their eyes shielded from the wind. She'd remember the sound of snow crunching beneath their feet, the bite of the wind against her cheeks. She'd remember Seung walking far ahead of them, holding a cricket bat in his hand, a cricket bat that he had found in Raja's closet, and Raja a few yards behind, and then her, right on Raja's heels, her coat pockets filled with two cans of shaving cream. She'd remember wanting to say something to him then, wanting to talk to him, but it was too cold to talk, too cold to do anything but duck her head and walk.

Earlier, Seung had looked up Tyler's dorm room in the campus directory, had written it down on the palm of his hand, and as they approached his dorm, she remembered Seung checking his palm again, then motioning for them to stop. He was standing beneath a lamppost, steam rising from his head, his eyes looking up.

They gathered beneath an awning on the side of the dorm, then

Seung said something about Chloe following them, waiting until they entered, then coming in a few minutes later herself with the shaving cream. She remembered Raja looking down at his feet, saying nothing. She remembered trying to catch his eyes, trying to touch his arm, but he was somewhere else now, and before she knew it they were moving inside, then up the stairwell, then down the hallway of Tyler's floor.

Nobody saw them. Nobody saw them enter the stairwell, and nobody saw them walk down the hall. Nobody had even seen them earlier as they'd walked across the quad. Later, this would seem like an amazing stroke of good fortune, but at that moment she remembered only feeling numb. Her mind had checked out. She was no longer a part of herself. Raja was looking around nervously. He was saying that they should stop, that they should go back, that this was crazy. He was saying that they'd come to regret this later.

This is nuts, he'd said at one point, and then she remembered him grabbing Seung's arm and Seung pushing him back. They were standing outside the door now, everything quiet.

Seung gave Raja a look, a look that said *Don't screw this up,* then he put his finger to his lips and motioned for Chloe to move down the hallway away from the door. Then he lifted his bat.

A moment later, Raja looked at her, she remembered, looked at her as if to say he was sorry, then he turned back to Seung and nodded.

What happened after that was a blur. It all happened so quickly that she could barely process it. She remembered seeing Seung knock and then, a few seconds later, seeing the door crack open. The room inside was dark, she could see that much, but she could only see a tiny slice of Tyler Beckwith's face, his nose and chin, his profile, before Seung pushed him forward, and then Raja followed, pushing Tyler Beckwith back into his room. She heard Tyler say, *What the fuck?* Then the door slammed shut behind them, and the hallway was quiet. For a good thirty seconds at least, it was perfectly still. For a good thirty seconds, before the screaming started, before Chloe ran, before everything in their lives would forever change, for a good thirty seconds the world was perfectly still.

Part Six

I

IT SEEMED STRANGE to think about now, but in the beginning she had liked so many things about him. She had liked the way he smelled, the way he touched her, the way he exuded a certain confidence in everything he did. And she had liked the way that he had basically taken control of their lives from the start, the way that he had covered every bill, paid for every tab. He seemed so much older than her, so much more worldly and experienced, and it made her feel safe, in retrospect, to be around him. It made her feel safe to know that he owned a house, that he had a steady job, that he had money saved up in the bank. It made her feel safe to know that he would always keep their refrigerator stocked with food and their cabinets stocked with booze, that he would always have enough money to take her on vacations, and that he wanted to have kids, too, like she did, and that he would do whatever he had to to provide for those kids.

And yet somewhere along the way, things had changed, though it was hard for her to say now when this was. Was it after Richard was born? After Chloe? For so many years her life had been consumed by the children, by their needs, by the responsibility she felt to take care of them, and she was even surprised, at times, by how easily she had come to accept this, how easily she had fallen into this role. While her friends were still in college, she was nursing Richard, and by the time these same friends had entered graduate school, or law school, or started working, she was already pregnant with Chloe. It seemed that the strange uncertain terrain of her early twenties was something she had missed. She had not had to contend with finding a job, or discovering who she was, or negotiating the single dating scene. She had had Elson and the security that came along with being married to a man who was forever moving upward.

Sometimes her friends would come to visit her on their winter breaks, and as they sat over beers on the back veranda, overlooking the pool, they would talk about their failed relationships, their growing credit card debt, their student loans, all the while marveling at her house, her pool, her children, at how together she seemed, how grown up. And yet, whenever they left the house, she'd feel an emptiness filling her up, as if she'd somehow been left behind, cheated out of a life she hadn't thought she'd wanted until she'd realized it was lost.

Meanwhile, the women she did hang out with on a regular basis were all friends of Elson's, wives of his colleagues and friends, all older women who seemed to take pity on her, who spoke to her like older sisters or mothers, giving her advice on where to find the best bargains on clothes for her children or what to do if Richard was sick or who to call if Chloe was acting out. They spouted off names and addresses, gave her business cards, but never asked her once about herself or what she wanted. These were all women who had long ago resigned themselves to their marital roles, who somehow, like Cadence herself, had lost themselves in the lifelong pursuits of their husbands.

And, of course, it had never occurred to Elson to ask her if she was happy. If he had, she wonders even now what she would have said. Probably nothing. Or maybe she would have told him the truth. Maybe she would have told him that at night, after he'd fallen asleep, she wandered around the house aimlessly for hours on end, trying to fight back the anxious thoughts that crept into her head, thoughts of Richard and Chloe and what type of children they would become, what type of adults they'd turn into, whether they'd end up resenting her or whether they'd inherit her propensity toward sadness or whether they'd end up being poisoned by the residue of a troubled marriage. She had long ago convinced herself that she had ruined them, that by allowing them to live together under this roof she had somehow stunted their growth, their emotional growth, and though they were children, and relatively good children at that, she knew that they must have somehow sensed the growing distance between her and Elson and internalized it, stored it away in the darkest recesses of their minds. Just as she had been corrupted by her own parents' marriage, they would be corrupted by hers, doomed to repeat her own mistakes, doomed to reinvent their own neuroses, doomed to live a life spent searching for a better model, a better paradigm, of love.

She never expressed any of these thoughts to Elson, however, and had he ever asked, she probably wouldn't have even then. Instead, she spent her days paging through clothes catalogs and books on parenting, researching summer camps for Richard, hosting Brownie-troop meetings for Chloe. She took up running on the weekends, joined a bridge group in the winter of Richard's seventh year, hosted parties for Elson and his colleagues, organized dinners and luncheons for their wives. She learned how to do Pilates, how to macramé, how to plant a sustainable eco-friendly garden. She bought the children the clothes they wanted, took Richard to swim practice, Chloe to ballet. She made sure to pay the bills on time, made sure to be home whenever the pool guy showed up to clean, made sure to keep the air-conditioning unit filled at all times with fresh filters.

But throughout it all, she never felt happy, and with each passing day it seemed that her sense of regret only increased. She thought a lot about college and how she'd never finished. She thought about Elson and how he was only the third man she'd ever slept with and how unfortunate that was. And she thought, of course, about her children and how despite their good grades they seemed to be falling behind their classmates in terms of their emotional development.

And then, for many years, she'd simply stopped questioning these things. She engaged instead in a kind of denial, an elaborate charade, a game of make-believe that Elson and the children had decided to participate in as well. The family meals on Sunday nights, the yearly trips down to Galveston, the daily rituals of sitting in front of the TV and watching the news together. They had grown up inside this routine, had even begun to enjoy it, to take comfort in it, and as long as nobody there decided to break the spell, as long as nobody there decided to point out the simple fact that none of it was real, then it all seemed to work just fine for all of them. Richard and Chloe were in middle school by then and still too young to drive, and so for a while there they had had these years, these precious years when the children were now old enough to talk to them as adults and yet still young enough to be controlled. It was a funny time, she'd realize later, a time that she thought about with both fondness and regret.

It was also during this time that she'd first begun to have thoughts of cheating on Elson, though she'd never mentioned this to anyone, not to Peterson and certainly not to Cheryl. She had never even mentioned it to the men themselves, the men who had made their interest in her clear. One was a colleague of Elson's from Sullivan & Gordon; another was a man who she had met in her Thursday-night book group. And then there was David Stine, a man who she had sat next to during Chloe's ballet recitals for several years, a single parent whose daughter was in middle school with Chloe and who had asked her out to lunch on several occasions. She had never actually done anything with David, though she'd thought about him often, and once, after a particularly bad fight with Elson, she had called him up out of the blue and asked him to meet her for a drink. David had agreed, but halfway to the bar, she had chickened out and turned around. A month later, she had found out from a friend that David Stine had been offered a job in Phoenix and never heard from him again.

Later, when they were going through the divorce proceedings, she had taken some pride in the fact that she had never acted on any of her impulses, that she had never technically been unfaithful to Elson, though she had also wondered at times whether this was actually true. I mean, if you thought about cheating, if you actually fantasized about being with another person, then wasn't that in itself a kind of betrayal? As for Elson, she had always assumed that there'd been other women, though she'd never actually had proof of his indiscretions. It was possible that he'd been faithful to her, too, though the truth was she'd never pursued the matter deeply, had never really wanted to know what she might discover if she scratched beneath the surface of his life. And besides, at that point, Elson had had another mistress anyway, his job, and for a long time she had considered this his greatest infidelity. The long hours he poured into projects, the weekends he spent on site, the lengthy trips he took for out-of-town projects. His heart seemed to be divided three ways, between his children, his job, and her, and for many years she had always felt that, of the three, she had been given the smallest slice, a tiny sliver that he had given to her more out of a sense of duty, or nostalgia, than anything else. And yet she still found herself admiring him at times, still took a certain pride in the fact that he was her husband and that they had managed to keep things together for all these years.

· · ·

Still, it wasn't until later, after the kids had gone off to college and she and Elson were left alone in the house, that she actually began to think about divorcing him. It seemed strange to her now, in retrospect, that she hadn't thought about it earlier, that it had taken the kids' leaving for it to even occur to her. And it wasn't something that had occurred to her all at once, in some grand epiphany. It was something that had snuck up on her gradually, like a secret, during that first semester Chloe was away. She remembered Elson coming home from work one night and sitting across from her at the kitchen table, and she remembered looking at him then as she poured herself some wine and thinking, *I don't love you anymore, I can honestly say I don't love you anymore,* and that's when she'd brought it up for the first time, just kind of mentioned it casually, like she was presenting her latest idea for their next vacation. *What if we just take a break,* she had asked, *some time apart,* and that's when Elson had stood up and walked out of the room and later driven off in his car to meet Dave Millhauser. When he got home later that night, she apologized and said that she was simply under a lot of stress right now and didn't mean it, but the question she had posed remained there, lingering between them, and over the next several months she would pose it again on several occasions, when they were driving home from a party one night, when they were sitting over breakfast one morning, when they were lying out by the pool one afternoon sipping drinks. And each time she posed it, Elson would react the same way. He'd stare at her for a long time and then retreat into himself, until finally one night during the fall of Chloe's sophomore year he had brought it up himself. He had been thinking about it for a long time, he said, and he agreed. There was no animosity in his voice at the time, only sadness, and it was then that she first began to have her own doubts. They were sitting out by the pool late at night, drinking coffee and reading their respective books, and he had just looked at her then and said that all he really wanted was to make her happy, and if getting divorced would make her happy, then that's what he wanted. Later, there would be ugliness, later there would be painful and contentious disputes over ownership and money, the division of assets, the allocation of funds, and so forth, but at that moment there was simply a strange civility between them, something almost sweet. "I've tried the best I could," Elson had said, standing up and looking at her then, "and apparently I've failed."

And for a long time she would tell herself that he had failed, that they both had, and yet now, as she walks across her bedroom, her back to Elson, who lies supine on the bed, his naked back a clear reminder of her latest mistake, she wonders if she should have tried a little harder, if they both should have, if she should have maybe given him a little more slack or tried a little harder to forgive him. All she knows now is that she has somehow, for better or worse, let him back in. At some point between the moment he showed up at her door tonight, the moment he showed up in a drunken stupor, holding out a bottle of wine like a peace offering, the moment he pulled her into his arms and embraced her, at some point between that moment and the moment she decided to kiss him, she had let him back in.

It is this that she's thinking about as she puts on her T-shirt and panties and walks to the bathroom. Outside the house, the neighborhood is quiet and dark, the only sound coming from a distant sprinkler system on somebody's lawn. She stands at the open window in the bathroom and presses her face against the screen, breathes in the crisp night air, her mind still spinning from the sobering realization that she has just added yet another major problem to her life. After a moment, she goes to the pantry and pulls out the small bag of marijuana that she had confiscated from Richard's room earlier that day. She fishes out the rolling paper, then starts to roll a joint, staring at her face in the mirror as she does this. The bathroom mirror is warmly lit, a soft amber light that makes her face look younger, maybe ten or fifteen years younger, and as she stares at her face, she thinks about Richard and how she had admonished him earlier that day about the dangers of doing drugs and how he had simply stood there, staring at her, as if to say, *Are you really going to lecture me about bad behavior?*

He had come home early that morning, clearly distressed about something that had happened, and he had spent almost the entire day lying on his bed, reading comic books. He used to get this way back in high school whenever he failed a test or whenever he lost a swimming meet. He would always retreat to the world of his youth, to the cluttered shelves of comic books and graphic novels that had once provided him such comfort. But that day it had struck her as strange, even sad, that he would do this, a grown man hiding away in his room, reading comic books. She had tried on several occasions to get him to talk to her, but he wouldn't, and when she'd later invited him to come downstairs and have a drink with her, he'd told her he had other plans. This distance that had grown between them in the past year, this strange, ineluctable wall, this intransigent barrier, it seemed to have come from somewhere deep within him, a place she couldn't name. He had never rebelled back in high school, had always been the perfect model of civility and grace, and yet now, lately, he seemed to have become someone else, another person. She couldn't describe it, couldn't put a finger on it, but it was there, and it was very real. Sometimes it struck her as sad that this had happened, and often she missed their closeness, their long conversations, the way he used to confide in her about everything, the way she used to go to his swimming meets back in high school, and the way he used to always wave to her right before his race, and the way that afterward they would always go out to dinner together, just the two of them, and talk for hours on end. Back then, back in high school, he had come out to her long before he had ever come out to his friends, or even to Chloe. For a long time it had only been she and Chloe who knew, and they had talked about it a lot, the three of them, over dinner, while Elson was off on a project or staying late at work. She had almost wanted to remind him of that this evening as he came down from his room, freshly showered and off to a party, but instead, she had brought up the pot and held it up before him, held it up like a cruel reminder of his recent failures, and he had simply looked at her and then shrugged and walked out the door.

Now, pressing the joint to her lips and lighting it, she feels her own hypocrisy, feels the sudden weight of her own admonitions. They had brought up their children in a world of excess, after all, in a world of wild parties and late-night drinking, and so why should she be surprised that they had embraced this world themselves? She sits down now on the toilet and stares out the window, fans the smoke in that direction. She thinks of Elson asleep in the other room, oblivious to her indiscretions, sleeping happily in her bed. Shortly after Richard had left for his party, Elson had shown up with his wine, and though she had worried about Richard returning, she had let him in anyway. To say that she was thinking at all at that moment would be a lie. What had happened between them had happened out of instinct and out of recklessness and out of fear. It didn't mean a thing that she had kissed him in the kitchen or that she had led him up to her room and allowed him to undress her. And it didn't mean a thing, now, that he was lying in her bed, or that she was hiding away in the bathroom, smoking her son's pot. If you could account for human behavior with simple explanations, a man like Peterson would be out of a job, and yet there was no explanation for what she was doing now, for the way she had allowed her daughter's absence to turn her into the type of person who hid away in bathrooms at three in the morning, doing drugs.

Outside the door, she can hear movement now, the sound of footsteps on the floor, a drawer being opened, then shut. She drops the joint between her knees, then flushes, then stands up and turns on the shower fan, pushing the smoke upward toward the vent, then outward toward the open window. A moment later, she hears her name being called, Elson's groggy voice saying something about the heat and whether or not she had turned it on. Then there's knocking at the bathroom door, a soft, hesitant knock, and this time she answers.

"Just give me a minute," she says, feeling suddenly panicked.

There's a long silence, then Elson says, "I smell pot."

"What?"

"Are you smoking pot in there?"

She moves toward the window and makes another dramatic motion with her arms, fanning the smoke and feeling suddenly caught. She doesn't answer.

"Cadence."

"Just give me a second."

"Jesus Christ, Cadence. What the hell are you doing in there?"

Realizing now that she's caught, she doesn't answer. She thinks of telling him to go away, to go back home, but she doesn't. Instead, she just tells him to go back to bed and that she'll join him in a second.

There's another long silence, then Elson says, almost gently, "Are you okay?"

"What?"

"Are you okay?"

"What do you mean?"

"Our daughter's gone missing, Cadence, and you're sitting in the bathroom smoking pot, so what I'm wondering is whether or not you're okay."

There's no scorn in his voice now, no disapproval, just genuine concern. She thinks of answering him honestly, but doesn't.

"Why don't you just open up the door," he says. "Okay? Just open it up and we can talk."

But when she looks at the door, it seems at that moment too far a distance to go. The ramifications of opening that door are simply too great, and so she just sits there, staring at the wall.

Finally, she says, "Can I ask you a question?"

"Of course."

"Why did you come here tonight?"

"What do you mean?"

"I mean, of all the places you could have gone tonight, why did you come here?"

"Because I missed you," he says, "because I wanted to be with you."

"That's not the truth, Elson," she says. "Please. Just tell me the truth. This is important, okay. Why did you come here tonight, honestly?"

There's another long pause, and then he says, very softly, "I don't know."

IT IS AN ATYPICALLY QUIET NIGHT at Beto's. At the far end of the blue-lit pool, three boys float languidly on their backs, like corpses, and above him he can hear the gentle slapping of palm fronds in the wind. Someone is playing an early eighties dance mix in the cabana house, and there is the occasional sound of laughter and applause. He leans back drunkenly on his small chaise longue chair at the edge of the pool and tries to avert his eyes from the man who has been talking to him for the past half hour. High on something, this man is telling him about his failed acting career, about how he should have never left L.A., about all of the major roles he'd almost had. He lists off the names of various actors and movie directors that Richard has never heard of, talks about parties at their houses, lunches with their agents, the endless series of broken promises and duplicitous dealings. But still, the man says, he should have never left L.A. It had been a mistake. He realizes that now. But wasn't that the thing about life, the cruel irony of it? Once you made a mistake, you couldn't take it back, and Richard nods, thinking suddenly of the man he'd met at the Hyatt Hotel, the only significant thing in his life he'd ever regretted.

Ever since it happened, ever since the morning before when he'd woken to the sound of a maid at the door, asking to change the sheets, he'd been able to think of little else. The room had been empty when he awoke. No sign of the man, or his bags, not even a note by the bed. Just a crisp stack of hundred-dollar bills pinned beneath a glass. He'd stood up quickly and dressed, then grabbed the cash and opened the door for the maid. He hadn't even been able to look at her, hadn't even been able to meet her eyes, he was shaking so much.

Later, on his drive over to Brandon's, he had tried to reconstruct it in his mind from what he remembered, had tried to replay it like a dream, but what he saw was only himself beneath the man's naked body, crying. He remembered earlier that night their awkward conversation at the bar, a strange attempt at civility, and how he'd lied about just about everything, how he'd told the man that his name was James, that he had grown up in New York, and that he was currently studying internal medicine at Rice. He had told him that he was an only child, that both of his parents were dead, and that he was only doing this to repay a late tuition bill. About the only thing he'd told the man that was true was the fact that he'd never done this before, but the man seemed neither surprised nor excited to learn this.

Later, when they got up to the room, the man had taken off his wedding ring and placed it on the dresser; then he'd turned on a sports station and watched the tail end of a college basketball game while Richard had sat beside him on the bed, drinking scotch. The man had said very little, and Richard had wondered at one point whether this was all he'd have to do, just sit here with the man and drink scotch and watch a basketball game. At one point the man had even drifted off, had fallen sound asleep for almost half an hour, and Richard had felt himself relaxing, too, had even turned off the light and fallen asleep himself. But then at some point later—he couldn't remember—he had been awoken by the sound of the man talking in his ear, yanking off his jeans, and then pushing himself on top of him. He'd felt the man's callused palms on his face, and then his mouth, as he'd tried to stop him from crying. *Shut the fuck up!* the man had said at one point, and Richard had then bitten the inside of his cheek so hard that he could taste the bitter tinge of blood in his mouth.

Afterward, the man had taken a shower and then left the room, saying he needed a smoke. Richard had thought about leaving then, too, of just taking off, but that wasn't part of the deal. If he wanted the money, then he'd have to spend the night, and so he'd pulled out the scotch and continued to drink, drinking to the point that he couldn't remember anything else, not a single thing, from the rest of the night.

Now, standing up from his chair, he promises the man sitting beside him that he'll be back in a minute, then starts around the side of the pool and wanders back toward the house. The back patio of Beto's house is covered with empty wine bottles and hors d'oeuvres trays, the leftover debris from an early afternoon party, it seems. On the outside edge of the sliding glass door is a sign that reads WATCH OUT! GLASS! in big bold letters, and as he opens the door he finds the kitchen filled with strangers, faces he vaguely remembers from other parties, people who he may have once spoken to but whose names he no longer recalls.

He fixes himself a gin-n-tonic, then starts down the hallway toward the library—the "book room," as Beto calls it—a large, dimly lit room filled with leather furniture and antique bookshelves and Persian rugs that smell at all times of smoke. Here, slumped against the leather couch in the corner, he finds Brandon, paging through a book, a cigarette dangling from his mouth. He looks blitzed.

"You drunk?" Brandon asks.

"On my way," Richard says, nodding at his glass.

Brandon smiles, then sits up on the floor.

"Pretty quiet round here tonight, don't you think?"

"Yeah." Brandon nods. "Has been all week. You know, ever since that girl cracked her head open."

Richards nods. "That's right," he says, suddenly remembering the horrific scene. "Any word about that?"

"What do you mean?"

"You know, about what happened to her."

Brandon looks at him, then shakes his head and ashes his cigarette. "Not that I've heard."

And suddenly this strikes Richard as sad, even reprehensible, that no one has even bothered to check up on the girl, that nobody even cares. For all they know she could have died on her way to the hospital that night or be dead right now, buried six feet under the ground.

"So let me ask you a question," Brandon says, leaning forward now. "How many of these books do you think are real?" He motions around the room at the enormous bookshelves along the walls.

"How many?"

"Yeah, how many."

"I don't know." Richard shrugs. "I kind of assumed all of them were."

"All of them?" Brandon laughs. "Right. Try none."

"None?"

Brandon stands up then and walks over to one of the bookshelves and then slides out an entire row of books like a drawer. "They're all hollow," he says, tapping the covers. "Can you believe that shit? It's all for decoration."

Richard looks at him and shrugs. "Well, I never took Beto for much of a reader, you know."

Brandon shakes his head and sits back down. "I know, man, but shit, why even bother to have a library if you're not going to have any books in it?"

Richard shrugs again and puts down his drink, lights a cigarette.

"So you still feeling freaked out?" Brandon asks after a moment.

"Who told you I was freaked out?"

"Nobody," Brandon says. "I can just tell."

"I don't want to talk about it," Richard says and looks away.

"You know, it's totally normal," he says.

"Normal?"

"To feel freaked out at first. You should have seen me the first time I did it. I couldn't sleep for like a week."

"Well, there's not going to be a second time," Richard says.

"That's what I thought, too, but then after a while, you know, it just kind of starts to feel normal, you know, kind of like sliding your punch card in at work."

Richard stares at him and suddenly feels the need to leave, to go back to the kitchen and pour himself another drink. This isn't a conversation he wants to be having right now.

"Can we talk about something else?" he says finally.

Brandon stares at him for a moment, then shrugs. "Sure," he says. "Whatever." He steadies his glass. "What do you want to talk about?"

"I want to know where you took them," he says finally, sitting down.

"Who?"

"My sister and Raja."

"I took them down to the warehouse district," he says, "like I told you."

"I know," he says, "but where exactly?"

Brandon throws up his arms. "Fuck if I know, man. I'd never been there before. Like I said, it seemed like they were just meeting a couple guys down there, and then they were probably going somewhere else."

Richard nods and suddenly feels his deepest suspicions confirmed. He thinks of the passport he picked up for his sister that morning and where she might be now. Maybe halfway down to Mexico or possibly on her way to Canada. It was impossible to say. All he knows now is that he has played a part in it, that he is now responsible, that he is now a complicit party. And he wonders then how he'll possibly explain this to his parents or to the authorities, when they ask, what he'll tell them.

"Why?" Brandon asks after a moment. "You have some idea where they might have gone?"

Richard looks at him and almost says something before he finally thinks better of it. "No," he says calmly, picking up his glass and starting back toward the kitchen. "No idea."

At the start of the night his goal had been to get obliterated, to numb himself to the point that any memory of the man who had assaulted him the night before would be eviscerated from his mind, and after several gin-n-tonics, and another several beers, he feels fairly close to attaining this goal. He is lying now in Beto's bed, all alone, no trace of Brandon in sight, no trace of anyone for that matter, feeling more or less completely trashed. In the morning, he knows, he'll have to make good on his promise to Michelson. He'll have to work on his application. He'll have to put together his transcripts. He'll have to write out a statement of purpose. He'll have to get all of these things together and in the mail by five, and yet at this moment he can think of nothing more disheartening than the idea of sitting in a room full of poets, listening to someone talk about this aesthetic or that, about line breaks and endjambs, knowing all the while that he doesn't belong there, that he's an impostor, that he's not the type of person who deserves this opportunity, but rather the type of person who sells his body off to perfect strangers at three in the morning in some luxury suite at the back of the Hyatt Hotel.

It was like a large dark cloud that had come over him, and yet what seems strange to him now, what bothers him the most, is not the fact that he did it, but the fact that he'd taken the money. Had he just gone home and left the cash, he could have justified it to himself later, could have passed it off as just another drunken blunder, an unfortunate lapse in judgment, a one-night stand that had gone terribly wrong, but when he'd seen that money on the table, he hadn't hesitated for a second. He had grabbed it quickly and then taken off, not realizing until much later that he had just taken payment for being assaulted, that he had just given the man who had assaulted him permission to do what he had done.

He wonders now where the man might be, what he might be doing, pictures him coming home to his wife and children, placing a kiss on their cheeks, then settling down for a family meal. He pictures him sitting in front of his TV, watching another basketball game, totally oblivious to what he's done. And then he thinks about his own father and how oblivious he'd been during his own childhood, how unaware he'd been of his mother's unhappiness, how wrapped up he'd been in his sports games and his work, and of course how surprised he'd been when Richard finally came out. Just as he'd been surprised when his wife finally left him. What was wrong with these men's minds? he wonders. What prevented them from seeing the pain that they caused?

Thinking about this now, he feels suddenly disturbed, and as he opens his eyes and begins to sit up, he notices a person sitting across from him on the other side of the room, a vague silhouette, staring back at him. Startled, it takes him a moment to make out the person's face, and then he remembers: it's the girl from the week before, the girl he smoked pot with. Angel. She is backlit, sitting mostly in the shadows, smoking a cigarette and holding up a magazine between her knees.

"Hey," he says, sitting up. "How long have you been there?"

She looks at him and smiles. "I don't know," she says. "Maybe an hour."

"An hour?"

"Yep. Just wanted to make sure you didn't pass out, or, you know, like die from alcohol poisoning or something."

He looks at her. "What have I been doing?"

"What have you been doing?" She laughs. "Nothing. Just lying there."

"Just lying here for an hour?"

"Yeah," she says. "Pretty much. Maybe longer."

"What time is it?"

She shrugs. "No idea. Maybe three or four in the morning."

He looks out the window. The sky in the distance is lightening along the horizon, a cool, pale magenta.

"Anyway," she says, "my job here is done, so I'm going to go now, okay? And you probably should, too. By the way, do you need a ride or something?"

He shakes his head. "How old are you?"

"Huh?"

"How old are you?"

"Why?"

"I'm just curious."

"I'm seventeen."

"You're lying."

"Okay," she says. "I'm sixteen, but I'll be seventeen next fall."

"And your parents let you stay out like this?"

She looks out the window, but doesn't answer, and he can suddenly see that her parents are a touchy subject.

"Look," he says. "Can you do me a favor?"

She looks at him.

"Can you just come over here and lie next to me?"

"Lie next to you?"

"Yeah, just for like a couple minutes."

She looks at him suspiciously, then finally stands up. And he doesn't know why he asks her this, or what it means, but as she comes over and joins him on the bed and puts her arm around him, he feels for a moment strangely comforted, feels the layers of guilt and shame falling off.

"Is everything okay?" she asks finally, rubbing his chest.

He looks at her for a moment, then closes his eyes. He wants to disappear at this moment, wants to fade away into the night forever, or else to stay here in her arms forever, he doesn't know which. Finally, he says, "Can I ask you something?"

"Of course."

He pauses, props himself on an elbow. "Have you ever felt like you've lost a part of yourself because of something you've done?"

"What do you mean?"

"You know, because of like a decision you've made?"

"All the time."

He looks at her. "And how do you deal with it?"

"Deal with what?"

"I mean how do you get it back, that part of yourself you've lost?"

"You don't," she says, looking out the window.

"You don't?"

"No," she says. "You don't. You just have to figure out a way to live with it."

"And what if you can't?"

"Then you come here," she says, smiling. "To Beto's. You come here and you get shitfaced so you don't have to think about it anymore."

He stares at her.

"I mean, do you honestly believe that any of the people who come here on a nightly basis are here because they actually want to be?"

He leans back on the bed, but doesn't answer, suddenly feeling the sadness of this place. Then he thinks again of the last time he was here, in this room, the gruesome scene below them, the blood floating around in the pool, the girl's pale face.

"Remember the last time we were here?" he hears himself saying now. "That girl who cracked her head open on the side of the pool?"

Angel looks at him, but doesn't answer.

"Did you ever find out what happened to her?"

"What happened to her?"

"Yeah."

Angel shakes her head. "No. Why?"

"I don't know," he says. "I'd just really like to know whether she's alive or not."

She looks at him now with concern. "Are you sure everything's okay?"

"I don't know," he says, and then closes his eyes. "I don't think so."

"You don't think so?"

"I think I may have done something really messed up."

She looks at him. "To yourself or to someone else?"

"Both."

"Do you want to talk about it?"

"No." He shakes his head. "I don't think so." Then he puts his arm around her. "But I would like you to stay with me here a little longer. Do you think you can do that?"

She nestles her face in his neck and holds him tightly. "Yeah," she says, moving closer. "I can do that."

"BECAUSE YOU HELD MY HEAD."

"What?"

"That night we met. It was because you held my head while I got sick. No one had ever done that for me before. That's how I knew."

She is sitting across from him at a small picnic table outside an outdoor icehouse in south San Antonio, the loud pulse of Tejano music filling the air, the smell of fish tacos and fried tortillas floating down to them from the neighboring food stands. Teo is off with a group of men on the other side of the street, trying to track down the girl who was supposed to meet them here, the girl who is supposed to be accompanying them the rest of the way down. The air is slightly warmer here in San Antonio, slightly drier, and she can sense the pull of Mexico, the pull of the border, in the distance. She raises her beer to Raja and smiles, then takes a big sip and finishes it off, her fifth of the night.

"So, what was it for you?" she continues.

Raja smiles at her, then puts the sweating bottle of Negra Modelo to his lips.

"It wasn't just one thing," he says. "It was everything."

"For example?"

"Are you fishing for compliments or something?"

"No," she says. "I'm just curious."

He looks at her, smiles again, then pauses. "Well," he says, "for example, this." He motions around the bar. "The fact you're sitting here with me now, the fact you're doing this. I can't think of anyone else in my life who would do this for me."

"Not your parents?"

He laughs. "Are you kidding me? My parents? No way. Not my parents, not my friends. I mean just look at the way everyone reacted back at school. All concerned at first, and then as soon as the police got involved, it's like, nothing. Nada. Won't even look at me anymore."

Chloe looks at him plaintively, touches his hand. "And that still pisses you off?"

"Of course it does," he says, calming down now, speaking softly. "But I also understand. I mean, it's not what I would have done to one of my friends, but I can understand why they did it."

"And what about Seung?" she says. "Do you understand about that, too?"

He looks at her, something in his eyes darkening. "That's a different situation."

"Why?"

"It just is," he says.

"So you forgive him?"

"I didn't say that."

"But you're admitting he did it."

"Did what?"

"That he was the one who hurt Tyler."

"Why are you so hung up on that?"

"I'm not. I just don't understand why you won't at least tell me the truth. I mean, what difference could it possibly make now?"

He stares at her coldly, and she can suddenly see that she's ruined the moment. Ever since he'd come down here, they'd avoided the topic of Seung, and yet now, for some reason, she can't let it go.

"Look," he says finally. "Seung did what he thought was right, and I did what I thought was right. It's not for me to judge him. Whatever he might have told them, that's something he's going to have to live with for the rest of his life."

"So you're admitting that he lied to them."

"I'm saying that we were both there that night in the room, and in this way we're both guilty."

"But you didn't hurt Tyler."

"Like I said, I was there. Being there is guilt enough."

This is the closest he's ever come to actually acknowledging his own innocence, but she knows that no matter how hard she pushes she'll never get him to say the words.

She feels almost sick with frustration now, with his stubbornness, and yet at the same time relieved that he's finally confirmed, at least on some level, her deepest suspicions. How he could protect such an asshole like Seung, though, is beyond her.

"And do your parents know?" She looks at him. "Did you tell them the truth?"

He sips his beer. "It wouldn't have mattered what I told them," he says. "They would have believed I was innocent no matter what."

"And they weren't angry at you for protecting him?"

"I never said I was protecting him."

"Okay," she says. "Then they weren't angry at you for not talking?"

"At first," he says. "Yeah. At first, they were. But then they understood."

"I find that hard to believe."

"Why?"

"I just do."

"You don't understand my parents."

"Well," she says. "Do you think they understand now?"

He looks at her. "I don't think that's fair."

He picks up his beer again and sips it, staring out at the flowering cacti and the bright pastel houses that line the street. Finally, he turns back to her.

"My mother said, *Aap bhalaa toe jag bhalaa.* which means 'If you are noble, you will find the world noble.'"

She steadies her beer. "There's nothing noble about martyring yourself for a guy who's just sold you down the river."

"I'm not martyring myself," he says.

"No? Then what do you call it?"

"I don't call it anything," he says and sips his beer. "If I truly believed myself to be innocent, then I would protest, you're right, I'd testify against him, but I don't."

"You don't consider yourself to be innocent?"

"No."

"Because you were there."

"Yes," he says. "Because I was there."

On the other side of the icehouse, she can see a group of young Mexican girls in leather skirts dancing by the side of the bar, waving their beers at a group of boys in the distance. The boys wave back, thrust their hips dramatically, then laugh. She feels suddenly sick with the thought of going to Mexico, of running away from a situation that could have been so easily resolved, if he'd only told them the truth, if he'd only been honest. And she wants to say this to him now, wants to tell him that everything can be resolved right now, if they simply go back to Stratham and talk to the cops, explain it all in detail, the real story, but she also knows how it would look, how it would seem unlikely that a boy who had just run away from the law could now suddenly be innocent. And besides, she knows that Raja is resigned to his decision, regardless of the consequences. He's made up his mind, and once he made up his mind, it was nearly impossible to dissuade him from anything.

She looks over again at the boys in the distance, who are now approaching the girls who had been waving at them. They are laughing wildly and swigging their beers, and then a moment later there's a group of men who appear—perhaps older brothers of the girls or maybe uncles—from behind the icehouse. They come out from beneath the shadows and confront the boys, get up in their faces, and just like that, there's a scuffle, the sound of bottles breaking on the ground, someone yelling, and then the girls screaming. Pretty soon there's a circle forming around them, and someone is yelling to call the cops, a fight breaking out in full force right before them. Chloe looks over at Raja, but he is looking down, and then, before she knows it, there's a hand on her shoulder, and when she looks up, she sees Teo.

"Let's go," he says, looking first at her, then at Raja.

"Where?" she says.

But Teo doesn't answer. "Come on," he says, yanking her up now, forcing her to stand. "It's not safe here."

Earlier that night, on the long ride from Houston to San Antonio, as they sat there quietly in the back of the van, unable to see each other's faces, he had talked for the first time about the guilt he now felt for what had happened. He talked about Tyler Beckwith and what he had learned about his family, about how he hadn't come from money, as they'd assumed, but rather was born into a family of immigrants, just like him. How his parents had immigrated to the States from Northern Ireland when he was five and how he had grown up poor, moving around the country for most of his childhood while his father looked for work. Everything that Tyler had earned—his scholarship to prep school and later Stratham—he had earned on his own accord, by working hard and by trying to assimilate into the world of his privileged peers. Raja had learned all of this stuff by doing research, he said, by reading the various articles posted around the Internet and by reading the various testimonials on the website that had been set up for Tyler.

Still, Chloe said, it didn't justify what Tyler had done, it didn't exonerate him.

No, Raja had agreed, it didn't exonerate him, but it did mean something, didn't it? The fact that he had never taken the time to get to know Tyler, the fact that if he had, it might have all turned out differently.

"You don't know that," Chloe had said. "He may have never even acknowledged that he did it, you know. He may have denied the whole thing."

"That's true," Raja said. "But I guess we'll never know, will we?"

And for a long time after that, he said nothing, and for the rest of the ride down to San Antonio, they had simply sat there, holding each other, bracing themselves against the threat of a falling box or a tumbling crate every time the tires of the truck hit a bump.

Even at that moment, however, the thought of going to Mexico had still seemed exciting to her, the thought of making a life for themselves down there, the thought of everything that they didn't know that still lay before them. Her entire life, it seemed, she had always known the next step, had always known where she would end up in a couple of months, or a couple of years, but now it all seemed so elusive, so vague, so undetermined. It wasn't until they had arrived in San Antonio, however, that she'd actually begun to have some second thoughts about it, some doubts. And yet, the more uncertain she became, the more resolute Raja appeared, the more determined.

"I can tell that you're scared," he'd said to her earlier as they'd walked from the truck to the icehouse.

"I'm not scared."

"Yes, you are," he'd said. "But that's fine. It's natural."

She looked at him. "And you're not?"

"I don't know," he'd said, and shrugged, and she could see then that all of the worry had vanished from his face, all of the anxiety she'd noticed earlier, when they'd first left Houston. "I had a thought on the way down," he continued abstractly. "I feel like I see things a lot clearer now."

"What things?" she'd asked.

But he hadn't answered, and before long they were at the icehouse, and everything was loud and chaotic, the Tejano music, the children shrieking, the men and women playing dominoes and laughing over steaming plates of food. He had gripped her hand tightly and then led her over to the bar, and then he'd whispered to her very softly, *"I will never let anything bad happen to you, Chlo. Okay? I promise."* And then he'd turned around and ordered them both beers.

The place where Teo takes them is an old, abandoned apartment complex down the street. Nearly every room in the building is vacant, from what Chloe can tell, but Teo has told them it's safe, that he knows the owner and that it's safe for them to be here, at least for the night. He's gotten hold of the girl, he says, but she's still a few hours away, coming down from someplace north of them. She'll be here by morning, he says, but for now, they'll just have to wait it out, stay here until morning, and then make the crossing then.

This is the most Teo has said to them the entire night, and now that he's left the room, now that he's off somewhere else, talking to his friends, a group of older men in dark blazers and cowboy hats, she asks Raja what he thinks about it all.

"Could be worse," he says. "I mean, he could have made us sleep in the van, right?"

She looks at him and nods. The room they're sitting in is filled with painting supplies, buckets of dried paint, a ladder, a few rollers in trays, some bedsheets bundled up in the corner. Everything smells of turpentine and old chemicals, and above them, a lone lightbulb dangles loosely from the ceiling. Someone must have been working on the room earlier that day, she thinks, the walls still wet with primer, the crisscrossed patterns of roller marks across the ceiling. They're sitting at what appears to be a kitchen table, and across from them, in the corner, is a dusty mattress, covered in a clear plastic sheet, where Teo has told them they can sleep.

"I think I might have actually preferred the van," she says.

"Really?"

"Well, at least the van had blankets."

He laughs. "We'll be fine."

She looks at him and shakes her head.

"Someday we'll look back on this and laugh about it," he says. "Someday we'll think about how romantic it was, right?" He reaches over then and squeezes her hand, and suddenly she feels tense.

Earlier that night as they'd made the three-hour trip from Houston to San Antonio, they'd sat in the darkness of the van and talked, mostly about Mexico and what they'd do once they got there. Raja had told her that he'd always had a romanticized vision of Mexico, but the more he talked about it, the less realistic it seemed. It was clear that his vision of Mexico had been informed by the movies—by films like *El Mariachi* and *Touch of Evil*—and she'd tried to explain this to him then, that she'd gone down there a lot as a kid and that it wasn't what he was thinking it would be. Yes, it was beautiful, she said, but it was also very dangerous in parts, especially in cities like Laredo, and that it was also very poor. She suggested they try to go down to the coast, to one of the cities along the Gulf, a coastal town, where there would be more American tourists and people who spoke English, but Raja had said no, he wanted to find the smallest, most out-of-the-way town in the country, someplace right in the middle, where no one would look for them. He talked about finding a little casita to rent, looking for work in the fields. *There aren't many fields out there,* she'd said to him. *Not in the middle. It's mostly desert.* Though she hadn't actually known if this was true.

Well, whatever, he'd said. *There's got to be some type of local industry, right?*

But the thought of this then, of Raja working in a field or picking up some random job at a factory, depressed her. Only three months before, he had been a straight-A chemistry major, on his way to a lucrative job in chemical engineering, and though he'd never truly embraced this path, at least it was a path, right? At least it had a future. At least it made sense. And the fact that he was so willing to give that all up so easily confused her.

I've never thought that the happiness in my life would come from my job, he'd explained. *And so, you see, it doesn't really matter.*

But she hadn't really believed him when he'd said this, or perhaps hadn't wanted to believe him. All she knew now was that the closer they got to the border, the worse this whole idea seemed to be. At one point Raja had even talked about the fact that they might have to change their names once they got there, once they arrived in Mexico, and what those names would be. Chloe had said she'd always wanted a Russian name, something like Anya or Natasha, something sexy, but Raja had said he'd actually go the other direction, something plain and inconspicuous, something like John or Doug.

"No offense"—Chloe had laughed—"but you don't really look like a Doug."

"And you think you look like a Natasha?"

She'd laughed.

It had been fun playing this game, thinking about the idea of reinventing themselves, and in some ways, she was kind of looking forward to the idea of switching her identity, of becoming someone else. It would be almost like acting, like playing a role, just as she'd done back in high school, and she felt certain she'd be good at it, that they both would. But on the other hand it also seemed somewhat strange, even frightening. After all, if she was no longer Chloe Harding, then who would she be? And would she begin to forget after a while who she truly was and who Raja truly was? Would their false identities, their make-believe lives, begin to blur with their real ones, and what would this mean in the end? She thought of the way that Simone had completely transformed herself into somebody else, the way she'd completely eviscerated any trace of who she'd once been. Was it really as simple as that? Could a person really erase who they were? And if they could, was that something she even wanted?

She wants to ask Raja about this now, wants to beg him to change his mind, but somehow in the dim light of this room, as he sits across from her smoking his cigarette casually, she can see that any mention of going back now would be pointless.

"And what about Teo?" she says finally. "Do you still have a bad feeling about him?"

He looks at her and shrugs. "Not really," he says and draws on his cigarette. "Not anymore." He smiles at her. "We talked."

"You talked? When?"

"Earlier, when you were in the bathroom at the icehouse."

"I didn't see you talking to him."

"Well, I did," he says, and winks. "And I think it's okay. I mean, I think it's all going to be fine."

And suddenly all of the nervousness in his face is gone, almost like he has resigned himself to something that even she doesn't yet understand.

"So you and Teo are tight now?"

"I didn't say that."

"Well, what did you guys talk about then?"

He looks at her, shrugs. "Nothing really," he says, and then he smiles at her again.

Earlier she had gotten a funny feeling about Teo. When Raja was up at the bar, getting them another round, she had caught him staring at her from across the street, looking right at her, just as he had when they'd first arrived in San Antonio and he'd let them out of the van. And later, when he'd led them down the street toward the bar, she'd felt his eyes on the back of her legs and twice caught him staring at her breasts. Beneath the finely pressed suit that he wore, beneath his polished exterior, she could sense a muscled physicality about him, an animal nature, as if his suit were just a façade, a secret skin.

"Look, let's talk about something else, okay? I want tonight to be a nice night, okay? Our last night in the States, right?"

And the sound of those words, the finality of them, unsettles her. She thinks about the ride down again, about the darkness of the cargo space in the back of the truck and how frightening it had been, how uncomfortable, how she'd used the clock on her cell phone to chart their course, imagining in her mind the various towns they were passing through, and how for a long time they had just sat there in silence, holding each other, calming each other's nerves. When they arrived in San Antonio, she could tell by the way the truck slowed down, the sound of cars honking outside the narrow walls. She had tried to explain to Raja how she had come here all the time in grade school, and then later in middle school and high school, how every other class trip she had ever taken seemed to involve a stop at the Alamo. And Raja had laughed then and nodded, saying that he had only ever seen the Alamo in films. *Well, it's a lot smaller than you'd think,* she'd told him. *And like so many other things you hear about, kind of disappointing, you know.* And then the truck had stopped, and there had been the sound of Teo opening up the back door, unlocking it, and then yanking it up, and there was a moment when the lights from the streetlamps were so bright that they had had to close their eyes and squint against them, and then there was the sound of Teo stepping up into the cargo space and moving around the boxes and crates. Like something from a dream, he had stood there, a looming silhouette. *Time to get out,* he'd finally muttered and then he'd smiled at them and winked.

· · ·

Later, lying with Raja on the mattress in the corner, she kisses his eyelids and tells him to sleep. They are lying side by side, his arms wrapped tightly around her.

"You look exhausted," she says.

But he shakes his head. "I'm not sleeping," he says, "but you should."

Up above them, the lone lightbulb dangles from the ceiling, casting shadows against the wall, and in the distance, outside the window, she can hear the sound of police sirens and people shouting, the fight at the icehouse breaking up, people heading home to their houses along the dark empty streets. Raja places his hand on her hip and squeezes it, then brushes her hair with his fingertips, and a moment later, everything is silent, and she feels herself relaxing, listening to the lilt of his voice, she feels her eyelids growing heavy, and then, just as she's about to drift off, she hears a rapping at the door, a violent knock, and then Raja is up and walking over there, standing in the open doorway and talking to Teo. She can't hear what they're saying, but she can see the top of Teo's head bobbing, and then a moment later the door slams shut and Raja is coming back to her.

"Let's go," he says. "Come on." His eyes are suddenly wild with excitement. "She's here."

"Who?"

"The girl," he says, smiling now. "She's here."

4

OUTSIDE THE KITCHEN WINDOW, Elson can see the first rays of dawn lightening the horizon, the sky above him overcast and dark, a few random lights going on in the neighboring houses. He is bracing himself for the long day ahead, the long day of interviews and meetings with the police, the second round of interrogations, but for now he feels strangely at peace. He is standing in the kitchen of the first and only house he'd ever bought, and he is no longer a stranger here. He is not an unwanted guest. He is here because his wife has asked him to be here and because she needs him at this moment, because she's opened her arms to him once again, and the thought of this now, the thought of Cadence asleep in their room while he is down here in the kitchen, about to make breakfast, the thought of this is so comforting to him at this moment that he almost has to smile. Despite all of the chaos in their lives, despite all of the uncertainty surrounding his daughter's absence, despite the profound fear that he now feels for her well-being, despite all of that, there is still a momentary glimmer of hope in the air, a possibility that they might all come out on the other side of this okay.

He places the skillet on the stove and cracks two eggs, then pulls out a carton of orange juice from the refrigerator and begins to grind the beans for their coffee. He hasn't made breakfast for himself or anyone else in several months. When Lorna used to stay over, they'd always go out to eat, and when he was on his own, he'd typically skip breakfast or sometimes grab a bagel with his coffee on the way to work. The ritual of breakfast, however, was something he'd reserved solely for his family, for his wife and kids, and it was a ritual, he now realized, he'd dearly missed. He could still remember, when Chloe was young, the way she'd wake up early on Sunday mornings and grab the newspaper and then begin to check off the important football games of the day, the games that might have serious playoff implications for the Oilers, back when the Oilers were still in Houston, or later, when she was in high school, the Texans. Football had always been a thing they'd shared, a father-daughter thing, a subject that Richard had little interest in. She would always sit there, reading off the latest injury reports or casting her own projections while he would stand at the stove, making them omelets or pancakes or sometimes, when Chloe begged, his famous French toast. Meanwhile, Cadence and Richard would come down a little later, usually a little groggy, and lie on the couches in the family room doing *The New York Times* crossword puzzle together. Later, when the kids were older, they seemed to do this less and less, but for a while there it had been a ritual of theirs, a thing that defined them as a family, and it occurs to Elson now that if they had simply kept this up, if he had maybe made it mandatory, just like their weekly meals, it might have been enough to save them.

It is this that he's thinking about when he hears the sound of Cadence's minivan in the driveway and then, later, the sound of the laundry room door opening. Upstairs, Cadence is fast asleep, so he knows it must be Richard, and were he not so caught up in his own distant memories at this moment, were he not so distracted by the past, he might have reacted a little more quickly, might have run up to the bedroom and hidden from his son, but at this moment it doesn't even occur to him that there is anything wrong about the fact he's standing here in his own kitchen making eggs, and so when Richard walks in, looking strung out and dingy, his entire body reeking of booze, he doesn't think twice about extending his hand to him and greeting him.

Richard stares at him for a moment, confused, like he's looking at an apparition, then scrunches his nose.

"What the hell are you doing here?" he says finally, ignoring his outstretched hand.

"I'm making us some breakfast, buddy," Elson says. "Have a seat."

Richard studies his body, his pajama pants, his wrinkly T-shirt, putting it all together.

"You slept here?"

"I slept on the couch."

"But you slept here?"

"Your mother didn't want me driving."

Richard shakes his head, and he can see he doesn't believe him.

"What the hell?" Richard says. "What are you guys, like, together again?"

"Richard."

"I can't fucking believe this."

"It's not what you're thinking." Elson walks over to him now and tries to touch his shoulder, but Richard jerks away. "Just sit down a second, buddy."

"Don't touch me," Richard says, and then they stand there at a stalemate, neither of them saying a word. Finally, Richard sits down at the counter. "So, what is this, like your master plan or something? To keep messing with our heads until we all go crazy? Haven't you done enough?"

Elson stands there, motionless, his son's words stinging him, reminding him once again of how much the boy hates him. Ever since he first came out, ever since Elson had suggested that he see a shrink to fix his problem, the boy had never forgiven him. Even when he'd come around to it, even when he'd come to accept it, even when he'd come to even admire his son's courage for embracing a lifestyle that surely wasn't easy, even when he'd told him these things, the boy had never forgiven him. He'd held on to that phrase, *fix your problem,* and had used it against him like a tool.

"Let me make you some breakfast," Elson says, staring at the skillet, which is starting to fill the room with smoke, with the smell of burnt butter. "You like eggs, right?"

"I'm not hungry."

"You need to eat something."

"I'm not fucking hungry, Dad."

Were the circumstances different, were Richard still in high school and were he and Cadence still together, he would have never tolerated this type of thing, this type of recalcitrance, but he is not in any position to argue these days, and Richard knows this, has been using it against him now for several months.

"Where's Mom anyway?" Richard says finally.

"She's upstairs sleeping."

"I think we should wake her up."

"I don't think that's such a good idea."

"I think we need to talk about this."

"Richard."

"I think we need to have a little family sit-down. Isn't that what you used to call it? A *sit-down?*"

Elson says nothing, feeling even more powerless than he had a moment before. He walks over to the stove and turns off the heat, then puts the skillet down in the sink. Finally, returning to the island counter in the middle of the room, he sits down across from his son and tries again to extend his hand to him, to touch his shoulder, which this time Richard lets him do. "Look," he says finally. "I think we're all just a little confused right now, buddy. Your mother's confused, I'm confused, and I'm sure that you're very confused, too. And when you're confused, you sometimes do things that you shouldn't do. And that's all this is. I think we're all just scared to death right now for your sister."

Richard looks at him, and he can suddenly see something in his eyes softening, giving way, a sign of recognition perhaps, or maybe hesitation. He knows his son well enough to know when he's scared.

"What is it?" Elson asks finally.

Richard shakes his head.

"What is it, buddy? What's on your mind?"

"Nothing."

"Just tell me."

Richard turns away, then walks over to the patio doors and stares out at the pool. A moment later, Elson walks up behind him and again touches his son's shoulder, squeezes it until he finally relaxes.

"I think I may have screwed up, Dad," Richard says finally, without turning around.

"What are you talking about?"

"I think I may have really screwed up."

"Is this about your sister?"

Richard turns to him then, but doesn't answer.

"Well, whatever you did, buddy," Elson says, feeling suddenly nervous, trying to choose his words carefully. "Whatever you did, I'm sure there's a way out of it, okay. But you're gonna have to tell me what it is."

Richard looks down at his hands for a moment, then looks away, and he can tell that he's lost him.

"Buddy?"

"It's nothing," Richard says finally. "Forget it."

"Look, Rich—"

"Dad, I gotta go. I got stuff to do." And just like that, he walks out of the kitchen and up to his room, and Elson is left there alone, staring at the kitchen, the charred remains of his failed breakfast.

At various times during their childhood he had been a strict disciplinarian, but he had never struck his children, and this was something he often took pride in. Several of his friends had admitted to him on various occasions that they had occasionally lost their cool, let a hand slip, or grabbed their child too intensely, and he could see in their pained expressions how much they now regretted it. But Elson had never done this. He had never even abused his children verbally, from what he could tell. He may have lost his cool from time to time, may have raised his voice, but he'd never put them down, never degraded them in the way that his own father had degraded him. And yet, they had still come to resent him, even despise him, in recent months, and he wasn't entirely sure why this was. Cadence had told him that it was all in his mind, that they didn't really despise him, that it was only a phase, a natural part of the healing process when two people broke up. But Elson had sensed it long before the divorce, had seen it in Chloe's expressions in high school, had heard it in Richard's voice when he first left for college. And now, when the three of them were together, when they were together without Cadence, he often felt like a prison warden holding his children against their will, making them eat dinners with him, forcing them to talk about their lives, when it was perfectly obvious to everyone that they'd rather be somewhere else.

It is this that he's thinking about as he cleans up the kitchen and, later, as he sits with Cadence out on the back patio by the pool, drinking coffee. It is an overcast morning, the threat of a storm coming in the late afternoon. The rhododendron bushes on the far end of the yard look sickly, and just beyond the pool he can see that all but one of the azalea bushes have died. It seems that the entire yard has gone to shit since he left, no one around to take care of it anymore, no one around to weed or fertilize or rake out the beds. He considers mentioning this to Cadence, but he can tell that she's already somewhere else. Only moments before he had explained to her what had happened with Richard in the kitchen, what he'd told him, and he can tell she's upset.

"So he knows," she says finally.

"He knows."

"And you told him."

"I didn't tell him. He guessed."

She looks at him, shakes her head. "I knew this was a mistake," she says.

"Cadence."

"Seriously, Elson. What the hell were we thinking?"

"I don't know that we *were* thinking," he says. "Wasn't that kind of the point?"

She puts down her cup and looks around, and he can see that he's losing her, that she's not in the mood to joke around anymore.

"Look," he says. "It doesn't have to be."

"What?"

"It doesn't have to be a mistake."

"Elson."

"I'm just saying." But he knows, in a way, that she's right. As much as he wants to believe that this is all just the start of something bigger, a new beginning for their relationship, a part of him knows that there's too much damage still to repair. And besides, the timing couldn't be worse. With everything that's going on right now, with everything they're being forced to contend with, this is the last thing that either of them should be thinking about. Still, looking at his wife now, he finds it hard to let go.

"Do you regret it?" he asks finally.

She looks at him. "That's not the point."

"Just tell me."

"No," she says softly. "I don't regret it, but I also don't think that this is something we should be wasting our time talking about right now."

"Fair enough," he says and crosses his arms.

She picks up her coffee then and sips it. "Did he say anything else?"

"About?"

"About, you know, Chloe."

Elson shakes his head. "No, but I think he knows something."

"Why?"

"He seemed like he wanted to tell me something."

"About her?"

"I don't know. About something. Earlier. In the kitchen."

"Maybe we should have him talk to the detectives."

"You really want to put him through that?"

Cadence pauses. "I don't know. What other choice do we have?"

And it is then that he hears his cell phone ringing in his pocket and pulls it out. Glancing quickly at the caller ID, he sees Lorna's name flashing across the screen, feels a sudden rush, then quickly closes it. As he turns off the ringer, Cadence eyes him suspiciously.

"Who was that?" she asks.

"Nobody," he says. "Work."

"They're still bothering you?"

"Yeah," he says, and shrugs. "You know, loose ends and stuff."

She nods, but he can tell she doesn't believe him.

He sits there and stares out at the yard.

When he first moved out, he'd told himself that he was catching a break, a second chance at life. He'd told himself that the woman he was leaving behind, his wife of twenty-five years, was too old, too needy, too intense, and what he needed right now was someone else, someone younger and more like him. And in his quest to find such a person, he had found Lorna, who was exactly that, the polar opposite of Cadence, but he wonders now, looking at his wife, if this is in fact what he wanted after all. Was there ever an ideal person in the end, and if so, was it possible that that person for him had been Cadence all along? She was certainly far from perfect, and they were certainly far from perfect together, but they were *something* after all, weren't they? In a very fundamental way, they worked, and in another very fundamental way, he needed her, found it hard to exist without her, and he was pretty sure she felt the same.

And yet now, thinking of the cell phone in his pocket, the message that Lorna has surely left, he feels an irrational desire to sneak off and listen to it, to find out what she wants, even as Cadence stares at him suspiciously, dubious of his intent.

"We need to meet the detectives at three," she says finally.

He nods. "Okay."

"So if you have something to do before then—"

"I don't."

"Well, I do," she says.

"What?"

"Homework."

He stares at her.

"For my business class."

How she can do homework at a time like this is beyond him, though he senses by the way she averts her eyes that this is simply an excuse, a way to get him to leave.

"Fair enough," he says finally. "Mind if I stick around?"

"I'd rather you didn't."

He stares at her again, trying to meet her eyes, but she looks away. Finally he stands up. "Okay," he says. "I'm not going to push."

She nods.

"But you're sure you meant what you said?"

"About what?"

"About not regretting last night."

She looks at him now. "I told you I didn't."

"But you always have some regrets, don't you?"

"Well, that's just me, Elson," she says. "You know, that's just my nature."

He looks at her now, suddenly remembering the strange scene from the night before, standing outside the bathroom door, whispering to her through the keyhole, the pungent odor of marijuana filling up the room. When she'd finally come out, almost an hour later, he was lying in bed, reading a book, waiting for her, but she didn't even look at him. She just asked him to turn out the light, then she slid into bed and put her arms around him very tightly and began to weep. And as he lay there, holding her, comforting her, he began to think about what a strange testament this all was to family life, to life in the modern age, that you could have a family torn apart by tragedy, you could have a son who despised you, an ex-wife who smoked marijuana in the bathroom, and a daughter who was very possibly going to jail, and yet you could still take simple pleasure in the fact that you were somehow a part of something larger and that the people around you needed you, that they depended on you, even if they didn't know it.

"You know, if you'd like, I could stick around and work on the garden," he says.

"The garden?"

"Yeah, it's a mess if you haven't noticed."

"Elson."

"Okay," he says. "I'm leaving. I was just offering. But look, sooner or later someone's gonna have to take care of it, okay. In fact, there's a lot of things around here, Cadence—if you haven't noticed—there's a lot of things around here that need some work."

She smiles at him then and rolls her eyes in that wry, ironic way of hers. "Yeah, Elson," she says, sighing. "I've noticed."

5

STANDING IN LINE at Kinko's, Richard feels suddenly nauseous. The thought of his parents getting back together, the thought of them actually being civil to one another, the thought of that combined with everything else, with the very real possibility that he has just enabled his sister to leave the country, that she is quite possibly standing on foreign soil at this very moment, the thought of all of these things put together, it's almost too much for his mind to process at this moment.

All around him people are jockeying for position, moving around frantically, holding large stacks of documents in their arms like babies or waving desperately at the attendants behind the counter, trying to get their attention, voicing their complaints, explaining that what they're trying to do here is very urgent. He closes his eyes and tries to block it all out and then looks again at his cell phone, rereads the text messages that have been sent to him in the past half hour, each one more cryptic than the last, all of them sent from a number he doesn't recognize.

The first arrived as he was leaving the house, just as he was pulling out of his parents' driveway in his mother's minivan, his poetry manuscript on the seat beside him.

rich, where r u ? pls call!

He had tried to call back immediately, assuming it was Chloe, but the phone call had gone to some anonymous voice-mail account, and when he'd tried again, a few minutes later, to send her a text, the text had been rejected.

A few minutes after that the second text arrived.

in trouble, pls call

But again he'd had no luck. He had tried the number probably a dozen times, but each time the call had gone directly to the same voice-mail account, and each time he had left a message for his sister, begging her to please call him, but she never had.

And then, just a few minutes earlier, he'd received the last message, the longest and also the most baffling.

> need ur help. not safe now. will call fr landline.
> pls erase these messages! -c

But he hadn't erased them, fearing somewhere deep inside that this might be the very last communication he ever had with his sister. Now, however, he isn't sure, and as he stands in line, feeling utterly absurd about his reason for being here, about the fact that he is somehow attempting to apply to graduate school in the midst of all this chaos, he begins to wonder if he should have tried to do something else, if it's finally time to come clean to the cops or to let his parents in on what has happened.

In front of him, a woman is arguing dramatically with one of the cashiers, claiming that they have ruined her daughter's invitations, that they have essentially destroyed her daughter's debutante party, and that it's too late for them to do anything about it. Beside her, a young teenage girl with blond hair, probably only a few years younger than Chloe, is staring down at her feet, clearly embarrassed. The woman demands to speak to the manager, and as the cashier disappears sheepishly into one of the back rooms, Richard feels a sudden desire to pull this woman aside and explain to her how lucky she is, to let her know how fortunate she is to even know where her daughter is at this moment.

But instead he just turns around and heads out the door, and it's then that his phone rings, and he feels a jolt of adrenaline rushing through him. Moving over into the shade of the Kinko's awning, he reaches quickly for the phone in his pocket, almost dropping it as he fumbles to answer.

"Chloe?"

"What?" says a male voice.

"Who is this?"

"It's Brandon, man. Look, you gotta get over here."

"Where?"

"To my place." He can hear the anxiousness in Brandon's voice.

"What's going on?"

"Dude, things are fucked up."

"What are you talking about?"

There's a long pause. Then Brandon says, "Look, man, just come over."

Richard moves out of the shade and starts over toward the minivan. "Can you at least tell me what's going on?"

"I don't know," Brandon says. "Can I? I mean, is my phone being tapped?"

"What are you talking about?"

"I'm talking about two detectives—or I don't know what they were— two guys in black suits, okay, coming over here and grilling me for like half an hour."

"When?"

"Just now."

"Just now?"

"Yeah, just *now*."

"What were they grilling you about?"

"What do you think?" Brandon pauses. "Look, man, they were doing some Internet surveillance or something. I don't know. But somehow they figured out that Chloe was using the Internet at my place. Traced the ISP or something. I don't know. But they're like *We know she's here*. And then when they looked around and saw she wasn't, they're like *Where is she?*"

"So what did you tell them?"

"Nothing, man. I mean I told them jack shit, but they were pissed. I mean I had to admit that she was here, of course. They knew that much already, but that's all. That's all I said. I just told them that she'd stopped by here for a couple hours."

"And what about Raja?"

"Nothing, man. Didn't say a word. Acted like I'd never heard of the guy."

"And do you think they believed you?"

"Who the hell knows?" He can hear the panic now rising in Brandon's voice. "Look, man, I told you before, I can't have this shit sticking to me, okay? I can't be having detectives, or whatever the hell they were, sniffing around my apartment, tracing my Internet and shit."

"I know," Richard says. "I'm sorry."

"I just can't have it."

Opening the door now to his mother's minivan, he feels the heat of the day, the cold drops of sweat on the back of his neck. Brandon is silent on the other end of the line.

"Look, Bran, give me ten minutes all right. Ten minutes and I'll be over there, and then we can straighten all this shit out."

Brandon is still silent on the other end of the line, and it takes him a while, almost several seconds, before he recognizes the lack of music in the background and realizes that Brandon has in fact hung up.

Backing out of his spot in the Kinko's parking lot, Richard hits the AC, then pulls out slowly onto Montrose Boulevard, his mind still trying to process what Brandon has told him. The strange reality of it all, the fact that Brandon is now getting dragged into this shit as well. Detectives? Internet surveillance? It seemed absurd. Had it really come to that? And how many of his own recent actions had been observed, surveilled? Did they know about the money he had given Chloe? Did they know about his night at the Hyatt Hotel? It seemed ridiculous to even consider such things, and yet how much did he really know about modern technology, about the means by which various authorities could obtain information? All he knows now is that there are bigger problems at hand, bigger problems than even Brandon knows about, and as he pulls up slowly to a stoplight, he looks again at his silent cell phone, scans the messages, then puts it away. In all of the confusion, he hadn't even bothered to mention to Brandon the most recent development and is no longer sure that he should. Why, after all, had Chloe asked him to erase her messages? Who, in the end, was she afraid of? Was there a third party involved? Another element he hadn't considered?

Driving through Montrose, he feels suddenly on tilt, his mind racing, the world around him a silent blur. If anything ever happened to his sister, he would never forgive himself. He realizes that now, just as he realized earlier, talking to his father, that everything he had done in the past two weeks, every poor decision he had made, every risk he had taken, had all been for her, for the sole purpose of protecting her. She was, for him, the one sole connective tissue in what was otherwise a difficult and absurd world, a world that seemed to blur around the edges, a world that rarely made sense, a world that was impossible to negotiate without her. Chloe. She had been for so many years the only person he could talk to, the only person he could tell about the boys that he liked, the only person he could complain to about their parents, the only person who would stay up with him late at night, after their parents had gone to sleep, and listen to him as he hypothesized about this thing or that, as he tried to work out the complex, fragmented pieces of his life. And as he drives along the narrow streets of Montrose now, he can see his sister's face, smiling at him from the edge of his bed. He can see her sneaking downstairs to steal vodka from their parents' liquor cabinet, lighting up her very first joint, lying out with him by the pool on one of those endless summer days. He can see her smiling at him from the end of the dinner table, throwing him a wink, telling him to calm down now, relax, telling him that everything is going to be fine.

Pulling over now on the side of the street, he feels his heart racing and has to stop and get out. Fumbling for his cigarettes, he lights one, then looks out at the neighborhood around him, a neighborhood very close to his own, a neighborhood that he must have driven through a dozen times but that suddenly seems unrecognizable. He checks his messages again, dials the number, then waits, hanging up as soon as the computer-generated voice comes on. He thinks of calling up his parents, of coming clean, then he thinks about Brandon, alone in his apartment, waiting for him. He thinks about the way that in the comic books he had read as a child, the concept of time had always been malleable, fluid, something that could be reversed or revised. That life itself was something revisable, and if he had that power now, he suddenly realizes, if he had the power to turn back time, he would have never given Chloe that money, would have never believed that he was helping her out. He would have recognized, as he recognizes now, that her judgment had been clouded by love, just as his own judgment had been clouded by love, and just as his parents, back in the house, playing their old charade, just as his parents' judgment had been clouded by love.

Looking down at the phone, he tries to catch his bearings, tries to get his thoughts in order, but the world around him seems suddenly surreal, moving in some ways very fast and in some ways very slow. Was this how his father felt when he had one of his famous panic attacks? Had he inherited his father's propensity toward anxiety? He'd only felt this way once before, after his first fight with Marcos, and yet, even then, it wasn't like this. It hadn't been this bad.

Leaning against the side of the car, he closes his eyes and tries again to breathe, first very slowly, then quicker, counting to himself, trying to calm down. And then all at once there's the sound of someone honking behind him, a car trying to pass, a car, which he realizes now, he's blocking.

"Hey," the woman behind him yells, rolling down her window. "What the fuck is wrong with you?"

Brandon is sitting on his front stoop when Richard finally arrives at the apartment. There's a large backpack on the ground beside him, and, behind him, leaning against the door, is a tall blond boy in military fatigues and a Fugazi T-shirt, smoking a cigarette. The boy glances at Richard suspiciously as he gets out of the car, then moves over next to Brandon in a proprietary way and sits beside him. As Richard approaches, Brandon introduces the boy as Griffen and then explains that they're on their way out. Richard looks at Griffen and nods, then says, "Where you headed?"

"That," Brandon says, "I can't tell you."

Richard stares at him. "Well, can you at least tell me how long you're going to be gone?"

"No," Brandon says. "Unfortunately, I can't."

Richard looks then at the backpack on the ground. "I thought we were going to talk."

"Talk?"

"Yeah, you said you wanted to talk."

Brandon stares at him. "No time for talking now, my friend. We gotta head out."

"Look, Bran, I'm sorry I was late."

But Brandon ignores him, slings the backpack across his shoulder.

"What's in there anyway?" Richard says, pointing at the backpack.

Brandon looks at the backpack, then pats it. "In here?" he says. "In here is basically everything I wouldn't want some motherfucker finding in my apartment."

There's an edge to Brandon's voice now that makes Richard feel guilty again, ashamed. "Look, Bran, let's just go inside."

But Brandon turns away. "I'm going to need you to cover my shifts while I'm gone, okay?" He looks at the ground. "I told them I was going out of town for a few days, okay? Some family emergency. So you're going to have to work doubles till I get back."

Richard nods.

"And if those guys come back, you have no idea where I've been, okay?"

Richard nods again.

Griffen looks away then, almost in disgust, and Richard feels a small pang of annoyance, then jealousy, not knowing who this boy even is but assuming he's probably one of Brandon's recent conquests, a pickup from the Limelight, a boy who is unknowingly being implicated himself.

"And there's one other thing I didn't mention to you on the phone," Brandon says. "I didn't want to freak you out or anything, but these guys seemed to think your sister might be in some type of trouble, okay?"

"Trouble?"

"Yeah, like danger, you know."

"What do you mean?"

"I don't know," he says. "I'm just telling you what they said."

"Were they talking about Raja?"

"I have no idea, dude."

And Richard thinks again of the messages and feels his mind begin to race, wondering what the hell he's done. He almost wants to say something to Brandon about the messages, but when he looks at Griffen, he thinks better of it.

"Okay, man," Brandon says, standing up. "We're heading out now."

Griffen stands up beside him then, and they start over to Brandon's car, Richard following.

Richard wants to apologize again, wants to say something else to Brandon to let him know just how sorry he is, but instead he just stands there, watching, as Brandon and Griffen get into the car. Brandon doesn't even hug him, doesn't even shake his hand, but after he starts up the car, he rolls down the window and looks at him.

"And another thing," he says, looking around the street suspiciously. "Don't try calling my cell phone, okay, because I'm not even bringing it with me."

"How will I know when you're back then?"

"You won't," Brandon says and shrugs.

And then he rolls up the window and turns on the radio, and a moment later, Richard is standing on the curb, watching the back end of the car as it disappears around the corner.

He waits there for a moment, not knowing where to go next, thinking of his application materials on the front seat of his mother's minivan and how he's never going to mail them and then about Brandon heading off into hiding and then about his parents back at the house, trying in their own misguided way to figure things out, and then finally about his sister and the words that Brandon said to him, how she might be in some type of danger, a sentence that only seemed to confirm what he already knew.

His thinking calmer now, he lights a cigarette and looks back at Brandon's apartment, at the third-floor window, where only days before his sister had probably sat, staring out at the street, planning her escape, designing some elaborate scheme with Raja. Why he'd trusted her so much he didn't know, but it is this that he's thinking about as he turns around and feels the slight vibration of the cell phone in his pocket, then hears the shrill ring, which he'd set to maximum volume just to be sure he wouldn't miss her. And when he first hears her voice, it is muffled and faint, like a whisper from the afterlife, like the voice of an apparition, and he is shaking so much with excitement that he can barely bring himself to speak.

"Chloe?" he says. "Where the hell are you?"

"I'm at a pay phone," she says faintly.

"No, I mean where the hell *are* you?"

"I don't know, Richard," she says calmly. "Honestly, I have no fucking idea."

6

THEY HAD WANTED to meet downtown this time, at the Houston Police Department on Travis Street, an old stone building that Cadence had never been to before, that she had never had occasion to enter before, just as she had never had occasion to enter the courthouse or the numerous bail bonds buildings that surrounded the neighborhood. This was a part of Houston she rarely visited, a neighborhood as foreign to her as another country, and yet, here she was, sitting in what she could only assume was some type of interrogation room, waiting for her husband and the two well-dressed police detectives from the Stratham Police Department who had greeted her earlier.

Elson had called her only an hour before, promised her he would meet her outside the building at a quarter to three so they could review very briefly what they wanted to say, but he hadn't shown up, and now, almost a half hour later, he still hadn't shown and hadn't answered any of her voice messages either. It wasn't like him to just disappear like this, and yet, in some ways, it was so much like him, so typical, to flake out like this at the worst possible moment, to drop the ball just when you needed him most. She'd found herself remembering all of the times he had missed Richard's swim meets or Chloe's orchestra recitals, all of the times he had told her that he would only be a half hour late for dinner and then never shown up, all of the times he had disappeared on business trips, all of the times she had had to cancel family vacation plans or go to dinner parties alone. It had always been because of work, or so he claimed, and yet he wasn't working now, was he? No, he wasn't doing anything at all. There had to be another reason, she realized now, but whatever it was, whatever it was that he was doing that was somehow more important than this, well, it better be fucking good.

She leans back now on the cold steel chair and looks out the window at the two detectives from Stratham Police Department who are now standing casually in the hallway, talking between themselves. They had greeted her rather cheerily when she'd first arrived, and yet now she can tell they're pissed, just as annoyed as she is by her husband's absence, by his total disregard for the seriousness of this meeting. And of course, without him, she has no idea what to say. After all, it had been Elson who had taken the reins from the start. Elson who had spoken to Albert Dunn about what might be damaging—or "deleterious," as he put it—to their case. It was Elson who had assured her only a few hours before that he would do all the talking, that he would handle it all, and yet now he had almost certainly abandoned her, left her to fend for herself, left her as the sole guardian and protector of their daughter's life. That she'd slept with him the night before, that she'd been foolish enough to convince herself that he had changed, that she'd allowed herself to let him back in, well, this was something she'd have to contend with later, on her own. What she needed to do right now was concentrate on her daughter's case, to think about the best possible way to get themselves out of what was certainly a trap.

Glancing back at the detectives in the hallway, she shrugs and smiles apologetically, then looks back at her watch, staring at it until the door finally opens and the taller detective enters.

"We're going to get started here, Mrs. Harding," he says coldly, pulling out a folder and then walking over to the table and sitting down beside her. "We'd like to wait for your husband, of course, but it's starting to look like he might have had second thoughts. Don't you think?"

Cadence says nothing to this but nods.

"In fact, what we'd really like to do is have you both come back tomorrow night, if that's okay. And maybe this time you could make sure to bring your husband along."

Cadence nods again, feeling ashamed, and then begins to apologize, but before she can finish her sentence, the detective waves her off and picks up the folder.

"I'd just like to ask you a few questions about your daughter, ma'am, and then I'll send you on your way, okay? But I should let you know first that there have been a few developments in the past couple of days, a few things we'd like to talk to you about."

"Developments?" she says, staring at him. "Good or bad?"

"Well, that depends on how you look at it."

"Tell me the bad first," she says.

"You sure?"

"I'm sure."

The detective looks back at his folder, then picks up his pen. "Well, it's hard to know at this point, ma'am, but if I had to guess, I'd say your daughter's probably looking at a pretty nasty civil suit at this point."

"A civil suit?" she says, puzzled. "What do you mean?"

"Do you know what a civil suit is, ma'am?"

"Yes, of course I do. But you're saying she's not looking at a criminal suit anymore?"

"Well, no," he says. "I mean, from everything we've heard about the Beckwith boy, he's in pretty stable condition right now. That's what they're telling us at least. He has some residual dizziness, of course, and there's a hematoma in the membrane of his brain, which they'll probably have to remove through surgery, but all of his criticals are fine, and from what they've told us, there's no sign of brain damage."

"No sign of brain damage," she says, almost laughing. "You're serious?"

"Like I said, it's too early to say for sure, but yes, it certainly looks that way."

"And he's conscious?"

"He's conscious, ma'am, yes. But he's still got a tube in his throat. They're trying to wean him off the ventilator gradually, you see. But he's writing now, writing pretty well, in fact."

"Oh, thank God," she says softly.

The detective smiles weakly.

"So that's the good news?"

"That's the good news."

"And they're not filing assault charges?"

"No, they are, ma'am, but that shouldn't involve your daughter, since she wasn't present when the incident occurred, and it should only involve the Kittappa boy in a marginal way, since he wasn't the one who delivered the blow. That is, if he's willing to testify, of course."

"What do you mean by 'blow'?"

"The blow to the Beckwith boy's head, ma'am. The blow that knocked him out. They've determined that the blow came from a cricket bat that belonged to the Kittappa boy but that didn't have his fingerprints on it."

She looks at him, still confused.

"The bat was found in the apartment of the other boy's girlfriend. A Bae Lin. Are you familiar with her, ma'am?"

Cadence shakes her head.

"Well, apparently, he'd rubbed it down afterward, the bat, but our team, the forensic folks, they were able to pull off about three or four solid prints, all clean, and they all matched the Cho boy, you see."

"So he did it?"

"From what we can tell, yes. But that doesn't completely exonerate the Kittappa boy, ma'am, and it's likely he'll still be looking at some charges himself. That is, unless he's willing to testify, which we suspect he will be."

Cadence looks at him. "What do you mean?"

"Well, I can't make any promises, ma'am, not at this point, but I'm guessing the DA will be willing take the jail time off the table if he's willing to testify. Basically give him time served, you know? He'll still have the charges on his record, of course—"

"But he'd be free to go."

"Yes, essentially."

"And no charges for Chloe?"

"Not at this point, ma'am, no, especially if she's willing to testify."

Gripping the edge of the table, Cadence can barely compose herself. The elation she feels at this moment, the knowledge that Chloe is essentially free to come home now, free once again to live a normal life, to have a second chance at a normal existence, it's almost as surreal as the concept of her going to jail had once been. And suddenly, despite all of the resentment she'd felt only moments before, she wants Elson to be here now, wants him to be here to hear this.

But before she can say another word she's halted by the expression on the detective's face, which is one of concern, not elation.

"Look, ma'am," he says finally. "We have another issue here, and that issue is that we still have no idea where your daughter is at this point, or where the Kittappa boy is for that matter, if they're in fact together, which we believe they are."

"What do you mean?"

"Well, ma'am," he says, pausing. "Look. Let's just say that we have reason to believe that they may have tried to leave the country earlier today, or perhaps last night, we're not sure. In fact, it's possible that your daughter might already be in Mexico right now."

"Mexico?"

"Yes."

"How do you know that?"

"I can't tell you that, ma'am, and it's not really relevant. I mean, that's not really the issue right now."

She looks at him. "But someone must have told you this, right? I mean, someone must have tipped you off."

The detective looks at her, but doesn't answer.

"Was it Simone?"

He pauses again. "Let's just say that Ms. Walsh was very helpful to us, yes. But, as I said, that's not really the issue right now. The issue right now is finding your daughter and making sure we get her home safely. Wouldn't you agree?"

"You think she might be in danger?"

"I didn't say that."

"But you think she might be?"

"We think it's a possibility, ma'am, yes. But look, that's where we're going to be needing your help."

"My help?"

"Yes," he says, looking at her calmly. "What I need you to tell me, Mrs. Harding—and I need you to be honest with me now—what I need you to tell me is whether you know of anyone who may have aided your daughter in getting across the border illegally. Anyone who might have had the means to do that."

At this, Cadence feels her heart quickening, the elation she'd felt only moments before turning into something else, a strange mixture of panic and confusion, the absurdity of what this man is suggesting floating loosely in her mind like a joke, a trick that someone is playing on her.

"She wouldn't do that," she says finally because she believes at this moment that this is true.

"I know you might believe that, Mrs. Harding—"

"No, I *know* that," she says, breaking in. "Look, even if she had—let's say she had, okay—even if she had, she would have certainly told Richard, and Richard would certainly have told us."

"I know that this might be a little hard to process at the moment, Mrs. Harding. Believe me, I have two children myself. But in my experience, siblings can have pretty tight bonds, and you told me yourself that your daughter and son are very close."

She stares at him now, the frail wall of her convictions giving way, the memory of Richard asking her for money the other day at lunch, the cryptic nature of it all—their conversation. *Two thousand dollars,* he'd said. *I need two thousand dollars, but I can't tell you why.* And she had suspected it even then, hadn't she? Hadn't she known that something was wrong, that this was somehow connected to Chloe? And yet why hadn't she acted on it? Why hadn't she pursued the issue further? Was it possible that her faith in her son's allegiance to her was so strong that it had blinded her from the truth? Or was it simply that she hadn't wanted to believe it, hadn't wanted to believe that he would actually deceive her? Thinking about this now, she feels unnerved.

"Have you spoken to him yet?" she finally asks.

The detective picks up the file, stares at her. "We've tried, ma'am, believe me, but if you don't mind me saying, your son's a pretty elusive character."

And though he says this with a smile, the implication disarms her, unsettles her in the same way Peterson's implications always unsettled her. She tries to consider what he's saying. Sneaking across the border illegally? What did that even mean? Crawling through a muddy tunnel on her hands and knees, one of those elaborate labyrinths like the ones that she'd seen on *60 Minutes,* or maybe riding in the back of some truck, huddled beneath a canvas tarp with a group of other fugitives? If it wasn't so disturbing, it would almost seem comical, the type of story that they might laugh about years later over Christmas dinner. But at this moment, even in the wake of her daughter's exoneration, the unbelievable luck of it all, she can only imagine the worst, and her concern for her now, for her safety, her well-being, is matched only by her sudden resentment of Richard, her anger at him for withholding what he knew, for letting Chloe go astray, for not protecting the one person she had always trusted him to protect.

"Are you saying you think your son might know something about your daughter's whereabouts?" the detective says finally.

Cadence shrugs. "At this point I have no idea."

"I know this is a lot to process right now, ma'am."

Cadence nods.

"Maybe you'd like to take a break."

Cadence looks out through the window at the other detective, who's watching them now with a slight grin. She shakes her head. "No," she says calmly. "I think what I need to do right now . . . I think what I really need to do right now is find my son."

7

LATER, WHEN SHE PLAYED it back in her mind, this is what she'd remember: She'd remember the way Raja had sat with her on the curb outside the apartment complex in downtown San Antonio, rubbing her shoulders and whispering into her ear, telling her it would all be fine, telling her it would all be over soon. And she'd remember how quiet it had been that morning, how peaceful, the sky just beginning to lighten above the small buildings that made up the downtown San Antonio skyline, and the way the streets had been so empty, so bare, and the way the world had seemed to pause there for just that moment, the way everything, at least in that instant, had seemed so sane.

A few minutes later, though, it had all been disrupted by the sound of Teo coming out on the curb with a few of the men he'd been talking to the night before, all of them still drunk and laughing uproariously, moving around quickly as they loaded several additional crates into the back of the van. Sitting there, Chloe had wondered how much space would be left for them to sit, especially now that they'd be sharing the space with someone else, that girl who still hadn't surfaced from the back of the building. She'd looked at Raja then, but his expression had been blank, expressionless, his eyes strangely calm.

Eventually, after they'd finished loading up the van, Teo had come over to them and told them that they were now free to get in. He'd apologized for the tightness of the space, then explained that he'd be back in a minute with the girl. They had entered the van slowly, squeezing their bodies tightly between the tall rows of boxes in the cargo space, then inching along cautiously until they'd reached the small dirty blanket at the back of the hold where they had sat only hours before on the ride down from Houston.

The space was considerably smaller now, and it seemed hard to imagine how they'd fit another body in there, but Chloe hadn't said a word about it, hadn't said anything in fact until Raja had squeezed her hand and winked.

"It's only for a few hours," he'd said. "I know it kind of sucks, but whatever. It'll be fine."

She'd nodded. Then she'd said, "Do you think he's drunk?"

"Who?"

"Teo."

Raja smiled. "Might be," he said. "I don't know. They were partying pretty hard last night." Then he'd started to laugh, as if remembering something she hadn't seen.

"This isn't funny," she'd said. "I mean, this is all we need. A fucking DUI."

Raja winked. "It's gonna be fine," he said, and then he'd moved in closer to her and pulled her toward him.

When the girl finally arrived, Teo didn't even introduce her. In fact, he just stood there at the steps of the cargo space and directed her toward the back of the truck. Chloe had seen her face for only a minute, a young, sallow face that made her think of Russian war films, of prison camp survivors, of long, cold Eastern European winters. And this picture was only intensified by the fact that when the girl finally did speak, her words came out in a thick foreign accent—Lithuanian? Polish? Ukrainian? She couldn't tell.

"'Ello," was all the girl had said, smiling weakly, and then the door had slammed shut behind her, and they had all been surrounded by darkness, fumbling to make space for each other.

Raja had slid up tightly against her, and then the girl had crammed her body into the small space left behind, pulling her knees to her chest and exhaling softly. Everything around them smelled of mildew.

"You okay?" Raja had asked her when he finally turned on the flashlight.

The girl nodded shyly.

"I'm Raja," he'd said, "and this is Chloe."

The girl nodded again but said nothing.

"Do you speak English?" Raja asked.

The girl shook her head.

Chloe could see that Raja wanted to engage her more, to make her feel at home, to let her know that they were not here to hurt her, that they were not the type of people she should be afraid of, but the girl had averted her eyes from them both, had stared down at her knees until the van finally started to move and they were on their way.

For the first half hour or so, they had just sat there, the three of them, perfectly still, not talking. Somehow it had seemed rude to speak to Raja in English while the girl was just sitting there quietly, and so Chloe had just leaned her head against his shoulder and let her mind wander. At first, she'd found herself thinking again about Mexico, about what their lives would be like once they got down there.

The night before it had begun to seem like a horrible idea, and though she still had reservations, now that they were moving closer and closer to the border with each passing minute, now that it was beginning to seem inevitable, she'd suddenly stopped questioning it. It no longer seemed like a choice that they had. It no longer seemed like a decision that could be reversed. And so she'd found herself instead trying to imagine the beautiful countryside outside of Oaxaca, the pristine beaches of Puerto Escondido, all places she had been to before and still remembered with fondness. But the more she tried to imagine these places, the more disjointed the images seemed, the more hazy, the more vague, and before long she found herself thinking instead about Stratham, about the snow-covered quad and the wood-paneled classrooms, and the prodigious buttresses that lined the ceiling of the campus library. She saw the students bustling noiselessly between classroom buildings, their bodies shielded by woolen jackets and knitted scarves, their messenger bags slung loosely across their shoulders. She saw her old professors, standing at the front of the room, lecturing to a group of sleepy-eyed freshmen, talking about Shakespeare and Heidegger and Marx. She saw it all very clearly, the world that was right now continuing without her, the world that had been disrupted but not forever changed by their absence. It would all go on without them, of course. She realized that now, just as she realized that she could never go back. It would all keep going, and her friends, too, would keep going. They would keep taking their classes and writing their papers, and eventually they would all go on to graduate and move on to their respective careers. They'd get married, have children, and begin what might seem to anyone else a normal life while she and Raja would be where? Doing what? How she suddenly longed to be back there right now. How she suddenly wished to be sitting in her dorm room, cramming for some exam or writing some stupid twenty-page paper on something or other.

Turning back to Raja, she found herself urgently wanting to say something to him, but the flashlight was off, and she couldn't see his face, and it wasn't until he finally turned it back on that she could see that he was worried.

"What's wrong?" she asked.

"I think she's sick."

"Who?"

"Who do you think?"

He shone the light on the girl's face, and she could see that it was drenched in sweat. The girl squinted, then turned away.

"Are you okay?" Raja asked, the light still shining in her eyes.

The girl looked down.

Raja reached across and touched her arm, and the girl flinched, then jerked away violently.

"I think we need to stop," he said finally.

"What are you talking about?"

"Look at her face," he said. "There's clearly something wrong."

"Probably just carsick," Chloe said.

"Do you want her puking in here?"

She looked away. He had a point there, and though she didn't want to stop, didn't want anything at this point to disrupt what had otherwise been a fairly smooth journey, she finally nodded and agreed.

"Do you have the phone?" he asked.

"What phone?"

"The cell phone."

She nodded and then reached into her backpack for the small, temporary cell phone that Dupree had given her the night before. The girl was starting to dry heave now.

After Raja dialed the number, there was a long pause, and then he said. "We got a situation back here, bud." There was another long pause, and then he explained to Teo about the girl, about how he thought they should pull over. She watched his face as he listened to whatever Teo was telling him, then he finally said, "Okay," and hung up.

"What did he say?"

"He said he'd stop in twenty minutes."

"Twenty minutes?"

"That's the next exit."

Meanwhile, the girl in front of them was covering her mouth with her hand now, her eyes filled with fear.

"It's gonna be fine," Raja said to her, reaching out again to touch her, but then stopping himself just before the girl jerked back. "We're gonna pull over," he said. "Okay? Twenty minutes."

The girl stared at them both blankly, and then there was a long period of time, maybe twenty minutes, when neither of them spoke and when Raja, she'd realize later, must have been devising his plan.

But at that moment she was only thinking about the girl and what was wrong with her, what they'd eventually have to do with her once they got down to Mexico, whether Raja would insist on caring for her, as she suspected he would, or whether they'd just abandon her at some bus station outside Laredo. It was this that she was thinking about when the van eventually slowed down and then, a few minutes later, ground to a halt.

Raja turned off the flashlight, and then a few seconds later, she heard the lock on the back of the van being unlatched, and then a few seconds after that, the back door flew up, and she had to squint against the brightness of the early morning sunlight. The girl looked startled now, and when she turned to Raja, she said, *No, no,* then gripped his arm tightly.

"We're just going to get you some air," he said, and then motioning toward his mouth, he said it again. "Air," he said. "You know, oxygen?"

Teo was standing now at the front of the cargo space, clearly annoyed, glancing at his watch. "Five minutes," he said to Raja, and then he stepped back down and disappeared around the front of the van.

Raja helped the girl up and then led her down the narrow aisle, Chloe following close behind.

"Why don't you take her around to the bathroom," Raja said once they'd stepped down from the van. They were parked around the back of a small building, a mini-mart, Chloe assumed, with a gas station attached to the front. She could see a Dumpster and a few empty cars parked behind the building and, beyond that, in the far distance, the lonely stretch of highway and the brown, dusty fields that seemed to go on forever. She had no idea where they were. Somewhere between San Antonio and Laredo, she assumed.

"I don't think she wants to go," she said finally.

"Just take her hand," he said. "She probably has to puke."

Chloe looked at the girl then and smiled, but when she tried to take her hand, the girl jumped back violently, then walked all the way back to the edge of the cargo space and stood there by herself.

"We're not going to leave you here," Raja yelled to her.

But it was no use. It was clear that this girl's distrust of strangers was too deeply ingrained.

Raja looked at her then and shrugged, and it was this that she would think about hours later, the expression on his face, how calm he'd been. "Why don't you see if you can get her something," he said. "Maybe some Dramamine and some water. Something for car sickness."

"I doubt she'll take it."

"Well," he said, shrugging again. "We have to do something, right?"

She looked at him. To be honest, she didn't see why they had to do anything at all, why this girl's troubles had suddenly become theirs. "We need to conserve our money," she'd said finally.

"Oh, come on now." He'd laughed. "Dramamine is, what, two bucks?"

And so she'd left, started around the side of the building toward the front of the mini-mart, not realizing then what was happening, not realizing then that this would be the very last conversation she'd ever have with him.

When she returned with the Dramamine a few minutes later, the back lot was completely empty, no sign at all of the van, just an empty expanse of concrete and a small rock with a piece of paper pinned beneath it. She looked at the rock, then out at the rest of the parking lot, and what she felt at first was not panic, not fear, but a cold, sobering numbness, the realization of what had just happened gradually settling in. Later, she would describe this sensation as a kind of sickness, a confusion, a disorientation, but at that moment there were no words to adequately describe what she was feeling, no words that could adequately capture the level of devastation she felt. After a moment, she walked over to the rock and picked up the piece of paper that he'd left, the words on it scribbled in haste, like the writing of a young child.

Chloe,
You know me and so you know why I've done this. Please don't hate me. Later you'll be grateful, I promise. This is not the end.
Yours devotedly, in love forever, Raja

For almost half an hour she had sat there on the ground, on the cold concrete surface of the back lot, completely stunned, rereading these words and trying to imagine what they meant. Though, of course, she knew what they meant, why he'd done this. To protect her, he would probably reason later, just as he had when they'd first fought about it in Brandon's apartment. To give her another chance at a better life, he would say. To keep her out of his own misfortune. But how had it come to this? How had she not seen it?

She could imagine what he'd done, how he'd run around to the front of the truck and talked to Teo, maybe slipped him a few extra bills, explained to him why he was doing it, how it was honestly in *her* best interest for them to leave her. Or maybe they had planned it all out the night before while she was in the bathroom at the icehouse, talking about it in hushed whispers. Or maybe this had been his plan from the start, his plan all along. All she knew now was that he was gone and that she had let him go. She had let him disappear. And yet, as angry as she was at Raja for leaving her, she was even angrier at herself for not seeing it, for not recognizing how obvious it had been. I mean, of course he wasn't going to actually let her go down to Mexico with him. Why had she ever thought he would?

All around her the world was quiet and bright and perfectly still, the sky above her a bright, expansive blue, the wide-open Texas sky that they showed in movies. In the distance, across the street, she could see a few dilapidated ranch houses and an abandoned storefront with a faded sign, advertising fresh empanadas, and beyond that a long stretch of fenced-in field grass, browned and brittle still from winter. From time to time, a car from the interstate would pull into the gas station, or a truck from the fields would drive by, but otherwise this place felt empty, empty and abandoned, a nowhereland, a place that had maybe one time been important but had long since been forgotten.

Later, in the mini-mart, she had learned exactly where she was. *A few miles north of the Cotulla border,* the gas attendant had told her, *halfway between San Antonio and Laredo.* He had said this with a slight smirk, as if this fact alone had made his gas station important, and then later, when she'd asked him the best way to get to a bus station, he had looked at her askance—as if the concept of bus travel in America were a foreign concept to him. Finally, he'd explained to her that the only one he knew of was in Cotulla, a few miles away. Six, to be exact. A walkable distance, if you were willing to do it, which she suddenly realized she wasn't. And without a credit card, and with only a few dollars cash to her name, she wasn't sure if she would even be able to afford a bus ticket once she got there. Opening her wallet then, she saw that she only had about fifteen dollars cash, the majority of their money now traveling with Raja down to Mexico, and it was then, staring at those few flimsy bills, that she finally processed what had happened, that it finally hit her, the cold reality of it all, the full extent of his betrayal.

"Are you okay?" the man behind the counter had asked her, because she was crying now. She was holding her stomach tightly and crying into her hands, though she wasn't sure if she was crying out of anger or sadness, if she was crying because the man she loved most in the world had just betrayed her or because she realized at that moment—with a certainty that made her stomach ache—that she would probably never see him again, maybe never even speak to him. She would never again get to touch his skin or run her hands through his hair or sit with him in a smoky bar over drinks. She would never again get to imagine having a house with him or a child with him, would never get to grow old with him, as she'd always envisioned, and take care of him. She'd never get to see the person he'd become or the person she'd always imagined he'd become, because he was already on his way down to New Laredo, already transforming himself into someone else, a new person with a new identity and a new name. A name she'd never even know or be able to look up, because he hadn't told her what it was.

"Maybe you'd like a paper towel?" the man behind the counter continued, but she had shaken her head and then reached for two of the forty-ounce beers in the ice chest beside her. Then she'd asked him for two packs of cigarettes and a pack of matches.

The total came out to more than she actually had, but the man behind the counter simply smiled at her, then slid the beer and cigarettes into a bag.

"Are you sure you don't need some help?" he'd asked.

But she had shaken her head and then dried her eyes with the sleeve of her sweatshirt and, without saying another word, had walked out the door and across the road to a shaded bench, where she had sat down and proceeded to drink the beer. In fact, it wasn't until she'd finished off the last sip of the second beer that it even occurred to her that she still had the cell phone on her, the cell phone that Dupree had given to her the night before. Still, she waited almost a full hour, staring out at the empty road, still believing that they might turn around and come back for her—she had waited there almost a full hour before she finally picked up the phone and sent her brother a text.

8

INSIDE LORNA'S APARTMENT, the late-afternoon sun is forming strange geometric patterns along the floor and across the walls, and as Elson sits there at her kitchen table, sipping his cold iced tea, watching her as she paces back and forth across the back veranda, talking on the phone, he feels momentarily numb. He wonders who she's talking to, what she's saying, but mostly he finds himself trying to recall the conversation they'd had only moments before, trying to replay it in his mind, as if replaying it might reverse the outcome, might change the sobering truth of what she'd said. That she was not two weeks, not three weeks, but six weeks late. Late. She'd said the word as if she could have been referring to anything: an overdue library book, a late-afternoon lunch, a meeting at work. And he had almost misunderstood her at first, had made her repeat herself twice, before it finally sunk in, what she was saying and what it meant. And then he'd asked her the one thing he should have never asked her. He'd asked her if she was sure it was his, and she had answered him by walking into her bedroom and closing the door.

There she'd remained for the past half hour, ignoring his desperate pleas to come out, to talk about it, to forgive him for asking. Meanwhile, his voice mail was filling up with messages, messages from Cadence, he was sure, messages filled with vitriolic bile and accusations, messages wondering where he was and how he could have so callously ignored the situation at hand. And the truth was he didn't have an answer for her, which is why he hadn't answered her calls. All he knew now was that his responsibilities seemed to lie elsewhere, with Lorna and with the baby she was carrying, and that leaving Lorna now, after what she'd just told him, would be far, far worse in the end. Maybe even irreparable.

That it would border on unforgivable. And so he'd rationalized it in his mind, told himself that he was doing the right thing, though even at this moment he isn't sure.

Outside on the back veranda, Lorna is sitting down now, nodding solemnly and gripping the phone tightly with her hand. Only minutes before, the phone had rung loudly, and she had come rushing out of her bedroom door, passing him without making eye contact, then slamming the sliding glass patio door behind her. Staring at her now, he wonders who she's told, whether she's told her mother and what this might mean. Given her Catholic upbringing, and given the fact that she had looked at him with such scorn earlier when he'd asked her if it was his, he can only assume that she's decided to keep it. And though he'd initially felt a kind of terror at this thought—a sobering realization that any type of future with Cadence would now be dashed—he now feels only sadness, sadness and guilt. He knows what this will mean, of course, knows what it will mean for Cadence and for the kids, knows what it will mean for any type of future plans he might have had. Whatever he might have been imagining that morning as he sat with Cadence out by the pool, whatever he might have fantasized about the night before as he lay beside her in the bed, all of that is gone now. Any hope for a second chance, a fresh start, all of that is gone.

On top of that, he has to consider the more practical matters at hand—the financial and emotional costs of raising yet another child, especially at such a late stage in his life, of saving up for college, of paying for child care, of rationing off what remained of his meager assets. And of course there is also the matter of Chloe and the guilt he now feels for ignoring her situation, for putting Lorna before her. There was virtually nothing in his life he would have ever put before Chloe, and yet here he is now, doing just that. How can he reconcile these two types of guilt, these two responsibilities? It seems like some type of cruel test that he is being given, one of those impossible conundrums that one faced in Greek mythology. No matter what he does, no matter what he says, he'll be disappointing someone. And yet, hasn't it always been this way? Hasn't he always been the fall guy when things went wrong? And hasn't it always been because of matters beyond his control? More and more, he is beginning to feel like an animal caught in a trap, and more and more he is beginning to realize that the only logical way out of this situation is to compartmentalize it, to deal first with Lorna, then later with Cadence. The cops, after all, will still be waiting there after Cadence is done talking to them, whereas Lorna surely won't.

Leaning back now at the kitchen table, he watches Lorna as she finally turns off her phone and flips it shut. She looks at him with something like dismay, then slowly opens the door and enters.

"What's going on?" he says as she walks past him, but she doesn't answer. Instead, she goes over to the fridge and opens the door, then begins to pour herself some juice.

"Who was on the phone?"

Carrying her glass over to the table now, she sits down. "Your wife."

"Cadence?" he says, staring at her. "How did she get your number?"

"That's a good question," she says, staring at him.

"It wasn't me."

"Well, then she must have called my work."

"She knows where you work?"

"I told her," she says. "You know, that night at the hospital." She looks at him. "Anyway, she seemed pretty upset."

"Did you tell her I was here?"

"No, but she wants you to call her right away."

He looks at her. "Did she say why?"

"She said something about Mexico. I don't know. She was kind of hysterical."

"Mexico?"

"Yeah," she says. "Something like that."

He stares at her, trying to figure out what this means. Mexico? What the hell is in Mexico? Is Cadence finally losing her mind?

"You know, she's a nice woman," Lorna says after a moment. "Your wife. You're lucky to have her."

"What's that supposed to mean?"

"Just what I said. You're lucky to have her."

"What makes you think I *have* her?"

"I think you've always had her," Lorna says vaguely. "Even when you thought you didn't."

Elson shrugs, wondering if this is yet another test.

"So are you going to call her now or what?"

"Are you still mad at me?"

Lorna looks at him and sips her drink. "Just call her, Elson."

"I'll call her in a minute, but first I want to talk about this, okay?"

"There's nothing to talk about."

"On the contrary," he says. "I think there's a fucking lot to talk about."

Lorna reaches for the magazine in front of her then and begins to page through it. "I haven't decided anything yet," she says finally, without looking up. "I just wanted to let you know, okay? That's all this is."

"And what if I told you I wanted you to keep it?"

"Then I'd say you were lying."

"I'm not."

"Elson," she says, her eyes softer now. "Look, I appreciate what you're doing, okay? I get it. You're trying to do the right thing. I understand that. But it's not that simple, okay? I mean, it's not like I expect you to marry me or something."

"Why not?"

"Elson."

"What?"

She pauses then and stares at him. All around them the room is filled with sunlight, unbelievable amounts of it, a soft amber light that casts them both in a hazy glow.

"Elson," she says, softer now, staring at him earnestly. "Just call your wife, okay?"

And so he does. Standing in the shaded cool of Lorna's back veranda, he pulls out his cigarettes and lights one, then reaches for the phone in his pocket. In the distance, he can see a group of workers cutting down tree branches at the edge of her narrow back alley and, beneath them, a group of kids on bikes, watching. The simple pleasure of a simple task, he thinks. The simple pleasure of doing a simple job that has a simple end. How he longs to be back at the office right now, or off on a site, doing just that. A simple task with a simple end. How he longs for the days when that was all he had to contend with. He looks back at Lorna, who is watching him now through the sliding glass doors, then looks back at his phone. Finally, finding Cadence's number in his directory, he pushes S E N D, bracing himself, knowing that whatever she has to tell him will not be good, but when she answers the phone, her voice is surprisingly calm, almost groggy, as if she'd just woken up.

"Elson," she says. "Jesus Christ."

"I'm sorry."

"Where the hell have you been?"

"It's a long story," he says. "A story for another day, okay?"

"Another day?"

"Yes."

She pauses for a moment and, to his surprise, doesn't persist. "You know what?" she says finally. "It doesn't matter. I don't even care right now. You're not going to believe this, Elson. You're not going to fucking believe this."

"What?"

"He found her."

"Who?"

"Richard. I just spoke to him on the phone, and he's on his way to get her right now."

"Chloe?"

"Yes, of course, Chloe."

"Where is she?"

"Cotulla."

"Cotulla, Texas?"

"Yes. And don't ask me why she's in Cotulla, Texas, because I have no idea. And I don't care, Elson. Honestly. I don't care right now. All I know is she's coming home."

And at this moment he can't bring himself to do anything but stand there, gaping out at the yard, the enormous weight of everything he's been carrying these past three weeks peeling off him like layers of skin, almost not believing it at first, and then feeling a strange sort of elation, a dizzying calm, like nothing he's ever felt before. He can hear Cadence's voice on the other end of the line, saying something about the police detectives, the Beckwith boy, exoneration, but he is no longer listening to her. He is staring back at Lorna, who is watching him through the sliding glass doors. He waves to her, smiles, then gives her the thumbs-up.

A moment later, she comes up to the door and opens it, then mouths, *What? What is it?*

Putting his hand over the receiver, he smiles at her and winks. "Good news," he says.

"What?"

"Good news," he says again. "Good fucking news."

9

THE DIRECTIONS RICHARD had found on the Internet had taken him west to San Antonio, then south along Interstate 35 toward Laredo. Chloe had told him to take exit 68, the first exit before Cotulla, and then to pull over at the first gas station he saw. It would be a small off-white building on the right, she'd said, and she'd be waiting out front.

Now that he's here, however, she's nowhere in sight, and he's beginning to wonder whether he maybe made a wrong turn somewhere or whether he'd maybe gotten the directions wrong. He'd been so excited, after all, when she'd first called, so overcome with joy, that he'd barely processed what she'd said. It was very possible that he'd written down the exit number wrong or maybe mixed up the numbers, written down 68 when she'd actually said 86. He picks up his phone again and dials the number of the cell phone Chloe was using, but there's no answer. He stares at the building in front of him, a tiny white mini-mart attached to a gas station, and wonders if she's simply inside, using the bathroom.

On the ride down, he'd tried her phone again several times, even though she'd told him not to, even though she'd told him she was throwing it away as soon as they hung up. She hadn't told him why she couldn't talk on it or why she even had a temporary cell phone to begin with. In fact, she'd told him very little at all, only that she was in trouble right now and that she needed his help. He'd asked her if she was safe, and she'd told him she was, at least for now, but then she'd urged him to hurry up. There was a desperate kind of panic in her voice, something he'd never heard before, and the longer he'd tried to keep her on the line, the more antsy she'd become. *I have to hang up now, Richard,* she'd finally said, and then the line had gone dead. It had struck him as strange that she'd never mentioned Raja's name, that she'd used the singular "I" instead of the plural "we," and he wondered then if he was even with her or if he was in fact the very thing she was scared of.

In the end, it had taken him almost five hours to get here, and though he'd sped the entire way and rarely hit traffic, it had still been a long and arduous trip, the endless series of small Texas towns with names like Buda and Kyle, the flat barren fields that surrounded the road, the occasional exits advertising historic locations or sometimes bars, the occasional roadside food stands selling fresh empanadas or barbecued ribs. Eventually, feeling frustrated and bored, he had called up his mother and told her the news. Even though Chloe had warned him against this, even though she'd begged him not to, he'd felt a sudden need to throw her a bone, to give her something. Earlier that day, when he'd first pulled out of Houston, he'd listened to the message she'd left him on his phone, a message filled with such stern admonishments, such violent disapproval, such profound disappointment, that he'd had to put the phone aside and stop listening. They had stung him, the words that she'd said, and he realized then that he'd gone too far, that he'd kept her in the dark far too long. When he called her back a few hours later, however, her voice was much calmer, and when he told her the news, when he told her where he was going and who he was picking up, she had simply grown silent, and then a few seconds later, he'd heard her weeping, weeping so loudly he'd had to pull the phone away from his ear.

"Are you joking with me, Richard?" she'd said finally. "Please tell me you're not."

"Why would I joke about something like this?"

"I don't know," she said. "But just promise me."

"I promise."

"You're sure?"

"I'm sure."

There was another long silence, and then his mother began to cry again.

Eventually, she'd come back on and asked whether or not he knew if Chloe was still with Raja, and when he told her he didn't, she'd started talking about the police investigation again and some detective she'd talked to earlier that day and how the charges were now being dropped. It was very important that he told them this, she said. It was very important that this information was conveyed.

"The charges are being dropped?" he'd asked, a little dumbfounded.

"Yes."

"Against both of them?"

"No, just against Chloe. Maybe Raja, too, but definitely Chloe."

"Jesus."

He'd wanted to ask her more then, but he could tell that she was getting emotional and didn't want to get her any more worked up than she already was. So instead he just told her not to tell anyone, especially not the police, and when she suggested contacting the authorities down in Cotulla, he told her that he didn't think that was such a good idea. *She wants to keep things quiet,* he'd said. *And I think we should respect that.* His mother had grown silent on the other end of the line, but then finally agreed.

"Just promise me you'll bring her home," she'd said finally.

"That's the plan."

"Promise me, Richard."

"I promise."

"And Richard," she said. "About what I said on that message."

"It's fine, Mom."

"No," she said. "It's not."

"Mom," he said, and he could hear her sniffling again now. "Mom, you know, seriously, it's fine."

And then he'd hung up and turned on the radio and tried to block out everything else for a while, tried to forget the very reason he was driving to Cotulla, Texas, in the first place.

Now, staring across the street, he can see a tiny barn covered in flowering vines and wisteria, and beyond it a long stretch of lonely field peppered with loquat trees and live oaks. Above him, in the sky, the sun is starting to lower. He stares back at the mini-mart and checks his watch, then decides to get out, feeling for the first time a sense of panic, a growing uncertainty, realizing that he's either made a wrong turn somewhere or else something has gone terribly wrong. Either way, he feels a sudden sense of urgency now, a surge of adrenaline, and as he gets out of the car and starts toward the mini-mart, as he reaches the door and thrusts it open, he enters the building so quickly that the man behind the counter almost spills his drink.

"Hello?" says the man, a little startled.

Richard stares at him, a short Mexican man with weathered skin and a fading hairline and a small, serpentine tattoo at the base of his neck.

"Can I help you?" the man continues.

"My sister," Richard blurts.

"I'm sorry?"

"Has anyone been here?"

The man stares at him, perplexed.

"I'm looking for my sister and I'm wondering if she's been here."

"Just now?"

"No, a while ago. Maybe a few hours," he says. "She said she was calling me from across the street. Did you see anyone over there?"

The man stares across the road and squints, then looks back at Richard. "Blond hair?"

"Yes."

"About this tall?" The man raises his hand above his head.

Richard nods.

"Drinking beer?"

"I don't know. Maybe."

"She was here this morning. Bought some cigarettes, beer. Then she sat out there for about an hour. Then she left."

"Do you know where she went?"

The man shrugs. "Got in a truck. That's all I know. But earlier she was asking me about buses. Guess she didn't need one."

"A truck?" Richard says, suddenly panicked. "What type of truck?"

"White truck," the man says, then, extending his arms, adds, "Big."

"Do you know when that was?"

"A few hours ago."

Richard stares at him. "And did you see who was driving?"

"The truck?"

"Yes."

The man shakes his head. "Didn't see." Then he looks at Richard. "Do you think that's her?"

"I don't know," Richard says. "Maybe." Then feeling his stomach tighten, he looks through the window down the road. "Are there any other gas stations around here, you know, on this road?"

The man shakes his head. "Just us," he says, smiling at him plaintively. "Are you okay?"

"Huh?"

"You're sweating."

But Richard is already turning around now, already heading out the door and back to the van.

Sitting in the front seat, he rolls down the window and lights a cigarette, wondering what to do now, wondering what he will tell his mother, and then wondering if the girl the man had described was actually Chloe or somebody else. And, if it was Chloe, where was she now? Who had picked her up? And where were they going? Suddenly he feels foolish for ever believing that it would all be this easy, for ever believing there wouldn't be a catch. And then he begins to wonder if it had all been a trick from the start, a setup, an elaborate charade to throw them all off.

Shifting into gear, he pulls out of the mini-mart parking lot and starts back toward the highway, realizing that sooner or later—at some point between now and the moment he pulls into his mother's driveway back in Houston—he'll have to tell her the news. He'll have to sit there and listen to her as she questions him, as she breaks down, as she asks him why he hadn't just let her call the cops in Cotulla as she'd initially suggested, why he'd insisted that she trust him. And he'll have to tell her then that he doesn't have a good answer for her, that he doesn't even know where his sister is at this moment. He'll have to acknowledge that on a very fundamental level he has failed her.

And the thought of this conversation now is almost as upsetting to him as the very real possibility that Chloe herself has just vanished for good, just disappeared into nothing. And he wonders then how a person could do that, just disappear like that, just cancel out everything else in their life—their family, their friends, their future—just give it all up, for what? A boy? A romantic idea about love? And he thinks then about all of the times he has done this before, all of the times he has protected his sister, covered for her, defended her in front of their parents. All of the times he had picked her up at parties in high school when she was too drunk to drive, all of the times he had written her fake notes to get out of class, all of the times he had rewritten her papers for her, all of the times he had lied for her, misled their parents deliberately, just to keep her out of trouble. And what had it gotten her now? What had he given her but a false sense of entitlement, a false sense of security, a naïve belief that where there were actions there were not always consequences.

It is this that he's thinking about as he pulls onto the highway and later as the phone on the seat beside him begins to ring. He's so overcome with frustration at this moment, though, so overwhelmed with dread, that he just lets it ring, believing at first it's his mother, or perhaps his father, calling to get a report, but when the caller calls back, he realizes, against all logic, that it might in fact be Chloe and quickly picks up.

"Chlo?"

"Richard," says a voice he recognizes immediately as Michelson's. "I'm so glad I caught you. I was afraid that something might have happened when you didn't show up at our meeting."

"Our meeting?"

"Yes, our workshop. You were the only one who didn't show. You and your friend . . ."

"Brandon."

"Right, Brandon. Well, I'm so glad I caught you because I have some fabulous news."

"I can't really talk right now," Richard says, suddenly feeling sick.

"This will only take a minute, Richard," Michelson continues, and then he goes on to talk about something—a conversation he'd had with someone earlier that day, a space that has just opened up at Michigan, financial aid—but it all begins to blur now, the thought of Chloe filling his head, the absurdity of talking to Michelson at a moment like this.

"Did you hear what I said?" Michelson says. "It's already a done deal. You're in. You just need to send them that stuff. Have you mailed it off yet?"

"I have to go," Richard says.

"Richard, are you hearing me?"

"My sister's gone," Richard says then, his mind growing numb.

"I'm sorry?"

"She's gone," he says. "She might even be dead."

"Dead? What are you talking about, Richard?"

But before Michelson can continue, he hangs up the phone and turns it to mute, then floors the pedal of his mother's minivan, weaving through traffic so recklessly that he no longer feels like a person who's connected to the road, the earth. He no longer feels connected to anything. And as the sun in the distance begins to fade along the horizon, turning daytime into night, he braces himself, remembering the last thing his sister said to him before she hung up, the last words that came out of her mouth. *I can't wait to see you, Richie,* she'd said. *You have no idea.* And then she'd said, *Look, Richie, I have to hang up now, okay?* And then there'd been a loud sound in the background, a horn, and then the line had gone dead.

10

AT THE EDGE of the kitchen sink, Cadence pours herself another cup of coffee and stares out at the backyard where Elson, even at this late hour, is still working on the yard. Bathed in the artificial glow of the backyard floodlights, he is laying down sod, smoothing it out with a roller, then soaking it with water. He'd come over earlier that evening with a bottle of champagne tucked beneath his arms, fresh flowers, a cake. Then he'd gone out to his car and carried in several patches of fresh sod, which he'd proceeded to set down on the deck. He wanted to cover up the bare spots at the back of the yard, he'd said, wanted to make everything look nice for Chloe. This was long overdue, he'd said. This was a problem that needed to be fixed. And as she stares at him now, she wonders what it was about men and lawns. It was like they saw the health of their lawn as some sort of outward reflection of their own ability to provide, their manliness. Or at least that had always been the case with Elson. If the lawn was in trouble, he'd spend the entire weekend just working on it, fretting over it, wondering if he had burned it with chemicals, watered it too profusely, cut it too short. And it would almost seem comical at this moment—the sight of him now—it would almost seem endearing, if it weren't for the fact that it had been almost eight hours now since she'd last heard from Richard.

Staring at the clock above the counter, she tries again to do the math. Five hours to Cotulla and five hours back. Even with traffic, they should have been back by ten at the latest. And now, with the hour hand moving closer to one—one in the morning—she can only assume that something is wrong. Earlier she had stood out in the yard with Elson as he lay down the sod, talking about what they would do, how they would celebrate, agreeing that they would not even mention what she'd done, how she'd worried them. There would be no accusations tonight, no reprimands. Tonight would be a night for celebration, nothing more. And they would all be together again, at least for tonight, and though she didn't take this to mean what Elson took it to mean—a new beginning, a new start—she'd still felt giddy at the thought of it. A momentary reprieve from what had otherwise been a very dark time in their lives, a momentary vacation before they had to get down to the business of dealing with the aftermath, the fallout: the civil suit, the inevitable interrogations, the media. But for tonight, at least, they'd keep all of these things far from their minds. Tonight, they would simply welcome back their daughter.

This had been the plan, at least, and Cadence herself had felt so nervous, so excited, that she'd barely been able to keep herself still. Moving around the house in a flurry, vacuuming the living room, fixing up Chloe's bed, ordering pizzas, calling up Richard every half hour, even though he never picked up, then starting all over again. But somewhere between then and now, between the moment that Richard first called her and the moment she'd begun to notice that the cheese on the pizzas she'd ordered had started to congeal, she'd lost that sense of optimism, that sense of hope.

Now, staring through the patio door at Elson, she catches his eye and waves. Brushing the dirt off his khakis, he waves back, then takes off his gloves and starts back toward the house, smiling.

"It looks nice in here," he says, as he enters, glancing around the room at the fresh cut flowers she'd set up earlier, the table setting, the votive candles arranged in a row.

"It's one o'clock," she says.

Elson looks at the clock. "They probably just stopped to get something to eat, you know."

"For three hours?"

"I don't know." Elson shrugs. "There's traffic, too. You have to consider that."

"Elson, he hasn't returned *any* of my calls."

"You told me he didn't want you calling him, right? He said not to call."

Cadence looks at him, nods.

"Look, you need to stop worrying, okay? They're coming home. They probably just got held up."

Cadence moves over to the counter and picks up her coffee, and as she does this, Elson walks past her toward the hall.

"Where are you going?" she calls after him.

"Out front to my car," he yells back. "Five more patches to lay down, then I'm done."

A moment later, the front door opens and slams shut, and she walks back to the island in the middle of the kitchen and puts out the candles that are starting to fade.

Through the patio doors, the backyard looks pristine. Elson has not only filled in the bare patches at the back of the lawn but has raked out three of the beds and weeded two others. He has swept up the pool deck, power-washed the patio, added new mulch. This is perhaps his own unusual way of dealing with stress, with uncertainty, but if it is, it's certainly not something she's seen before.

Still, it occurrred to her earlier that there was no way to account for a man like Elson, a man who could snake his way back into your heart in the most unorthodox ways, a man who could inexplicably miss out on one of the most important meetings of his life and then try to make it up to you by spending several hours out in the backyard, laying down sod. That she'd chosen to forgive him, that she'd chosen to ignore what he had done, that she'd chosen to overlook his negligence, this was not something she could explain. It was like trying to explain twenty-five years of marriage to a person you'd never met. These habits were simply ingrained in her. They were as much a part of her as anything else. And Elson, too, was a part of her. As much as she wanted to pretend that he wasn't, she couldn't. They were inextricably linked, the two of them, bonded like tissues in a single body. And no amount of separation or betrayal or even divorce could ever change that.

It is this that she's thinking about as she stares out at the backyard, at the stillness of the pool water, and then at the darkness of the sky, and then later at the flashing screen of her cell phone in the distance, which is blinking now, beckoning her.

It had entirely slipped her mind that she'd left her phone out there, on a small glass table by the side of the pool, and as she rushes to it now, as she pushes open the glass door and starts toward the pool, she feels that giddiness returning. *Richard,* she thinks. *Thank God.*

But when she finally picks up the phone, the caller ID says "Restricted." She stares at it for a moment, then answers.

"Mrs. Harding?" says a voice on the other end. It's a young voice, male.

"Yes."

"You don't know me, but I'm here to relay a message from your daughter."

"Who is this?"

"She wanted me to let you know that she's safe and that she loves you and that she's very sorry. These are her words, okay: *I'm sorry, Mom, but you need to trust me. I'll call you when it's safe.*"

Staring at the still water in the blue-lit pool, Cadence feels sick.

"This is ridiculous," she says finally. "She's coming home right now. My son is bringing her home as we speak." But by the time she finishes, the line has gone dead, and the caller is gone. She tries to call back, but a voice comes on to tell her that the number she is trying to call is no longer in service. Panicked, she turns back toward the house and starts inside, thinking at first that this is all just a prank, some cruel prank. But who would pull such a prank? Who would be that cruel? The voice was not a voice that she recognized, not a voice she had ever heard before. Racing now through the kitchen, she calls out for Elson, but he's nowhere in sight. *Elson,* she calls again, her heart sprinting now, but he doesn't answer. And then she remembers that he'd just stepped outside to get the sod and starts back toward the hall. But when she opens the front door what she sees in her driveway is not her husband pulling out sod from the back of his car, but her own minivan, parked at the edge of the curb. And that's when she notices Richard, his body drenched in sweat, his red T-shirt and baggy jeans hanging loosely off his hips, and then she sees Elson, moving toward him, his body still covered in dirt, and then the two of them hugging, embracing, at the edge of the lawn, beneath the streetlight, two looming silhouettes, their bodies convulsing, sobbing, a sight she has not seen in many years. And she realizes then with a certainty and a terror built into her from years of disappointment that something here—something at this moment—is terribly wrong.

Part Seven

WHEN THEY WERE KIDS, they had devised the game out of boredom, or perhaps out of a desire to keep their own relationship at a distance from the relationship they shared with their parents. This creation of alter egos, this invention of names. She had been Blaise—a name that she thought suggested wealth and intrigue—and he had been Sean, a name that he had borrowed from a book he'd once read. They had played the game constantly, on family vacations, in the hallways at school, sometimes even at the dinner table, surreptitiously slipping each other secret notes full of cryptic messages, addressed to the other person's alter-ego. Some psychologist would probably have a field day with this, he used to think, trying to interpret it, perhaps defining it as a worrisome sign of things to come, but Richard himself rarely considered it.

In fact, it wasn't until he'd received an e-mail during his second week of classes at the University of Michigan, almost three months after Chloe had disappeared, that all of the memories came flooding back. The e-mail had been sent to him from an address he didn't recognize (bl7462@ hotmail.com) and the subject line was blank. Normally, he would have just discarded this type of e-mail without even reading it, but for some reason he opened it, and when he did, his mind went numb.

Sean,

Do you hate me? Please tell me you don't.
Love, Blaise.

He stared at the computer, rereading the message several times, his mind still not processing it. Initially he had wanted to write back right away, tell her how much he missed her and that, no, of course he didn't hate her, couldn't possibly ever hate her, but he'd been sitting in the campus library at the time, surrounded by undergraduates, and he was late for his four o'clock class, and so instead he'd logged off his computer and gone to class, figuring he could just write her back later, when his mind was a little clearer and he'd had a little more time to process it.

In the end, he had spent almost an hour crafting his response. He wanted to make sure he didn't say anything that might make it obvious that he was writing to Chloe, in case his account was still being monitored, but at the same time he had so many questions for her. Was she safe? Was she still with Raja? Could she tell him where she was? First and foremost, he wanted to emphasize to her how happy he was to know that she was still alive, not that he'd ever doubted it, and how much he had been thinking about her these past few months. He also wanted to tell her, in case she wasn't sure, that it was safe for her to come home now, anytime she wanted, that she hadn't technically done anything wrong, at least not in the eyes of the law. He'd wanted to assure her of this, that the Beckwith boy was fine, that the charges against her were now being dropped, and that she and Raja could get full exoneration if they simply came back to the States and testified. He'd written the e-mail very carefully, including the dates of Seung's trial, the name of the district attorney, and even the PO box of the private investigator that his mother had hired. Then he'd emphasized again how much he'd missed her, and signed it *Love, Sean.*

He sent the e-mail off at ten o'clock that evening and waited for her response, but her response never came. The following day he sent off another e-mail, asking her if she was okay, but again heard nothing. Finally, two days later, he received an e-mail in his in-box informing him that the account he was trying to contact no longer existed. He wondered if Chloe had even received the message or whether she'd canceled her account long before he'd even replied. He'd tried again to send her a message, but again the message was denied. He stared at the screen. If she was protecting anyone, he realized then, she was protecting Raja, not herself. Raja, who was still facing two assault charges back in the States. But still, he wondered, why would she have even gone to the trouble of sending him a message, and then canceled her account?

For the next several weeks her message had haunted him, had made it hard for him to do anything else, to concentrate on classes, to hang out with friends, to prepare for the undergraduate course he had been assigned to teach. Every few hours, he would check his e-mail, hoping for another message, but he never received one. He even thought about calling up his mother and telling her about it. His mother, who was convinced that Chloe was dead. It would have been the humane thing to do, after all, but he also knew where this would lead and how Chloe would never forgive him. His mother had hired a private investigator almost as soon as she'd learned that Chloe was gone, and she had been calling Richard every two or three days just to inform him of their progress. So far, they had no solid leads, she'd told him, but they had narrowed the search down to a remote part of Mexico. That's what she'd told him the last time they spoke, though he could tell, even then, that his mother was skeptical, that she was preparing herself for the worst.

Meanwhile, his life in Michigan had turned out to be better than he'd expected, or at least better than anyone could have expected given the circumstances. At Michelson's insistence, he had finally sent off his materials to the program, and when he'd received a phone call a few weeks later from the director, he had been charmed by her demeanor, by her genuine friendliness, and by the fact that she didn't seem to be pushing him in one direction or the other. *You can come or not. It's your choice,* she'd told him. And a few days later, he had called her back and accepted the offer, realizing then that there wasn't much keeping him in Houston anymore and also wanting to get as far away from his parents and the memory of what had happened as possible.

And since he'd been here, it hadn't been that bad. The town itself was very cute—a sleepy college town filled with independent bookstores and coffee shops and more bars than he could count. He'd found a small apartment near the river, which ran through the center of town, and in the afternoons and evenings he'd sometimes take walks along the river, the leaves in the trees already starting to change color now, the first brisk winds of autumn biting his cheeks. Often he thought about Chloe and the way she'd described Stratham to him when she'd first arrived there. *You have no idea what it's like to have seasons,* she'd written. *Real seasons. It would blow your mind, Rich.* And he would wonder then, as he walked along the river, if this is what she meant. Making his way back toward town, he would sometimes stop at a bar where all the poets went, a small, smoky dive that played a lot of Velvet Underground and Leonard Cohen. You could always count on a regular crowd there, young men and women just like him, slamming down amber shots of whiskey and eager to talk about anything from Robert Hass to Jorie Graham. He'd had some great conversations there, conversations that had made him want to go back to his apartment and write, conversations that had inspired him in a way that Michelson never had. And he'd met some wonderful people, too, in particular a young visiting poet who was teaching one of the graduate workshops that semester, a man who had twice asked him out to dinner and who had told him that his work showed "remarkable promise." He wasn't sure if this man was just delivering a line, a loaded compliment designed to get him into bed, but he didn't think so. This man wasn't like Michelson. There was no sleaziness there. He was young and handsome and probably could have been with anyone he wanted, and that he'd chosen Richard, Richard believed, was simply luck, or, at the very least, a sign—a sign that he might actually be capable of trusting another human being again.

On the first night they went out, the man had taken him to a small Indian restaurant on the other side of town. Over steaming plates of curry, they had talked about the man's work and then about Richard's work and then afterward, as they stood outside in the chilly night air, the man had kissed him beneath the awning of a neighboring bar. The man's lips had been cold, and soft, and Richard had realized then, as he kissed him, that this was the first time he had willingly kissed another human being since Marcos.

It was strange. When he was out at the bar or sitting in class or standing in line for a movie or lecturing to the group of sleepy-eyed freshmen he'd been assigned to teach, he felt strangely at peace. He took a certain comfort in the fact that he had a reason for being there, a purpose. It was only later, when he got back to his apartment and sat down to write, or make himself dinner, that he felt that old sense of loneliness coming back, that he felt his mind drifting back to the past, to Houston. And the truth was, he didn't want to think about Houston. He didn't want to think about Brandon, who was no longer talking to him, or his father, who had recently moved in with his girlfriend, or his mother, who was sinking obscene amounts of money into her pseudo-investigation. He didn't want to think about any of it. He wanted to pretend that the past was the past, that that life had been another life lived by another person. He wanted to pretend that the person he was now was the person he would always be. But inevitably his mind would drift back to the past, replaying the events of the previous spring, and at these moments he'd find himself standing up, lighting a cigarette, sometimes pouring himself a glass of wine, then sitting down at his computer to write. He'd pull up his e-mail account and begin a new message. *Dear Blaise,* he'd begin, and then he'd start writing, letting it all out, everything he wanted to tell her, everything he'd wished he had said, his regrets, his fears, his anger, all the while knowing that the person he was writing to, the account he would later be sending this e-mail to, no longer existed.

WHEN SHE THOUGHT about it now, what bothered her the most was the fact that Chloe never knew. She had never had a chance to talk to her, had never had a chance to explain to her that the charges against her were now being dropped. If she had, she wonders if Chloe would have even cared, if she would have changed her mind and come back home, or whether it would have even made a difference. The truth was she didn't know and might never know. All she knew now was that Chloe was gone, and though in her darker moments she'd occasionally allow herself to consider the worst, she believed in her heart that her daughter was alive. She believed this in the same way that she had once believed that her marriage to Elson was going to work, with a kind of willful denial. To believe the opposite, after all, would be to throw in the towel, to give up on the only thing in her life that actually gave her hope.

She had tried to explain all of this to Peterson the last time they met, but Peterson had simply sat there, staring at her blankly. She had started seeing him again these past few months, mostly out of a sense of boredom and loneliness. She had so few people in her life to talk to right now. Richard was off in Michigan, Elson had moved in with Lorna, and Gavin, after their last painful meeting, had decided to stop returning her calls. Peterson was at least a person to talk to, a person who would listen, though, in typical Peterson fashion, he offered very little.

During their last meeting, she had told him about her idea to sell the house, about how she'd already started looking for apartments in Montrose, and about how the money she earned from the sale would not only keep her afloat financially for a while but would also help to fund the ongoing investigation, her search for Chloe. Like Richard, Peterson had been skeptical of the man she had hired, the private investigator, and of the investigation in general, and like Richard, he also wondered if she wasn't becoming a little too obsessed. But instead of saying this, he simply asked her what she thought Elson would think about it.

"Elson will not have to know about it," she'd said.

"Well, I imagine he'll have to know at some point, right?" Peterson had smiled. "I mean, his name is still on the house, right?"

"Whose side are you on anyway?" she'd asked.

"It's not about sides, Cadence," he'd said and smiled. "It's never been about sides."

Frustrated, she'd left her meeting with Peterson and gone to a wine bar near her house and proceeded to spend most of the night there. The truth was she had wanted to sell the house precisely because it reminded her of Elson, precisely because it reminded her of her former life. How was she expected to move on when she had to pass her daughter's bedroom every morning, when she had to spend her life inside the hollow cavern of her past? *It's like living in a tomb,* she'd wanted to say to him. But instead she'd gone to the wine bar and gotten drunk and then gone home alone.

In the past three months, her kitchen had been transformed into a kind of office. All of the information the private investigator had acquired lay strewn across the counters, organized in files, taped along the walls. It looked like the house of a crazy person, she'd thought that night as she came home from the bar and poured herself a beer. And of course, most of the leads had turned out to be garbage anyway. Inquiries that had turned up nothing. People of interest who had turned out to be totally useless. Former classmates and friends of Chloe who refused to speak. She had been surprised at how quickly it had all gone away, the way the college had swiftly covered it up, the way the newspapers had soon lost interest. Their sympathies had all been with Tyler Beckwith, after all, and now that he was better, now that he was back in school, finishing his senior year, the whereabouts of Raja and Chloe seemed to fall off their radar. Even the Stratham Police Department had relegated her daughter's case to a low-priority file. After a somewhat-tertiary investigation in Mexico, an investigation that seemed to involve little more than a few phone calls to the Mexican authorities, they had called her up to let her know that they would be in touch as soon as they learned anything, but that, in the meantime, she shouldn't keep calling. *We're pretty sure they'll eventually turn up,* they'd told her. *Sooner or later, they always do.* And then they'd given her the number of a detective who had been assigned her case, a man who never returned her calls.

Finally, at Elson's initial insistence, they had hired the private investigator, a man named Deryck Lowe, who had been recommended to them by Albert Dunn. But after a few fruitless meetings with Deryck Lowe, even Elson seemed to have given up. Even last week, when she'd told him what Deryck Lowe had discovered, that he now had reason to believe that Chloe and Raja were now hiding out in southern Mexico, even then Elson had grown silent on the other end of the phone and then finally asked her, "How much are we paying this guy again?"

"Is cost really an issue?" she'd asked.

"It's not when we're getting results," he'd said, "but it's been, what, three months now?"

"You want to give up?"

"I didn't say that, but maybe there's someone else, you know, another person we can talk to."

She'd hung up on him then and hadn't spoken to him now in almost a week. It would be wrong to say he didn't care. She had had enough conversations with him in the past month to know that he was just as obsessed with the case as she was, maybe even more so. But somehow he had found a way to move on, to keep going to work, to continue his liaison with that twenty-something girlfriend of his. It was a thing she'd come to resent, his resilience, his strength. Wasn't it always his nature to fall apart in situations like this? Why had it fallen on her? She had never considered herself a jealous person and had never honestly believed that things with Elson would ever work out, not even after they'd slept together, but a part of her still felt tricked, misled into believing he'd actually changed.

In the past month alone, she'd met with him over a dozen times, and each time they met he'd seemed even-keeled, relaxed, hesitant to get overly excited or overly depressed by any of the information Deryck Lowe had supplied. It was just that it all seemed so contradictory, he'd told her the last time they met. One minute he was telling them that she was hiding out in southern Mexico, and the next he was saying that she was back in the States. And she had to admit that Elson was right. The information just didn't add up, none of it did. And none of it was solid. None of it was verifiable. The last time they'd met, she'd almost conceded this point, but a part of her couldn't. After all, to give up on Deryck Lowe at this point would be to essentially give in. It would mean acknowledging that on some level all of the work they'd done together these past several months had been useless, and a part of her just couldn't do that. And besides, who was to say that the next person they hired would do any better? After all, hadn't all of her own meager efforts been fruitless? Her attempts to talk to Simone at her store, her countless phone calls to Raja's parents, who refused to talk to her, her e-mails to Chloe's classmates at school. She'd even tried to contact the dean of student affairs up at Stratham, a quiet man who had told her that now that Chloe was no longer a student there, there wasn't much he could do. And yet, in the midst of it all, here was Elson, placid and controlled, thinking it all through, deliberating over it, questioning it, discussing it like he was discussing his latest plans for a new building, not like a man who had just recently—just in the past several months—lost his daughter.

It was this that she was thinking about that night she came home from the wine bar, blitzed out of her mind, and it was this that she was thinking about later as she sat out by the pool and received the phone call from Richard. His voice had seemed nervous at first, talking in clipped sentences, starting and stopping, making her tense. Finally he said that he had some information about Chloe, but that if he shared this information with her, she would have to promise him that she wouldn't tell anybody, not even the private investigator, and especially not Dad. She could tell that he felt nervous even saying this much, guilty about betraying his sister, and she saw no other choice but to promise.

He paused for a long time after that, and then he finally explained to her that he now had proof that Chloe was alive, and though he wasn't certain, he was also pretty sure that she was safe. Of course, she'd asked him how he knew this, and of course he'd told her couldn't tell her. He'd simply said that he thought she should know, that she would want to know, and that he owed it to her to tell her. She'd thanked him for telling her, and then she'd closed her eyes and leaned back in the chair, all of her deepest suspicions suddenly confirmed.

Over the next several days she'd call him again and again, hoping to get more information, and each time she called he would stonewall her and beg her to stop asking. And though she'd wanted to tell Deryck Lowe, too, she'd respected her son's wishes and not mentioned it. Still there was something that Richard had said to her that first night that stuck with her, that haunted her. She'd been asking him why he was so resistant to telling the authorities, or Deryck Lowe or Elson for that matter, and Richard had simply paused for a long time and considered this. Then finally he said, "I was thinking about that, Mom, and I was thinking that maybe we should just let her be lost for a while."

"What are you talking about?"

"I mean, maybe," he'd said, his voice growing quiet then, "maybe she's not ready to be found."

"What do you mean she's not ready to be found?"

"I mean just that," he said. "Maybe she's just not ready to be found."

3

NOW THAT LORNA was in her second trimester, he knew that sooner or later he'd have to tell Cadence. Sooner or later they'd run into each other at a restaurant, or sooner or later someone they both knew would see him out with Lorna and report back to her. It seemed inevitable, and yet every time he thought about calling her up, every time he tried to imagine that conversation, a part of him would panic, realizing just how painful it would be for both of them and also understanding what this would mean for their relationship. It would essentially be setting in stone the final chapter of their life together. Not that he wouldn't still see her. Not that he wouldn't still be a part of the children's lives. It's just that it would never be the same. Any hope they may have once harbored about getting back together, about reuniting as a group, any hope of that would now be gone. And though he wasn't sure whether Cadence had ever held on to this hope in the same way he had, he knew that it would inevitably unsettle her, maybe even devastate her, the knowledge that in a few short months he would be a father again, that he would soon be embarking on a new life with a new family.

Of course, the fact that he hadn't told Cadence yet, the fact that he was still keeping it a secret from her, this had been the one source of major contention between him and Lorna these past few months. Lorna of course had seen it as a worrisome sign, a sign of things to come, an indication that he still wasn't over her, and though he'd tried to explain to her that he was only trying to be sensitive to Cadence's feelings during what was already a very stressful time, he could tell she didn't buy it. *You're still in love with her,* she'd said to him the other night. *It's so obvious.* And though he'd tried to assure her that he wasn't, he knew that the only way to truly convince her was to tell Cadence about the child, to make that final leap. And so he'd walked up to Lorna the night before and put his arms around her. He'd said, *I'll tell her this week, okay? I promise.*

Still, aside from these occasional fights about Cadence, things had been remarkably smooth between the two of them these past few months. On the night that he moved in she had told him that this would be the first step in what would be a long journey toward regaining her trust. He would have to earn it back, she'd told him, but she would also have to let him. And this gesture of letting him move back in, this would be the first step. She had spoken very solemnly as she said this, and he had taken her admonition to mean that he was on a sort of one-strike-and-you're-out basis, but also that she was taking this whole thing very seriously, that she not only wanted to try very hard to make it work, but that she also saw him as her partner for the future, the man she wanted to be with. And so he'd tried very hard to be supportive, to be attentive, to show her he cared. He had driven her to all of her doctor's appointments, had taken her to all of her prenatal exams, had bought her books on parent-ing, had assured her when she worried that all of the things that worried her—the baby's kicking, the hiccups—were perfectly fine. He had been through this before, after all, had been through it twice, and though he often wanted to mention this to her, often wanted to compare what she was going through with what Cadence had been through, he never did. Instead, he'd tried his best to be supportive, tried his best to assume the role of a first-time parent himself, and in a way he kind of enjoyed it. The giddiness and uncertainty, the simple pleasure of simple things, like an ultrasound picture or a very first kick. He had even enjoyed some of the less glamorous parts, like driving Lorna to the drugstore when she was feeling nauseous or talking her back to sleep after one of her second-trimester nightmares. This was all part of the deal, after all, all part of the game, and though he occasionally found himself worrying about some of the more practical matters ahead—the financial strain, for example—he tried for the most part to ignore these things. It would all work out in the end. He knew that, just as he had known the min-ute Richard was born that he would find a way to make things work. Once a child arrived, after all, it was never an issue of *if* it could work, but *how.*

He had been thinking about this the night before when they came home from Lorna's latest ultrasound test, a test that had revealed to them both that they'd soon be the proud parents of a lovely baby girl. A daughter. The thought of this had unnerved him at first, had made him think immediately of Chloe, of what this would mean to her, and to him. In a way, it almost seemed like a punishment. A kind of cruel cosmic joke. After all, what would this be if not salt in his wounds, a constant reminder of his own recent failings? Another daughter who would grow up to resent him, another daughter who he'd fail to protect. The more he thought about it, the more agitated he became, and perhaps Lorna had sensed this because after a while she had turned off the lights and gone off to bed without saying good night.

Sitting alone in her kitchen, he had fixed himself a drink and stared out at the yard. In the other room, he could hear Lorna turning on the television and getting ready for bed. He could hear someone on the television saying something about Lyndon Johnson and then wildflowers, and then everything became very quiet, and as he sat there at the table, filling his glass with more Tanqueray, he began to wonder if he wasn't thinking about this whole thing the wrong way. Maybe this wasn't a punishment but a gift. Maybe he was being given a second chance, a chance to do things right. Whereas he had just lost one daughter, now he was being given another. And how could he not see this as an opportunity to make good on all the mistakes he'd made with Chloe? How could he not see this as a second chance?

But somehow thinking about the baby this way, and thinking about Chloe this way, made him feel funny. It was a messed-up way of thinking, when you got right down to it, a perverse type of logic informed by gin. And besides, what did the one have to do with the other? Human beings were not like buildings. They could not be replaced and remade. And even if they could, could he have ever imagined a child more perfect than Chloe? Even with all of her recent mistakes, she had turned out so much better than he could have possibly hoped for, had made him proud in ways she'd never know. And when he rehearsed the conversation with her that he rehearsed in his mind at least once every day, it was this that he told her. How proud he was, how unequivocally proud he was of everything she'd turned into. But he wondered then, that night, if he'd ever actually have the chance to tell her these things. From everything Cadence had told him, his daughter had disappeared off the face of the earth. She had erased any trace of herself. She had vanished into the darkest corners of Mexico or was maybe living back in the States under an assumed name. It didn't matter. All that mattered now was that she was gone, and when he allowed himself to think about this too much, as he did that night, sitting in Lorna's kitchen, he felt such an acute sense of sadness, of loss, that everything else in his life seemed to fade away. It was almost dizzying when you tried to wrap your mind around it. That this had happened to them. That their daughter had gone to such an extreme measure to extricate herself from their lives. That she thought so little of them. That she hadn't even bothered to call.

Walking out to the back veranda, he lit a cigarette and sat down at Lorna's patio table, staring out at the backyard furniture illuminated by the lights from the alley. He thought about Lorna, asleep in her bed, and how in so many ways she had been right to be concerned, how on a certain level he would always be in love with Cadence, and how a part of him would always hold on to the idea of regaining what they'd once had. Even if it was impossible now, even if Richard was off in the chilly Midwest, trying to be Jack Kerouac, even if Chloe was off in some foreign country, living under an assumed name, even if he would soon be the father of a newborn baby girl, even if their lives, and everything that had happened these past six months, was irreversible, he still found himself fighting against it, this notion of time, still willing his way back into the past.

And at moments like this, when he found his mind drifting back, there was one memory in particular that he always returned to, a memory of the four of them eating together on the night before Chloe left for college her junior year. The memory, which took place over a year ago, was the last time he could remember the four of them being together as a family. It was long before he and Cadence had ever announced their divorce, long before Richard had ever talked about going to graduate school, long before Chloe had even met the boy she would later be accused of hurting. It was long before all of that, and in this memory, which is unremarkable in almost every way, they are sitting together at the table, eating fresh corn on the cob and hamburgers, which Chloe has helped him prepare on the grill. They have all participated in different ways in the assembling of this meal, Richard husking the corn, Cadence making the salad, he and Chloe out in the backyard, grilling the burgers and lining up the condiments. And now they are sitting here together to eat, the four of them, as a family. In a year from now they will barely be talking to each other anymore. They will not even know the smallest details about each other's lives. They will not even know where Chloe is living. But for now, they are here. For now, they are simply sitting together in a room, around a table where they have sat a thousand times before. They are eating a meal together, in silence. And they are together in this moment. They are doing what they believe, what they've been taught, families do.

4

AT A SMALL CYBER CAFÉ on Wörther Straße, across the street from the School of Fine Art and Design, Chloe is trying yet again to explain to her brother why it was she left. In the six weeks since she and Raja have been here in Prenzlauer Berg, in East Berlin, she has written over twenty versions of this e-mail, each one over a page in length. In the only one she actually sent him she'd simply asked him if he hated her, but a few days later, she'd panicked and canceled her account. She knew that if Raja ever found out what she was up to, if he ever discovered what she was doing, he'd never forgive her, and yet here she was again, trying once again to explain it.

In most of the e-mails she'd already drafted, she had found the tone too defensive, too cold. She was trying to explain with logic something that couldn't really be explained. She was trying to give justification to something that couldn't really be justified. This time, though, she is simply trying to describe in detail what actually happened, hoping their actions will speak for themselves. She is trying to explain to him that somewhere outside of Laredo, somewhere between the moment they left her and the moment the van began to slow down outside the border, Raja had had a change of heart. He had changed his mind. This is what he'd told her at least. Something inside of him just snapped. He described it as a moment of weakness, of course, a wavering of his convictions, but she had never seen it that way. She had always seen it as something else—a testament of his love for her, a sign of his inability to live without her. He had banged on the wall of the van for nearly twenty minutes, he'd told her later, banged until his knuckles were bloody and bruised, banged until the girl who was traveling beside him began to cry. And when Teo finally pulled over, he had begged him like he'd never begged for anything else in his life. He had begged him to turn around and go back.

Later, he would get angry when she'd ask him to retell it. It was a moment of great embarrassment for him, he'd claim, the way he cried in front of Teo, the way he stood there and begged. But it was this story that she most wanted to tell Richard. It was this story that best explained why she was where she was, and why she'd done what she had done.

He wouldn't need to know everything, of course. He wouldn't need to know how they had spent less than a month in Nuevo Laredo, then Mexico City, before finally deciding to leave the country. He wouldn't need to know how easy it had been for Raja's friend in Palo Alto to wire them the money they needed for their plane tickets or how easy it had been for Raja himself to obtain a passport or how they'd both changed their appearances—Raja growing a beard, her dying her hair—or how they'd made it through the customs terminal at the Berlin Brandenburg Airport without a hitch. He wouldn't need to know about the first week they'd spent at the Generator Loft in East Berlin or how they'd managed to find three American art students who were willing to put them up for the past few weeks. He wouldn't need to know how friendly everyone had been to them since they'd first arrived in Berlin or how much they loved the city or how they'd both recently found jobs—Raja washing dishes at the Morgenrot Café in Prenzlauer Berg and her waiting tables at Luxus Bar—or how they were now only a few weeks shy of being able to make a first month's deposit on a small one-bedroom apartment in Friedrichshain.

He wouldn't need to know any of that. Just as he wouldn't need to know that she now went by the first name Anne, or the last name Leigh. For now, all he needed to know was that she had done what she had done not out of fear but out of love, because the man she loved most in the world had banged on the metal wall of a dirty cargo hold for nearly half an hour. This was the only story he needed to know.

But even as she sits here now, staring out across the street at the rain-drenched sidewalks in front of the School of Fine Art, even as she sits here at her tiny terminal, typing out the final lines of her latest e-mail, even now she knows she can never tell him this story, can never send him this e-mail. To give him this amount of information at this point would be tantamount to turning themselves in. Even sending him that initial e-mail had been a risk. And so instead, she logs off her computer, saving the e-mail as a draft, and then goes back to the counter for another cup of coffee.

Of course, she knew what would happen if they ever went back. She had been following the story on the Internet for months. She knew about Seung, about how he'd been indicted, and she knew of course about Tyler and how he'd gradually recovered. And she knew that if they ever agreed to testify they could probably get immunity from the district attorney. Richard had made all of this very clear to her in the e-mail he had sent her, an e-mail that had included the trial date, the name of the attorney to contact, and even a post office box for the private investigator her mother had hired. But none of this mattered to her now. Even when she'd mentioned it to Raja the previous week, he'd simply smiled at her and said, "Yeah, we could do that. We could go back. But that doesn't mean I'm going to testify."

And she knew when he said this that he meant it, that no amount of exoneration would ever change the simple fact that he was never going to betray a friend, even a friend like Seung, who had already betrayed him. It wasn't in his nature. It wasn't in his makeup. And though she used to resent it, she'd recently grown to accept it, even admire it, this stubbornness. It was simply a part of who he was. Thinking about this now, she picks up her coffee and returns to her table.

The café itself is small and dark, filled with German art students typing away at their computers, chain-smoking their Gauloises cigarettes, talking in earnest voices about things she doesn't understand. On the walls around her, there are symbols of a bygone era, black-and-white photographs depicting the neoclassical buildings that had once stood on this street, bright-colored advertisements filled with Communist propaganda, a World War II gas mask framed in a box. This is a city that will forever live in the past, she thinks, a city that will forever be defined by its history. Even in its newly revitalized state, even with its burgeoning art scene and urban renewal, it will never fully move on. And perhaps that's the point. Perhaps that's the point of all these reminders hung along the walls: that no matter how hard we try, no matter how far we go, we can never truly escape what's happened before.

But if this is true, she wonders now, sitting down at a small table by the window, then how could she account for what she'd done or for the exhilarating sense of freedom she'd felt since leaving the States? Was it possible that the only true way to escape your past was to erase it, to erase yourself, to invent a new identity, to sever all ties from your family and friends, your country of origin? And if this was true, then how long could it last? Was it possible she could go on forever, living like this, or would she eventually feel the need to return? If there was anything standing in her way, it was only guilt, a strange sense of familial obligation, a responsibility she felt to her mother and to Richard, a sense of remorse for leaving them so little. A cryptic e-mail sent to her brother in haste. A phone message to her mother, relayed from Teo to Dupree, which had probably scared her mother more than it had assured her. It was something that she thought about often, a question that plagued her, whether or not she'd ever return. And she knew the consequences, of course, but it wasn't about that. It was about whether this new life she'd created, this new life she'd just begun, would be enough to fulfill her.

All she knows now is that in less than an hour Raja will be getting off work and meeting her here. As soon as he arrives, they will switch over from coffee to beer, and then they will go off to another bar on the other side of town where they will meet with a small group of friends, new friends, who they've only just met and who they don't know very well, but who they'll know a lot better by the end of the night. They will use whatever money they've saved up for going out to buy as much beer as they can, and they will stay out as late as their bodies will let them, trying to speak what little German they've learned, trying to remember the lyrics to the German songs their new friends have taught them. The bar will be small and warmly lit, and the air will be thick with cigarette smoke, chaotic with laughter, and in that moment, sitting across from her new German friends, sitting beside the man she loves, the idea of returning to Houston will seem impossible to her. She knows this now, just as she knows every time she looks up the cost of transatlantic flights, every time she calculates the distance between here and Houston, every time she thinks about her parents' divorce, or the trouble back at Stratham, or her brother's handsome face, every time she considers the damage that's been done and the bridges that have been burned and the utter irreversibility of time, every time she thinks about these things, she knows, as she knows now, staring out the window at the rain-drenched streets of East Berlin, the foreign signs of this foreign city, that even though she will soon have enough money to buy a plane ticket, even though she will soon have the means to go home, it is simply too far a journey, too great a distance, to go.

Acknowledgments

I would like to gratefully acknowledge Trinity University and the Artist Foundation of San Antonio for their generous support during the writing of this book. I would also like to express my deepest gratitude to my brilliant and tireless editor, Diana Coglianese, and to my generous, wise, and always supportive agent, Terra Chalberg. Finally, my most profound thanks to my friends and family and to my wife, Jenny, without whose love and encouragement I would have never been able to write this book.

A NOTE ABOUT THE AUTHOR

Andrew Porter is the author of the story collection *The Theory of Light and Matter*. A graduate of the Iowa Writers' Workshop, he has received a Pushcart Prize, a James Michener/Copernicus Fellowship, and the Flannery O'Connor Award for Short Fiction. His work has appeared in *One Story*, *The Threepenny Review*, and on public radio's *Selected Shorts*. Currently, he teaches fiction writing and directs the creative writing program at Trinity University in San Antonio, Texas.

A NOTE ON THE TYPE

This book was set in Scala, a typeface designed by the Dutch designer Martin Majoor (b. 1960) in 1988 and released by the FontFont foundry in 1990. While designed as a fully modern family of fonts containing both a serif and a sans serif alphabet, Scala retains many refinements normally associated with traditional fonts.

Typeset by Scribe,
Philadelphia, Pennsylvania

Printed and bound by Berryville Graphics,
Berryville, Virginia

Designed by Soonyoung Kwon